FIVE MAN FUGUE

A Mystery in Five Voices

By C.D.Peterson

Five Man Fugue
By C.D. Peterson

"Fugue—a procedure in which a motive is exposed in an initial ... dominant relationship, then developed."
– **Timothy A. Smith, D. M. A. Professor, Music Theory, NAU**

"Fugue—a combination of amnesia and physical fright. [An] individual flees from his customary surroundings [but] what he is really trying to escape is his own fear."
– **1965 Rosen & Gregory Abnormal Psychology**

"The lunar eclipse, which will visible in Chicago beginning at 10 o'clock this evening, will turn the face of the moon a deep rust color. Once thought to be a sign of impending doom, we now know
that the reddish hue is simply a product of light penetrating the Earth's dense atmosphere. In other words, don't panic— this is not the end of the world."
– **WGN Morning News**

Overture

For some of us, the only love story we'll ever get is the one we write for ourselves—this was going to be mine. And if that had actually come to pass, we all might have been better off. Unfortunately, instead of love, I got deceit. The passion I'd anticipated for so long was lost as my muse slipped away from me ... and the story changed. Now it has less to do with any sense of romance than it does with five disparate men, a series of tragic mistakes, and a lunar eclipse. For that, I should apologize.

You see, there were bikers in my favorite bar last week. A great many of them—what you might call a gaggle, if they had been geese (which they were not), or a cluster, if they had been a headache (which they also were not, although that's closer). For lack of a better word, however, let's call them a throng—clad in studded black leather and stained denim, holding tightly to overflowing mugs of beer and wiping foam from the bristles of beards that stood out from their chapped faces like unruly hedgehogs. They stamped their feet and shouted with laughter when they saw me clutching my notebook and staring at them through the bar's front window. They barked insults at me in biker-ese and thumped the table as they laughed. Thumped *my* table.

I've been a regular at Lonnie's long enough to feel like I belong there; that I fit in as well as one of the cherry-red barstools or chunky, amber candle holders, even if that belonging hasn't helped me fit the color scheme. Lonnie's, for me, has offered both safety and opportunity. But because I always beeline straight to my table in the rear corner, curling myself around my notebook to left-hand-crimp words onto the page, most of the regulars overlook me in favor of the heady pleasures of Old Style. Not that it matters. Not that their acceptance is what's important.

What's important is this: I found my muse at Lonnie's on that very first day nearly three months ago, and that is what has kept me coming back, despite the obstacles. Crouched at a corner table, my agoraphobic eyes keeping the crowd at bay, my life was suddenly transformed. For too long I had been filled with blank pages and paragraphs, unable to find words to fill them. Then one day, with the heart-quickening immediacy of an opened door, I discovered the story that I had always yearned to tell. The story that I deserved to tell: my own love story.

I had words again. My muse had presented herself.

After an initial rush of adrenaline, I felt my muscles relax as a sense of calm washed over me. And that sense of calm allowed me to collect and twist the jumble of desires that seem to constantly be clamoring for my attention into something that was, for once, less crinkled-up anger and more … intellectual origami.

It made my words come alive. To the point where, now, if I shift my chair away from the table to shield my eyes from the sharp tang of the neon sign that hangs in the front window, the magic ebbs away. And without that magic, I become diverted. Divested. I lose sight of my muse. I lose control.

So I take great care in centering myself: I secure my table and point my chair toward the front door, waiting for my inspiration. Crouched over the page, I twist my elbow toward the ceiling to keep my traitorous left forearm and palm from smudging the graphite trails I leave on the paper, and I alternate sips of Dewar's neat with Bitters and Soda (because the Dewar's gives me a stomachache). And I write my love story.

Ever since last week, though, that has not been possible. I have been cut off, my muse withheld and my story stolen by the presence of the aforementioned bikers in my bar.

They stole my calm, sullied my refuge, and crushed my intellectual origami, driving me away to search elsewhere for inspiration; to look elsewhere for a muse and for a love story. And, as is so often the case when one searches fruitlessly for love, what I found (and where I found it) proved problematic. The bar stools here are stainless steel and pleather and there are no candles to speak of. I don't belong here, but this is where I find myself. And that has left my story forever changed.

I'll tell it anyway, though I may have to spin my yarn contrapuntal to fully capture the complexity of the situation—a deep breath and a hard right turn. A new starting point, a new muse; a new beginning. I trust we'll navigate these snowy streets to find a fitting end, even if we have to sacrifice a character or two along the way. Kill your darlings, after all ...

And because I control the future—as long as I'm writing it, at least—it doesn't feel right to start this tale off with "Once upon a time" or "Call me Ishmael" or even "The day broke gray and dull" (although that's closer). They all feel like standing starts, while opening this at less than tempo seems a mistake (and there are already five of those coming, along with that lunar eclipse I promised you). So, instead, let me take a breath and begin *allegro vivo* as we introduce the first of the five men in our fugue. We'll start just east of the beginning and just north of Armitage Avenue. Just around the corner from Lonnie's, actually. It may not feel like love at first sight, but perhaps I can find a way to twist this story back into a romance before it has the chance to resolve itself into something more foreboding.

Puck

Eclipse in 50 hours

Puck is hot.

He can feel beads of sweat collecting in his armpits, building up the weight to slide down his ribcage and the undersides of his arms.

Puck is panting, his breath coming in shallow huffs. Each gasp punctuated by a small grunt of effort that springs from deep in his chest.

Puck is being chased. And not even the syncopated thud of his heart, nor the slap of his feet against the rain-wet pavement can force away the sounds of his faceless pursuer.

Puck is terrified. And he can't run fast enough to escape that terror. Not even when he forces his footsteps to come faster, the heat to intensify, the sweat to flow down his face unchecked.

Puck can't get away because he is dreaming ...

And then, suddenly, he is awake. But still hot.

Air from the rusted metal duct behind him burns against his back, pushing him out of his dream. He twists away from the heat, muttering under his breath.

"No. No, no, no. Nonononono. No." The rhythmic denial bounces across his tongue like grease on a hot griddle. Like blood on ice. "Nope. Nonono. Nnn ... no you can't. Can't, can't trust it ... "

He struggles to his feet, brushing snow stained with alley grit off his pants. The heat disappears almost immediately, leaving him numb with cold, the winter night nipping at his cheeks and making icicles of the rivulets of sweat running down his back.

He shakes his head, tossing beads of moisture from his thick, brown beard, lately streaking with gray, and watches the droplets fall. Imagines them freezing solid moments before they hit the ground, then shattering with an icy crash. A beautiful sound.

"Can't, can't, can't," he mutters again. "Can't d ... depend on it. Ca ... can't be sure. Can't come to need it when you don't kn ... know."

He stoops to retrieve the fatigue jacket that he had pushed away during his dreams and shrugs into it, reassured by its weight on his narrow shoulders. Over the years, the jacket has grown thicker and heavier, its lining bolstered by swatches of flannel and fleece and linen. Scraps that Puck traded for or scavenged from piles of thrift-shop discards and attached with careful knots, twisted bits of wire, or even needle and thread, when available. He runs a calloused thumb along the inside of the jacket, stroking the small, tattered piece of cashmere he has carefully stitched there, losing himself in the smoothness of his past.

His moment of calm is short lived, though. The emptiness of the street makes the nightmare that woke him feel all too true—The Bogeyman turns suddenly real when he's whistling "The Man That

Got Away" and rhythmically jingling his keys in the pocket of his coat as he follows you home.

Puck chews absent-mindedly on the inside of his bottom lip, stained deep burgundy by red wine, making it pooch out in the pursed-lipped kiss that has earned him his nickname. Pucker. Puck. He sucks on the shredded bits of skin that cling to his gum line as he thinks—a small act of self-cannibalization that always seems to calm the frenzied pounding of his heart.

As his breathing slows, his eyes focus on the giant clock panel of the American Bank Tower, and he reads its scrolling numbers: *8:50 ... pm ... 12°...* The sight pulls him from his stasis and touches off his ramble again, this time with a new tenor. "Nine. Nnn ... ine. Nine, nine. Nine is time. Nine is time." He is chanting now as he shifts his weight from one foot to the other. "Nine is time, is time, is time at nine. Nnn ... nine-time."

He dances to the chant for a few minutes as he watches the clock's glowing numbers move: *8:54 ... 8:57 ... 8:59 ...* He shoots an anxious look back at the crumpled pile of newspapers, old blankets, and black plastic that marks his nest. He has the best spot in the city, tucked between a small corner taqueria and an office supply store. With a knot of blankets packed against the grill of the restaurant's heat escape and his coat pulled over his head, he's safe and warm. Heat, shelter, and camouflage, with stacks of empty boxes on one side and a dumpster on the other, the open air above the alley providing a clear view of the stars overhead and the clock across the way. Perfection. The oven-heated air always left him smelling like taco meat and onions, but even that didn't do any harm, except to make him hungry as a newborn.

Puck hesitates a moment longer. Moving even a few feet can be dangerous, especially in the winter; especially at night. Since they tore down his building, this six square feet of alley is the closest thing that he's had to a home, and the more buildings fall, the more intense the competition for that space gets. He needs his nest to survive, but nothing can be gained without risk.

He pulls off his stocking cap, letting damp gray strings of hair fall around his shoulders as he drifts away from his home and toward the busier street. He glances up again. Now the clock reads *9:01 pm ... patience ... patience ...*

From down the street he hears a woman's voice rising above the clamor. "I thought I told you to quit following me." A low voice mutters unintelligibly in the background before hers rises above it again. "Don't call me that. It's creepy." A pause, then, "Well then, fuck you, Prince Charming. Stay the hell away from me."

Puck leans against the cold brick wall of the taqueria to better see the woman as she approaches. He unzips his coat just enough to more easily caress the cashmere patch and his lips pooch out again as he scrapes them gently against his teeth, finding comfort.

He runs a hand over his matted hair, smoothing it against his neck and looking around absently for a mirror, before smiling at his own disorientation. Even after so many years, the street is hard to get used to. Not the basics—it only took a few days for him to be able to sense a police car before the siren announced its presence. Not long after that he could count a man's change by the jingle of his pockets. By the end of the month he'd learned how to disappear against a brick wall. But there's no time to waste reminiscing. She has arrived, right on schedule.

As she comes into view, Puck steps out of his alley, forcing words past the nervous stutter that threatens to derail them. "Hi, Jamie," he says. His voice sounds odd to him—quiet and frail. Not like he remembers it. Not purposeful or anxious or brusque. Not even sad. Just soft.

"Not now, okay Puck? It's already not a good night." A sigh. Her footsteps slow and then stop as she looks back over her shoulder. "Ah shit, now what?" She notices that Puck is still looking at her and turns her full attention to him. Her eyes find his for the first time.

Jamie is hard—angular and sharp—her bleached hair a sharp contrast against her bronze skin. But she is so full of strength that Puck can feel his entire body puff and swell in response to her with a swiftness that makes his ears pop. His eyes dance and his tongue bounces word fragments against his palate, but he remains nearly still, with only a subtle vibration to suggest his body's need to dance.

The two stay locked together for several seconds until, finally, Jamie blinks the connection away. She gives him an affectionate half-smile and impulsively grabs his hand. "Later. Okay, baby? I need to move. I've got some problems to take care of before work." Her smile becomes an apology as she glances back the way she came. Then her eyes return to his and she squeezes his hand. "Later, Sweets. You're okay." A statement, not a question.

And then she is gone, cut off from his sight by the mass of the brick wall, leaving his mind to idle, tossing up snatches of sentence fragments that twist in the winter breeze, hanging so close that he can almost reach out and touch them. But, as always, the words skitter beyond the clumsy sweep of his mind, giggling at the way his eyes roll around to follow them as he tries to glue a sentence together. His frustration builds as he sputters, his cracked lips momentarily moistened by his efforts. "Mmmm ... ahh ... ha ... hhhe ..."

"Hi, Jamie!" he finally manages to repeat, still smiling at the empty sidewalk where she had stood. He steps back into the alley, his anxiety retreating, replaced by the joy of the encounter and the anticipation of their next meeting.

Puck exhales slowly, sagging against the alley wall as he allows his eyes to return to the bank tower. The clock now reads *9:08 ... pm ...* . But he's not concerned. It's hard to know exactly when Jamie will be back, but Puck knows that he won't see her before *2:00 ... am ...* His feet tap out the pent-up tremors that he had buried, mimicking the double beat of his racing heart. This is what Jamie does to him. It occurs to him that he could follow her to the bar one night—just stand to the side and watch her work—but the thought makes him jittery. A relationship born in the seconds it takes her to pass his alley could not bear the weight of those expectations. Though she may be his only regular chance to practice being human, he's meant to be with Jamie only at the mouth of this alley—the only place he's ever seen her. This is the place where they belong together. He nods compulsively to himself, wishing that he could do something for her that would be as significant as her nightly presence is for him.

Just as the thought touches him, however, he hears again the click of high heels approaching the alley. Confusion clouds his eyes, and he takes a tentative step forward, shooting a look at the clock still stuck at ... *9:08 ... pm*

As he stands, frozen in puzzlement and indecision, an angel drifts past his alley. Her golden hair, backlit by the glow of the streetlights, falls softly over her shoulders, which are draped in a long white coat that likewise falls softly over her slender frame, practically sweeping the snowy street. She moves lightly, but with purpose, and it dawns on Puck that she has been sent to watch over his Jamie. A protector.

Jamie and her Angel. An Angel for Jamie.

He smiles and unconsciously reaches up to touch his hair again. His movement catches the angel's eye and she turns her head, seeing him but not breaking her stride. She smiles as she passes, though, and the smile is enough to tell Puck that he has been blessed. It is enough to fill him with warmth.

Smiling quietly to himself, he drifts back into his alley. But moments later he hears footsteps approaching for a third time. This time he feels no compulsion to approach the street. Instead, a growing dread pushes him deeper into the shadows.

As he watches, the streetlights seem to dim, as though a fog has descended. Then a new walker steps into Puck's sight and the world fractures, slipping into excruciating slow motion.

The man wears a knee-length gray coat that hangs off him like a shroud drying on a pitchfork, his thin frame poking odd angles into the leather at the shoulders and elbows. His step is decisive but erratic as he jerks down the street, his head down but his eyes up and focused, hands thrust into his pockets. His gaze is fixed on the street in front of him and his taut lips move in a constant, silent narration. Puck stops breathing, unsure whether he has done so for the sake of silence or because his breath has been stolen from him.

Like the angel only moments before, the man abruptly swivels his head to stare down the alley without breaking stride. Beneath a flat leather cap, Puck can see small, wire-frame glasses, nearly frosted over from the cold, the man's eyes cutting through the pinpoints of clear glass at the center of each lens. Puck has been in danger before—in street fights, in the cold—but he has never felt closer to death than he does when he sees those eyes.

The man passes from sight, moving down the street in the direction that Jamie and her angel had gone, but not before Puck sees the curl of a tight smile that tells him that he has been seen and remembered.

And Puck is terrified again.

"No. Nonono," he stammers, but it is not what he wants to say. He scurries back up the alley to his nest. "Noo no ... n ... "

He crouches, curling his blankets and newspapers into a loose pile, pausing to place his cheek close to the heat for what might be the last time. "Don't lose it. Can't. Can't lose it." But then he shakes his head, amending his words, chastising himself. "Can't lose ... hhh ... her. Her. Her. Can't, can't, can't."

His decision made and his course set, Puck quickly drags several large boxes over to the twist of blankets and trash that he has molded to resemble a man's body, curled up in sleep—a paper clone to protect his nest until he can return. For a moment he sits, freezing in the cold and staring out at the city, the jagged pitch of the rooftops standing out like broken teeth against the deep indigo of the sky; grinning a challenge at him.

Summoning up his courage, he hurries down the alley away from his home and the delicate doppelganger he has built to protect it. As he walks, he wrestles his tongue, struggling to say what he means.

"No. Nonono. Nono ... nnn ... now. Now. Now, now. Move now. Now you need to move. Need to now, now you need to, now."

He throws one last look over his shoulder, stroking the cashmere patch of his coat and letting his eyes rest longingly on his alley, knowing that, if things go according to plan, he may never be back. Then he hurries away down the street. His Angel has appeared at the right time. She will keep the demon at bay. But only for a while.

He's not running yet, but Puck is sweating again.

Author's Note: I know what you're thinking. I see it in your eyes as they flick across the page, following these words. And I can't say that I disagree. This is, undeniably, a digression. But it's beyond my control. The story that I want to tell has no need for this vagrant and his delusions, but where the muse walks, the writer must follow. And so this is where we begin.

To tell the truth, I'm hoping that's the last we'll see of him. I'm hoping that I can be rid of him before he has the chance to do anything problematic. After all, these streets can be dangerous at night.

But I sense determination. I read patience in the length of his hair and the gray in his beard. And because he is the first in our fugue, he sets the tone for all that is to come. And that makes me worry.

He may prove problematic; the syncopation of his stutter may disrupt the rhythm of my writing and the footprints he leaves in the snow may not lead us in the right directions. He may prove more detriment than detritus, more obstacle than observer. So, rather than avoid him, better perhaps to put him to use …

Ben
Eclipse in 36 hours

Gradually, through the black of unconsciousness, music emerged, snaking forward to twine around the old man's synapses.

Music, no matter the genre, had always seemed to take hold of Ben in a way that set his foot tapping and his head nodding a rhythmic agreement. Even now, in sleep, his lips wrinkled into a grin as a wave of melody washed over him, the supple interlude twisting him into a pirouette and dipping him low to the ground, the gray metal of his bridgework winking in the stray shafts of sunlight that found their way around the drawn shades.

In his mind, he swung a succession of beautiful girls across the floor. They spun like soft cotton thread through his confident hands, growing long and lean; tall and trim, drawn out by his mastery of the dance.

But as they wove past him—girl one, girl two, girl three, four, five—he found himself suddenly partnerless, standing alone in a cocoon of empty space, separated from the rest of the dancers with an abruptness that stilled his inertia and left him rooted to the floor. As he stood there, trapped in the bizarre paralysis so common in dream, a path through the crowd opened in front of him.

The smiling, lightning-eyed girl leaning casually against the armory wall returned his gaze with a composure that left him mesmerized, wonderfully captive to her even before she had a chance to speak. She touched him the instant he became aware of her and cemented that awareness with her first words:

"Ben?"

The old man's eyes fluttered and he mumbled something that sleep made indecipherable.

"Ben?"

He rolled over, twisting a blanket over the pillows beside him, fashioning a delicate body to support the weight of his arm.

"Ben, get the hell out of bed, it's late! Drag your lazy old ass down here."

Ben Dawes opened his eyes and, though his body complained, sat up, blinking away sleep. "Coming, sweetheart ... " he called.

Dragging himself to his feet, he staggered to the bureau and considered his reflection in the mirror, peering at a face that, over the years, had grown progressively more foreign.

"You're not looking too good, old son," he muttered. "I'm thinking you need some more rest. What do you say?"

The face in the mirror nodded in weary agreement and Ben studied it a minute longer, noting the bags under his eyes, the loose skin at his neck, the exhaustion that read like a computer manual: all-encompassing and overwhelming. He ran a hand over the rumpled tangle of white that his hair had become and sighed, then let his gaze go slack, blurring the discomfiture of the picture as he listened.

No sound from downstairs. That was odd.

His brow creased, digging rifts and chasms across his forehead.

"Elle?" Ben called, listening to his voice reverberate through the house, feeling suddenly hollow, as though a piece of himself were missing. Or that he was forgetting something.

The phone at the bedside rang sharply, the sound cutting through the silence as it rattled against the nightstand, the first fragment of reality since he'd awoken. But something kept him from answering: he didn't have the patience to listen to a too-quiet voice on the other end whose whispers made him feel guilty and tired and alone.

Instead, he lifted the phone a few inches off its cradle and dropped it back down again, then shuffled toward the bedroom door, still fighting the lingering fog of sleep and straining to hear music.

Over the forty-six years of their marriage, Ben and Elle had slipped into a solid but soothing repetition, rarely jumping the channel cut into the granite of life by their day-to-day routine. Over time, the random and unusual had eroded away, leaving their days feeling safe and rounded, and Ben and Elle mostly content—everything smoothed under a constant current of music.

Elle, the lighter sleeper, always awoke first. In doing so, she took on the challenge of waking her somnolent husband by six-fifteen in order to have him off to work by seven-thirty. More often than not, she accomplished this by combining the smell of breakfast—of coffee perking and bacon frying—with music: swing, big band, the occasional waltz, intermittent bursts of rock and roll, and once, when she'd been in a particularly impish mood, rap. But always music.

Ben could hear no music today.

He stood in the doorway, listening to the silence. A silence that said, *"Something is wrong."*

He sniffed, searching for the odor of popping grease, but smelled nothing. *"Something is wrong, and you know what it is."*

He shook his head, then vocalized his disagreement. "I don't know."

His voice rattled down the long hallway, ringing the emptiness back at him, echoing a mocking *"Yes, you do ... "*

Ben sighed again and moved toward the stairs. "Must be getting old," he muttered, softly enough to avoid the disquieting echo. As he approached the landing, the wall clock at the head of the stairs began to chime.

He peered at the clock in confusion. The face, inexplicably, said ten-thirty. It said, *"Something is wrong and you do know what it is."* It said, *"There's no bacon, no coffee and no music."* It said, *"This is the seventeenth day in a row that your wife has been dead, and you're going to have to get used to it."*

Ben didn't put on any music. He made his own breakfast, the coffee bitter and the bacon burnt, but he couldn't bring himself to play any music. Instead, he hummed softly under his breath as he cleaned up the kitchen, searching through the identical white cabinets to find where Elle had kept the dish soap and the paper towels. From time to time the telephone hanging just above the counter would come to life—clamoring for his attention—but he ignored it.

Eventually, though, he ran out of things to clean. When he found himself methodically polishing the same spot on the mantel for ten minutes, he slipped reluctantly into his wool coat and scarf and pushed out the front door into the winter air, his breath puffing out in clouds of steam that reminded him of the train that he and Elle had taken from Paris to Lisbon on their honeymoon. For the seventeenth day in a row, habit made him call, "See you later, sweetheart" over his shoulder as he left the house. For the seventeenth day in a row he heard her reply in his head: "So go already. And try not to drive like such a maniac. You're going to kill somebody someday." For the seventeenth day in a row he sat in his car for ten minutes before he could see well enough to pull away from the curb.

>**Author's Note:** Ben was meant to be our beginning; the first voice of this story and the genesis of all that is to come. I'd planned to juxtapose the tragic death of his love story with the joyous beginning of my own. But it seems everything has been delayed—our arrival, Ben's comprehension of his wife's passing, and certainly the beginning of my own love story. Even so, there is much we can still learn here. There are important insights buried amid the orange rinds and

coffee grounds in Ben's trash. And because he is too discombobulated to play his part, I'm happy to be the one to sort the relevant from the refuse.

Two things, to me, are vital:

First: Elle's funeral was the most maddening time Ben had ever experienced, and not simply because he'd lost his wife of more than forty years. The day was made more difficult by the cacophony that came along with it.

There were demanding in-laws and ingratiating guests. There were sympathetic glances and empathetic back pats. Worst of all, though, was the put-on-a-good-face phoniness of it all. For a man who had always been stolid; quiet, focused, and thoughtful,
the parade of partially remembered acquaintances and extended family offering him apologies and advice without taking the time to understand the complexity of his remorse set his teeth on edge. Their demanding placations drowned out the Thelonious Monk record that Ben had arranged to play during the viewing (and which Elle would have adored).

Ultimately, though, Ben couldn't come to terms with the naive suggestions that he "get on with his life" and "put it all behind him," because none of the guests could know that "getting on with his life" was the primary reason that his grief was tinged with guilt.

To clarify: By the time she died, Elle and Ben were no longer in love. She'd grown petulant and quick to anger and he had been unable to change his habits. She had become consumed by suspicion and accusation, and he had proven more talented at evading her questions than at allaying her fears. At some level, the love was still there, but something had changed. They had moved from passion to accepted parameters, from meaningful conversation to comfortable squabbling.

 And then Elle got sick. With terrifying rapidity she became disoriented and confused, and Ben grew more and more tired of answering the same questions over and over again, even as he found himself less and less able to recognize the woman that he had loved for so many years. Near the end, they had begun to live separate lives in the same house, divorcing within the context of a marriage.

 I don't know whether that knowledge will change your view of the man that Ben is now. I don't know that it should. Maybe you'll like him less to know that the only way he could deal with the increasingly frequent shifts in his wife's mood was to escape, avoiding the house for hours, sometimes even days at a time, leaving her to her doctors and nurses and caretakers. Maybe you'll like him more to learn that mourning her gave him a sort of self-inflicted Alzheimer's of his own as he pushed the discord that had dominated their last few years out of his head entirely, replacing it with a gleaming white pedestal just her size. You might find it noble that he stuck out a difficult situation, or sad that in the last years of Elle's life Ben was essentially carrying on an affair with the memory of the woman that she had once been.

I can't know what you'll think of him any more than I can know exactly where Ben is driving. I could hazard a guess, but until it appears on the page, it lives in potentiality. No more certain than the shifting wind, the throw of a die, or an abrupt change in personality. No more certain than what might happen when he gets out of his car, which, I promise, will be far more interesting than where he's actually going.

What is certain is this: the fact that Ben can't remember why he and Elle started fighting in the first place will become much more important once he lets himself remember that they fought at all.

Incidentally, he's driving to the grocery store. And, to be fair, not even he knew that.

#

Ben drove aimlessly. During Elle's illness, there had been too many destinations every time he got in the car. The drug store, the library, the doctor, the grocery. Her death had changed everything. He no longer had pressing needs or hurried errands. So he had begun to take long, looping trips through town, going nowhere and looking for a reason to stop.

As was the case every day, he didn't notice that he'd arrived at the grocery store until he found himself puttering through the aisles of peanut butter and green beans with no memory of parking or the chilly journey from the car to the store. The blank spots in his day had frightened him at first, and he'd wondered if it was his turn to lose his mind. But lately it didn't seem to matter.

Ben pushed his cart around the large store, the quiet muzak fusing with the murmurings of his fellow shoppers into a soothing drone of background noise. He moved slowly, occasionally dropping something into his cart—a box of spaghetti, some tomatoes, a pot roast—sometimes pulling something back out, but mostly just meandering through the semi-populated aisles and finding a small amount of relief in the side-stream company.

Eventually, he did what he had done every day since the funeral. He left his cart, stocked with enough food for two weeks' worth of "meals for two" standing alone at the end of an aisle, picked up a single can of soup from a crowded shelf and trudged toward the front of the store to pay for it.

He made it to the end of the aisle without incident, but there, surrounded by cans of Rosarita refried beans and Heinz Tomato Ketchup, his world came apart.

To Ben, everything seemed to slow and blur, as though he'd stepped through a thick, pliant cobweb. There was a sense of hesitation in the world around him that made him stumble, and he clutched weakly at a metal shelf full of taco shells for balance.

Another step forward and the world fell utterly out of sync, slipping out of focus.

As a corporal stationed near the front lines in Korea, he'd been badly injured when a platoon member had tripped a land mine. In the explosion, fragments of shrapnel and bone had perforated Ben's stomach and lower intestine. The army surgeons had given him ether and, for a moment, just before he went into surgery, he'd felt a numbing vibration pass through him, a sense of frenzied detachment. A moment when his mind was alive and awake but his body was empty and cold, floating in an icy sea of alcohol. He'd felt tranquilized. He got that again, now.

Ben found himself paralyzed but vividly aware, feeling clearly the weight of the can of soup in his hand as he tilted forward in an eternal dive, absorbing every sound around him: the muzak from the store's overhead speakers untwining from the conversations of the people sharing his aisle to form separate threads of sound that then spun back together, in and around conversations long past; exchanges that had once defined him but now made him feel the desolation of who he had become.

"Ben, get up. You're going to be late for work."

"Hiya soldier, what's your name?"

"Like a samba that swings so cool and sways so gentle ... "

"Don't frown, you never know who might be falling in love with your smile ... "

"Remember to get bread, Ben. You always forget the goddamn bread."

"I watch her so sadly. How can I tell her I love her?"

"There must be something wrong with my eyes ... I can't take them off you ... "

"I smile, but she doesn't see."

"I've wasted my life waiting for you to become someone worth my time."

"Are you going to ask me to dance or just steal looks at me all night?"

"She just doesn't see."

"Hey soldier, wake up! You're about to hit the floor pretty damn hard."

"No, she doesn't see."

All fuzzy, but familiar, ringing true in his ears but overlapping, each snatch of conversation obscuring another as they swapped places and partners, overlapping until Ben could no longer keep up. He wondered idly whether he might finally be dying or if this was just another detour.

His mind roiling, Ben never felt himself hit the ground. Awareness returned to him seconds after impact, soon enough to see the dust sweep across the checked tile, blown out in a silty wave that encircled his body. The breath chuffed out of him and he lay there for a moment, his cheek pressed against the cool tile floor, mildly disappointed to find that he was more surprised than hurt.

He glanced up to find that his vision remained unfocused. Images swam before him: twin figures side by side, sliding together to form a unified body before splitting apart again: Homo Sapiens Mitosis.

Four men in dark coats became three men glaring at him through sunken, skeletal eyes and round, wire-framed glasses. His vision swam again and they merged into two, closer now and regarding him with alarm. For a moment, they threatened to become one, before finally resolving more cleanly into two very different men. The first of them was young and robust, his perfectly coiffed blonde hair matching the expensive weave of his denim and practiced wear of his leather jacket. The other was rawboned and sallow, his long trench coat seeming both perfectly matched to him and wildly out of place. Both were transfixed by something behind Ben, out of his vision.

He closed his eyes and caught his breath. He was summoning the strength to rise when he felt a light hand on his shoulder and heard a woman's voice.

"Are you hurt?"

Ben blinked. There was a third man at his side now, wearing an anxious expression, the other two still rooted in place among the mustards and steak sauces. Ben found himself suddenly grateful that neither of them had stepped forward to help, as the man in the leather jacket looked glossy and ineffectual and the other man pinched and intense. As he watched, vision clearing, the first man—leather jacket—seemed to become aware that he was staring and turned away, striding briskly off down the aisle. The second man—pinched—took a moment longer, studying Ben carefully before winking at him through his round framed glasses (in greeting? in confirmation? Ben wasn't sure) and disappearing down the aisle and around the corner out of sight.

"Sir, can you hear us?"

A woman's voice from behind him.

"He seems a little out of it. Maybe we should get someone?"

That was the man standing beside him.

"I'll go." The woman.

Ben fumbled for words, but managed only, "Observing?"

"What?" The man knelt in front of him. "What was that? Sir?"

"He said 'observing.' What does that mean?" The woman again. Ben had a sudden desire to see her. Swept up by that desire, his mind became clear. He turned his head.

The face before him was one he felt certain he'd seen before, and for a moment he was possessed by the thought that the woman staring at him with such concern could only be Elle. But as he watched, he became aware that his recognition of her was a finer thing. He was reminiscing as much as recognizing, allowing his fitful memory to draw gossamer parallels. Ben could see warmth and wisdom and humor in the woman's gaze, but missed the five decades of shared memories that Elle's eyes had carried. This woman was stunning—her white-blonde hair falling across the smooth skin of her forehead, partially eclipsing eyes the dark blue of deep water—but she was not Elle.

On the subject of her beauty, though, the man tending to Ben seemed to agree. Despite his best efforts to focus on the problem in front of him, his eyes were repeatedly drawn to the woman kneeling beside them. And Ben couldn't blame him. He listened to the two, a smile flickering across his lips.

"He seems okay, I think," the man was saying.

"I don't know," the woman replied. "He looks a little dazed."

"Well sure, I would be too. But I don't think he broke anything."

"I didn't see him fall," she continued. "Did he hit his head?"

"I don't know. I don't think so. Honestly, it just looked like a little spill ... " The man hesitated a moment, gaze still flickering between Ben and the woman beside him. "Uh ... I'm Cort, by the way."

The woman nodded, attention still fixed on Ben.

"And, you are?"

"Seriously?" She straightened, turning to face the man—Cort. "Can we at least get him on his feet before you turn on the charm?"

"Sure," Cort stammered. "I wasn't ... I didn't mean ... "

She turned slightly to face him, skepticism in the arch of her eyebrow.

His mouth dropped open, and he seemed to search for words for a moment, then went on. "Okay, maybe I was. Sorry. Bad timing." He pulled a small silver phone from his jacket pocket. "Hold on, I'll call an ambulance."

And with this, Ben's attention snapped back to the present, from whatever corner of life's movie theater it had retreated to. "No," he said, as distinctly as he could.

The other two turned to face him instantly, Cort's expression guilty and the woman's face hot with embarrassment.

"What was that?" Cort said. "Sir, are you okay?"

"Help me up."

Ben struggled to his feet, his body coming awake in fits and starts until he was standing, braced against a grocery shelf. But once he had proven himself mobile, his caretakers seemed to forget him again; or, at least, to acknowledge his existence while forgetting his presence.

"We should probably stay with him for a while," the woman was saying.

"Definitely," Cort replied, unable to hide his enthusiasm. He flushed. "I mean ... " Again he paused, as though his voice was fighting his thoughts, tripping over his tongue before managing to salvage a sentence. "I mean, no. It's okay. I'll keep an eye on him. You go ahead."

"Are you sure? It's not a problem ... "

Cort hesitated, and Ben could almost see the air shift as magnetism twisted the area between the two young people. But the younger man shrugged off the moment.

"Thanks, really, but don't worry about it. He seems okay. We'll get him looked at and be safe, but there's no need to drag you along."

"Okay," the woman replied. "If you're sure."

"I am," he grinned, "but only if you tell me your name. I mean, he is on his feet now ... "

She hesitated for a moment, then smiled cautiously in return. "Fine. Only fair, I suppose. I'm Allison."

Allison. Ben's mouth shaped the word soundlessly.

But Cort got the words out first. "Allison. It's nice to meet you. Thanks for ... Well, thanks. Don't worry, we'll be fine." A pause, as the man seemed to struggle to pull his gaze free from hers before he turned to Ben. "Can you walk, sir?"

Ben allowed himself to be turned and led a couple of steps down the aisle. Then he stopped.

"Sir?" said Cort.

Ben turned. The woman, Allison, was walking away slowly, the rhythm of her steps unconsciously matching the muzak playing "The Girl From Ipanema."

"Allison?" Ben said, haltingly. She stopped, turning to look at him over her shoulder, her blonde hair falling lightly against her cheek.

Ben took a moment to let himself smile. "You, my dear, are the most beautiful woman I've seen in seventeen days."

Her smile, radiant through its puzzlement, gave him the strength and balance to execute a small bow. She laughed, then offered a slight wave of her fingers in return before her gaze returned to Cort. Her smile changed, becoming almost shy before she turned to move away again, her long white coat swishing behind her.

After a moment, suitably barren of sound, thought, or breath, Ben turned back to face Cort. He studied the younger man, weighing carefully the exquisitely coiffed hair and manicured chin stubble against the warmth in the man's eyes before nodding quietly and allowing himself to be led away.

#

"Feeling better?"

Ben glanced up, taking in the cautious smile of the young man across from him and nodded, somewhat wearily. "I'm fine."

"Good. That's good." Cort drummed his fingers on the table between them, the corners of his mouth still turned up slightly, clinging to his smile until he could find a more appropriate expression. "You know, I'm still not sure how I let you talk me out of taking you to the hospital."

Ben let his gaze roam the small café tucked into the corner of the grocery store, practically empty in the quiet hours between breakfast and lunch. Without people filling the booths, the starkness of the bright blue and white tile made the room feel clinical—chilly and over-sanitized. "Trust me," he said, "I don't ever need to be in a hospital again."

Cort laughed. "Well, that must be nice, huh?"

Ben stared at the other man for a moment, watching his wide smile fade into uncertainty, and then turned to look out the window, listening to the wind batter at the pane, scratching to get in. Such a thin barrier between warmth and winter; between life and death. He shivered.

"You cold?" Cort asked.

"You perceptive?" Ben snapped in reply. He watched Cort's eyebrows rise and his mouth drop open. But before he could respond, Ben cut him off with a sigh. "I'm sorry, son. I'm just a little out of sorts. I don't mean anything by it. Trust me, I'll need a hearse before I need a hospital."

Cort's smile had returned. He nodded at Ben. "It's okay. You had a pretty bad spill. I'd be surprised if you weren't a little rattled."

"It's not that. I'm fine. It's ... " Ben's voice drifted off. How to explain that the problem wasn't some stumble in a grocery store aisle but an accumulation of stumbles. The adding up of arguments, illnesses, misunderstandings, and collapse.

"Ben? You still here?"

He blinked, then nodded, leaning forward to sip from his glass of water.

Cort looked skeptical, his eyebrows high enough now that they were almost a part of his hairline. "Okay ... But stay with me, yeah? You freak me out when you wander like that."

"Well, we wouldn't want that. I promise I'll do my best to keep you calm."

Cort laughed again, his chuckle settling into a genial grin that sat slightly lopsided on his face. He paused like that for a moment, head cocked as though mulling his response, before coming back to life. "Okay, then. I'm picking up the sarcasm, but I appreciate the sentiment."

Ben snorted and allowed silence to fall between them. After a moment, he looked up at the younger man again. "And don't feel like you have to stay. I'll be just fine, if you've got somewhere else to be ... "

A shrug was his only answer. Curious, he pressed on. "Middle of the day and a young man like you has nothing else going on? Pretty sure you didn't leave a basket behind when you dragged me over to this booth. Why're you wasting your time at the grocery in the middle of the day, anyway?"

"It's not a waste," Cort replied. "I came in to pick up something for lunch and I ... Honestly? I'm not working at the moment, and I get cabin fever. So I don't keep much food in the house—forces me to get out. Meet people."

"That sounds familiar, at least," Ben allowed, then lapsed back into silence. He could feel Cort looking at him, eyes full of curiosity. After a moment, the younger man seemed to come to a decision and leaned forward in his chair. "So, what happened to you back there? I didn't see it, but it seemed like it came on you pretty sudden."

"It did," Ben replied. "It was ... very sudden." He closed his eyes, feeling the sensation of the supermarket's cold tile floor pressing against him again, the clamor of voices and the interplay and overlap of past and present shaking the air and throwing tremors through him.

Eyes still closed, he spoke. "You know how people say your life flashes in front of you just before you die?"

Cort was frowning. Ben's eyes were still closed, but he could feel it from across the table, hear it in the other man's cautious, "Yeah ... "

He sighed. "Well, it must happen to people who aren't dying, too. Or maybe I'm just dying slowly, because I've been seeing mine replayed over and over, wearing me down for the last seventeen days. Sometimes it trips me up."

Ben opened his eyes to see Cort wearing his usual smile, but twisted—nearly a smirk.

"What?" Ben snapped.

"Nothing, nothing," Cort replied, but his smile widened.

"Nothing, bullshit," Ben said. "What is it?"

"Honestly, it's nothing," Cort said. "It's just that this is the second time you've used that time frame: seventeen days. No big deal, it's just ... a little odd. Random."

"Unless there's meaning behind it."

Cort frowned again. "Okay," he said thoughtfully. "Okay ... " He trailed off, then shook his head. "Nope. Sorry, I don't get it."

"You don't have to. I do. It's a moment of tuning for me."

"Okay," Cort repeated again. A pause, then, "Meaning?"

Ben let out a tired breath. "There are times," he said, "moments in your life that stand out. But before every life-changing event is a time of tuning, when you're consciously or unconsciously preparing yourself for the decision that you're about to make." He paused. "The thing is, if you let those moments slip past, all of the decisions that follow will be wrong. Your life, after that, will be wrong."

"Uh-huh," Cort said. "So, a few weeks ago you were tuning. But that doesn't explain what happened just now. What set you off?"

Ben thought a moment, though he already knew the answer. Knowing was the easy part. "It's hard to say," he began. "Everything happened all at once. And over the course of fifteen years." His voice trailed off even as the words brushed past his lips, the truth of them stunning him for a moment as memories that he had kept walled off for years found a chink to pass their barbed messages through. In the distance he could hear Cort's voice: "No, I mean your fall ... " But it didn't matter. The past had claimed his attention.

"The boy was so quiet. Too quiet. Timid, really. And he never grew out of it. Got out of school and couldn't find a job, didn't have a knack for interviews. So, I brought him in to work with me. And then things went bad, and ... we never got over it. The guilt or the regret or the frustration. It kept popping up and getting in the way until we couldn't be in the same room. The same house. Or maybe I just couldn't have him near me anymore. Either way, that was the end.

He sighed. "It was a mistake. In a moment of tuning. It changed things."

He stopped, struggling to find the words to explain.

How quickly a son's wide-eyed admiration could take on colors of suspicion, and how that could make a wife's bright, easy smile begin to harden. How that hardening could penetrate a marriage, affecting every conversation, twisting every interaction, infiltrating every intimacy. The strain of that wore on a person. It led, invariably, to overreactions and outbursts, exploding small mistakes and exacerbating minor misunderstandings. When the dust had cleared—when you couldn't imagine things getting any worse—that was when you would realize that you hadn't factored in the prospect of illness or the effect of seeing someone you love alternate between openly hating you and not remembering you at all. And even though it may have taken decades to get from there to here, it will also have taken only one mistake, made at the wrong moment.

But if you couldn't say anything while it was happening, what is there to say after the moment has passed?

Ben clenched his eyes shut, his life flashing before him for perhaps the millionth time in the past two weeks. He could hear his heart beating in his ears, the slow rushing of blood booming like the deep thud of an immense drum, the sound enveloping him. He shuddered.

"Ben? Hey, Ben! Come back, buddy. Talk to me."

The voice hammered at him, insistent. "Come on, Ben. Talk to me."

"She would have been fine if you hadn't left us. Now I've lost both of you," Ben snapped. He opened his eyes to see Cort's face, his expression a mix of surprise and concern, and sighed again, his shoulders slumping in exhaustion and defeat.

"I'm sorry. I got ... caught up. It's nothing."

"It's not nothing." Cort stared at him a moment, head cocked as though he were running through options, selecting his words carefully. "I want ... I'm going to take you to the hospital now," he said, finally.

"I already told you no."

"Well, I'm not listening to you then." Cort shifted in his seat. "Look, at best you had a nasty fall. At worst ... honestly, I don't even know. In my opinion, you should already be in an ambulance."

"Well," Ben replied, "you're entitled to your opinion. But your opinion is wrong."

Cort sighed. "Ben, I'm serious."

Ben glowered at him. "So you're finally serious. Good for you. Now, listen to me. We're not going anywhere. It won't do a damn bit of good. Besides, if I was going to go to a hospital, I would have let Elle take me earlier."

Cort frowned. "Wait, wait ... Who is Elle?"

Ben paused, letting memories sift through his fingers, searching for something solid. "Allison. I would have let Allison take me." He smiled at Cort. "You're a handsome kid, but she's got you beat by a mile in the looks department."

Cort shook his head. "I swear. Just when I think you're losing your mind." He leaned across the table, lowering his voice as though they were not the only people in the café. "Seriously, though.

When you bowed? I was sure you were going down again, and right after I got through promising her I'd take care of you."

Ben studied the boy's face, assessing him, before allowing only, "She deserved it."

The statement seemed to rattle Cort, and he stammered momentarily before rallying to say, "Well sure, but ... "

"Besides, someone had to salvage things. You're terrible at flirting ... "

"Oh, come on," Cort protested. "I wasn't flirting. We were both just worried about you."

Ben nodded thoughtfully, then sank back in his seat. "What color were her eyes?"

"What?"

"Her eyes," he repeated. "What color?"

"Blue," Cort replied. "Dark blue. Why?"

Ben closed his eyes. "And mine?"

There was a long pause, then: "Fine. I was flirting. And badly. You win some, you lose some. But hey, you can't win if you don't play, right? That's the dance."

Ben smiled to himself. "The dance ... "

"Yeah. It's all just one big dance, right? Everyone showing off for everyone else ... You don't have to be the best in the world, you just have to be better than anyone else in the room."

Ben just smiled quietly.

"And, of course, sometimes you realize that you're actually the only one dancing and everyone thinks you're an ass."

"This woman in particular," Ben added.

"Allison ... " Cort agreed, his voice low, almost testing out the name.

Ben nodded. "Cort and Allison."

"What?"

"Cort and Allison. Say it."

"Come on ... "

Ben gave him a tired smile. "Humor me."

Cort sighed. "Cort and Allison."

"Good. Now do it again, but without the condescension."

"Ben ... "

"Please. I may be old and lonely, but I'm not senile. Do it."

Cort smiled, shaking his head. "Cort and ... "

"Close your eyes."

There was a moment of potential protest, but then Cort nodded and allowed his eyes to close.

A breath, long and drawn out, as though he were deflating. Then,

"Cort and Allison."

Ben inhaled deeply as the words lingered in the air, floating, the buoyancy of each name mingling with the other. Cort and Allison. Elle and Ben. It felt right. Predestined. He smiled. After a moment, he broke the silence. "You see?"

Cort sat, eyes still closed. "Wow."

"That's right."

"So you're ... What are you saying?"

"Mostly, I'm saying that you were an idiot to let her leave." He held up a hand as Cort opened his mouth to interrupt, and continued, "Particularly when you had the perfect excuse to get her to stay—a delusional old man who needs constant supervision to keep him from collapsing again."

"That's crazy," Cort said. "I mean, no offense, but I just met this woman. And she may be stunning, but our conversation was pretty limited to whether the ambulance that picked you up was going to need to use its siren or not." He winced. "Sorry. Tactless, but true."

"You know what I think?" Ben snapped.

Cort shrugged.

"I think you're looking for an easy way out. I think you're pretty good at fooling people, but fooling yourself is even easier. And I think that you should go try to find that girl before it's too late."

"Why her?" Cort asked. "And why is this so important to you? You just met me—you just met both of us."

Ben thought for a moment. "People are connected," he said finally. "Tied to each other by ... invisible threads. Not literally. Stop looking at me like I'm crazy." He stared thoughtfully at Cort for a moment. "You know how sometimes you know someone, but you can't remember how you met? Sometimes, I think maybe you actually haven't, but you know them anyway. We all have deep connections to the people who are most important to us. And I think sometimes those connections might exist before we actually meet. Allison could be one of those people for you."

"How could you possibly know that?"

"Because I recognize the look. I had it the first time I met Elle. You had it fifteen minutes ago, and," he said, holding up a finger to silence the potential protest, "so did she. Believe me, there are people that you haven't met yet who are going to play very important roles in your life, and there's nothing you can do to change that."

Cort was silent for a moment, then shrugged. "Maybe you're right. But even so, I don't think that means—"

"Don't," Ben interrupted.

Cort blinked. "Don't what?"

"Don't do that. Don't pretend to agree with what I'm saying when it's obvious you think it's horseshit. Don't humor me. And for God's sake don't wait."

Cort threw up his hands. "Don't wait for what?"

"For whatever you want to do! Don't wait. You're rambling through a mundane life because you don't have anything to coax you out of it. So do it yourself. Do the things that you want to do now. Today. Meet the person that you're meant to be with, today. Make a decision about where you want to go and what you want to do, right now, today. Because you don't have near as much time as you think you do."

Cort threw an anxious glance around the nearly empty room, then leaned forward, his voice low. "Okay, okay. I get it. But I can't control when I'm going to meet someone."

"You already met her," Ben hissed. "So take action. Find her before she disappears. Or find someone else, if you think you can."

Silence sat at the table with them for a moment, then Cort straightened. "Okay," he replied. "Maybe you're right. Maybe there was something there—or maybe not. But we're never going to know because she's gone, and there's nothing either of us can do to bring her back. At the end of the day, all I know about her is that she was a pretty girl in a grocery store. And she's not the only one. And so ... I rise to your challenge."

Ben shook his head and started to rise. "Son, that's not what I meant," he began.

"No, no. I'm not trying to be flip, really. But I don't subscribe to the idea of love at first sight. I don't recognize the definition of the word smitten. Anyway, it's always better to have options," Cort said.

Ben sank back into his seat. "Fine. Do your worst."

Cort smiled at him and sauntered away and Ben closed his eyes, unwilling to watch. He let out a long, emptying sigh, and then found himself unconsciously humming along to the muzak that permeated the store.

"'Girl From Ipanema,' right?"

Ben's eyes snapped open as he recognized the melody of the voice. And there she was, standing beside the table, looking at him with a blend of amusement and tenderness. Elle. He blinked. Not Elle … Allison. He smiled anyway. "'Girl From Ipanema.' Yes, that's right. I'm surprised you know that song. It was popular so long ago. Before you were born."

She let her fingers rest on the table beside him. "I love music. My parents used to play that song all the time."

"Your parents have good taste."

She laughed. "So they keep telling me." She cocked her head, suddenly serious. "How are you?"

Ben nodded. "I'm fine. Didn't hurt anything but my pride, at any rate."

"Sometimes that hurts more than anything … " One of her hands fluttered up as though to brush his cheek and Ben felt his heart quicken, but she drew it back to her side, startled, as though it had moved without her permission. "Anyway," she continued, her cheeks coloring. "Don't worry, the bow was very elegant."

"Sure," Ben replied. "For all the good it did."

Allison's puzzled smile gave a short, sharp twist to the knife that Ben's memories of Elle had become.

"What do you mean?" Allison was saying. "What good was it supposed to do?"

Ben shrugged noncommittally. "Well, it didn't get you to linger with us, did it?" he said. "Not that I blame you. Hard to see the point in a tête-à-tête with a strange old man and his young compatriot, especially when they're both flirting with you rather shamelessly." He saw her expression and added, "Each in his own way, of course."

She sank into Cort's vacant seat opposite him and held up a finger in reproach. "Hold on, now. I didn't abandon you—and certainly not because of any flirting. I don't believe for a second that that's what that bow was about."

Ben smiled. "Perhaps not."

"And as for your 'compatriot'—anyone who thinks he's smooth but is that oblivious deserves what he gets."

"He meant well," Ben said. "Just got distracted."

Allison snorted. "Pretty easily. Most people don't go looking for love in the middle of an accident."

"Which, if you ask me," Ben interrupted, "makes the people who do even more interesting."

"Really?" She leaned back, laughing at Ben with her eyes. "What are you trying to say? He seemed nice enough, but I don't know that I'm buying hidden depths."

"He was willing to give up on a budding romance to attend to a frail old man ... " Ben held up a hand to cut off her interruption. "Fine. That's overstating. But here you are, talking to me and looking disappointed about it. Maybe you came to see how I'm doing, but you were also coming to give him a chance to improve on his first impression. Yes?"

"No." She shook her head, then smiled. "Okay, mostly no. Either way, he's screwed it up again by abandoning you. Where did he go?"

Ben sighed. "That's my fault. I made the mistake of questioning his intentions, and his definition of fidelity."

"And what does that mean?"

"It means that I've managed to look like an ass in front of you twice now." Cort appeared behind her, his smile oddly cautious. He shrugged helplessly at Ben.

Ben had been focused on Allison, allowing himself to savor the small moments of nostalgia that it brought him. But that focus also gave him vantage to observe how carefully she concealed her pleasure at the sound of Cort's voice. Ben smiled to himself.

"Oh," Allison said, feigning the same surprise that had been real only moments earlier as she turned to face Cort. "I thought you'd left."

The coolness of her tone did nothing to detract from Cort's mood. If anything, his grin widened. He pulled a chair over from a nearby table and dropped onto it, letting his hands drape over the backrest. "I said that I come off like an ass, not that I am one—no way I'm ditching this guy. At least not until he proves that he's not going to take another dive."

Allison flushed. "I'm sorry. I didn't mean that." She shook her head and sighed. "Honestly, if you've been an ass, then I'm sure I've come off like a bitch."

Cort shrugged. "No sweat, we make a perfect couple." Then, as he noticed her exasperated eye roll, "Yeah, see? My verbal censors are not on the ball today. This is me with no seven-second delay." He let out a breath. "No more," he said with mock solemnity, crossing his heart with two quick swipes of his hand. "I swear."

Ben could see flashes of amusement in Allison's eyes, but she buried it a moment longer. "It's okay," she replied. "You just have a strange sense of timing."

Cort's distinctive bark of laughter echoed through the small café. "You can say that again!"

The outburst was the perfect antidote to the awkwardness that had dominated the conversation, but even as Ben watched his table-mates find common ground he found his gaze lifted from the sparring couple to the woman sitting alone at the café's counter. The woman that Cort had been talking to only moments before. Her chop-cut dark hair could not hide the suspicion in her angry stare. Her scowl looked like trouble to Ben. He fought the perverse urge to stick out his tongue at her.

"I don't know what that's supposed to mean," Allison was saying.

Ben's eyes snapped from the dark-haired woman's anger to Cort's suddenly trapped expression. He watched the boy open his mouth to reply, then hesitate, as though carrying on an internal debate over the dictionary definitions of honesty versus truth.

"It means," Ben intoned, startling both of them, "that I challenged him to be more impetuous. To take more risks." He traded glances with Cort. "And he took me at my word, even as he completely misunderstood me.

"But that doesn't matter," he continued, pleased to have stunned them into silence. "Turns out I was challenging the wrong person."

Much of the delight that Ben had sensed in Allison's voice and demeanor had aged into exasperation at this point. "See, and what the hell is that supposed to mean?" she asked. "It's like the two of you worked up a routine before I got here, but the plot makes no sense. You," she pointed at Cort, "are the high school superstar who doesn't realize he's not eighteen anymore, and you," she continued, pointing at Ben this time, "are half self-help guru and half ... I don't even know."

"Crazy old man," Cort finished. "Other than that, I'd say you nailed it." He turned to Ben. "Sorry. Censor's off."

"No offense taken," Ben replied easily. "All I meant is that if you were any more consciously disagreeable we would be in some awful romantic comedy. And the last person that I had that kind of adversarial relationship with, I married." He held up a hand to ward off protest. "I'm not making grand predictions, just drawing an old man's conclusions." He turned to Cort. "You, I already talked to, for all the good it did." He turned to Allison. "But you. You remind me so strongly of my wife that I can't imagine that you won't eventually have to cross a gymnasium to tell some idiotic young man what he's supposed to do next. Just don't expect anyone to do it for you. Other than me, I suppose." He sank back into his seat, watching them.

Surprisingly, Allison spoke first. "Okay," she said, "I'm not sure that made sense, but what the hell." She turned to Cort. "I give up. If you're interested, I have two tickets to a fundraiser for the Chicago Homeless Coalition tomorrow night and no plus one. It's fancy, but it should be a good time. And it's for a great cause, if that's something that's important to you."

Ben glanced at Cort, who had shown no reaction, other than a slight widening of the eyes and slackening of the jaw.

"So, what do you think?" Allison continued.

A slow smile spread across Cort's face. "Are you serious?" he asked.

"What?" Allison replied. "Of course. Why?"

"You're not putting me on?" He looked at Ben. "Or you?"

"What?" she repeated. "No. What are you talking about?"

Again, with Cort, Ben saw a moment of hesitation. One second where he had words poised for delivery that he bit back as he searched for something else.

"It's just ... weird," Cort said haltingly. "Truth is, I'm already going. I'm a ... my family donates."

"Oh!" Allison replied. "Well, that's great. Maybe we can meet up there, if that ... "

"And," Cort continued through a tight smile, the words seeming to emerge against his own will, "I already asked someone to go. Invited someone ..." He hesitated, then added "Like, five minutes ago." He made eye contact with Ben briefly, his expression reading, *Don't say it, I know I fucked this up* loud and clear.

"Oh," Allison said again. "Oh. Wait. Five minutes ago?" Then, manufactured disinterest took the place of her surprise, "I mean, sure, that's okay."

"No, it's not," Cort said. "Clearly, I actually am a jackass. Sorry."

"Don't be," she replied. "You didn't know. How could you know?"

Cort shook his head. "Still. Not cool. If I'd known you were coming back, I ... " He cut himself off, flushing slightly. "You know what? I'll just cancel with this ... other person, and you and I can—"

She cut him off. "Absolutely not. You asked her first. I'll see you there. Maybe we can grab a drink, and I can meet your date. Everything else ... " She blushed. "Anything else is for another time. It's probably better that way."

Ben watched the conversation, amused, and allowed himself to fade into the background. For a while he hid behind oxygen molecules and particles of light and simply listened, relishing the clumsiness of Cort's "I'm such an idiot" narrative and the sincerity of Allison's "Everything happens for a reason" rebuttal. Eventually, though, their conversation closed the doors to the outside world and sealed the two of them in, and so Ben slipped away, out of the grocery store and into the cold. But he didn't notice the chill, warmed as he was by the vision of two young people who seemed so completely taken with one another. While he could make no guarantees about what might happen, he was pleased that he had managed to switch the music back on, at least. It didn't matter whether this was an end or a beginning or something halfway through.

It was all a part of the dance.

Puck

Eclipse in 36 hours

Puck wakes up again.

This time, however, he has not been tormented by dreams; no nightmare visions of running until his lungs catch fire, growing thick and heavy with soot and ash and effort.

At least he cannot remember any dreams, and to his mind, that's just as good.

He wonders briefly whether his jumbled memories are, perhaps, dreams themselves, fueled by liquor and paranoia: the advancing clock, Jamie and her angel, the skeletal demon and the enveloping fear—like so many of his memories, no more than drunken fantasies.

But he doesn't remember having a drink, or even finding the money to buy one, for that matter. And his visions are as sharp and clear in his mind as the glassy shards of ice that cling to his beard. As sharp as his frozen tears. Besides, his feet are tired from walking. There is a flat box sitting beside him, but he has no memory of where it came from. More significantly, he does not feel the warmth of his nest. In fact, he's not sure where he is or how he came to be there.

These feelings are unsettling, but they will pass. In the winter, an old engine needs time to turn over. Eventually, a spark will catch. Puck glances around curiously and rubs his hands together for warmth as he lets his thoughts idle.

The spot where he has wakened is not as comfortable as his own. There is heat, but it is dim and diffuse and he doesn't feel warmed by it. He stands, his knees and feet cracking a painful complaint, and turns to find the heat's source.

He stands for a moment, blinking in the bright light of morning and squinting at a drab gray building that he vaguely recognizes as the Clean and Bright Laundromat. His nose seconds the recognition, as the commingled scents of detergent, fabric softener, and scorched dryer lint find prominence in the crisp winter air.

A weak gust of heat brushes the exposed flesh of Puck's cheek, and he turns to regard the wall that he had been sleeping against and the duct just above his head. He snorts, derision flooding his eyes. The heat escape is too far from the ground. Warmth from the spinning clothes dryers inside blows out and downward, but it is swept away by the wind before it can fully warm a body leaning against the wall beneath it. Wasteful.

He regards the duct for a moment, scorn revving his mind's engine until it is churning at full throttle, no longer in danger of stall. Then he turns, moving away from the building. As he does, his foot nudges the flat box, jostling it along the pavement. Puck stoops, brushing his fingers across the lid. But now, his thoughts are running more cleanly. He notices the writing across the top: De-Lish Donuts. A grin splits his face. Puck has reached speed. He has a plan, a mission. He stoops to pick up the box as memories flow back to him, filling in the gaps.

Every evening just after midnight, the teenagers working the late shift at De-Lish Donuts throw out the overstock, the unsold donuts that would otherwise go stale. Most nights the dumpster is left unlocked on a quiet corner of a little-traveled side street, almost an alley, just down the block from the Clean and Bright. After the store has closed, there's no one to notice if a passerby happens to pull a bag out of that dumpster. Certainly no one who cares.

This is vital information, and Puck feels lucky to have it, residue of a time when he'd taken shelter on a nearby block, before the weather forced him to retreat to his warmer nest beside the taqueria. During those summer months, he'd feasted on day-old pastry every night and had missed the sweetness of the crullers and bear claws ever since. But the four-mile walk from Division to Irving Park was too far to travel and too great a risk. It wasn't worth it, not even for free and plentiful pastry. Not under normal circumstances.

But today is different. Today it is worth the risk. Today, for Puck, free and plentiful pastry is Step One.

He scoops up the box, pausing for a moment as his stomach recognizes the logo and rumbles a request. But he steels himself against the hunger pangs, instead sliding the box onto the heating duct above him. It fits perfectly on the makeshift shelf, as he had known that it would. He takes a moment to scan the ground around him, the snow clean and unbroken—no footprints. The demon has not followed him—cannot possibly know where he is or what he is doing. Which is for the best. While the thought of the mirror-eyed monster from the previous night sets him trembling more vigorously than the chilly morning air, it also motivates him. Makes his mind quicker and his stride more certain. He runs a hand inside his coat to stroke his cashmere patch, muttering softly to himself under his breath

After his moment of calm, he walks to the street and fixes his eyes on the barbershop on the corner. After a few minutes, the sign in the window flips around, "Sorry, pal. We're closed" becoming "C'mon in, we're open!" Puck nods to himself, then shuffles back to collect the donut box, now wonderfully warm to the touch. He scoops it up and then crosses back to stand at the mouth of the alley, his feet refusing to move any closer to the small shop, his mind spinning and worry tugging his mouth into its familiar pucker. What if things have changed? What if he no longer belongs here? What if, somehow, his memories are make-believe and he has never belonged? He can feel the warmth of the box beginning to dissipate and knows he has to make a decision, and so he stares down at his feet, desperately trying to talk them into Step Two.

Author's Note: "You can't go home again." One of life's ostensibly undeniable truths that, for whatever reason, we seem stuck with. And you're either nodding your head in agreement or frowning as you question the context and dispute the definition of "home" (or, for the more literary minded, bemoan the short tempers of the folks in Libya Hill). Me, I'm one of the frowners.

I've always found that phrase to be insipid, trite, and all the more bothersome for being such obvious bullshit. Travel costs, burned bridges, unexpected tenants, or a bad sense of direction notwithstanding, home is nearly always within reach. Metaphorically—that's tougher. Whether you take the phrase to mean "you can never rediscover your innocence" or "things will never be simple and charming and easy again" or "you'll never remember which nondescript exit sign takes you off the highway and back to your own, particular, podunk town," it still comes down to this: Of course you can. That town may be stuck 60 years in the past, the people may stare at you with a too-familiar mistrust (or not recognize you at all), and the house might look as ramshackle as the day you left it, but you can go back—it just takes effort. And, of course, sometimes you'll get there only to find that you can't bring yourself to walk through the front gate.

Ultimately, though, you have to retreat to move forward. You have to work through your repeats before you can reach the coda. To rediscover your past—to go home again—you have to accept the risk that everything may have changed and that you no longer fit the scenery. If you can manage that, you'll be home—it just won't feel that way. You're going to be hit by that eerie mix of alienation and déjà vu. You're going to come face-to-face with the possibility that your home does not belong to you anymore.

And honestly, why would you put yourself through all of that? Isn't it better to shed the past—shuck it off like an old coat—and find a home that suits you better? Rediscovery can be traumatic. And I promise you that it will be, for Puck. Traumatic, but perhaps still worthwhile. While it may be monotonous to follow him as he trudges back and forth across the city, I think it may prove insightful. Regardless, eventually Puck will need to go home again. I can't tell you why because, frankly, I don't know yet. It's just one of a long line of things that has to happen. And so it will.

It does raise the point, however, that before you decide to go home again, you should take care to know exactly where, and what, home is. And it might also be worthwhile to make sure that you know who will be waiting there for you.

#

The bell on the door jingles a greeting as Puck steps inside, warmth wrapping around him like a mother's hug, smothering and safe. From the back he hears a voice call out, "With you in a moment, sir or madam," and he takes that moment to scan his surroundings, reacclimating himself. Searching his erratic memory for an understanding of how he fits into this place. It feels homey, without being home. He sways from foot to foot, letting his eyes sweep the small shop as thoroughly as the push broom propped casually in the corner. He silently takes in the twin silver barber chairs, their cracked vinyl seats showing slivers of the foam padding beneath. A collection of combs in electric-blue liquid perches beside a large glass jar of Atomic Fireball Jawbreakers on the shelf by Ino's chair. A towering stack of old magazines sits quietly in the corner. Puck is riveted, watching the objects around him, not moving, his expression a cross between amusement and reverence. His nose is tickled by the amalgam of smells: the warmth of cinnamon, the dry, medicinal smell of dead hair and old men, and the sharp tang of aftershave. He sneezes; twice in quick succession.

"Bless you!"

He turns to the curtained doorway that separates the shop from the stockroom in the back as the old man standing in the doorway beams at him, his white teeth flashing from a heavily wrinkled face the color of expensive bourbon. Behind the smile the old man's eyes widen in surprise.

"Puck? Is that you?"

"H ... hi, Ino," Puck replies, relieved that he is sober—as though he somehow knew that sobriety would be important here. He is startled at the ease with which he is able to find his words, having forgotten how simple it is for him to think and speak in the warmth of this place.

"How've you been, boy? We miss you around here. I was sorry to hear ... " Ino frowns, cutting his words short, then looks Puck over with a slow, appraising eye. "But you. You look pretty good. Rugged, but good. You come in for a ... " He pauses, completing his sentence with a series of knocks on the counter at his side: tap, tap, tatap, tap.

Puck grins. "Sh ... shave and a haircut. Yeah." He pulls off his hat, letting his tangle of hair spill down over his shoulders.

Ino whistles. "Wow, mijo. You *have* changed. You want to take it all off?"

Puck nods. "I think so. I need to look ... good." He hesitates a moment, then continues. "I'm g ... going home."

Ino's eyes widen at this, but he says nothing. Just nods curtly and sets about preparing for the procedure to come.

Puck watches for a moment, then interrupts. "Ino?"

Ino has bustled over to his chair, but he turns to look at Puck over his shoulder. "Yeah?"

"Ino?" Puck repeats, nervousness reawakening his stutter, "I ... I don't h ... I don't h ... have ... "

Ino's smile somehow manages to grow. "It's okay. I saw the doughnuts. At least I hope they're for me."

Puck nods again, gratitude in his eyes.

"Still warm, too, I bet."

Puck smiles and passes the box to the older man, the motion conjuring up a multitude of memories, traditions of a time not too long past. Recent enough that Ino looks mostly the same: a bit more creased, a couple of inches shorter, and his hair more salt than pepper, but with the same twinkle and bounce that he'd had a lifetime ago when Puck had spent his weekends crouched amid the old magazines watching the older men laugh. He is fairly certain that his friend knows where the doughnuts come from, but he's never said anything about it.

"Okay then. Let's get you in the chair and get started. How short you want to go?"

Puck dips into the pocket of his coat and pulls out a laminated card, letting his eyes skip briefly across it before passing it over. It says "Illinois Department of Motor Vehicles." It says "D.O.B. 4/28/64." It says "Expires 4/28/03." It has a name printed on it that is not "Puck" and a picture on it that many would swear is also not Puck. Even so.

"Like this. Like it was."

"Right you are. Have a seat." And Ino goes to work.

Forty-five minutes later, it's over. The grime has been shampooed out of Puck's hair and the hot towel that loosened the alley dust and coaxed color back into his cheeks is cooling on the arm of the chair. The sink is full of stubble-flecked shaving foam and the floor is littered with long strands of gray-brown hair. And Puck feels naked. Freshly born into the world, a wholly new person. Or perhaps the reincarnation of a person he'd thought long dead. A man he can recognize but hasn't seen in years.

"That did wonders for you, son. You look like a new man."

Puck smiles at the old man's reading of his thoughts. "Thanks, Ino."

"Yep. I'm a miracle worker all right." Ino is beaming again.

Puck slips his coat back on, absently thumbing the patch of cashmere with one hand and rubbing his naked jaw with the other, the familiar and the foreign combining to jolt him with anticipation and fear—trepidation. He nods agreement.

"Hey, before you go ... You want to take a crack at those magazines? Take some of them off my hands?"

Puck smiles at the words, reveling in tradition and memory. He nods. "Okay."

Ino grins and jerks a nod at the towering stack in the corner of the shop. "Go to it!" he says, then disappears through the curtained doorway, leaving Puck to his task.

Puck kneels beside the stack and scans the spines of the volumes of *Life* and *Time*, some of which date back to the day that Ino had opened his shop more than four decades ago—many of them untouched. It's a running joke among the regulars. No one comes into Ino's to read the magazines.

Puck's eyes dance over the titles and dates for a moment, and then his hands come alive, darting among the stacks, decisive and confident. Selecting, discarding, piling, repiling, and sorting, and every so often flipping a particularly pristine copy into a small but steadily growing pile. And the more he engages in his task the more he is able to let go of the complications of life. The faster his hands move, the less likely he is to notice the old men who come in to complain about the weather, the world, and the price of gas. In his mind, he has left the reality of the barbershop for the familiar memory of a cramped office where his fingers could freely roam the stacks of files. Where he could learn everything about the people living inside of those files without ever having to speak to them. Where he could carve out a world where he could feel at ease, at least for a while.

When he finally looks up, he has sorted the piles of magazines into stacks separated by title and year and has flipped a stack of fifteen magazines off to the side: his payment for the service.

He stands. "Done, Ino!"

Ino reappears from the back room. "You're still the best, Puck. Two hours flat. Takes me a whole day."

Puck grins, flushed with embarrassment at the compliment, aware that his new shave and haircut allow his blush to be seen. "Mm ... ha ... Okay," he manages, forcing a cautious smile.

Ino rests a casual hand on Puck's shoulder. "Thank you, Sammy. Really."

Puck nods, neck still burning with the lingering effects of the aftershave.

"You going to be okay?" A question. A different inflection than the last time he heard those words, but it flashes Puck back to his most recent conversation. Makes him think of Jamie, and the Demon and the Angel. Makes him remember his purpose.

He nods, feeling the hurry. "I'm fine. I'll be ... fine. I just have some st ... stuff to do."

Ino nods in reply, his grin looking oddly serious now. "Okay. Don't let me hold you up. But you come in anytime. Anytime. And don't be afraid to ask me for anything. Anything. You know that, right?"

Puck feels moisture prick at his eyes. He swallows hard. "I nnn ... I know."

Ino watches him turn to go, but the chime of the door spurs him to further action. "Puck? You want to know anything? About ... about anything? A lot's happened."

Puck turns slowly, internal struggle etched on his face. "No. Th ... thanks Ino. I d ... don't. Don't want to hear it. But I'm ... I think I'm going to have to. Pretty soon." He looks at Ino for a moment and then turns to go. This time there is nothing to stop him.

#

The wind bites Puck's neck as he hurries down the street toward the hectic uncertainty of downtown. He stares for a moment at the morning commuters streaming in and out of the Sheridan El stop, but then turns his back, tugging his wool cap down over his ears to approximate the protection from the cold that he lost with his haircut. The confined space of the train cars makes him uneasy, whether due to the close quarters or to the attention that he attracts. Perhaps both. His cargo of magazines feels heavy under his arm, weighing him down, but it also pulls him forward, accelerating him toward his ambitions.

He catches a flash of his reflection in the window of a bookstore and the sight startles him. With his razor Ino has scraped away two years of beard and twenty years of fatigue. In the window's mirror Puck is seventeen again, blissfully unaware of the conflict ahead. He closes his eyes and tucks a non-existent swatch of hair behind his ear as he stares at the memory of who he had been. The wind on his neck is as sharp as it had been the first time he'd walked out of Ino's barbershop. His reflection blurs and changes in front of him, his face smoothing and his hair lightening until he is once again a towheaded boy of five or six wiping tears from his eyes as he watches drifts of snowy blond hair skitter around the barbershop floor, the old men in the shop laughing at his consternation.

His father's voice rises over the clamor. "Well, at least it looks like the waterworks have dried up ... You're not scared anymore, are you Sam?"

Puck and the boy in the window both shake their heads, fighting to keep the tears at bay and forcing a smile under the steely gaze of their father, his face impassive and unreadable.

Ino's laugh had sounded friendly, even then. "C'mon, now. Give the kid a break!" he'd chortled. "Even Sampson had a tough time getting through his first haircut."

Puck's father pats Ino on the back. "Sure. But Sampson had a lot to lose. Getting a haircut isn't going to make this one any weaker."

The men had fallen into laughter then, young Sam still smiling through his confusion, too taken with the spiky new texture of his scalp to wonder what the joke was and too pleased at what he took for his father's pride to care.

Things had changed when they had gotten home. As his father laughed his way through a description of the scene at the barbershop, Sam had sat hidden on the stairs, listening to that laughter fade under his mother's tight glare, her murmured "I don't understand how you can say things like that about your own son" putting a damper on the conversation.

Sam listened as the clock counted off seconds of awkward silence, his chin slowly sinking into his hands as realization crept over him.

Ice rattled in an empty whiskey glass, and then finally his father answered softly. "Jesus. It's not like he understood what we were ... "

His mother's voice was still sharp with anger. "Maybe not, but that doesn't make it any less awful. He wants so badly to impress you. If you want to see change, help him. If you would spend more time ... "

His father's voice was an explosion. "Come off it. That's not going to do a bit of good, and we both know it. You could see how that kid was going to turn out the day he was born. Won't play with the kids in the neighborhood. Goes to pieces at the idea of a haircut, in front of God and everyone. Our Sam is no Sampson, I'll tell you that ... "

Sam drew a sharp breath, the air darting in as though anxious to fill the hole in his heart. Even so, he heard the ringing slap from below and his mother's hasty footsteps hurrying toward him. Seconds later, his father's weary sigh.

But he ignored all of it, scurrying up the stairs and hurling himself onto his bed, tears flowing freely down his cheeks as he mourned the loss of something that he couldn't quite name, feeling an emptiness that was new to him; that made his comfortable solitude suddenly feel lonely.

Days later, when the raw emotions of the day had begun to scab over and, more importantly, when his father was out of the house, Sam's mother had sat with him on his bed. She'd pulled him tightly against her and kissed his hair. "You're so smart, Sammy," she'd murmured into his brow. "If you just relax a little, people will see that in you. Stand up for yourself. You might be surprised by the result."

Sam had promised to try. But some things don't come naturally.

Puck opens his eyes to find himself once again staring at the boy, Sam, his head newly shorn. He blinks away tears and sees young Sam's image blink in reply. The motion snatches his attention, and Puck leans in to look closer, noticing the dirty jeans and patched coat that the boy wears. Sees the clutch of magazines under his arm and the age worn into his cheeks. He's changed, Sam has.

As he watches, the boy's lip pooches out in a familiar approximation of a kiss. Puck blinks again, slowly coming to recognize himself as he would recognize a man he had met only briefly, and a long time ago.

For as long as he can remember, Puck has not looked like himself. Or, more accurately, he has never looked like he felt. Not when he was five-year-old Sammy learning the paired feelings of betrayal and loneliness; not when he was a fifteen-year-old feeling forty, matured to the point that he could no longer identify with or relate to his schoolmates; not when he was twenty-five but teenaged, simultaneously conquering scholarship and alcoholism; and not when he was thirty-five disguised as twenty-one masquerading as eighty, a confusing union of anxious ambition and anthrophobia. Somehow, staring at his reflection today makes him feel more himself than he has in a very long time.

Puck smiles at himself in the bookstore window for a moment before he notices that it is no longer a bookstore window. He looks around. The street that he is standing on has changed as the sun slid through the sky. As he has navigated his memories he has managed to leave wandering footprints in the snow that stretch all the way across town. Three miles ... no memories.

He sighs, affected but unconcerned. In the past, he has chalked these mental lapses up to liquor or exhaustion or insanity.

Nothing he can help, at any rate. This time, he's just happy to have missed out on even a few hours of cold and worry, both of which return full force with the onset of reality and the weight of Ino's magazines.

He glances around again, fixing on his location—Armitage and Sheffield—and smiles to himself. He adjusts the magazines again, taking care not to scuff or bend the pages, and hurries down the block, racing the sun to the horizon.

#

The pawnshop Puck enters may technically be the same temperature as Ino's barbershop, but it has none of the warmth. Puck feels chilled even as his face and hands thaw.

He moves hesitantly toward the dingy glass counter, where the rodent-faced owner of the shop is talking heatedly with a large Black man in a denim jacket, the sleeves pushed up to his elbows. He stays carefully separate from the pair as their argument catches fire.

"What do you mean, fifty?" the Black man demands. "It's worth twice that, at least."

The smaller pawn shop owner does not back down in the face of the bigger man's fury but counters the anger with boredom. "Hey, I'm doing you a favor. There's no way I can resell this. You shouldn't even have it inside city limits. I'm offering you fifty because we've got history. Otherwise, I'd just throw you out."

Puck's eyes follow the man's gesture and fix themselves on the handgun lying on a dirty piece of chamois on the counter. His eyes widen, and he hugs his thin stack of magazines tighter to his chest, unable to drag his eyes away from the dark metal.

The Black man's gravelly rasp cuts into Puck's reverie. "That's horseshit. You know it's horseshit. C'mon, work with me here …"

But the shop owner doesn't seem to notice. "Sorry, Spider. That's my best. Take it or leave it."

"So what am I supposed to do?"

The shop owner spreads his arms and shrugs, saying nothing.

"Fuck," the customer mutters, folding the gun into the cloth and stuffing it into a pocket. "Never mind. Thanks anyway." With that, he pushes away from the counter and toward the door. As he brushes past Puck, he seems to notice him for the first time, and his eyes flicker over Puck's battered coat and stocking cap. And although Puck feels himself shrink under the man's gaze, he cannot turn away. After a moment, the man sighs impatiently. "You need something from me, friend, or you window shopping?" Puck makes a futile effort to speak, but his tongue balks at the request and instead sticks resolutely to the roof of his mouth.

"Hey," the scrawny shop owner interjects, "don't peddle your shit in my store. If you can't sell it to me, you can't sell it."

The customer nods in disgust, then his eyes return to Puck, who has not yet been able to look away. "Yeah, well, take a fucking picture. It'll last longer." He pushes through the door, leaving Puck to watch it swing shut, the jingle of the bell signaling the end of one opportunity and the beginning of another. A shudder runs through him, and for a moment he feels caught between the present and the future, uncertain whether to jump time or just give up and allow himself to be run down by the past.

The man behind the counter sighs, not watching the other man leave but focusing on his own hands. "Shit," he says under his breath, then looks up and seems to notice Puck for the first time. "Now what the blue fuck do you want?"

Puck's shoulders bounce in an involuntary series of shrugs as his attention is jerked back and forth between the door where the Black man has just exited and the task at hand. He doesn't try to speak, knowing that it is pointless in this place. Instead, he holds the stack of magazines out and waits, eyes on his shoes.

The man sighs again. "Magazines? All right, let me take a look."

He grabs the stack from Puck and drops them on the counter, where he begins leafing through them. As he looks, however, his examination becomes less cursory, and he slows to inspect each magazine closely.

"Hey, these are pretty old, you know?"

Puck can only nod.

"Not bad shape, either. Nice." He finishes with the stack then looks up at Puck, eyeing him appraisingly. "Tell you what. I'll give you ... say ... thirty bucks for the stack. How's that?"

Puck's gaze returns to the floor and he shakes his head slightly. "Nnn ... nnn ... " he mutters.

"What, you want more?" the man says, irritation coloring his voice. "Look, dude, I'm being pretty generous already ... "

"Nono." Puck manages. "I ... nnn ... "

"You what?" The man watches for a moment as Puck dances from foot to foot, struggling for words. Then he says, not unkindly, "You don't want cash?"

Puck sighs with relief, nodding his head, his eyes finding the man in gratitude.

"Fine," the other says. "You want to do trade? You can have, say fifty bucks to work with. That fair?"

Puck nods, moving away from the counter to scan the store, searching.

Five minutes later he's back at the counter, holding three vinyl records and a small stack of baseball cards—Rod Carew and Pete Rose hanging out with Louis Prima and Stan Getz on the dirty glass counter of a Chicago pawn shop.

The man eyeballs the pile, then nods. "That's fine, man." He hesitates a moment and then adds, "Honestly, though? You only got about forty bucks worth. You need anything else?"

Puck shrugs and shakes his head, but then the memory of struggling across town with an armful of magazines changes his mind and he snatches a large straw handbag from a small rack of women's purses. Big enough for the records. After another moment's thought, he returns to the counter and stares down at one of the small items inside: thinking of a gift for Jamie. Something that will communicate what she means to him. He points at the small gold bauble, and the man behind the counter scoops it up with a grin and passes it to him.

"Nice, man. Real nice. Good choice. We're even, okay?"

Puck nods and turns to go.

"Hey, you ever get any more of those mags, you come back and see me, okay? Talk to me first!"

Puck doesn't stop walking. He knows he'll never come back. There is no need. His plans have changed slightly, but he'll adjust. Regardless, he is halfway home. He smiles softly at the joke as he steps back out into the cold. Halfway home indeed.

Cort

Eclipse in 34 hours

Author's Note: Too often, life seems to come down to who is first. Too often for it to be random, at any rate. And that's not fair. So that will not be the case in this story. For Cort, it is all going to come down to who is second. Poetic, really.

In this case we're talking about a close-run race, the photo finish blurred at the end to rob the victor of the trophy. But perhaps that's how it has always gone. Perhaps Bell's patent application landed on the appropriate desk moments after Meucci's but got shuffled to the top as they were filed. Perhaps Adam beat Eve to the apple tree by a snake's length but handed over the prize out of gallantry (or a preference for Golden Delicious). Perhaps I'm getting ahead of myself ...

Let's begin with the fact that Cort is a square—though not in the way that teeth-gratingly clichéd 1950s jargon would have it. Only in the sense that things seem to happen to him in pairs.

When he was a child, if he made a new friend, it was a sure bet that he'd wind up in a fight by the end of the day. As a teenager, if he made the honor roll, it was only a matter of time before he got expelled. Minutes after he got the news that his mother had passed away he learned that the man he'd always known as his father was, in fact, not. And hours after learning who his real father was, he found himself arrested on charges of breaking and entering (more on that later). Everything in pairs, multiplying impact. Misfortune times misfortune. Luck times luck.

Even on this particular day, every second moment had seemed to be full of import and opportunity; each meaningful encounter followed by another that casually recharted his course. The time shared with Allison in a random grocery store aisle would have come and gone had it not been for Ben's collapse. And if not for the old man's ramblings in the café, Cort would not have spoken to Theresa, who was sitting alone at the counter, her dark hair a curtain shielding her from his attention. She'd looked so aloof that even Ben's goading might not have coaxed him into approaching her ... if he hadn't been looking for a second moment to complete the square.

Now, he can't take his mind off the two women, or reconcile the fact that, for better or worse, he's going to see both of them tomorrow night.

But I'll tell you this: Cort's life goes in one of two directions, starting here. And this time around it will be better for him if he settles for second. At the end of the day, someone has to win, and Cort is a second-place kind of guy—even if he doesn't know it yet. He is charisma without class. He is shine without substance and charm without character. And whether that impresses you or makes you angry or, in some walled-off section of your psyche, arouses you, he's simply not the kind of guy you root for. At least he's not the kind of guy that I root for, and this is my story.

He may be smart, there is plenty that Cort does not know. For example:

He doesn't know it, but this upcoming two-date night is possibly the most important of his life.

He doesn't know it, but he's going to have a decision to make, one that will cement his future (and the last few chapters of this story).

Cort doesn't know it, but there are more exciting things in store for him than even he had hoped for. Certainly more exciting than second place—though second place is precisely where the excitement begins.

Cort doesn't know any of this because it's all in the future, yet to be written.

So let's watch. And bear in mind that, unfortunately for Cort, it might have been better for him if this time it had actually come down to who was first.

#

Cort laughed out loud as he shrugged into his jacket, steeling himself against the January chill that waited outside the warmth of the grocery store. The events of the afternoon had sent him somersaulting down the far side of belief to the degree that he found himself checking every few seconds to confirm that life was continuing on in a timely and linear fashion and not twisting him into a knot for the sheer pleasure of watching as he struggled to untie himself later.

From where he stood just outside the glass doors of the supermarket he could see Allison's long white coat retreating down Clark Street, gliding along the snowy sidewalk until she disappeared into the crowd. He stared at the remnants of her footprints in the snow for a moment before they were obscured by the crush of midafternoon traffic. He watched for a moment before he realized that he was grinning like an idiot and laughed self-consciously, turning back toward the store. He glanced through the window into the small cafeteria, hoping to replace his lingering image of Allison with a glimpse of Theresa, to trade one budding romance for another in the hopes that it could unwind the threads of fascination that Allison's presence seemed to have woven around him.

Theresa was still sitting at the counter where he had left her after Ben's halfhearted dare, and Cort felt a small thrill watching her engrossed in her life, unaware of his attention. She was stirring her coffee with one hand as she flipped brusquely, almost angrily, through a magazine with the other, not seeming to care what she was looking at. As he watched, she half stood, turning slightly toward him before stopping herself and dropping back into her seat to tear at the magazine again.

Cort hadn't moved, riveted by her angry beauty, her cheeks flushed and her body tight with checked ire. As though she could feel him watching, she reached up to flick a wayward strand of her heavy pixie cut away from her cheek. And although he was certain that she couldn't fail to see him if she chose to turn and glance out the window, he couldn't bring himself to move away.

Just as she brought her eyes up, however, someone walked through Cort's line of sight, the darkness of the man's coat cutting off his gaze. He blinked, startled at the abrupt break of his focus, then turned back to the window just in time to see the same man slide into the seat beside her. As Cort watched, this stranger began to talk, Theresa clearly not glad for the company but unable to escape as the man leaned on the counter, pressing his attentions. Whether it was the chill, the disconcerting feeling of being held separate from the conversation by the frosted glass of the store window, or the fact that his date for the next evening was being hit on while he watched, Cort found himself growing more and more irritated with each passing second. Finally, he gave up any pretense at nonchalance and started back into the store, not sure what he would say but determined to move the stranger along.

His intentions, however, were interrupted by a hollow-faced man lurching down the sidewalk toward him. Cort stepped back quickly, stumbling as his feet dodged one another in their haste to retreat. The man mumbled something that Cort couldn't make out, then blinked hard and took another step toward him. For a moment Cort thought the stranger meant to kiss him, as his lips puckered and his eyes drifted shut, his hands floating between the two of them. But then, as Cort watched, a sense of peace seemed to settle over the man and he straightened, his eyes opening. His pursed lips eased, and Cort found himself trapped by the man's eyes. While the rest of his face seemed plain, if somewhat haggard, his eyes rang with a beguiling emptiness. A heartrending sense of need backed with an unexpected, brittle determination.

The two men stared at one another for a moment before the stranger broke the silence. "You ... you ... " he sighed out heavily, and one of his hands stole up the seam of his heavy coat, gripping the lapel and rubbing it compulsively. His stutter eased a bit. "Y ... you luh ... love ... her?"

Astonished, Cort dragged his eyes from the man to glance back into the store.

"No!" the stranger demanded, inexplicably agitated, "Nono! Hh ... hh ... her!"

"No," Cort replied. "I mean, I'm sorry, I don't know who you mean."

"Her!" the man insisted again. "Th ... thhhh ... thhhhh. Ah ... Aa ... " He gestured spasmodically down the street.

Understanding came to Cort and he smiled cautiously. "Allison?" he said. "Do you mean ... Do you know her?"

The man gave a fitful toss of his head that Cort could not tell was meant to convey a "no" or was, perhaps, simply a gesture of disdain or dismissal or something else entirely.

"She ... she's ... shhn ... aan ... " the man sputtered.

"She's what?" Cort prompted.

"Hmmm ... " The man let out another sigh, his eyes again lighting on Cort's, carrying an intense sadness that made Cort aware of how cold the day had become.

"Please," the man sputtered. "Pl ... please help ... "

Cort sighed to himself. After all that, it'd been a hit up. "You need some help?" he asked, reaching into his pocket and pulling out some random bills, change from the coffee that hadn't made it back into his wallet.

The man's hands darted out, startling Cort enough to force him back another step, but he didn't snatch at the money as Cort had expected. Instead, he patted at it, seemingly unable to take hold of the thin paper. At the same time, a sense of agitation overtook him, his face retreating to the strange mask he'd been wearing when Cort had first seen him, eyes closed, lips puckered as though struggling to whistle as he mumbled indecipherable fragments of words: "Weh ... wh ... aaw ... "

Cort eyed the other man warily for a moment, but now he seemed almost frozen in place, a gentle rocking and a slight shake of his head the only observable movement. After a few seconds, Cort stepped forward and tucked the bills into one of the man's coat pockets, murmuring, "Hope this helps, man."

He continued down the sidewalk, then paused and turned to look back at the stranger, who was still standing where Cort had left him, swaying slightly and staring down the street. Cort watched for a moment, shaking his head in wonder.

"Weird," said a voice beside his ear.

He started in surprise, spinning around to see Theresa regarding him, her dark eyes flashing with curiosity.

"Jesus!" he exclaimed. "You scared the hell out of me."

"Sorry," she replied, not looking particularly apologetic. She nodded in the direction of the homeless man. "What was that all about?"

She was smaller than he'd remembered from their brief encounter at the grocery store's café, a full head shorter than him and compact, with deep brown eyes and hair so black it was nearly blue. Her body was tight with anxiety, her chin and chest pointing at him in accusation. Cort made the spontaneous decision that contrition was better than conflict and swallowed the first response that had sprung to his lips ("What was what about?"). He shrugged. "Beats me. I thought he was just trying to get some cash, but ... " He trailed off, remembering how the man had patted at the offered money. Perhaps trying to push it away? The idea worried him for reasons he couldn't put into words.

Theresa's voice cut into his daze. "Uh-huh. And the woman?"

Cort blinked, thrown by the shift in topic. "Who?"

"The blonde in the white coat. That you were talking to earlier? That your girlfriend?"

Cort hesitated, his tongue glued to the roof of his mouth and his mind whirling.

Author's Note: Let me interrupt for a moment to share a revelation: All people are different. (But wait, there's more!)

What we so often fail to realize is that, while all people are undeniably different, the gradation from one to the next can be shockingly slight. Life's infinite canvas may be cut through with swaths of blue and green, crisscrossed with crimson and shades of gold, but in the end, each point on that canvas is different from its neighbor in only the most subtle, imperceptible way. A trace of magenta produces a unique personality. The barest hint of cyan and a singular entity is born. And while, to the casual eye, the opposite ends of the spectrum may seem poles apart, the truth is that we individuals are not separated by swathes of color or by violent changes in tempo or tone. We are not divided by dramatic changes in light or shadow (although that's closer) but by only the barest of degrees. And so "every person is different" becomes "every person is only slightly different." The trick, then, is how to identify and interact with each "slightly different" individual.

And like any magic trick, it takes practice, dedication, and creativity. For example, to some, one might explain away a wayward look with a casual, "I think they used to work at my office." For others, "I was just thinking that would look amazing on you" would be a better choice. And for some, "Wow, they're fucking hot, huh?" would be perfectly acceptable. It depends on the circumstance and the individual ...

Reading what I've written, I see that this doesn't necessarily come off well. Callous is a word that people use. Manipulative. Shallow. But in my defense, I present this only as the narrative that I imagine has been going through Cort's mind as he scrambles to find a response to Theresa's very fair question.

There's a surprising amount to be learned from Cort, not the least of which is how the slight difference in gradation from person to person in no way makes those individuals interchangeable—it simply makes it that much more difficult to find a match, if such a thing truly exists.

Until now, perhaps. Though he's fighting it, there's a piece of Cort that wants to scrap the conversation that he's currently getting more and more deeply entwined in so that he can go charging off down the street, searching the crowd for a woman in a long white coat.

But while that may be good for Cort, it would not be as good for the story. And luckily for us, Cort is the type who will almost always play two hands rather than fold either before the turn. After all, "It's always better to have options."

Cort took another half-second to consider his options. Denial: "Wait, who are you talking about?" Honesty: "Damn, you weren't supposed to see her." Even Greater Honesty: "That's the woman I'd rather be talking to right now. Do you mind if I bail on our date tomorrow to be with her instead?"

Instead, he settled for "misunderstood":

"No, no. Not my girlfriend." He laughed, adding, "I don't have a girlfriend," and wondered, even as the words left his mouth, why he'd felt compelled to clarify that point.

Theresa eyed him suspiciously. "Uh-huh."

"Really!" he continued. "She's just a ... " He thought of Ben's collapse and the series of conversations in the grocery store aisle and café. "A friend of a friend," he finished with a gentle smile.

The ice in Theresa's gaze showed a few tentative cracks. "Really?"

"Really," he replied seriously. "Trust me. Not my girlfriend." In his mind, he added a silent "yet" that he felt immediately guilty for.

"So, I'm still meeting you at the party tomorrow night?" Theresa asked.

"Of course!" he replied, resting a hand on her shoulder as he bit back the rest of the sentence ("After all, I did invite you before I realized that I could have gone with the woman you're talking about. Incidentally, she'll be there too.") Instead, he said, "The party starts at six-thirty but I'm tied up until eight or so. If you get there at eight-thirty or so, that'll be perfect. Any earlier and I make no promises. You'd be shocked at the number of guys who turn up just to troll for women."

"Really," she replied, eyebrows raised. "Not like you ... "

Cort laughed, raising his hands. "Touché. I just want to make sure no one hits on you before I've had a chance to strike out."

She was smiling now. "I guess we'll see. You've done okay so far. But you knew that, didn't you?"

Cort shrugged in a way that felt modest.

Her eyes narrowed for a moment, and then she shook her head, smiling again, despite herself. "Fine. I'll look for you at eight-thirty."

"You better ... " he replied with mock severity.

"I will," she insisted, laughing now.

"Alright then." Cort grinned at her; the grin that had always made people fall in love with him; the grin that made him feel alive.

"Okay," she repeated. "Um, bye then ... " She backed away a few steps, then waved shyly and turned to continue down the street.

The encounter over, Cort felt his adrenaline fade and, with it, his interest. Even as he watched Theresa move down the street away from him, the easy sway of her hips guiding her through the crowd of passersby, the electricity of the interaction began to dissipate into the frigid air. And the instant it did, he found his thoughts sliding back toward Allison. He shook his head, as though that could rattle her from his thoughts, but there she was, eyebrows scrunched in amused disbelief.

For a moment, Cort considered calling after Theresa. Shouting, "Hey! You know what? Never mind. Don't worry about tomorrow. I met someone else." But something welled up inside him and he collared the impulse. Wrangled his tongue and squirreled the words away behind his grin. Instead, he settled for leaning in a too-casual-to-be-unrehearsed pose against a nearby bike rack and waved at Theresa's back.

"Til tomorrow!" he called. "And the dance!"

She waved over her shoulder, then turned the corner and disappeared from his sight.

Cort stood for a moment staring in the direction that both women had gone, shuffling from side to side to fight off the chill. He found himself smiling in anticipation as he let his imagination predict the future, his smile gradually dissolving into a thoughtful frown when he realized that, despite his best efforts to remain neutral, in his mental picture of the party he had only one date—and it wasn't the one he'd just made. "Well shit," he said softly, "it's always better to have options."

He shrugged, then flipped his collar up against the cold, blew warmth onto his chapped hands and began the walk back to his car, whistling "The Girl From Ipanema" under his breath.

#

The block and a half walk back to the parking garage went by practically unnoticed, with Cort's focus buried under a torrent of thoughts. The sight of his Jag parked serenely in a corner of the garage, however, was enough to clear his head of its turmoil. The thirty-two years since the birth of the bright yellow 420 had made it more decrepit than classic, but Cort's love for the car had erased the minor dings and scattered patches of rust on the body and the coughing rumble of the engine, and turned it into a thing of beauty.

He was just climbing into the driver's seat when his calm was interrupted by the cheerfully annoying chirp of his cell phone. He slid the key into the ignition, then dipped into the breast pocket of his coat for the device, glancing at the familiar number that flashed across the screen before answering as he backed out of his parking space.

"Hey Ryan," he said, sliding the phone to his left shoulder and pinching it there with his chin as he shifted into drive. "What's up?"

"Where are you right now?" Ryan demanded without any preamble.

"Good talking to you too, man."

"Fuck you, smartass. Where are you?"

"Delightful," Cort muttered, maneuvering the car through the catacombs of the parking garage toward the small booth at the front. Despite being worth more money than Cort could imagine, Ryan talked more like someone who worked on one of the shipping barges his family owned than the person due to inherit them.

"Well?" Ryan demanded.

"Jesus, settle down. I'm in my car, on my way home," Cort replied. "From the grocery store," he added, anticipating the next question. "Why?"

"You alone?"

"Ryan, what the hell?"

Ryan's sigh sounded like radio static through the phone's speaker. "Never mind. I withdraw the question. Besides," he continued, "you wouldn't swear if you were with a woman. Or am I interrupting something?"

"Yeah," Cort said. "My good mood."

"Glad to do my part."

"What's with the questions?" Cort asked. "Where are you?"

Ryan's voice shifted from bored to cautious as Cort guided the Jag up to the garage entrance, flashed his pass at the bored security guard, and swung out onto the street. "Doesn't matter," he said. "Nowhere worth mentioning."

For a moment, Cort considered pressing his friend, but he knew that once the note of evasion had entered Ryan's voice, the truth quickly became a no-fly zone. Cort had learned to recognize and adapt to that tone, which was one of the main reasons the two had stayed friends as long as they had—a shared love of what might generously be called personal fiction and more accurately labeled "bullshit."

Cort had met Ryan Dotson three years earlier at a community fundraiser. For months he'd turned down invitations to various art openings and silent auctions before finally breaking down and showing up at a dinner-dance benefiting a local museum that he'd never even been to. However, once that ice had been broken, he found himself addicted to the first-class food and liquor that was, ironically, given away in vast quantities to the wealthy by organizations that wanted their money. He found a kindred spirit in Ryan.

The Dotson family had been wealthy long enough to have forgotten where the money came from. Long enough to have accumulated countless stories about shipping strategies and business coups, immense gambling losses and money changing hands over everything from rat races in the Bronx to gun shipments abroad. All of which Ryan would laugh loudly about, winking at the wide-eyed blonde attached to his arm on that particular night and then shooting a more meaningful wink at Cort, who was left searching for anything even half as interesting to talk about with his own date.

The Dotson story was legendary. Cort's was significantly less well publicized, if even more unusual. But because it was not something he was eager to share, he had to work harder to earn his place in Ryan's circle, which made him savor every small moment in the spotlight and grab every opportunity he could to bring Ryan down a peg—just to keep them on something near equal footing.

"Honestly?" Ryan was saying, which meant that whatever came out of his mouth next was guaranteed to be at least 80 percent fiction. "I just walked past a girl that could change my life, if I give her the chance. I thought I'd give you a call to see if you were around to wing me."

Cort rolled his eyes and leaned back in his seat as he brought the Jag to a stop at a red light. "And you figured that now was the best possible time to ask me for a favor?"

There was a pause at the other end of the line and Cort could almost see Ryan's face in his mind, his brow knitting as he tried to make the mental shift from what he needed to what he might owe. It didn't take long ...

"Ah shit, you're not still pissed off about that, are you?"

"Not sure," Cort replied. "You think I should be?" He pulled the phone away from his ear and tapped the base lightly against the steering wheel. "Hey man, I've got another call. I'm going to go ... "

"So I left early," Ryan interrupted. "I bagged on you. Fine, I'm sorry—that what you want me to say?"

"I don't want you to say anything."

"Cort ... "

Cort missed the rest, as he had to hold the phone away so that his friend wouldn't hear the laugh that would give away the joke. Collecting himself, he returned the phone to his ear, only to hear Ryan's clamoring voice, sharp and indignant. Cort sighed, then tapped the phone against the wheel again and cut his friend off.

"Hey Ryan, I've got another ... "

"Let it go to voice mail!" Ryan interrupted. "Listen, you said it yourself: 'Never think twice when there's money or women involved.' Don't. Think. Twice."

Ryan's comic eagerness quickly restored Cort's smile, and his good mood with it. He waited a moment to set up the punch line, then said, "You finished?"

"Yeah," came the reply. "Yeah, I am. Now tell me I did right."

"Yeah, okay." Cort said easily. "We're cool. I'm not upset. Tell me about this girl who's going to change your life."

There was a long pause, then a burst of laughter from the other end of the phone. "Asshole!" Ryan shouted, the volume making Cort jerk the phone away from his ear and swerve to avoid introducing a parked Volkswagen to the right front fender of his Jag.

"You complete asshole," Ryan repeated at a more manageable volume. "Why do you do that to me?"

"Because I can, my friend," Cort replied easily. "Only because I can."

"Yeah, yeah. You're just pissed that I snagged a hottie and you had to clean up after me. Again."

"Whatever you say," Cort replied. He took a breath. "So, seriously, what's with this girl? And what happened to the one from the other night? I thought you two were hitting it off."

"Yeah. We were. We did. Maybe too much," Ryan replied. "This new girl today is just ... " Cort heard his hesitation and wondered what it meant—what he wasn't saying.

"Whatever," Ryan continued. "She's just someone who caught my eye. It's nothing yet. Forget I brought it up."

Cort opened his mouth to protest, but Ryan cut him off. "The girl from last night is a problem though—she called me twice today already. I'm not sure how I'm going to get rid of her."

Cort eased the car forward again, grinning. Time for a little revenge. "Question: Did you fool around with her last night?"

Ryan's voice was cagey. "C'mon, man. I'm a gentleman."

"I'm not talking about sex," Cort interrupted. "Just normal, everyday, parked-car/living-room-sofa fooling around. Window-fogging."

"Oh," Ryan replied, embarrassment flushing his tone. "No. None of that either, actually. We just talked."

"Well, that's your problem," Cort said. "Now she's filed you under 'relationship: potential husband' instead of 'one-night stand: wild monkey sex.'"

"Shit," Ryan muttered.

"I can't believe you saddled me with her friend for this. Do you know how long I spent listening to stories about that girl's cats?"

"I'm sorry," Ryan muttered.

"Lucky for you, I'm here to save your ass." Cort made the turn onto Norwood and pulled up at the curb in front of his building.

He leaned back in his seat and stretched his legs, savoring the moment. "So. You haven't kissed her yet, right?"

"Cort, I already said ... "

"I know, I know. Such the gentleman. But you know what that means ... "

"What?" Ryan asked.

Cort waited in silence, counting. He'd reached five before he heard Ryan's sharp intake of breath.

"Awww shit. C'mon, Cort no."

"You want to get out of this?"

A pause, then a begrudging, "Yeah ... "

"Well then—Kiss of Death."

Ryan sighed. "Fuck."

"Sure," Cort replied, laughing. "Go there if you have to."

Ryan tried force a chuckle, then cut the laugh off. "That can't be the only way."

"Maybe not, but it's the best way. Think about it: you go to give her that magical first kiss, and she closes her eyes, imagining Prince Charming, ... and then it's just soft, and gross. A dead fish. That's going to make her rethink everything."

Another sigh. "Yeah, I guess.

"That moves you from 'husband' to 'friend' territory immediately. And you can kill that by saying friends would be too painful—your feelings are too intense. I promise, you'll never see her again."

"Okay, okay." Ryan sighed, sounding miserable. "I'll give it a shot."

Cort shook his head in amazement. Sometimes the line of shit that people would swallow was unbelievable. He forced seriousness into his voice. "Good man."

"Thanks, Cort."

"Hey, don't mention it. That's what friends are for, right?"

"Yeah, I know. Hey, listen, I'm setting up a poker game for tomorrow night. Let me know if you want in. I'll spot you if you need it."

"I can't," Cort replied. "Got a Carlsbad event."

Ryan laughed. "When are they going to learn, huh? You don't even have the money."

"Yet. Yeah, I know."

"So, blow it off," Ryan pressed.

"Love to, but I can't. Sorry."

"You got a hot date?"

Cort laughed. "Actually, I think I might have two."

Ryan whistled. "Hey! Nice work! But be careful, Lucy. Sounds like one of your crazy schemes ... "

"Don't worry. It's under control. Besides ... " Cort trailed off.

"Besides what?" Ryan asked.

Cort opened his mouth to reply, then paused. He'd nearly let it slip that there was something different about one of the women. That she was special in a way he didn't yet know how to describe.

But even if it was true, Ryan was not exactly there to play confidante. No need to offer ammunition to your own firing squad.

"Besides," he repeated, "I'm not a redhead."

"Whatever," Ryan replied. "So, what do they look like, these women of yours?"

"Um." Cort called up a mental image of Theresa, looking up at him from beneath the heavy bangs of her blue-black pixie cut. "One of them is … edgy. Short, cute ... um ... forthright?" He laughed. "Pretty much exactly my type."

"Uh-huh," Ryan replied. "And the other one?"

And now, Allison dominated Cort's vision. "The other ... " Cort began, unsure how to explain her and not certain that he wanted to, either unwilling to confine her with his description or unwilling to share his perception of her with Ryan. Finally, grudgingly, he relented. "The other is blonde. Tall. Elegant." He hesitated. "And nice. Gorgeous, but really, really ... nice."

"Oh," Ryan said, sounding oddly disappointed. "Cool man. That's great." Then, "You need someone to ride shotgun? Entertain your extra lady? I got an invite to the shindig tomorrow, too. I wasn't going to go, but I owe you."

"Are you kidding? After what you put me through last night? Not a chance. And neither of these women are your type anyway."

"No?"

"No. They've both got class and taste."

Ryan laughed, adding "asshole" for good measure.

Cort took his foot off the brake and swung the car into the apartment complex's driveway, hitting the button of the garage door opener above his head with the antenna of the cell phone, then returning it to his ear. "Hey, I have to go. I'll talk to you later."

"Yeah, okay. Later."

Cort grinned his lopsided grin, the grin that marked him as simple to people who didn't know him, charming to those who thought they did, and sly to those who were truly dialed in. "Oh, and Ryan? That girl from last night?"

"Yeah?"

"Don't forget to 'not' brush your teeth ... "

A heavy sigh drifted through the phone, punctuated by one last muttered, melancholy "Fuck."

Cort thumbed the button that cut off the call, simultaneously pulling into the parking garage that would have done the same thing, smiling to himself all the while.

#

Cort was still smiling as he stepped into the minimal warmth of his one-bedroom walk-up. He dropped his coat over the back of an old armchair and made his way into the small kitchen, blowing on his hands as he cursed the apartment's unreliable furnace.

He paused just inside the kitchen door, nose wrinkling at the stale funk of the old paint peeling from the walls, smelling of spoiled milk and Windex. For the first time, he felt a twinge of guilt at the joke he was playing on Ryan.

He pulled a pot from a low cupboard, filled it with water, and set it on the stove to boil, pondering the amusing mental image of Ryan draping himself gracelessly over some beautiful, probably wealthy woman, planting dead-fish kisses on her unsuspecting lips and neck until she finally pushed him away. Cort laughed, despite himself, as he ripped open a bag of dirty rice mix and upended it into the pot. He stared into the boiling water for a moment, then shook his head ruefully. Truth be told, working to scuttle a friend's social life was hardly an appropriate hobby for a thirty-year-old man, even if your chosen target was consistently doing the same to you, and using his family's money like a bullfighter's cape to grab attention.

If he were honest with himself, Cort took more pleasure in tripping Ryan up than in anything else in his life, and if that made him an asshole, so be it. Maybe he wanted Ryan to have to work a little harder for everything that he would eventually get anyway—or maybe he just wasn't as nice a guy as he liked to think he was. Cort smiled mirthlessly as his thoughts drifted back to the two women he'd met that day. He looked around his apartment, taking in the bare white walls and the patched carpet, wondering how he could ever explain why his occupation was "don't get into any trouble" and why most of that work wasn't on his resume. The truth was a thing that he usually tried not to have to explain.

He shot one last scornful look around the small room, then pulled the rice off the stove, dumping it into a convenient bowl to cool. His stomach was twisting and knotting with what felt like nervousness or anticipation but was probably just hunger. He scooped up the bowl and flopped into a kitchen chair, staring at the gray, congealing mixture in front of him for a moment before he began to eat. With luck, a quick dinner would bury the queasy feeling in his stomach and give him new life. Even without luck, a cheap, unfulfilling dinner in his tiny, dim kitchen would at least provide him a sharp reminder that, ultimately, he was meant for finer things.

Ben

Eclipse in 33 hours

The couples wove together in whirling motifs of movement, complex and intimate, sweeping through the fluid circle-square of a waltz. And despite occasional pockets of uncertainty and eddies of hesitation, each melded smoothly into the greater tapestry of the dance, forging flawlessness from their imperfections.

Ben's gaze skipped lightly among them as he watched from the low balcony overlooking the cleared area of marble that served as dance floor. As he watched, his thoughts followed the lessons of the day's ballroom class, slipping him into each man's place as he led his partner across the floor. He cut in on college students and retirees, business-class button-ups on their lunch break, and a gaggle of teenagers left over from a school tour who clutched each other in helpless laughter whenever the recently learned steps eluded them. Ben danced with them all, even as he watched from above. And with each change of partner; with each shift from age and experience to youth and vigor and back again, the smile on his face grew wider and more solid.

He'd left Cort and Allison to build on the rapport already blooming between them and exited the supermarket feeling buoyant, as though he were floating several inches above the tiled floor as he moved down the aisle and out the sliding doors. At the first brush of icy air, however, the frail line that tethered him to Earth had snapped, leaving him to bounce and drift wherever the wind would carry him.

He'd wafted, dreamlike, through the busy downtown streets for a brief but exhilarating time, the clatter and the press of bodies ringing confusion in his ears and guiding him forward, until he was pulled back to reality by faint strains of music. It tugged at him, insistent, coaxing him through the doors of the History Museum.

The music should not have been unexpected. For years, he and Elle had come to the grand, open space at the museum's core for ballroom classes. They'd danced together every Thursday, until it had become impossible.

But memories fade in time, and Ben had seen his fair share grow dim and diffuse. So today, the music was mildly, if pleasantly, surprising. Ben let it lead him into the building and up the stairs to the balcony, where he now watched, rapt with wonder and wrapped in memory. Every so often, the music would stop, and Ben would blink, turning away from the action of the dancers to better see the past.

As he was studying his shoes during one such lull, mentally changing his scuffed brown loafers for glossy black oxfords, a change in the tenor of the room dragged his focus back to the present. He looked up, his gaze leaping over the railing to fall upon the crowd as they watched the dance instructors, a young couple in evening wear demonstrating the proper technique for a rumba. But Ben's eyes quickly located the flaw in the scene.

A group of teenagers had stopped watching the lesson and was now facing him, the boys regarding him warily while the girls giggled and whispered around shy smiles and cupped hands. He wondered, idly, what he'd done to get their attention and pulled his gaze away, slowly allowing his eyes to find their way back to the group. They were still looking at him. Or, more accurately, past him. He turned.

A girl stood across the balcony, just at the head of the stairs, and her steady gaze made his legs feel weak. He thought for a moment that it might be Allison, who had so mesmerized him after his accident in the supermarket. Seconds later, guilt turned her into Elle, looking at him with an expression that flashed love and argument. His old man's eyes teared up, fuzzing the image and obscuring the blonde hair and the soft pink sweater; the small, hesitant smile and the calm surety of her stare. And as her visage blurred under his rheumy eyes, the girl lost her age. She could have been seventeen or seventy, she could have been his daughter or his lover or his wife. Ben let go of the plastic cup of water he had been clutching as his hands fluttered to his mouth.

A tremor swept through him that made his breath shudder and catch in his throat; made his heart simultaneously stop and quicken. Doubt poured over him like dark water, suffocating him, smothering the world and blotting out everything that was not her. And in that moment, she took a step forward and he could see that she was, indeed, his Elle.

He had a flash of trepidation as he wondered whether approaching her would find them picking up where they'd left off, elbows deep in argument. But her eyes told him that all was forgiven, and so he breathed in deeply and allowed the past to envelop him.

Standing before his wife of more than thirty years as though for the first time, he found himself surprisingly bashful. He took a moment to study the floor, raising his eyes just in time to close them as her soft lips met his and he was nineteen again: awkward and nervous and elated and terrified, somehow kissing the most beautiful woman in the room, his hands resting lightly on her shoulders and then on the small of her back and then exploring the curves of her body like anxious butterflies, growing more confident with each new alighting, each caress.

Quite suddenly, they were standing together in their new home, everything in it belonging only to them; shared ownership of everything, including one another. Ben pulled the veil from her face and allowed his fingers to tangle in her hair, his eyes and his insides pulling him toward her, into her, the entirety of his being demanding to be a part of her. His knuckle stung where his wedding band had scraped away the skin in his haste to get it on, an effort to prove that all of this was real.

But life is finite—relentlessly so. Though the passion of the moment had made him swell to near bursting, his confidence vanished quickly, like morning mist burned away by the sun. Even so, Elle's eyes were a force, bolstering him, so open and trusting that his awkward fumbling with zippers and clasps seemed only momentary setbacks rather than crushing defeats, his own hurried disrobing no more than a formality.

And then they were fully together, her skin wonderfully cool to his touch, the lightness of her fingers on his back and arms simultaneously tickling and scalding him. Every sensation woke him further, until his thoughts evolved into a hyperawareness that threatened to remove him from his body, forcing him to observe what was to come rather than participate.

Ben had long been aware of the machinations of sex and had a broad understanding of the process. But his studies and suppositions had not adequately prepared him for reality. He hadn't expected his hands to turn clumsy, or for his passions to so overcome him that he became less tender and more anxious with each eternal second that ticked by, even as he grew more and more aroused until he thought he might burst out of his own skin. Eyes screwed shut, he swiveled his hips (as he felt he was supposed to) trying not to imagine what his new bride might think of his incompetence; of his immaturity and unreadiness. But his self-castigation was interrupted by a soft hand on his shoulder. He opened his eyes.

Elle was regarding him steadily, her expression a mixture of amusement and affection. Ben tried to formulate an apology for his inexperience, but she cut it off with a kiss that began as tender, then grew deeper the longer she pulled him to her.

He eased her back onto the pillows, her fingers tracing double helixes down his back then curling around his waist to his groin, holding him firmly but softly as she guided him slowly inside her.

At the moment of penetration, both gasped, Elle's eyes widening in a mix of surprise and satisfaction, Ben's mirroring hers in his shock. The warmth of her embrace, the explosion of bliss that began at his core and then washed over the whole of him left him stunned and gasping for air.

The two locked eyes, taking in each other's stricken expressions—eyes threatening to turn inside out and mouths gasping for air—and then they both collapsed against each other in laughter. Ben sprawled across his new wife and smothered her with kisses between the giggles. In time, their laughter died and instinct took over, the centers of each body beginning the quest for one another, exploring the possibilities of pleasure.

As they began their own, personal dance, Ben's mouth explored the unknown territory of Elle's collarbone, her earlobes, and the soft hair that curled lightly at the nape of her neck. His hands sought out her hips and her breasts and the backs of her thighs as they clung to him, encircling him at the waist. Each nibble brought a new sigh, each nip or pinch or caress produced a matching moan. And every involuntary twitch and gasp, each squeeze and thrust, pulled him deeper into her and brought him a fresh wave of ecstasy.

Encouraged, Ben quickened his pace, deepening his thrusts and pushing further into the delirium of pleasure. Eventually, he was no longer conscious whether the moans and cries from beneath him were from passion or pain. He had crested a hill and found himself careening toward the bottom, unable to slow his descent, much less stop it entirely.

Eventually, he reached his nadir and burst, his entire being contracting on itself before exploding. He collapsed, inert, and lay without moving for what felt like hours.

When he came back to himself, aglow with an excitement that was entirely new to him, he was surprised to find that Elle was not there. He listened for her but could hear nothing in the bathroom that adjoined their (now shared) bedroom nor any sound from downstairs. He threw back the covers to find that the sheets were stained with blood, that his legs were streaked with it.

Panic dropped over Ben and he leapt from the bed, flying through the house in search of his wife; fruitlessly, as she was nowhere to be found. It was as though she had melted into the walls or had never existed at all. After a time, the search began to wear on him, adding heaviness to his limbs and draping him in exhaustion until he was simply wandering from room to room without any purpose to guide him, more by habit than hope. He'd nearly forgotten what he was searching for when he heard a soft tread on the floor above. He forced himself up the stairs one last time, knees complaining with every step, to find Elle curled on the bed looking at him with a soft smile. Her face was now deeply lined with age, but her beauty was undiminished.

His eyes begged her for an explanation, and he took a step toward the bed, his mouth forming words of apology, but she silenced him with a shake of her head. She rose, unashamed of her nudity, and wrapped her arms around him, kissing him softly on his cheek. She bit him lightly on the ear, then walked to the hall, turned the corner, and was gone forever.

Author's Note: And this is the problem. This is why the grand experiment that is "falling in love" is always doomed to fail. Love is only the name we give our desperate need for intimacy and the shining beacon of hope that hangs just beyond the reach of the otherwise hopeless. In reality, love is nothing more than the downward spiral of coming to know the person you imagined you were destined to be with. This is why even the "perfect" relationship of Ben and Elle was always destined to disintegrate. This is why Cort and Allison cannot be "meant for each other" and why their burgeoning romance can never be fully realized. It's why romantic songs are written by the lost and alone, and it's why I will always struggle to find a muse who can give me a love story— because true love stories are so rare that they scarcely exist.

If Ben's love couldn't keep Elle alive, how can any of us expect to wake our own princes and princesses? If the only way for a man to hold on to devotion is to trick himself into believing that his partner is perfect—that his love song is beautiful when it actually went discordant years ago—then he's not living in reality, and perhaps not really living at all. And as much as I'm willing to succumb to life's infatuations where I find them, I know that the luster will always fade. Inspiration collapses and the muse must be replaced. The best we can do is craft temporary connections to keep ourselves alive—and be willing to put those connections out of their misery when we must.

Life will never let us abandon the search for love, and it is impossible to know if you've found it until the moment that you learn that you haven't. And that's why Ben has continued to tell his own love story, over and over, for the past seventeen days—in a desperate attempt to make true what has already been proven false.

But you and I both know that this isn't Elle that's standing in front of Ben. It's just a guilty conscience.

#

The sound of his cup rattling against the tiled floor was just enough to drag Ben from his reverie. The girl was still standing across the room from him, and even without wiping away the tears in his eyes he could see that it was not Elle; nor Allison for that matter. As he stared, the girl raised her hand in a half wave and started toward him. And with each step that brought her closer she grew younger, the skin of her neck and cheek growing smooth and fine beneath his gaze and her eyes brightening with the flash of teenage innocence.

To his surprise, however, the girl got no bigger as the distance between them closed, so that when she finally stood before him, smiling her tentative smile and looking at him as though waiting for something, Ben felt as though he could scoop her into the palm of his hand, curl his fingers around her and protect her from the world—from violence and war and pain and sickness. It was a wonderful feeling, but a power come too late.

His smile must have given the girl confidence, because she spoke, her voice surprisingly mature. Not the adolescent twitter he had been expecting.

"Hi," she began, her eyes darting nervously between the spilled water and the old man's face. "So ... sorry to bother you, but we noticed you watching the dancing and thought you might like to join in?"

Ben's smile widened as he came out of his daze, but he shook his head slowly. "Thank you, but no. It's enough for me just to watch. It's been too long since I tried to rumba."

She gave him a sharp look—at once arch, incisive and affectionate, and wise with years. But her smile was that of a teenager. For the first time Ben felt himself missing his wife without the pain that usually accompanied it. "C'mon, don't be like that," the girl was saying. "You wouldn't come and watch every week if you didn't want to dance."

"I'm not sure ... " Ben began.

"Well, I am," the girl interrupted. "Come on. They're playing swing next and I need someone to Cha Cha with. It's my favorite. You can be my new partner."

She leaned over, punctuating her request with a light tap on the chest that jolted Ben's heart into a quick double beat. He felt a small twinge of pain, and then he was following the girl down the steps as though she had run him through with a needle and drawn the thread tight through his core. He could feel the tug of it leading him down the stairs and toward the dance floor.

But in the seconds before the music started up again, just before the tug of the thread sent him wobbling through the swirl of couples, Ben stumbled into a moment of silence. One crystalline second of uninterrupted calm amid the chaos. In that moment, he found himself struck like a rung bell, resonating with belief. Something unusual was happening. Something spectacular. Better than that.

Since Elle's passing, he had felt swallowed. But today, he couldn't escape the short sharp slivers of wonder that seemed to surround him. They meant something, though he couldn't comprehend what. Perhaps he was moving on, or losing control. Perhaps he was a part of something bigger. Perhaps he was healing. Or perhaps he was slowly working his way through the process of dying.

With a jolt, the music lurched to life around him and the first few energetic chords propelled Ben onto the dance floor, leaving his thoughts behind to stand bashfully against the wall. Abandoned, they watched with jealous longing as he was pulled, half by the tiny hands of his young partner and half by the thread strung though his heart, back into the spinning maze of wonder that was the dance.

Puck

Eclipse in 32 hours

Puck is caught, frozen and immobile, his feet locked tight to the ground, trapped by his own indecision. He is stuck, skipping like a record needle that rides a scar in the vinyl back to repeat the same snatch of song again and again. And even as his roots burrow deeply into the cracked concrete of the sidewalk, words skim lightly over the gouge in his thoughts, tracing the grooves in a tightening circle.

"Where ... wh ... wh ... She's n ... nnn ... not ... Whe ... wh ... wa ... huh." He sighs out heavily. That he would see the Angel is not surprising to him, but he is stunned by the fact that she seems to no longer be watching over Jamie. And not even the gift of a few dollars from the man who was pretending to be wealthy could give him the strength to move again. He cannot break the grip that his toes have on the pavement. Instead, he stands, swaying, occasionally pushing bursts of half-formulated questions from between his pursed lips.

"Wh ... why were y ... www ... where's Jamie?" he sputters. "Yyy ... your turn. It's your turn! I'm n ... Not ... not ... nnnn. Not ready yyy ... yet." As he talks, his eyes sweep from side to side, trapped by the momentary paralysis his body. He scans the world for something that can spur him to movement, some catalyst that will set him on his way. Get him back on track and back to his quest.

As if in response to his searching, or possibly drawn out by the tidal motion of his eyes, a man appears, standing in the doorway of a large building just across the street, the stray ends of his explosion of white hair flicking joyously in the intermittent gusts of wind: Einstein gone supernova.

Puck squints, then rubs his eyes with a gloved hand, blinking against the wind and mumbling under his breath. "Whha ... nnn ... nono. Hmmm ... not ... y ... y ... Nnn ... not yet, nnn ... Hmmm." Behind his eyes, he feels a spark of curiosity fighting with something more alien—it has been a long time since he felt the bloom of true anger. These feelings mingle and merge with one another, then settle into a detached, fascinated antipathy as the man turns to walk away. Almost against his will, Puck follows, stumbling along behind at an accidentally discreet distance, stroking the cashmere patch on the inside of his coat as he attempts to bring balance back to his world.

As he walks, he feels his senses reawakening, shrugging off the numbness of cold and indecision. His fingers tingle as the world pops back to life around him, sounds and smells becoming more vivid, the clamor of shoppers ringing a perfect complement to the explosion of red and white from a bus stop Coke sign. The tired ache in his legs and back eases as the city comes back to life around him. Frowning to himself, he trots down the street after the old man.

But this familiar man moves in an unfamiliar way, lurching forward in a strange amalgam of stops and starts, pauses and accelerations that Puck struggles to mimic from half a block behind. The man swaps speeds with a peculiar suddenness, first moving slowly as if in dream, weaving his way through pushy crowds who are put off by his oblivion, then quickening his step to jerk along with almost spastic purpose, leaving Puck to trail doggedly behind.

And then, abruptly, the man stops, a hand to his temple, as though he's forgotten something. Convinced that he will be seen, Puck steps into a convenient doorway and disappears as only someone who has lived on the street can. But instead of turning around, the man stands unmoving for a moment or two. Then he shakes his head as if to clear it and pats his pockets in an absentminded routine. Reaching into one of them, he retrieves a set of keys, walks to the driver's side of the car he has paused beside, unlocks the door, and climbs in.

Puck smiles. He doesn't recognize the car and knows that he can't possibly hope to keep up with it, but that doesn't matter. He turns around and hurries back the way he came, toward the El platform on Clark and Division. His curiosity has been piqued enough to quell his anxiety, to divert his focus and even bury his distaste for the train, at least temporarily. Some fires burn with warmth and some with destructive force. Both are important. The trick is telling which is which.

An indeterminable number of minutes later, Puck has been herded back off the train at Kimball, the end of the line, and is standing across the street from a small, nondescript house that a real estate agent might call taupe or eggshell but which is actually a dirty beige. He's breathing heavily, partly as a result of his hurry to get here but also because of where here is, the nearness of his past making him anxious, making him eager, making him fluctuate between grimace and grin. There's a core of pleasure and anticipation blooming in his chest, but there's anger and resentment behind his eyes, and the dichotomy is difficult to reconcile. More to the point, he knows that he's getting ahead of himself, and that to do so is dangerous, but he can't seem to help it.

He stares at the scene in front of him, frozen by indecision. The car that he hadn't recognized is parked in front of a house that he does, and that seems right. The small neighborhood feels quiet, as though holding its breath, somehow separate from the commotion of the nearby city, and that seems right. But the old man is now stranded on the front lawn, staring at the house, unmoving, and that feels wrong. Feels odd even to Puck's admittedly shaky sense of reality. His eyes drift over to the curtained front window, hopeful that some movement from inside will signal to him that all is well, but simultaneously worried that he will be spotted and forced into a confrontation before he is ready. The longer he stares, though, the emptier the house feels. Puck shoots a nervous glance around the quiet neighborhood, worried that life here has been somehow upset by his presence. That once again he is to blame for whatever has gone wrong.

He is about to leave, in the hope that his absence will allow the scene to slip back into normalcy, when the man on the lawn moves again, raising one arm to reach toward the silent house. Arm outstretched, parallel to the ground, the man proceeds to stroke the air in front of him, as though dancing or searching for something he has misplaced in midair. Puck watches, his skin pricking the way it does when he leans up against his heating duct after a day spent fighting the chill. After a few moments, the man pulls his hand away, moving it with painstaking deliberation to his face. Seconds later, he drops his head into his hands, his shoulders shaking as he moves up the walk to the front door of the house, which he unlocks and opens.

Once he has disappeared inside, Puck crosses the street to stand in the spot the old man had occupied. He stares at the house, chewing on his lower lip, puckering.

He thinks of summertime and feels the heat sinking into him.

He thinks of music swirling around him in a desperate rhythm that almost demands that he dance.

He thinks of the house before him and the years behind him.

He thinks, momentarily, of the concept of right and wrong and wonders how anyone can tell which is which as it is happening.

After a moment, he raises his hands, casting a worried glance at the front window. But the curtains are drawn, the house and its inhabitants, blind. He pats the air in front of him, tentatively at first, molding and sculpting, searching as the old man had seemed to for something that he isn't sure he'll recognize even if he finds it. But there is nothing there for him to find: no understanding, no new information, only air.

He stares at the house quietly for another minute or two, but now, after all his searching, just being near it makes him feel less confident, almost childish, and so he moves quickly away in his distinctive half-stumble. He has arrived too early. There is still a great deal to do, and moving forward is better than standing still.

#

Another mix of minutes and blocks later and Puck is standing in front of Merrill's Consignment Store replaying the past few hours in his mind, laying spade to earth and turning over his life. The future has simultaneously grown brighter and more confused. Easier, but less certain. It makes him cautious, but energized.

He bounces lightly on his toes in a small, impromptu dance of celebration, then lets out a childish pop of laughter, almost a giggle, as he pushes through the door and into the thrift store, his bag of treasure still clutched tight to his chest.

He walks quickly to the back corner of the nearly empty store, where the men's clothes hang on crowded racks, crushed together and smelling faintly of mothballs and mildew. He sifts through the hangers as best he can, pushing aside the rejects with an impatient *shick,* occasionally examining a tag or rubbing a piece of material between his thumb and forefinger. Every so often, out of habit, he shoots a glance over his shoulder at the mismatched pair of clerks at the front of the store, the taller one neatly combed in pressed slacks and a bright blue tie, the other's jet-black hair sticking up in gold-tipped spikes, the nails of his right hand long and painted black, those on his left ragged and bitten down. Puck smiles. He belongs here.

He sifts through the racks a moment more, then selects a conservatively cut blue suit and a white dress shirt and moves up to the front of the store.

Barney, the cashier with the gold-spiked hair, greets him with a nod and smile. "Hey Puck, I like the haircut. Looking sharp! You selling today?"

Puck shakes his head. "Nnn ... no. Not today, Barn. B ... buying."

Barney takes the clothes from him and whistles low. "Nice. Classy. You getting married, Pucky?"

Puck can feel himself blush at the question, and he shakes his head quickly. "N ... no! Just need to d ... ress up a little."

Barney lets out a bray of laughter. "I know, man. I'm just kidding you." He turns to address the other clerk. "Hey Neddy, check out Puck's new threads."

Ned, the well-scrubbed cashier, wanders over. "Fancy," he says seriously. "You need a tie with that though. Hold on a sec ... " He turns to walk into the store, but Puck stops him.

"Nnn ... No thanks. No ties."

The two men look at him, their curiosity evident.

"P ... promised myself," Puck says in explanation.

"Okay then," says Ned. "Looks like you're going to owe us fifteen bucks." He looks at Puck, compassion in his eyes. "Do you have that, Puck?"

Puck doesn't respond, instead reaching into his bag to pull out the small stack of baseball cards he'd gotten at the pawn shop and fans them out on the counter.

Barney frowns. "Awww, Puck man. We can't take these. They're not—"

"Hold on a sec," Ned interrupts. He scoops the cards up and sifts through them quickly, almost professionally, as Puck waits. After a moment, Ned's eyes move up from the cards to fix themselves on Puck.

"These'll do fine."

"Seriously, dude?" asks Barney.

"Absolutely," Ned replies. "You sure you want to give them up, Puck?"

Puck nods.

"Okay then. You got yourself a deal. New shirt, new suit, no tie. Enjoy." He smiles and walks away, fanning through the cards again.

"Nice work, man," Barney murmurs as he wraps Puck's purchases into a large plastic bag. "It's not everyone that can sucker Ned into a deal."

Puck smiles quietly. It's not worth explaining the value that can be found in simple observation. "Th ... thanks."

"You going to tell me what you need the suit for?" Barney asks.

Puck's smile widens, and he shakes his head, eyes dancing.

"I didn't think so," Barney laughs. "Hey, you take care of yourself out there, man. It's cold, you know?"

Puck nods. "I know."

"You're okay?"

He nods again and Barney regards him appraisingly. "You know, I think you are. Something different about you today, man. Apart from the shave, I mean. You seem ... I don't know ... taller or something."

Puck looks at him curiously, then shrugs.

"Shit, what do I know?" Barney laughs. "So go ahead, get out of here then. Go to your wedding or your dance or whatever. Do your stuff. And bring in some of them doughnuts next time ... "

Puck nods. "Okay."

He moves toward the door, pausing momentarily to carefully tuck the plastic bag holding his new suit and shirt into his own bag.

Ned waves to him as he pushes out the door. "Thanks, Puck. And hey, be careful. With that suit and haircut you're going to have to beat the women off with a stick!"

Puck hears Barney's good-natured laughter, but it is secondary, as everything around him retreats to the background and the thought of Jamie springs back to the fore. Seeing the old man earlier had thrown Puck off his rhythm. Rushed him, flustered him into forgetting what was important. He'd let go of the purpose behind his machinations and filled the last several hours with empty action. Now it had been too long since he had checked in; Jamie was not safe without the Angel watching over her. He feels a flush of guilt, of negligence, and his insides feel hollow with worry. With a murmured goodbye, Puck is out the door and jerking down the street, alternating between a stumbling run and a rolling half-jog that eats up ground as quickly as possible.

As he runs, his fears intensify, gripping him with stainless steel claws as he imagines the demon-man from the previous night just ahead of him, the cold, hard discs of his eyes fixed on Jamie as he closes in on her. Puck stops, heart hammering, eyes locked on the tiny corner bar where she works, just a few yards away in his mind. Behind the bar the buildings of the city rise like jagged, broken teeth. Before him, the demon nods a mockery of greeting and licks his thin lips, revealing his own crooked teeth as the flickering neon makes cold, blood-red mirrors of his glasses.

Puck feels himself shrivel in response, his scalp constricting, his shoulders hunching and his testicles shrinking under the chill of the man's gaze, his entire being retreating to seek protection at the core of his body as tears begin to slide down his cheeks.

He falls to his knees, muttering softly under his breath. "Jamie ... I can't ... I'm ... sss ... Hmmm." He clutches the small metal pin he has purchased for her, desperate for its thin promise of safety and his eyes once again find the bar, fixing on the door. He senses the demon's presence before him and closes his eyes to shut out the possibility. Deny the danger.

But with his eyes closed, he finds himself trapped in dream, overcome by his fears. He winces as he is thrown into his own past, his memories cutting at him, the sound of teeth tearing at roasted flesh as his own mouth waters then goes dry, before the sound changes from the soft torment of abundance to the sharp crack of desperation, a grimy man breaking scavenged bones in two to suck out the precious marrow, furtively avoiding the stares of the passersby.

Puck's heart flutters as those passersby begin to crowd around him, pressing in, at once confining and demanding, pawing at him, pleading for something he can't identify or hope to provide. As his helplessness builds toward the panic of claustrophobia, he feels the demon's presence draw closer, elongated fingernails scraping across his arms, chest, and face, taunting him for his inadequacy.

His nose tickles and flares at the envelope of smells that surrounds him, fed by his fear and memory, but also by the nearness of his enemy. The sickly-sweet smell of floral perfume masking the deeper odor of something rotten and decaying.

Evil, all of it. The demon swims in his vision, demeaning and insistent, and Puck begins to shiver against the cold that is sinking into him, sure that he will never be warm again.

He is so shrouded in terror and delusion that he doesn't immediately notice the man who steps out of the bar in front of him; not until the man blows warmth onto his hands and Puck can see the whorls of intricate tattoo that peek out from the cuffs of his dark denim jacket.

Puck comes back to reality with a start. He blinks, his vision clearing. And, as though somehow cowed by the large, bearded man standing a few feet away, the specters that had tormented him retreat to the background, where they seem content to wait. For now.

Puck doesn't move for a moment, watching as the man turns to leave, and then his eyes drop to the man's jacket pocket, where he catches the barest glimpse of cold black steel wrapped in a dirty chamois. The jacket hangs heavily, flapping against the man's side with each step, and Puck cannot pull his gaze away from that dark metal. He clenches his eyes shut for a moment, biting his tongue as he shapes the future in his mind, making sure things will line up the way they must. He remembers the excited beat of his heart in the dingy pawn shop, and before he can change his mind, he spits the word out.

"W ... www ... wait?"

The man stops, turning slowly to face him, still wearing his suspicious scowl. Puck conjures a smile and moves toward him. Signs are signs, and must be taken advantage of. Besides, something—perhaps something that doesn't even come fully from his own consciousness—is telling him that it's always best to have options. Puck thinks for a moment, then gestures at the man's pocket as he brings words to his lips, carefully shaping them into what he hopes is an acceptable offer.

Author's Note: At the beginning of a story, much must be taken on faith. A writer must trust their instincts, their inspiration, their muse. As an author invents their characters, they also invest in them—deeply, building each a place in the world even as they uncover the details of the story. The last thing an author would expect is for those characters to be withholding. For them to keep secrets or conspire together. The last thing an author should expect is betrayal. And so, as we learn more and circumstances change, the arc of the story may shift. When a muse is no longer supplying inspiration, decisions must be made. Decisions, and sometimes sacrifices.

And while changing tack mid-tale is dangerous, it makes the myriad possible. Anything can happen—inspiration can be reborn, some storylines may end even as the possibility for love is kept alive. And so, for us, there is still a chance to redeem this "love story." But if we're going to bring this to a satisfactory finish, something dramatic must be done. I'm tired of standing in the cold, watching and waiting and writing. It is time for action.

Perhaps bringing the fifth man into our fugue will help regain some degree of control. Perhaps he can draw our conspiring characters back into line.

It's no great trick to bring a defiant dog to heel; it takes only a demonstration of who is master. Once a mongrel is broken, he'll walk unbothered into his own cage.

The Imposter

A Series of Episodes – Out of Time

Cities do sleep. I know what you've heard—trust me. There are moments in the slow hours of early morning when the pulse of life slows; the hum of breath grows even, and the eyes of the city fall shut. That's not to say that systems shut down entirely; there is always an undercurrent—isolated individuals who continue to move; synapses that continue to fire. And so there are dreams—and, in some cases, nightmares.

Against the still landscape of this sleeping city a figure moves, the darkness of his coat cutting into the snowy facade of the quiet streets—a moving tear in the smooth shroud of winter.

Looking closer, one can see the flush in his cheeks that suggests that he's been out in the cold too long; the circles under his eyes from worry or lack of sleep. Look closer still and you will see his mouth moving in a silent narration, putting forth a constant description of what is happening around him. Which, to be honest, I find discomfiting. Those words belong on paper, not whipped away by the winter breeze.

Still, the venom with which he spits his invective into the brittle air nearly demands that the words be heard, inaudible as they may be, and there's no one else around. So, watch with me as he stalks the streets and listen with me as he spouts his black poetry. Then study the differences between his nighttime ramble and his daytime demeanor and see if you can understand him, and how important he may be. After all, a lot can be learned from overheard conversations.

#

"
I am the imposter.
I am the adversary.
I am the misinterpreted interpreter.
I see others stumbling ahead, and
I am here to guide them,
even as they run from me; hide from me.
And though wrong to run, they are right to fear.

I am the unexpected enemy. The unpleasant surprise.
With each word I am expanding, expounding,
my spirit seething in a turmoil of the unfulfilled.

And though the others may stutter and stagger and
dream away the night,
in the end their lives belong to me.
As surely as I can see the future.
As surely as I can change the future.

Believe.

I am no idle dreamer.
I am the razor's edge.
I am sharp charm and piercing insight.
I am focus.
I am creation.

And yet ...
Even for the enlightened there can be new light.
There is much to take from
the old man, the poor man, the beggar man, the thief.
And much to learn from the man who rests on the lip
of life—
watching his own story unfold.

There is so much to take away
so long as you are willing to take ...
And I am willing,
I am able.

I am everything and everyone.

I *am* the rich man and the poor man,
the old and young man,
the beggar-man

and the thief.
I am the people you see every day.

I am the quiet man standing too close to you in line.
I am the passerby you catch with his eyes on you.
I am the smile that takes you by surprise,
The compliment that makes you flush,
The attention that makes you quicken your pace.
I am the last person you expect,
And first willing to end a life.

I am lust.
I am torrid.
I am the magic man
and the mountebank.
I am the danger and the passion,
the student and the teacher,
the privilege, the pleasure and the pain.

I am always listening,
I am always watching,
I am always learning.
And I am always moving
Toward resolution
even as we move toward eclipse.

Believe.

"
#

The bar door bangs open and a harried woman steps in, closing it quickly behind her and leaning against it as though the frigid breeze that chased her inside might force its way through. After a moment, she stands up and shrugs out of her coat, dropping it onto the back counter. She eyes the few customers scattered throughout the small bar and lets out a deep sigh, everything about her sagging with the expulsion of breath—her shoulders slumping, her cheeks and chest wilting, and her eyes threatening to close as she sways on her feet. Her too-short skirt hikes further up her thin thighs, and she absentmindedly tugs it down, then ties an apron around her waist and heads into the back room. She feels many years older than she is, today.

"That you JJ?"

Carl is out of sight in the cooler, stacking cases of beer by the sound of it.

"Yeah."

"You're ten minutes late—your boyfriend's looking for you."

She starts to apologize, then stops. "Reggie was here?"

Carl emerges from the cooler wiping his hands on the dirty towel that hangs from a hook on his belt. He squints at her, the blue of his eyes barely finding its way past his thick white eyebrows. "Naw. I mean your other boyfriend. The skinny guy with the glasses. Been waiting for you for the past hour—asks every ten minutes when you're coming on."

"Fantastic," she sighs. "Alright, I'll go take care of him."

"Hey," Carl calls after her. "Price of being popular, right?"

Back in the bar, she scans the thin collection of patrons dotting the tables, letting her eyes fall on a man near the back, his head bent low but his eyes up and searching. When they find her, they dart quickly away, then creep tentatively back. He smiles a thin, cautious smile.

For the third time in five minutes, she sighs—a bad sign. She fills a glass three-quarters full of Club Soda, then taps a few drops of bitters into it—the drops pearling as they hit the water, slowly picked apart by bullets of carbonation as they sink through the glass.

She sets the concoction beside a small book at the man's table. Though it is warm in the bar, he is still wearing his long coat, and she can see that he is sweating; can pick out individual beads on his cheeks and forehead—on his glasses, even. She stands there a moment, not sure what to say.

"Thank you," the customer says softly, his eyes not moving up from the book in front of him.

"No problem," she replies awkwardly. Then, "So what are you reading?"

"Poetry. And I'm writing it, not reading."

"Oh. Sorry." She turns to walk away. "Well, good luck."

"I don't need it," he replies, and something in his voice stops her.

"What do you mean?"

For the first time since she has been standing there, his eyes come up to meet hers—a connection she cannot return, as the bright glare of the neon in the window turns his glasses opaque.

He smiles tightly. "I mean that I don't need luck—I have you."

She rolls her eyes and starts to turn away. "Don't."

"Don't what?"

"Just knock it off," she replies. "Leave me out of it—whatever "it" is. And don't be asking when I'm coming in either. It's creepy. You don't know me. You don't get to write poetry about me. If you keep it up, I'll have Carl throw you out."

She stares at him defiantly until he shrugs and closes his book. With that, she nods, turns on her heel, and walks away, retreating behind the bar, trembling slightly for reasons she can't fully explain to herself.

Behind her, the man reopens his book, muttering under his breath. "Not to worry, not to worry. We'll get there. You'll see."

He smiles again, and if she had still been watching Jamie would have had a better understanding of why she was trembling.

#

Easter

"

A miniature night,
A black coral sea.
Nude, she approaches – the city child.
How intense this unpaved time,
Thrusting savagery into the air to the
Drunken drum's tattoo, pulsing mahogany and
Churning out a desperate music
That snakes and shakes and rides to the rhythm
Of the beat.

And she cuts through the frail congestion –
This girl who shines like the highly polished night,
Piercing my smothering shroud with
Her bubbling giggles and sky-blue pops of laughter,
Perfect in her complexity.
And yet,
For me –
For my city –
A lazy waltz, with violins would do;
A release from the suffocating sense of now.
Gone, instead, to the garden, where the music rides
forever
Trailing hellos and goodbyes,
Nestled in memory,
Warm and safe –
Folded in an anodyne haze,
Not bled dry of consequence and abandoned.

Could we but transpose –
Plant flowers in the cracked concrete and sow seeds
of stop signs in the rich loam.
If we could twine the bump and grind with
Swish and sigh
And not allow the music to fade –
Each tune riding the other,

Nipping at their heels, and
Driving the derision out of our consciousness.
Out of all conscience.

Cautiously
This city child comes to me
Her sparkle pulling splinters through my spine,
And my waltz drifts off
(or my waltz drifts on, silently),
Leaving only the pulse of life as we lay curled together –
Twined in a ceremony of paradox and
I can taste her sweat.
I can feel the cool softness of her palm on my neck.
I can see flashes of color prick her eyes in the near dark
And though she is not there, there is music in it.
Music that endures past all sound fading.
Music that disappears off the tongue –
Leaving just the echoes
To sing her life's coda.

And so we sleep apart
As her pulse pierces the darkness and
I dream of my city child
Dancing bare through the garden to invisible music,

Reawaking my steady waltz with the bliss of her naked rhythm.
"

#

"Hey ... "

The woman stops walking and turns to take in the man behind her—the darkness of his hat and coat, the angular sharpness of his face, and the wire frame glasses that obscure his eyes, turning them to hard steel disks, shimmering and dead. "Yeah? What do you want?"

The man says nothing.

Her eyes narrow as she stares at him thoughtfully. "I know you, right? How do I know you?"

He smiles, the slight curl of his lip making the night somehow colder. "From the bar," he replies. "You're Jamie."

"Yeah, that's me. What do you need?"

He holds up a finger, asking an odd permission, then leans over to whisper in her ear. She stands frozen in the bitter evening, immobile, as though carved from ice— slashed at with a pick and then rubbed smooth by gloved hands. And, though she has been out in the ten-degree evening for some time without fully feeling the sting of the night air, now she struggles to keep from shivering.

After excruciating seconds of his breath on her ear and the suffocating envelope of his floral cologne, he finally finishes speaking and leans away. Jamie exhales in a great convulsive shudder and then squares herself, pulling away from him and blinking her hard edge back into place. "So that's it, huh?" she says with a smirk, tipping her head back in bravado. "That's what you've wanted this whole time?" She lets her eyes travel over the man's lean form—tracking down, then back up slowly—and then seems to reach a decision. "Only if I see some cash; otherwise, get out of my way."

Her answer seems to amuse the man, and he smiles tightly, not showing his teeth, and then lets the smile collapse into a sneer of disgust. He hesitates a moment, then jerks his head, indicating that she should continue on her way.

She stands her ground for a defiant moment, then pushes past him, muttering under her breath. "Alright, fuck you then, Prince Charming. Freaky fuck."

He stands silently, listening to her departure without turning to watch her leave, and allowing his face to go dead, abandoning any pretense of a smile. Anger flickers through him briefly, but he struggles to ignore it, focusing instead on the click of her heels against the pavement as she moves away down the sidewalk. After a moment, the clicks stop and he overhears an abrupt, jostled conversation that rekindles his grin. But still he stands, waiting.

Finally, he turns to follow, pivoting on his heel just in time to see ... Her. The One. His long-imagined ideal. Blonde and pale and, despite the clear white of her long coat, somehow standing out against the snowy backdrop behind her. Almost involuntarily, he follows, feeling a surge of excitement and insight, muttering under his breath as he walks. "Oh, you. Look at you ... The rest pale, my perfect. My trouvaille ... "

He passes the mouth of an alley and is forced to check his mumbled narrative as a homeless man scurries away from him, tripping wildly over trash cans and cardboard boxes, cowering as he watches the street with soft, fearful eyes. A vagrant, but perhaps not entirely worthless. He nods, grinning to himself when the man cringes away from him, but he cannot linger too long or he will lose track of Her. He strides away from the mouth of the alley, boots crunching in the snow, his steps quickening to take on the mechanical rhythm of fresh resolve. While the bitter taste of failure is still fresh on his tongue, he is certain that now, together, they can persevere. It takes only the end of one opportunity to spark the beginning of a new one.

Can't I Go

"

Delay creation a moment.
Sit silent and let the players play
As you watch—their stories similar.
So low and loud that the truth of life
Sinks beneath the narrative; reality sinks beneath notice.

Fallow soil offers opportunity to a scattered seed.
Roots take hold and build the preacher's pedestal.

So instead
Speak loudly,
Of my sin and of theirs, and yours.
Tell the truths of creation to illuminate the night and the lies.

Speak loudly of frigid footprints stamping pained significance
On the patina of the city,
And louder of men's eyes that prey on the unaware, that play
"Touch me, touch you" with the crowd and beg to be caught,

But go vacant when asked to explain.

Speak of ignorance and conflict—diversion fraught
with fury and zest, and of color arrested mid-fade.

Speak of false bravado and abandoned hope. Both
irredeemable offenses,
witnessed only by the innocent.

Speak of loneliness and jealousy –
Those flaws that seem futile but are so easily
sharpened.

And speak of my eyes and their fragile focus,
Of their dalliances and infatuations in the night.

Speak to silence the accusations—to still the
chatter—
To rise above those who choose lovers and heroes
with little care.
Nihilism, Infirmity, Malefaction, Greed,
(Chaos, Control ...)
Beauty overwhelms them and buries their attentions
under false hope.
But beauty will inevitably die. When she must.

All too similar ...

Speak loudly,
but not of me—I am not here.
I am waiting for you and moving on all at once.
The imposter will prove the truth, in the end.
The nothing that leaves no survivors—
No pictures, no sacrifice, no love, and no guilt.
Only a record that blots out the moon.

Speak loudly, love.
I forgive you, as you may forgive me, someday.
With regret, gratitude, and humility.

So speak loudly,
There's no one to hear you anyway.
"

#

"Has anyone ever told you that you have a beautiful body?"

"Leave me alone, creep."

The look on the young woman's face matches the tone of her voice perfectly, but the young man nods pleasantly, seemingly unconcerned by her anger. He ambles down the line of freezers, turning the corner into a long aisle filled with boxes of crackers and cookies. He runs a hand through his crown of blond hair, patting imagined stray strands back into the gelled tangle of golden curls that stand out against his deep tan—out of place in the midst of the Chicago winter—and sweeps the cluster of midday shoppers with a practiced eye. Behind him, unseen, a stranger in a long gray coat follows him into the aisle, his gaze turning from suspicious to curious, fixing more solidly on the younger man.

That young man grins as he approaches another unsuspecting woman, his blue eyes flashing. "Excuse me, could you help me? I think there's something wrong with my eyes ... "

This new woman looks up, brushing curly auburn bangs out of her own eyes, concern evident on her face. "Oh no! What's the matter?"

"I can't take them off of you," he finishes, grin widening.

She stares at him for a moment, then sighs, her disgust palpable. "I should have known," she mutters, turning away.

"What?" he protests, laughing. "What did I say?"

"Look," she interrupts. "You can save the lame pickup lines for someone else, okay? I'm married." She waggles a ringed finger at him. "Married?"

"No no," he replies. "No problem. Sorry." He moves away from her, but even once he is out of sight, the woman still feels the discomfiting sensation of eyes on her. She glances quickly over her shoulder, but if anyone had been there, they too have moved on.

The young man moves through the grocery store, eyes up and active, searching, then locking in on a new target even as his gray observer continues to trail him, unobtrusive and unseen, watching through thin glasses as his new mentor approaches a young woman with heavy dark bangs, crouched in front of a stack of cereal boxes. "Hey there, don't frown, you never know who might be falling in love with your smile ..."

The woman turns her head, squinting at him in disbelief. "Are you serious?" she asks.

For the first time, he seems embarrassed. He blushes and runs a hand over his coiffed hair. "Stupid line, I know," he says. "Sorry about that. But I didn't mean it as a line. You look worried, and I hate seeing a beautiful woman worry."

She rolls her eyes. "Please. You take the time to check in with everyone at the grocery store to make sure they're in a chipper mood? Sorry, not buying it."

Ryan watches her walk away, then mutters, "Not everyone ... "

She turns to face him. "What was that?"

"I said, 'No, not everyone at the grocery store.'" He shrugs. "But an attractive woman looking unhappy ... I don't know."

"You don't know when to give up, do you?"

He shakes his head. "Nope. But hey, you never know where you're going to meet someone—and you're guaranteed not to if you refuse to try. I'm Ryan, by the way." He hesitates a moment, then blurts, "So, could I buy you a cup of coffee? Give you a friendly ear to tell your troubles to?"

She cocks her head. "Your pickup lines suck, Ryan. And what troubles do you think I have that are only fit for random grocery store lurkers I've never met?"

"Fair," Ryan nodded. "Fair enough. So then, what if I promise great conversation with no pickup lines and throw in my recipe for the world's best spaghetti sauce?"

She sighs heavily, pretending to consider the offer, though anyone observing can see that she's already decided. "I'd say it would make you sound pretty desperate, and I don't love spaghetti, but fine. In that scenario I suppose I might have time for a cup of coffee."

"That's great," Ryan grins. "But not the cafe here, if that's okay. Grocery store coffee never did much for my spirits. I don't know about you ... "

There are still traces of trepidation in her laugh, but she seems pleased. "No, that's fine. I'm done here. Just let me hit the checkout line and I'm good to go."

"Cool. Should I meet you just outside?"

"If you think you can stand the cold ... "

His smile widens. "I'll manage. See you soon ... " He waits expectantly.

"Theresa," she supplies, and he smiles in return.

"Theresa. I'll see you soon then, Theresa."

She nods with a sudden shyness, then walks away, her step light. Both Ryan and his observer watch her go and then, almost in unison, their gazes fall on an unusual scene at the end of the aisle. An older man has collapsed onto the cold tile floor, where a man and a woman—a strikingly pale, beautiful and, to one of them, familiar woman—now hover over him. As affected as both men are, however, their reactions could not be more different. Ryan starts toward the group, a look of concern on his face, then focuses on the man beside the woman who had first seized his attention. Instead of approaching, he moves away, shooting glances over his shoulder every few steps and cursing his luck, his coffee date forgotten.

The other—the observer—is unable to look away for several seconds. After a moment, he shifts his gaze to the man kneeling in front of Her. Behind his thin glasses his eyes narrow in suspicion, and he slides around the corner to watch from a more discreet location. At no point does his gaze leave the scene, not even as Ryan disappears quickly out the front door and down the street, oblivious to the angry confusion of the coffee date he's left in the checkout line. Not even when the three people crouched on the tiled floor rise and go their separate ways. He stands, rooted to the spot, his mind whirling. He has found a new focus and learned a new lesson. Now he needs time to prepare. He needs practice.

All the same, it is time to speed things on their way ...

#

At the Station

"

She illuminates the fog of life
with simple movements,
gliding across the floor toward a terminal moment.

The other: vain and insincere, alight with guarded allure,
leaping to argument and speaking sweet lies:
their fragrance is gentle on your sin; my love.

He laughs like my father—mirthless and mistaken—
at once winning and lost, starving to salvage a last shred of hope.
I speak desperately,
silently, through my eyes, "Please don't leave.
Don't leave me, don't harm me, don't fool me, betray me.
Help me build the future.

I need you."

But simple words, spoken plainly, come more quickly

than mine can, and I dissolve under them

as the time for departure draws near.

And so, I get this and that, "what if" and "I suppose;"

modern legends and lore. Leftovers

and little else. As always.

And the joke is on me

as I fade into the fog.

But this ship has not sailed.

This story is not ended.

Time remains.

This joke will be retold.

"

#

"You look upset."

The woman sitting at the counter turns from the window she has been staring through, shooting a scornful glance at the gaunt, bespectacled man regarding her evenly from the seat beside her. "And who the hell are you?"

The man smiles a tight close-lipped smile. "I'm ... well ... You know what? It doesn't really matter. I just want to help."

The woman snorts. "I don't have time for this." She stands abruptly, knocking her silverware to the tiled floor in her haste.

"Please. This isn't a come-on. Stay." He stoops to retrieve the scattered utensils, then spreads his arms wide in entreaty. "Please. I really am just trying to help. Really. Stay?"

The woman scowls, her short, dark hair framing her face in a way that accentuates her ire, but she sits. "Help how?"

"This isn't a come-on," the man repeats. "You're worried about the man you were just talking to, yes?"

Her eyes burn white-hot holes through him and he rushes on to escape the glare. "The man you just met? Who's talking to the blonde woman outside the store. Yes?"

She glares a moment longer, then speaks. "So what?"

"And it's worse because that other man you were talking to earlier, he disappeared. And now this man is abandoning you as well."

Her eyes have widened during this, but now she darkens again. "You've been watching me? Who the hell are you?"

"Honestly?" he replies. "My name is Love. Funny, don't you think?"

Her laugh rings with sarcasm. "That's a new one at least." She sighs. "Okay, Love ... Love what?"

"Love is my last name." The man smiles his tight smile again and shakes his head. "And that's not the worst of it."

If he was expecting her to respond he's disappointed, but he doesn't show it, instead simply blurting, "I'm a doctor."

"A doctor." Her tone is bored, but he can sense the hint of a grin through the cynicism and the makeup she wears. Her mouth is painted with too much dark lipstick that cakes at the corners, but the grin is there, nonetheless.

Keeping his face cheerfully blank through her smirk, he nods.

"Doctor Love?"

A tight, apologetic smile this time, and an embarrassed shrug.

The woman puts a hand over her eyes. "Great. Okay, Doctor Love, diagnose me. What's ailing me, aside from the fact that two different guys have just hit on me and then bailed, and that you're wearing way too much of that flower perfume?"

The doctor smiles tightly and doesn't say "I'm not the one wearing a mask of Maybelline, Jezebel." Instead, he ignores the thin critique and replies, "Nothing, so far as I can tell, Miss ... "

"Theresa. Nothing?"

"Nice to meet you, Theresa." He extends a hand, leaving it to hang there, alone, for a moment before withdrawing it to his lap. "No? No." He clears his throat. "Well, as I see it, you've got no problem here."

"No problem," she repeats. "I'm being stood up for the second time in half an hour while the guy I just allowed to pick me up—against my better judgment—is standing outside talking to a beautiful blonde woman—"

"That he's not interested in," Dr. Love finishes for her.

"No?"

"Oh no. He can't be." The doctor glances quickly over his shoulder, then leans in closely—too close perhaps—to whisper, "The truth is, even while the two of them have been talking, he's been stealing looks in here at the two of us ... "

Theresa pulls away, half glancing over her shoulder, then stops, turning back to him. "Really?"

"Really," he replies. Then, "Go ahead and look."

She does, twisting in her seat to gaze out the grocery store window again. "You're right," she says. "She's not even there anymore. Now he's talking to some wino."

The doctor glances up sharply, eyes cutting the conversation short as he turns to stare through the window at the unique, two-man dance taking place outside. Then, just as quickly, his gaze softens and returns to his companion. "You're right. She's gone. So no harm done?"

She regards him with narrowed eyes for a moment, then relaxes, settling into her seat. "Yeah, I guess not."

He smiles, lips thinning over his teeth and turning up at the edges in a taut grin. "Exactly. And so, the best thing you could do right now is to go talk to your young man before you lose him. Rescue him from that vagrant." He pushes his glasses up on his nose and smiles more widely, still without showing his teeth.

Suddenly uncomfortable, she stands. "Okay, well, we'll see. Maybe I will."

He nods at her. "Well, I can't ask for more than that. Best of luck."

She allows him a cautious smile, her lingering discomfort making it feel phony and pasted on. "Well ... thanks, Mr ... Doctor Love." She laughs nervously at the name, then moves quickly toward the door and a confrontation between jealousy and indifference, shooting an occasional glance at the back of the man that she's left sitting at the counter, his long, dark coat hanging almost all the way down to the floor. But he doesn't notice her looks. The Doctor's gaze remains riveted on the two men talking outside the store window. He is still smiling tightly.

#

Harder Lament

"
See in soft focus what has been placed before you:
The young, yet to know temptation,
Their innocent and accusing stares carrying the mark of
The hapless led to slaughter.

See acquiescence and longing,
A demand for self-determination and open air.

See a quartet of obstinacy
And reams of paper, adorning the room like a garnish,
A maddening error on every page, with
The gallows work of repair ever looming.

See safely the imposter: the Doctor. The madman.
Observe with a patient eye as he reformulates his goals
And tremble as his words fall on the deserving.

See fragile death as she approaches.
See vitality masquerading as life.
See shadow as it gains prominence.

See our collection of men—the meek, the mad, the flawed and the flagrant—
And judge them all. But see clearly—your comfort is not free,
It is ushered forward in torrents of apathy
Before losing its legs.

It will be laid last rites at the altar of truth
As suffering and sacrifice mount the final podium.
"

#

"How you doing this fine evening?"
The woman turns, tucking her white-blonde hair behind an ear, and smiles. "I'm okay, thanks."

"You mean that you're fine, don't you?"

She had begun to turn away to resume distractedly stirring her drink, but the unexpected continuation of a half-conversation makes her pause, then turn back to face her California-tan admirer, looking out of place amid the suits and silk ties in his Chinos and battered (but clearly expensive) leather jacket. She smiles politely. "I'm sorry, what?"

The man slides up to the bar beside her, wedging himself into the compressed space between her stool and that of the rail-thin man drinking quietly next to her, and winks. "You're a fine woman on a fine evening—am I right?"

Her smile is a little more forced now. "Sure. Yes, okay. I suppose I'm fine, then."

"So, can I buy you a drink?"

Once again she starts to turn to face him, but then checks herself. "Actually, no. I'm meeting someone. He should be here any minute. Sorry."

"Don't be," the man laughs. "Having friends is a wonderful thing." He leans against the bar, scooping a handful of shelled peanuts from a nearby bowl. "You're okay to chat with me until he gets here, though, yeah?"

The woman hesitates—her pause just long enough for her tanned admirer to sense it. He smiles again and holds up his hands in concession. "Hey, if not, say the word. I'm just making conversation. Passing the time. I mean, I'm not trying to pick you up ... "

A snort from the thin businessman on the stool next to them draws a pair of looks, one amused and the other annoyed, and her bronze suitor is forced to repeat himself to trump the distraction. "Really. Not a pick-up line."

She swivels in her chair, turning her attention back to him and raises her eyebrows in skepticism. "No?"

He laughs in reply. "I swear! We can just have a conversation. I promise."

She hesitates again, and his laughter dies. "Or I could just leave," he says. "Sorry to bother you. I was just trying to be friendly." He stands, jostling the man beside him enough to spill some of the businessman's drink onto the notebook he's been writing in. The man emits a second grumble, this one ignored by Mr. California in his haste to leave.

"Hold on," she interrupts, stopping him with a hand on his wrist. "I'm sorry. I'm not trying to be rude. I'm just nervous—first date tonight."

"That's better!" The man smiles at her, rejection forgotten. "I'm Ryan, by the way."

"Allison," the woman replies, her smile less eager than his.

Ryan taps his neighbor on the shoulder. "Hey, you mind sliding over so we can talk? Thanks." The other man grumbles again, shooting a disgusted look over the top of his glasses, taking in the Chinos and leather, the deep tan and the loafers worn without socks, but he stands up and moves down as requested, leaving his seat vacant.

"So, first date, huh?" Ryan grins. "At a beg-and-brag event? Some date."

"What do you mean?"

"Well, the food is free. The show is free. The only thing that costs here are the drinks. Your date's getting off cheap."

Allison scans the room, her tone sharpening. "It's not really about that. Anyway, it's not a formal date. We both ... You know, it's not important."

"Don't know him that well, huh? Well, at least now you've got a pretty good idea that he's broke." He sees the expression on her face and shakes his head. "Sorry. I don't mean to be a jerk. Really. Here, let me buy you that drink—your guy might not even show up, for all we know."

But by now she is shaking her head. "You know what? I appreciate the gesture, but I'd rather just wait here by myself. Thanks."

"Hey, no problem," he replies, forcing out another laugh, this one falling somewhat short of jovial. "But if it turns out he's too cheap to take care of you, look me up. I'll be around. Yeah?"

She gives a quick nod, then turns her attention back to the half-empty drink in front of her, missing his sour expression and the way his lips shape the word "bitch" as he walks away.

"Don't you hate that?"

She turns to regard the thin man, now leaning on the end of the bar after having been displaced from his stool. "Pardon?" she says.

"Pick-up assholes," he replies. "Sorry to eavesdrop. But I can't stand it when people push like that—as though you've got nothing better to do."

She laughs. "You get that a lot?"

He looks confused for a moment, then startled, and then he gives her a thin smile and shakes his head. "No, no. Not me personally. But I see it all the time."

"He was annoying, but he didn't mean any harm."

"Maybe not. Maybe he didn't, but he did some."

She frowns. "Did he? What was that?"

He holds up his half-empty glass. "Spilled my drink." He glowers for a moment, then breaks it with a half-smile and nervous chuckle.

She joins him in laughter. "The tragedy!" She lifts her purse from its place at her feet. "Let me get you a new one ... "

"No, no," he protests. "I was only kidding. I don't need another. In fact, I should let you get back to yours."

She shakes her head. "That's okay. I'm just sulking anyway. I'll own this—I shouldn't have even engaged but I was bored. I usually like to meet new people—so long as they're not like the 'people' that just left."

"That's fair," he replies. "And, acknowledging that this is going to sound like a pickup line now: unlike pretty much anyone else in this room, I'm not here looking for anything."

She cocks her head at him, still smiling. "No?"

"Truth." He crosses his heart with a quick double flick of his wrist. "I am deeply committed to ending this evening at home alone."

Her laugh this time is real and full. "Fair enough. Can't get more truthful than that ... "

"Thanks." He clears his throat. "Anyway, I'm Robin."

The woman extends her hand. "Allison. Park. Nice to meet you, Robin ... ?"

"Love," he replies, shaking her hand somewhat awkwardly. "And the pleasure is mine, Allison."

"Robin Love?" she says, her hazel eyes sparking with amusement.

"Constantly."

Allison cocks her head, forehead wrinkling in puzzlement. "Pardon me?"

"Sorry," he says. "Habitual response. I am constantly Robin Love. Blind." He flashes Allison a timid smile. "Defense-mechanism joke."

Allison laughs again. "Love is blind. I get it. Funny."

He gives an abrupt nod, his expression going vacant for a moment—an expression she takes for embarrassment.

"So why are you so committed to being alone, Robin?"

He looks startled by the question but then relaxes, sinking in his seat until he is almost deliberately casual. "Oh, I'm not, really. Not forever, you know. Someday. Someday soon, hopefully. I've just got ... other fish to fillet at the moment. Right now I'm kind of ... "

"Happy enough on your own?" she finishes.

He half-stands, then drops back into his seat, anxiety bubbling to the surface. His hands wrestle one another on the bar, fighting for dominance as he stammers a reply. "Well ... Ha! You know, not ... In a way, I suppose."

"I understand. It is hard ... "

He shrugs. "It doesn't have to be."

"What do you mean?" she asks.

"Well, you just have to ... " Robin pauses a moment, shifting on his stool, and she picks up a faint and unexpected scent of rosewater, the smell making her think of old ladies and sewing circles, and her mind threatens to wander before she is able to refocus on the sharp angles of his face—out of place against the sadness of his eyes. After a moment, he continues, his gaze strengthening, his voice hollow but hard. "You just have to find the switch that shuts off your pain. Turns you into a machine. If you don't worry about anyone or anything else, you're indestructible."

Their eyes lock together, filled with gravity, before Allison finally crumbles into tense laughter. He smiles in response.

"Oh that's awful! I thought you were serious for a second."

He grins tightly back at her, his eyes obscured as his glasses catch the light. "Yeah, sorry. Bad joke. I'm not always good with people ... "

"No, no," she says. "You're fine. I'm the one being rude."

But now he seems flustered—unscripted and ill-prepared. He glances quickly around the room again before allowing his gaze to return to her. "No, you're not," he says. "Your date is the rude one."

"What do you mean?" Allison asks.

"Well, where is he?" he replies. "We've been talking for ten or fifteen minutes ... "

Allison is suddenly on her feet. "Oh shit. I totally forgot."

Robin stands as well. "Sorry! I didn't mean to distract you. Go look for him. I'll get your drink."

"You don't have to do that."

"I know. But I'm going to. No strings attached."

She smiles. "You sure?"

"Of course," he replies, eyes still roaming the room. "I'm going home alone, remember?"

The two stand there for an awkward moment. Then she glances over her shoulder. "Well, I should—"

"You should," Robin agrees. "Go. Don't worry. Go find your date."

"I feel like kind of a shit leaving you alone, now."

He shrugs. "Don't. Tonight is, and will be, exactly what I wanted and needed it to be. I'm positive."

She opens her mouth to speak, but he cuts her off. "Never mind. Forget that. Don't talk, just go."

"Thank you," she replies. "And don't sell yourself short, Robin. You're plenty good with people. You're a very nice, very clever guy." With that she turns away and moves into the swirling crowd of people, leaving him to stand at the bar watching until he can no longer see her.

He is nodding seriously. "You're right, Allison. I am a clever guy."

#

Work in Process

"

I am a very clever guy,

I am patience and control,
And now, I am knowledge.
We can begin.

I am real.

I am formulating.

I am coalescing.

I am creating.

I am intensifying, investing, and inventing the new.

And I <u>feel</u> new.

I have a new plan.

A new focus

A new muse and a new game.

And it is a game that I will win.

Believe.

"

Spider

Eclipse in 10 hours

Take a picture. The setting: an El car, red safety lights flashing past the smudged windows as the train dives subterranean. Two people seated in the foreground, blurring slightly as they jostle side-to-side with the motion of the car as it sways over the tracks.

Take that picture and move in closer on the pair: the man's face tightening with each shriek of the train's brakes, his hands clutching his knees. His stained denim jacket thrown almost into shadow by the light reflecting off the golden curls of the young girl sitting beside him, humming quietly to herself.

Take the picture and bring it still closer until you can almost pick up the tangy funk of too many people pressed together. The scent of sixty lives coming into alignment for ten minutes and these two isolated in that crush. The stale remnants of cigarette smoke on the man's breath and the bite of the peppermint hard candy he turns over and over in his mouth. The sticky sweetness of the girl's bubblegum lip gloss, freshly applied from the tube that she turns over in her hands, mirroring the candy's revolutions.

Take a picture and give it time to fully develop, then bring it right up close to discover what you missed the first time around: the rough calluses on the man's hands; his Black fingers standing out against the soft amber of the girl's shoulder, the dirt under his fingernails against the clean white ruffle of her party dress. Listen to the silence that has gripped the small car and feel the sudden, urgent need to do something, to say something about the inherent wrongness of the picture before you. Feel the suspicion; the outrage. Then feel the man's eyes on you, soft and calculating, but resting as heavily on you as his hand does on the girl's shoulder.

"Take a picture."

"What?" The nervous man in pressed gray suit blinks, running his hand along the sharp crease in his slacks, his eyes focused on the task before darting up to the large Black man sitting across from him. He takes in the shaved head and bushy beard; the denim jacket, sleeves rolled up to reveal the whorls of intricate tattoo that stand out on the man's forearms. He blinks again, noticing that the girl is watching him now too, her eyes wide with question.

"I said, take a picture. It'll last longer."

"I don't know what you're talking about. I ... "

"Sweetheart?" the giant man interrupts. The girl turns her head to look up at him. "Who am I?"

"Daddy!"

The giant's eyes are still focused calmly on the man's pallid face. "And how long have you known me?"

"Forever, daddy!" The girl's voice rings with sincerity and laughter, but also with repetition. This has happened before.

"And where's momma?" Eyes still fixed on the thin man across from him, their gazes locked through the thin barrier of the man's round, wire-framed glasses.

"Mindy-Yoda!" the girl laughs, and her father breaks his focus for a moment to regard her fondly.

"Close enough, Sweets. Minnesota is exactly right." He ruffles her hair with a tenderness that seems at odds with his heavy, calloused hands. "Put on your coat now. We're almost there."

The train jerks to a stop and the two rise to leave, the man helping his daughter with the sleeves of her winter coat, the girl's small hand disappearing into her father's as they turn toward the doors of the train. They stop at the door, and the large man curls one hand around the metal pole, his scarred knuckles just inches from the bespectacled man's face. "I'm a good father. And you can mind your own fucking business in the future."

The gray man shrinks in his seat and pushes his glasses up onto his nose, ignoring the stares of the people around him, muttering tightly under his breath as the giant leads his daughter off the train. The girl's voice rings clearly in the background.

"You said the f-word, daddy. That's bad."

"I know, Sweets," the giant replies. "Daddy's trying to be better, okay?"

#

Reggie Webb liked to say, with deliberate understatement, that he'd made his fair share of mistakes. In life, in love ... in general. But none of his choices had done more damage than the high school decision to allow his friends and classmates to call him

Spider. In his mind, that dubious label had steered him into a seemingly endless spiral of bad luck, fueled by a burning need to reshuffle the hand he'd been dealt and stifle a nickname that he felt strangely compelled to live up to.

As a kid, he'd made his share of rash decisions and poor choices, but somehow even the best of intentions seemed to leave him with the worst possible outcomes. He made friends easily but found himself gravitating to people who would ultimately turn out to be anything but friends. He was naturally funny and engaging but struggled with depression and alcoholism, and the blackouts that came along with it. As a teenager he'd been busted multiple times, mostly for "getting by"—for panhandling, for petty theft, for possession with intent… But he'd never had serious issues with the law until the night he found himself piss-drunk and sitting in the wrong car, with the wrong people, at what was certainly the wrong time, and realized that his nickname crossed with the neighborhood he grew up in made his skin color a prison sentence that not even innocence could prevent.

And then, in another blackout fueled moment a few years later, he'd managed to add fatherhood to his list of achievements. When he'd gotten the news it had nearly been the final hammer blow to the temple; the slaughterhouse end of a slaughterhouse life. Fatherhood, as far as Spider was concerned, would be a greater imprisonment than jail could ever be.

He'd been out of prison for two and a half months, barely long enough to settle into an apartment and get the electricity turned on and the phone set up. Long enough, though, to meet Carrie. It took Spider ten drunken minutes at a bar to persuade her to go out with him, ninety more for a movie neither could have told you the plot of, thirty in the tiny bedroom of his apartment, and twenty waiting for her cab to arrive after they'd finished. A grand total of three hours, counting travel time, that boomeranged three and a half months later when she showed up at his door to give him the news.

There was a lot more: conversations that evolved into arguments, escalated into shouting matches, and invariably ended in silence. His color and her conservative parents; his time in prison and her decision to transfer to a school in Minneapolis; his inability to find a job and her parents' desire to sweep the whole situation under an imported Turkish rug. On top of it all, there was Catheryn.

The instant Spider saw the tiny form of his daughter staring up at the turmoil around her with an infant's curious sobriety, he'd accepted the need for his own sobriety. He'd abandoned his protests and submitted to the will of Carrie's father; taken the offer of a small apartment, a part-time job, some cash, and a daughter.

And so, with one grand mistake, Spider—Reggie Webb—encased his previous collection of errors, bad luck, and worse timing in a cocoon of love and determination.

And though the job was long gone as the economy dove south; though the money had dried up as he struggled to find work and keep their lives together, his determination was renewed daily by the squeeze of his daughter's fist around his thumb, her halting first steps on the cracked pavement in front of their building, and his optimistic translation of her gurgled "Pa-da" into a first word. He couldn't pretend to understand the peculiar solemnity of his little girl as she studied the world around her, but he knew that she made him want to be a better person. And so he decided to be one. It seemed a much better life than anything Spider could have expected.

> **Author's Note:** Let me be clear: it can be noble for a good man to do something that falls outside the normal perceptions of "right" in order to accomplish a greater purpose. Robin Hood may steal from the rich to aid the poor; black ops may take down a dictator to prevent him from exterminating his own people. There are times when the ends can justify the means. And often, people doing questionable things to achieve noble ends can be misunderstood. But I don't know that that's what we've got here. We're not looking at a good man brought down by the system. We're not looking at a wronged man who never meant to hurt anyone. We're not looking at the guy next door arbitrarily destroyed by the powers that be (although that's closer). We're looking at a man who committed crimes because it was easier than the alternative, and who is paying the price for it.

Now, granted, since his release from prison, Spider has done his best to stay clean and sober. And since Cate has come into his life, he has mostly succeeded. But that doesn't make him a new man. It doesn't make him trustworthy. It doesn't make him honest, and it doesn't make him good. It just makes him someone who has realized that doing the right thing for the time being might just be the safest bet. It makes him a man who has temporarily found the ability to focus on the needs of others because, for the moment, it's also best for him. It makes him a father.

I'm just not sure I trust it.

I don't tell you any of this to make you root for or against him, just as I don't tell you this to make you love him or pity him or to make some grander point about Man's ability to rise above—to hoist himself up by the bootstraps and craft a life out of the pile of shit he's been given.

But at the same time, however good he might or might not be, he does have a hole to climb out of, collaboratively dug by his own actions and hundreds of years of history: he's got his neighborhood and his name; he's got his race and his record; he's got the challenge of living in this city and of dealing with this system, and that's something I can empathize with. But it's also something I can work with. It helps to make our larger story possible.

I think I know who Spider is. But let's see if we can get him to prove it. Let's test him, you and I. And if he's found wanting, well, then we'll convict and sentence him. That's our privilege. If you ask me, I hope it turns out that he has become a good man. It'll be all the more fun to watch him fall.

#

Spider emerged at street level like an overgrown schoolboy at the fair, tugged up the subway stairs by his daughter, his thick fingers entwined protectively with Cate's delicate ones as her exuberance dragged him from the gloomy press of distrustful stares into the cold, open air. Though he could still feel wary, watchful eyes on him, on the surface they were at least more widely spaced. On the streets, the mismatched pair of father and daughter could find some breathing room.

"Hurry up, daddy!" she demanded.

Spider smiled at the girl and allowed himself to be dragged down the street. "Relax, Sweets. We'll get there. We just got to make one detour. There's something daddy needs to take care of before we get you to your party." The words had barely left his mouth before he was wishing that he could call them back, as the girl's eyes flashed confused unhappiness and her lip began to tremble. "Come on," he said sternly, stooping down beside her and using one heavy finger to push a tendril of hair off of her cheek. "Don't be like that. You got all night to spend with your friends—we can make a quick stop. Tuck that lip in or some bird's going to sit on it." She smiled at that, the smile that set his heart alight, and he pressed on. "We'll pick you up a present before the night's over. I swear."

And just like that her trembling lip was replaced by a full (if gap-toothed) smile. He stood, knees cracking, and let her skip ahead, watching her small hops of joy and listening to her six-year-old singsong.

" ... Out came the sun and dried up all the rain, and the itty-bitty Spider ran up to spout again!"

Spider threw his head back and roared with laughter that came even harder when she turned back to face him, her arms akimbo and her face full of childish petulance at his outburst.

Unable to contain himself, he rushed forward, sweeping her up into his arms. He buried his face in her flaxen hair, inhaling the purity of her youthful scent, and snuffled like a bear as she shrieked with delight.

"Daddy!" she cried, giggling.

"Uh oh, little one," he growled in reply. "Daddy Bear's gonna eat you!"

She squealed again and the two tussled for a moment, then she turned, throwing her arms around his neck, hugging him fiercely.

The strength of her small body had always startled him. To think that she could hold him so tightly was wonderfully smothering and terrifying. He stopped walking, shifting her in his arms to hold her more securely, and pulled her tightly to his chest, planting a light kiss on her forehead.

She leaned away, bringing them eye to eye as she regarded him seriously. "Daddy, you're not a bear."

The solemnity of the statement nearly touched off his laughter again, but he fought it down. For a precocious child, Cate was easily hurt.

"You're absolutely right, darlin'," he replied. "I am not a bear. Very smart."

She beamed at him, then squealed again as he flipped her up to sit on his shoulders, observing the people around them from above, lifeguard of the city.

"When you're bigger," Spider said as he started down the street again, "you'll be able to ride with me on the bike, and then we won't have to ride the train anymore. What do you think of that?"

Silence from above as she bounced along on his shoulder.

"Cate?"

"Mommy said I'm not ... " she began.

Spider sighed. "I know mommy don't want you on the bike. But mommy's far away and she doesn't understand how safe it is. In Chicago daddy makes the decisions. When you're a little bigger, it'll be fine. When you visit mommy, she can make the decisions, okay?"

"Okay!" the little girl replied cheerfully, and Spider smiled, amazed anew at her ability to ignore the rift between her parents, or at least pretend to. He knew that he hadn't adequately explained her mother's absence, but could you describe prejudice and abandonment to a child? He gritted his teeth, grateful that she couldn't see his expression.

The bell on the door dinged as the two stepped into the small, dingy office. Spider looked down at his daughter. "You wait here by the door, okay?"

"Okay," she replied. "Can I play with your zippy?"

He smiled. "Yeah, sure." He reached into his pocket, handing her a battered Zippo lighter. Gripping it tightly, she retreated to a corner of the office, where she proceeded to flip it open and shut with innocent fascination.

When Cate had first come to him as a toddler, he'd had no toys, nothing that could hold the interest of a child. Panicked by her crying, he'd yanked the flint from his lighter and given it to her to quell the sobs. Since then, no matter how many teddy bears or Barbie dolls she accumulated, the lighter remained her favorite.

The small office was nearly empty, and Spider walked up to the counter without the usual hassle of taking a number and waiting in line, though he still felt smothered by the overwhelming air of depression that filled the small room. As he approached, the horse-faced woman behind the counter glanced lazily up at him and sighed, brushing her bangs away from her eyes as she cocked her head at him. "Help you?"

"Allison Park, please?" Spider replied.

"Name?"

"Reggie Webb," he supplied. "Reginald."

The woman glanced down at her computer and punched a few keys, the taps syncopating with the echoing click ... click of the lighter flipping open and shut in Cate's hands. After a moment, she looked back up at him, a frown forming. "Appointment?"

"Not exactly," he began. "I—"

"Is she expecting you?" Horse Face interrupted, managing to look simultaneously bored, scornful, and accusatory as she brushed the hair away from her eyes again.

Spider gritted his teeth, doing his best to bury the anger at being interrupted. "I told her I'd be in this afternoon," he replied.

She stared at him blankly for a moment, then sighed. "You can wait for her in Room B."

He nodded a curt reply, turning toward the front door. "Come on, Sweets, we're going to talk to the lady."

Catheryn looks up from the lighter. "The nice lady?" she asked, oblivious to the presence of the horse-faced woman.

Spider smirked. "Yeah," he replied. "The *nice* lady. Come on, now."

Cate trotted over, and they stepped through the heavy door into the cramped hallway beyond.

Allison was, in fact, already waiting for them in Room B, and rose from her chair as they stepped in, kneeling quickly to greet Cate. "Hiya Catie, look at you! You get bigger every time I see you. I love your dress. So pretty!"

Cate blushed, hiding behind Spider's legs, suddenly bashful, though not enough to keep her from shooting comically demure looks at the beautiful blonde woman every few seconds.

Allison stood, turning her smile on Spider, and he felt himself automatically smiling in response. "Reggie," she said.

"Hi," he replied, annoyingly tongue-tied in her presence.

She regarded him evenly for a moment, remnants of the smile still playing across her face; dancing in her eyes. Then she cut the moment in two with abrupt gravity. "So, good news," she said, returning to her seat and gesturing him into the one across from her.

He sat. "How good?"

"Very." She leaned over to retrieve a sheaf of papers from the briefcase at her feet, shooting a wink at Cate that sent her scurrying back behind Spider's chair giggling. "Your claim came through," she continued. "You weren't fired with cause, just laid off, so you're eligible for full benefits."

Spider sighed with relief. "Thank God."

She smiled. "I agree." Then, serious again, "Realize that you'll need to be actively looking for work. We'll need proof of that every week."

"No problem," he replied. "Absolutely."

"Good." Her gaze moved to Cate for a moment, who was sitting on the floor and playing with the Zippo again, then continued. "Three-fifty a week, food stamps, and a child-care subsidy. Think that'll work?"

Spider nods. "That'll work great. And I won't need it long. I'm looking every day. I'll find something soon."

"I know you will," Allison smiled.

He listened to his heart beating in his ears for a moment, then drew a deep breath and cleared his throat. "Um ... Ms. Park? One question."

"Of course. What is it?"

"Can you ... Is there any chance of some kind of an advance? Like, today? It's just that it's Cate's ... "

She bit her lip, thinking, but at the same time her head was shaking. "Sorry, Reggie. I'm really sorry. I wish I could, but there's no way to do it. All I can give you for today is the food stamps ... "

He stood, the abruptness of his action sending his chair clattering against the tiled floor, startling Cate, who jerked her attention back to him. "No, no," he stammered, "that's okay. I shouldn't have asked."

Allison rose from behind her desk, her eyes flashing concern. "It's totally okay to ask, Reggie. I just can't. It's not something we can do on the spur of the moment."

"Yeah, I get it. It's just ... Never mind. We ... we'll make do."

"I'm sorry, really," she repeated, then watched him a moment. "You'll be okay?"

He shrugged agreement, head down, flushed with hot embarrassment.

She opened her briefcase again and came out with a small stack of grocery vouchers. "Here, take these for now," she said. "Your first check should arrive by the twenty-eighth, but if you have any trouble, let me know right away. I'll do whatever I can. You have my number, right?"

He nodded again, then stooped to gather his daughter in his arms before heading for the door in silence. At the door, he stopped, letting out another deep sigh before looking back over his shoulder. "Ms. Park? Thanks. Very much. Seriously, thank you."

She smiled in return, full and warm. "Of course. We have to take care of the lovely Lady Catheryn, don't we?"

Cate's giggle echoed through the small room, but Spider could only manage a faint smile before quickly pushing out through the door before he lost his composure. Cate called "Bye, Ally!" over his shoulder, which almost set him off again, but he managed to distract himself, shifting his daughter in his arms so that he could deal with the heavy door of the reception area. Immediately, he could feel the weight of Horse Face's stare on the two of them, and even through the happy chatter of the little girl in his arms, he could hear the muttered, "Jesus help us. Poor girl."

Spider stopped in the middle of the room and set Cate down, crossing to the counter in two long strides and then shooting his hand through the gap in the plexiglass screen to grab the woman by the wrists. He pulled her close enough to see the fear in her eyes, their faces nearly touching, with only the plexiglass partition separating them. He felt the thin bones of the woman's wrists under his grip and imagined how easy it would be to simply snap them. But instead, he pushed the woman's hands lightly against the counter between them and pinned them there. He looked for a glimmer of resentment or hatred in her eyes that would justify more, but there was nothing there but terror.

"Don't," he said, "say anything about my daughter ever again."

Without waiting for a response, he released the woman's arms, turned to scoop Cate up and hurried out the door, clutching her to his heaving chest.

"Where are we going now, daddy?" Cate asked as the two stepped out into the dimming light of the early winter evening. Still shaking with checked rage, Spider didn't even hear the question. Couldn't feel the chill against his face as he stepped into the wind or hear the whine of rush hour traffic buzzing past on the crowded street. He drew in a deep breath, forcing himself to let go of his anger and concentrate on what was important: the night, the birthday party, his daughter.

"Hey, Sweets?" he said. She looked at him expectantly, and he couldn't help but smile. "I know I said this was the last stop, but I got one more. So, I'm going to leave you at your party while I run by the bar real quick—"

"To see your girlfriend?" Cate interrupted, her tone one of playful teasing, startling Spider with its maturity. He flushed slightly.

"Yeah, you got me. I want to stop by and see Jamie."

"Okay," she replied, adding with heartbreaking seriousness, "I love Jamie."

He hugged her tightly, not wanting her to see his expression, then held her at arm's length. "But I'll have a present waiting for you when you get home tomorrow morning, okay?"

"It's okay," she replied. "I have presents at the party, too."

He frowned. "You do? From who?"

She nodded. "Jenna's mom said everyone gets presents, just in case."

Spider did not ask, "Just in case what?" but was well aware of the answer, even if Cate was not. He gritted his teeth and doubled his resolve to track down something worthy of his daughter, trying not to imagine catching Jenna's mom alone and explaining to her the differences between generosity, privilege, and presumption. After the frustration of his encounters with the horse-faced receptionist and the judgmental prick on the train, he considered just bringing Cate to the bar with him, not sure that he was willing to abandon her to the wealthy parents of the well-fed white kids in her kindergarten class.

But before he could give it any further thought, she was hauling on his arm. "Come on, daddy, hurry!" She lunged forward, once again towing him down the street.

Spider did his best to put his worry and anger behind him. If things went as planned, he could drop Cate at her party and still have time to swing past the bar to see if Jamie could spare some cash to get the girl the birthday present she deserved before the stores closed. Not for the first time, Spider wished it were possible to move faster. There was never enough time—he felt always moments too late, eternally two steps behind, as though whoever was pulling the strings of his life had arranged to keep the best of everything tantalizingly, frustratingly beyond his reach. But he was beginning to realize that, as long as his daughter was beside him (or dragging him down the sidewalk at excited-little-girl speed), he could pretend that he had finally caught up. That his run of bad luck was over. He could forget about the past—and even the present—

and fix his foci on the future. Smiling again, Spider hurried along after his daughter, warmed through, despite the cold.

Puck
Eclipse in 24 hours

Author's Note: Technically speaking, the next person we should be watching is Cort. It's his turn. It's his right. It should be his night—he's got a lot going on. But I sense something big approaching and, at the moment, I don't feel comfortable taking my eye off of the jittery homeless man who has somehow taken over my story. He may be fragile. He may be broken. He may be a loose gathering of abandonment and anxiety, and he seems ridiculously dependent on a random stretch of dirty alley. But for some reason he keeps clamoring to the forefront. And for that, he makes me nervous. For that, he's worth keeping an eye on.

Besides. Cort isn't ready for us. He's busy primping, blissfully unaware that while he thinks he'll have his choice of two women tonight, he's really choosing which of two directions his story will veer.

So, let's follow Puck for now—Cort's opposite in so many ways. Let's see what a vagrant can bring to the party when he's given the opportunity to dream. And what happens when his dreams take over.

But first, let's recognize: it is possible to love opposites. To give your heart to the lawyer and the laborer, the flower and the filth, the Methodist and the madman. With devotion, you can ride the pendulum swing from fire to frost and back again. It is possible to love opposites.

And for some, it comes naturally. Take, for example, the weather.

In the Midwest, the weather is irrational. Off its rails and unpredictable. Manic depressive. A fleeting rush of long summer days—heat and humidity turning the streets into liquid and the air to steam—followed by a seemingly endless string of sharp winter nights.

But like a battered wife who clings to her abusive husband or an overeager schoolboy who idolizes his tormentors, Midwesterners: your Minnesotans, your Wisconsinites; your Iowegians and Clevelanders and Chicagoans—they all wear the schizophrenic nature of their weather like a badge of honor. It is their Alamo, antiquated and dusty but polished up with pride. "Sure, it's awful, but we like it that way." And they survive by focusing on the positives, blinding themselves to the misery in favor of the fantasy. They remember the bright, sunny days over the suffocating humidity; the suntan over the sweat. They forget huddling together against the sleet in favor of cuddling together by the fire and celebrate the beauty of the winter snow over the bone-brittling wind chill.

And they can do this because the sweltering summers and frozen winters are theirs. The tumultuous weather gives them unity; it makes them family. It somehow makes their city more their city. Makes their home more their home. And people will defend their home with a passion that they might not have known they possessed.

And that can make them both vulnerable and dangerous.

#

Puck is home. And it is snowing tonight.

He stands just inside the mouth of his alley, feeling the chilly kiss of each snowflake as it gives its life away. They light on his cheeks and neck, melting against the warmth of his bare skin where once they might have lived on, resting on a stray shank of his beard or curl of his hair.

He is staring down the alley, breathing heavily from excitement and exertion and, lately, from a new surge of anxiety. There is an intruder; curled up in sleep in what had been his nest. He moves closer, noting how his replacement has turned toward the heat of the taqueria's air vent, leaving his back to be covered by a clean, white blanket of fresh snow. Puck's thoughts dance with one another just behind his eyes, which remain locked on the motionless form, and his lips purse involuntarily, shaping themselves around silent words and forming unvoiced sentences that might begin with "Who are you?" or "Why are you here?" But might just as well be "Where do I go now?" or simply "No!"

Finally, after minutes of chewing on his lip and stroking the soft cashmere patch inside his jacket—long enough for his footprints to have been snowed over—he spurs himself to action, striding with vengeful purpose to the silent form of his usurper and laying a hand on what he makes to be the man's shoulder, intending to shake him awake.

Instead, the body crumbles under his touch, breaking down into its component parts: crumpled newspaper and black trash bags. Puck sinks back on his haunches, still working the inside of his lower lip with his teeth, even through his rueful smile. This is the body he'd built himself, the doppelganger he had created to protect his most valuable commodity, which had faded as quickly as his memory of building it, as quickly as his tracks had vanished beneath the snow. Over the past several years, Puck has grown accustomed to forgetting things, but he has never tricked himself before. He shakes his head, chiding. "Gotta guh ... Gotta, gotta, gotta. Got to pay attention Sammy. Pa ... pay attention. Gotta ... g ... get back to work."

His hands move quickly, remembering their time in Ino's barbershop and rediscovering their dexterity even in the cold, quickly taking the "body" apart. Making room for Puck by the warmth. As he settles against the grate, letting his back and sides relish the restaurant's heat, his eyes find the clock tower and the flashing lights that spell out 8:00 ... pm ... At the same time, his lower lip gently strokes his teeth from the gumline up to the lip and back down. Comfort. Jamie is due by again in a few hours and Puck, exhausted as he is, is electric at the idea that he will see her so soon.

He props himself up on an elbow, watching the snow that hangs in the air above him, picked out by the impersonal glare of the streetlights and thrown into beautiful relief by the red and green and blue of the local neon. From below, the snowflakes seem infinite. Billions of icy specks spinning through the darkness as though the stars had found sudden life. As though the heavens were dancing just for him, their revelry inspiring them to change their position in the sky; changing astrological meaning. Changing the future.

The snow-stars blur as Puck noddingly blinks himself awake once, twice, then again, each blink further from the one before it. He desperately wants to stay awake to see Jamie; to find any opportunity to justify his quest. But the warmth of the grate is seductive, and it draws him toward sleep. He feels confident that, for tonight at least, nothing can hurt Jamie—not while he is watching from his nest. But even as that knowledge subdues his anxiety, it dulls his edge. It makes it easier for the warmth to infiltrate his thoughts and lull him into sleep. And as the snow begins to build its gradual blankets once again, sleep drifts up and over Puck, blocking out the world and enveloping him in dream.

###

Though his eyes are closed, Puck can feel his awareness heightening, his senses sharpening. He feels more in control than he has ever been, his grasp of this dream world eclipsing any understanding he has ever had of the real one. He hears meaning in the buzz of traffic that zips past the mouth of his alley: each Camry hurrying to a sales call or soccer practice, each BMW ferrying its businessman home from work. He feels the bustle of the restaurant at his back and the torrent of people pacing the icy streets in front of him. And he also senses the stares; the eyes watching him, waiting to see what he'll do—what comes next.

He sits up, searching the alley, his eyes and ears telling him that he is alone, but his intuition telling him otherwise. He proves to himself that he is dreaming by sitting motionless—no twitches, no spasms, and no stutters—waiting for a movement that will reveal the person that is watching him. But not even the stars are moving anymore; or perhaps it has simply stopped snowing.

From the mouth of the alley there is a rush of air that tosses a fresh drift of snow his way, and now he is standing and somehow holding a gun, pointed down the alley toward the street. The stock of the rifle burns cold against his cheek. He traces the mouth of the alley with the barrel while searching for a better understanding of what is going on.

But nothing has changed. Nothing has moved. Just a gust of wind and a scattering of snow. Rifle still pressed tightly to his shoulder, Puck moves toward the street, every so often brushing his lower lip across his teeth, as though to remind himself of who he is.

The wind gusts again, filling his eyes with tears that he tries to blink away before they can crystallize, each blink shooting him down the alley, jumping frames to leave him standing at the sidewalk with his gun pointed skyward, his eyes scanning the street.

As he moves out into the city, his perception of the landscape shifts. He absorbs the empty eyes of the surrounding buildings, the canopy of multicolored awnings and the crackle of empty cigarette packs beneath his feet, brittle from the cold. He catches the scent of tires burning and of dying flowers. And through it all, he feels the eyes on him, watching.

The street before him is crisscrossed with cracks and pockmarks that spell out a Sanskrit message he cannot decipher. The flashing red neon of the restaurant on his right paints abstract pictures of light and shadow on a rough brick wall that seems familiar. But the bank clock flashes ∞ ... $\sqrt{I}$ ... 616.89 ... and it is so far away. Even the familiar mouth of his alley looks different. Smaller. As if it were closing in on him—sheltering him from the weather, the world, and its demons, but also hiding him from angels.

The thought gives Puck new resolve, and he steps out of his alley, away from his home and deeper into dream. He still feels watched, and so he moves down the deserted street toward Jamie's bar, not noticing as his alley closes up behind him, its dark mouth filling with brick until the wall is smooth and unbroken, leaving no sign that Puck's nest had ever existed.

Puck's gaze, however, is fixed on the bar, though the building is shrouded in fog, or perhaps draped in a thick canopy of leaves. He takes another step and the leaves fall from their stems to be caught up by the wind, spinning through the air even as they wither and die, becoming a sandstorm that cuts a swath between him and his destination. Another step and the grains of sand become flakes of snow, turning the air into a wall of white. At the same time, with each step, with each new barrier, Puck can feel the gun in his hand shrinking. The weight of the AR-15 compresses into a Winchester Sharpshooter, shortens into a 22 Magnum revolver, and then folds in on itself, turning into a Backup 380 and then an MP-25. He can see the bar far in the distance, and his eyes pick a path through the sleet. After a moment and a pair of heavy breaths, he puts his head down and begins to run, unable to hold himself in check any longer.

With his eyes closed, he can't see the fire or ice or thorns that he must plunge through. He can't see his destination or the ground that he covers as he runs. But it is better that way. For Puck, there is no past and no future. No patience or planning. Only the demanding immediacy of his mission and his lower lip scraping against his teeth.

Finally, exhausted, he stumbles to a stop and opens his eyes, finding that, in the magic of dream, he is standing less than a foot from the door of the bar. Through the small round window Puck can see the entirety of the small room. To his dismay, it is deserted, save for a smallish man huddled in the corner writing in a notebook.

Puck slumps against the door in despair, clenching his eyes shut and grabbing fistfuls of his hair, twisting himself violently around to face the street. He opens his eyes and tips his face up to catch raindrops and snowflakes on his lips and cheeks. And as he watches, the stars begin to move again, spinning above him and pulsing from dim to brilliant with a vitality that makes his knees weak. He wonders, desperately, whether he might be dying.

But even as the thought passes through him, the bar door slams open, jolting him to life. In the doorway stands a figure who, at first, looks like the white-haired old man he'd followed earlier in the day but then resolves into Puck's father, exactly as he remembers him: eyes hard and calculating; always watching.

Puck swallows hard, then speaks. "I wanted to ask you," he begins, "if you could let a friend of mine ... "

But his father cuts him off with a sharp look and snaps, "We're going to be late," before striding quickly away. Puck hesitates and then hurries to catch up, his legs shorter than he remembers.

As he draws near, his father turns to address him without making eye contact. "We'll take a cab from here. Your mother is waiting for us ... "

Puck nods, but his father is already gone, sliding into a pale taxicab, which drives quickly away. Still desperate to keep up, Puck climbs into another.

As his cab pulls away from the curb, however, Puck notices that the two have split, moving in different directions. He pounds against the glass partition, but the cabbie takes no notice, instead pointing the cab away from the bar, away from his father, away from his alley, his home, and everything that Puck has ever known.

After several moments of spastic, impotent panic, Puck sags against the seat, resigned to his lack of control.

The driving feels interminable, Puck's body filling the dead time with jumps and jitters, his tongue beating a metronomic pulse against the roof of his mouth. Finally, just as he is wondering whether he will spend the rest of his life tongue-tied and trapped, the cab comes to a stop and the door opens.

He finds himself standing in a nondescript, middle-class neighborhood, four or five smallish A-frame houses facing him, the road sloping away to his right.

He approaches the nearest house, half-expecting to find his father already there, but no longer certain what is real. Perhaps he'll find Jamie sitting on the front porch waiting for him. Perhaps he'll open the front door and step into Hell. Perhaps this is all just a continuation of a drunken dream, and he'll wake up at his desk in the offices above the press room to find that the payroll had never been lost and no records had gone missing; that he'd never lost his job or had to face his father's disappointment. Perhaps he will wake up, cheek stained with ink, fingers raw from filing, tongue thick with bourbon and sleep, wishing for a way out and unaware that it is the wrong thing to wish for.

Perhaps it's best if we all stop expecting ...

The door swings open to reveal a woman who takes Puck's breath away. She stands with her hip cocked and one hand resting on the door handle, either holding it open for him or preventing it from opening further as she regards him with curiosity and knowledge and suspicion and innocence. She stands straight and defiant, challenging him. Welcoming him. Inviting him in and demanding that he leave. Her gaze pins him to the floor, seizes his definition of beauty and erases it. She reads the past in his face and rewrites it.

He is speechless.

She is precisely his height, so that their eyes are perfectly level, hers bright blue and piercing in their intensity. Her features are sharp and angular and would make her seem hard, if not for the softness of her eyes, which are brown like her hair.

Puck looks down at her, a tiny blonde angel just like his Angel.

She is young. And wise with years. And roughly his age.

She is tender and tough. She is demure and detached.

She is every woman he has ever loved. She is his mother. She is his Angel. She is a cocktail waitress and a prostitute and a little girl that he once saw walking down a random street.

She is captivating.

The everywoman offers a smile that resolves her image, the innocence of the girl, the edge that is Jamie, and his mother's maternal love merging into something warm and safe and still somehow unfamiliar. She gestures for him to enter, and without a moment's thought, he does.

But things are different inside. The seconds tick sideways, at irregular intervals. And although he knows that he is sitting at a small table talking to all of the women of his dreams, the conversation trips and stutters along with the irregular tick of the clock.

"Now what did you say your name was?" she says.
"You okay, Puck baby? You look like you saw a ghost," she says.
"It's alright. I like you. You seem good," she says.

The voices assault him, clamoring for his attention, and he struggles to separate them. His mind swims as they twine together, each demanding that he listen only to it. To her.

"Something's happening and you've got to be careful. Don't trust anyone."
"There's no time."
"It's too much to ask. He's not ready."
"I miss you ... "

Puck blinks, trying to focus on one voice but unable to unbraid the conversations.

"Have we met?"
"I've got a secret. But I'll share it with you ... "
"You've always had a kind face, but you need to learn to be strong. If you can't fight, people will take advantage."

"Baby, you have to listen. You have to push through. There's trouble ahead and only you can stop it. But you have to be careful ..."

There is a knock at the door. The beautiful blonde woman glances over her shoulder, and the older woman turns back to face him.

"I'm so sorry. Could you wait for just a moment?"

She smiles an apology and stands, crossing from the room before he can say, "Wait, don't leave" or "I don't understand."

And then she is gone—and they all are gone. He may hear murmured voices from another room, or it might be the beating of his heart or the tick of the clock or nothing at all. So he waits, hunched in his chair, legs popping with jitters as his tongue chastises the inside of his lips for letting her out of his sight. After a moment, his eyes move to the small sideboard and a decanter of what he assumes must be whisky. After a brief, internal struggle, he crosses to it and pours himself a glass.

Time passes in more ways than Puck can keep track of. In minutes and hours, but also in degrees of light and temperature. In growing shadows and empty glasses, guiltily refilled. After too many of them all, Puck realizes that his host is not going to return.

He stands, unsteady and filled with indecision. The room is suffused with the thick musk of a million dead flowers—a scent that plants a ball of lead at the pit of Puck's stomach and makes his legs go suddenly weak. He collapses against the doorframe, feeling the burning desire to do something without having the slightest sense of what can be done. He stands, twitching, for a moment, and then, without warning, his legs come to life, launching him out of the house and into the street.

He runs aimlessly at first, then in a rigid pattern of crisscrosses and ever-tightening circles. He runs until he can no longer remember why he is running or whether his search is for a woman that he knows or a home he has mostly forgotten; for his father or his mother or Jamie; the Angel or the blonde girl. Eventually, he is running only because it is something he has always done. He runs to maintain inertia.

Finally, he staggers to a halt, collapsing to the curb, weeping from exhaustion and failure. Covering his eyes with grimy hands that turn his tears into rivers of mud, he sobs until he has nothing left. Until he feels as dry and empty as a seashell; no life of his own, no energy, and no purpose.

At that, he lowers his hands and looks up. Before him, covering the streets like a patchwork of lace, are crisscrossing trails of sand. Pure, white, interlocking lines that mark every inch of his frenzied search. From where he sits, Puck can see everywhere that he has been and, by extension, everywhere that he has yet to be. He looks down at his feet and finds that the sand has been spilling out of a pair of small hourglasses, one attached to each heel. But even when he is still, the timers continue to run. The pile of soft white sand beneath him grows larger with each passing second as the hourglasses empty. He scans the world before him for a place empty of sand, which he somehow knows will tell him where he needs to be. But as he looks, the last of the sand runs out, and the crisscrossed paths before him begin to fade, blowing away in the breeze, mingling with the grime of the street, or possibly just disappearing into nothingness, as seconds and years will.

And then Puck wakes.

This time, his sleep does not drop away like snowy blankets or the severed strands of his hair. It sticks in his eyes and feels thick in his throat. He feels drunk, or recently drunk. By the time he comes fully awake, he is already standing, his bag tucked under one arm and his coat thrown over the other shoulder, the sun bright in his eyes.

Puck blinks one last time for clarity and then shoots a glance back at his nest, still bearing the outline of his body against the dampness of the melted snow. He stares at the outline a moment, then back up at the sky, sitting just above the horizon, warming the city. Which is good; the snow is melting. But the sun is too high, the sky too bright, and Puck doesn't need the bank clock to know that he is late.

He spends more seconds than he can spare hastily rebuilding the false body that guards his home, frantic hands patting his double into tenuous life, but his mind is already several blocks down the street, eating up sidewalk squares with quick, syncopated strides as he rushes to catch up with his vision of the future, praying that he can run fast enough to get to the place he needs to be before it no longer exists.

Just as in his dreams, each blink of his eyes propels him forward. A blink to clear away the last of his sleep, and he is a block down the street. A blink to ward off a gust of wind, and he is hurrying past the mall; a quick series of blinks to keep the sweat from stinging his eyes, and he finds himself pushing through the door of a gas station, breathing heavily as he scans the small convenience store.

His eyes roam the aisles of candy bars, beef jerky and automobile accessories, but he quickly begins to feel watched again. He turns to face the sales counter and the man behind it.

Puck shuffles his feet, cringing as his chin dives toward his chest in a self-conscious spasm. He sets words on his tongue and gives it time to consider them. After a few seconds of rolling them around and shaking loose the debris, he finally is able to offer up, "Bathroom?"

"Yeah ... " the clerk says with narrowed eyes. "You going to buy something?"

Puck nods in relief, his hands patting his jacket pockets to confirm that he still has the money that the confused man had given him in front of the grocery store. Feeling the clerk's eyes on him, Puck dodges up an aisle, casting about for something suitable as he pulls the damp bills from his pocket.

He runs his lips across his teeth yet again. His eyes fall on a small travel toothbrush and tube of toothpaste. He pulls the package from the rack, smiling ruefully to himself, and moves to the counter. He sets his selection, carefully wrapped in a five-dollar bill, on the counter. The clerk picks it up disdainfully, his thick black eyebrows coming together as his nostrils flare in disgust. "Dollar sixty-eight's your change," he says, then jerks his head toward the rear of the store. "Bathroom's in the back."

Puck scoops up the toothbrush and his change and retreats toward the rear of the store, feeling the clerk's eyes on him all the way.

In the bathroom, he empties his bag onto the counter and undresses quickly, rolling his grimy jeans and shirt into a tight cylinder and stowing them in the recently emptied bag. He then hurries into his new suit, trying to avoid his own eyes in the small mirror before him.

When he has finished dressing, Puck turns to leave, then stops himself as he reaches the bathroom door. He hesitates, turning cautiously back toward the row of sinks that he has just left. The mirrors above them show innocent images of the line of bathroom stalls further inside, and Puck slides toward them carefully, approaching from the side to stay out of the mirrors' line of sight. He closes his eyes, forming a picture in his mind, and then takes one sideways step, planting himself firmly in front of the closest mirror before opening his eyes.

The image before him is closer to the one in his mind than he had expected, but the subtle differences are enough to make the picture jarring: the sheen of his cheek that shows the vestiges of his hurried run; his wind-mussed hair; the grime of the street that has already begun to find its way back into his cheeks. Collectively, they make Puck wince.

He sighs, a heaviness sinking into his shoulders. His eyes, unaware of his melancholy, roam the room via the mirrors, traversing the row of stalls behind him before returning to the row of sinks in front of him, each with its own small soap dispenser. His lips twitch in the vestiges of a smile, and then he strips off his shirt and coat and cleans himself as quickly and as thoroughly as one can at a gas-station bathroom sink. The water is cold but refreshing. Nothing compared to a night on the streets.

Five minutes later, he feels better. Newly scrubbed and brushed and once again dressed in his new suit. For confirmation, he pulls out the battered driver's license that he had presented to Ino as a model. The image in the mirror is slightly older and has seen things that the other could never have imagined, but for all intents and purposes they are indistinguishable.

Puck smiles again, driving home the resemblance, then slides his fatigue jacket over the lighter suit coat, takes a moment to rub the patch of cashmere under his lapel, and then walks out of the bathroom, confidence steadying his stride. He can feel the clerk's suspicious eyes follow him to the door, but the look slides off of him. Can't touch him. He is too young now to be bothered by the opinions of others.

A twenty-minute train ride later, talking to himself throughout the journey and ignoring the strange looks that the narration earns him, Puck finds himself in a familiar location. From across the street he can see the small house and the empty air in front of it.

He crosses the street slowly, unable to take his eyes off of the nothing in the air. As he steps onto the lawn, he considers pausing to see whether he had missed something the previous day; wondering whether finding whatever it was might make this process easier. Might make the coming confrontation less traumatic.

Instead, he finds himself suddenly standing at the front door. He pats the bag at his side, as though to remind himself that it is there and that his gift is tucked safely inside. He had been confident that his offering would be appreciated and accepted, but now he finds himself doubting whether it can possibly be enough to repay the favor he plans to ask. After all, he has no idea how long Jamie will have to stay here. How long before the demon forgets about her and seeks new prey. Before he allows himself the time to think about it, however, he reaches up and rings the doorbell. Wincing at the familiar, grating chime, he rubs his cashmere patch again, the action reminding him that he is still wearing remnants of his recent past. Not the image he wants. He shrugs quickly out of the fatigue jacket and stuffs it into his bag, immediately feeling the winter chill begin to creep in.

The house looms over him, threatening. He hadn't anticipated how nervous he would feel to be standing so close and for a moment he considers bolting, but he needs this. There is one final exchange to be made; one last trade to complete his quest. And so he presses the bell again, wondering which of them will answer the door and praying that it will be her.

He hears footsteps from inside, but they seem to take forever to reach the door, and with each echoing step Puck's newfound confidence shrinks and his stutter comes alive, sending him spinning wildly away from the urbane, suited professional he intended and toward the bedraggled street rat of a day ago.

Just as he begins to feel that if he is forced to stand there a moment longer he will dissolve into a limp body of crumpled newspaper and black trash bags, the door swings open to reveal the white-haired old man from Puck's dreams whom he had watched caress the air in front of the house only twelve hours earlier.

The two men stare at one another for a moment, and the old man's eyes narrow, widen, and then harden as they move up and down to examine Puck fully.

When his examination is complete, the man clears his throat and swallows before finding Puck's eyes again. Enough time passes for Puck to wonder whether the world has frozen again, and then the old man finally sucks in a breath through his teeth. "That's a second-hand suit," he says.

Puck fights the urge to flinch, nodding mutely instead.

Another endless period of time drags by as nearly visible thoughts and memories move across the old man's eyes. Puck's tongue offers up sentence fragments but his lips wisely choke off the words.

Finally, the old man seems to find some stability and he looks Puck in the eyes again, his watery blue gaze weaker than Puck remembers it.

"No tie," he says, fighting some emotion that Puck can't identify. "You look good, though." He pauses, scanning the gray suit again before finding Puck's eyes. "Your mother is dead," he says. "I suppose you'd better come inside."

Puck sways as his legs go weak and his mind catches fire. His future is once again overcome by doubt as everything he knows, everything he has built his reality on, begins to crumble. Through a growing fog of remorse, he steps through the doorway behind his father, once more feeling the rising sensation of panic.

Ben

Eclipse in 8 hours

There was a symphony in the brittle afternoon air. Ben could hear it: the whisper of the icy breeze like subtle strings over the percussive rumble of a train passing on its elevated tracks some blocks away and the syncopated crunch of a snow shovel around the corner. Life went on unflinchingly all around him, and every moment contributed to the music. Eyes closed, he let it enfold him as his hands floated up to shape the tune of the world.

He felt finally in control, forging beauty as a symphony conductor does, finding art where there had been none. He dug his fingers into it, separating each strand of melody from its counter, searching each thread for meaning.

At the same time, his hands shaped the sound to match the rhythms that he had danced to earlier and that still echoed in his memory, the elegance of his young partner making the dance effortless. The way it was meant to be.

And so, when he finally cut the music off with a flourish and opened his eyes to find that the beauty he had been so carefully sculpting had disappeared, Ben felt rubbery and spent.

He found himself standing in front of a house that might have been his own but that felt somehow foreign. The white siding, the green shutters, and the overgrown hedges were familiar but distorted, as though he were seeing them from a new angle or through an imperfect lens. Worse, the house looked empty—like an abandoned shell washed up on the beach.

It loomed over him, its hollow stare throwing out challenges: "Where were you?" and "Why do you leave me here by myself?" Each demand echoing with the rising tremor of Elle's voice in her later years. Ben shielded his face from the biting wind, doing his best to ignore the disquieting thoughts. He exhaled deeply, his body feeling loose and exhausted but his face tight and brittle from the cold. Through his watering eyes, the world took on a new shape, and Ben realized that he'd been wrong. The house before him was not a shell. It was a coffin. It had been Elle's for years and now it was his, watching him even as it waited.

And so he gave in, staggering to the front door and stepping inside, ignoring the ringing telephone and anything else that could spark a memory. He managed to drag himself up the stairs to the bedroom, where his legs finally gave out, dropping him onto the bed to see whether dream might be a better place to live out whatever time he had left. Clearly, reality was no longer the answer.

#

Seemingly, no time passed between Ben's collapsing into sleep and his eyes opening again to find himself propped in his favorite chair at the foot of the stairs, newspaper spread open on his lap, his pipe in the ashtray at his side. He blinked, mind still foggy, and picked up the paper to find an antidote to his disorientation.

The date was set in type far too small for him to make out, and he bypassed it (as he so often did these days) to scan the headlines, which were easier to read and to understand than the convoluted print beneath. Today he found nothing but well-worn topics: the growing homeless problem, child abuse and abandonment, murder and sexual perversity, pointless violence and street crime, and on and on. But when he folded the paper to put it away, he was surprised to find that he was unable to remember the specifics of anything he had read. War-torn countries' names had been erased from his internal map, crime-infested neighborhoods in his own city had merged into a large unnamed mass. Despite his best efforts to unlock his memory, the corrupt politicians and petty criminals all remained carefully anonymous. Faceless.

Frustrated, Ben tossed the paper to the floor at his feet. "Must be getting old," he grumbled to the air, "and forgetful." The phone beside him rang an interruption, its abrupt jangle jarring him from his thoughts, and he eyed it mistrustfully, sensing that he shouldn't answer but unable to remember exactly why.

He was just about to haul himself out of his chair and head upstairs, when he caught a subtle movement out of the corner of his eye and glanced up to see his son at the foot of the stairs clutching a book to his chest. Ben frowned as his disorientation returned and his vision swam. "Either I've been dreaming the past forty years or I'm dreaming now," he muttered to himself. He looked more closely at the book, the florid colors and cartoon graphics on the cover telling him that it was much too simple to hold the interest of a ten-year-old. Or had Sam still only been six then? Ben's frown deepened.

From the day his son had been born, Ben had found it difficult to reconcile the boy's age. When he'd looked at his newborn son and studied the wizened, wrinkled face and the wide, bright eyes filled with the wisdom that only one who has so recently touched the hand of God could possess, self-doubt had reverberated through him.

Ben Dawes had never truly understood his son.

As a baby, Sam had seemed old and wise; as a toddler, serious and reflective. As a preadolescent, he had been curious, then creative, then distant. As a teen, awkward and withdrawn. And through it all, he'd maintained a childish innocence that made him seem almost dim; made him seem eternally seven. At the same time, he had always been much smarter than his father. Ben had struggled to wrap his head around any of it.

And so now, regardless of whether this current moment was a dream—to see the boy again at six or ten, clutching a picture book intended for a three-year-old—it made Ben's frustration and disappointment rise up all over again. At the same time, he felt jealous—proud, even—of his son's sense of peace. And so he scooted up in his seat and patted the cushion beside him, shifting his weight to make room. He took the proffered book and set it on the table beside the ashtray that held his now extinguished pipe.

"You're more than capable of reading this by yourself, Sammy," he said. "How about I tell you a story instead?"

Author's Note: Let me start off by saying that this is not necessarily the story that Ben told. It is, however, the story that Ben would choose to tell his son today, if he could. And the detail of what he's dreaming about (since all of this is, of course, a dream) can tell us quite a lot about what's on the old man's mind. So, let me boil his story down to its essence and then put it to you as a sort of parable—take from it what you will:

> Once there was a young man—older than you are, though not by a lot. He was finishing up school and felt confident that he'd learned a tremendous amount. He knew the square root of 3,504 and how to spell "erroneous." He knew who Demosthenes was and how osmosis worked and how to rebuild a carburetor. More than any of it, though, he was proud of his understanding of love. Because, although he was still in his teens, this boy—this young man—knew how love worked. He'd never been in love himself, of course, nor had he been able to make someone else love him, but he'd watched as his friends fell in and out of infatuations and had studied their various flirtations. He'd seen the effects of love, witnessing heartbroken telephone calls filled

with desperation and bitterness. He'd observed love in action and concluded that it was a waste of time. "Why kill yourself to earn someone's love," he reasoned, "when the capriciousness of human nature makes it nothing more than a coin toss? Why waste time on romance when there are other pursuits so much more worthy of your energy? More than anything, why spend months or years searching for 'the one' when almost everyone on the planet is essentially the same: 70 percent water with a dash of carbon?"

No, he was certain that avoiding the whole mess would put him ahead of his friends and give him a life that few could hope for. And then he met Elizabeth.

The night of the commencement social for St. John's University and the College of St. Benedict's, his philosophies were shattered by the vision of a young woman leaning casually against a wall on the far side of the room. She seemed to catch him every time he stole a look at her, but he couldn't stop his eyes from finding their way back to her, over and over. He felt flushed, with a tightness in his chest that worried him. Eventually, though, he managed to get up the courage to cross the room to talk to her and, over the course of the next six months, to ask her to dance, to hold her hand on the train, to kiss her on her father's front porch, and to ask her to marry him. With each day and each hurdle overcome, he grew more and more confident, and more and more aware that he had never really understood love at all.

He'd never been happier, despite the fact that he sometimes made errors balancing his accounts and misspelled "paramour" or "immutable." He was a young man in love.

And he was a smart man, so although no one had explained to him the intricacies of love, he was able to pick his way through without making a mess of things. Though he'd never been told that maintaining a relationship took constant effort, he was driven to make his marriage a priority, pushing through arguments and misunderstandings toward harmony. It didn't hurt that he and his beloved were a perfect match—giving lie to his young belief that any couple could succeed if they were motivated to do so. No, this pairing had proven to him that there were those who were meant to be together, in part because he couldn't imagine abandoning his prospects for a career in engineering for the stability of a factory job for anyone else. Nor could he imagine anyone selfless enough to tolerate his peculiarities in the way she seemed willing to.

It was, indeed, perfect—and that's all there was to it. No matter if they occasionally quarreled over his late nights home from the factory or her habit of leaving dishes waiting in the sink for him. No matter that his devotion to schoolwork in his younger years and his quick marriage had given him little chance to enjoy his youth or that she seemed to take a perverse joy in teasing him about his early transition into stuffy old man— this was love.

And so it went. They grew older and had a child; they moved from an apartment into a house, reached middle age, and saw their child leave home. They fought about money, made up over coffee, and loved one another through it all.

Then, one day, everything changed.

This man, who had always considered himself rational, sane, and stolid, found his life turned unexpectedly upside down when he turned seventy-five.

For the past several years, he'd been feeling ... unusual. He'd found himself laughing more and noticed a new skip in his step. His body felt lighter and his thoughts sharper, and he began to notice that his wife of more than forty-five years seemed suddenly very old.

On his seventy-fifth birthday, it finally struck him: somehow, he had begun aging backward. And the instant the realization blossomed in his head, the truth of it became obvious.

He was, of course, surprised. It went against everything he'd ever believed to be possible. But there was no denying it—he was getting younger with every passing day.

He felt invigorated, cut from the tethers that had bound him to the stodgy timeline that most of us are forced to live along, and he was surprised to find that he actually had very little to do. He was retired and his son had left home long ago, but his newfound energy far outbalanced the "to do" list he'd made in preparation for his golden years. He wanted to think and dream and create, but had no outlet for that intellectual vigor. He wanted to meet people, exchange histories and hear stories he'd never heard before, but no one his age seemed to need or want new friends, and those younger than he tended to regard him with suspicion. He wanted to see new things, to travel and learn and explore, but Elizabeth seemed constantly tired and no longer had any desire for new adventures.

He began to take long walks alone through neighborhoods he'd never seen before, talking to the people he met there. He did some traveling alone. He saw Sicily and Athens; he visited London and Dublin and Wales. But when he got to Lisbon, it made him remember his honeymoon—made him miss his home and his wife and their lives. He grew nostalgic and lonely and flew back to Chicago to be with the woman he'd loved for more than two-thirds of his life.

When he arrived, though, she was no longer there. Oh, there was a woman in the house, but she was much, much older than he remembered and spoke to him in a sharp, unfamiliar tone. She shackled him to their house with guilt and dependence and tortured him with memories of the beautiful, brilliant woman she had been. And every so often, painfully, he'd see the sparkle in her eyes that he'd seen that first night across a crowded gymnasium. The burst of life that had transformed him by teaching him the truth about love. And every time he saw it, his heart would explode with hope and love and life, only to be smothered when the sparkle faded into dullness or sharpened into an attack.

This was a part of love that he had never known—because even through the pain and the attacks, he loved his wife with every fiber of his being. But time with her left him exhausted, as if he were taking on some of her age with every second they spent together. Despite it all, he loved on.

And then, with frightening speed, she forgot him—didn't know his name or why he was in her home. Or she remembered him but forgot their lives together. He told her the same stories a hundred times, answered the same questions a thousand:

"Who's this?"
"That's a picture of our son."
"What time is it?"
"It's two o'clock, sweetheart."
"Where's Sam?"
"I don't know, Elizabeth."
"What time is it?"
"It's two."
"Where's Sam?"
Silence.
"What time is it?"

Every story was interrupted with an impatient, "Who?" or cut off with the abrupt wave of her hand when she couldn't remember that she'd asked to hear it in the first place.

Through all of this he continued to grow younger, almost against his will now, until he could scarcely sit still with her—he needed to get out, to run away. He needed to feel the outdoor air fill his lungs, and because the woman he loved rarely remembered him anymore, that's what he did. He went back to his custom of long walks through the city, his guilt receding when he realized that she often didn't notice that he'd been gone at all. In fact, he found himself preferring the times when she did notice, her shrill voice carrying no trace of the melody she'd had in her speech as a young woman. At least on those days she had remembered.

As the weeks passed, however, those days grew less and less frequent and then disappeared entirely. And his walks grew longer. Until, one day in midwinter, he returned home after a brisk walk along the lake, his cheeks red from the wind and exertion. He stepped into the house, feeling its stillness and wondering, wearily, whether that meant she was asleep or sitting on her rocking chair, silently counting nothing.

He found her on the kitchen floor, a spilled mug of tea not far from her hand.

And at that moment, standing frozen in the kitchen door, all of the age he had shed over the past several years fell on him like a hammer, driving him to his knees. Every muscle in his body spasmed and then fell weak, like an over-stretched rubber band that's lost its snap. He felt exhausted, drained. He felt old.

Perhaps he'd been fooling himself all along, and his over-exertions had finally caught up to him. Perhaps it was the shock of realizing that he'd lost the only woman he had ever loved and that he had not taken advantage of the time he had been given with her. Or perhaps she had been shielding him somehow—taking age onto herself to allow him a second chance at the youth he'd missed out on the first time around. Regardless, it was over now, and he found himself suddenly old and frighteningly alone.

But despite his sorrow, the man continued to talk to his wife every day. Thanking her, asking her advice, telling her that he missed her, sometimes apologizing, and always reminding her that he loved her.

He came to understand love more completely than he ever had, and he tried to pass on that understanding on to those he met.

He finally recognized what age means and what death is, and that they are very different things—and that recognition allowed him to find peace.

He sometimes tried to get out to remember what youthful vigor and energy had felt like, even though his heart was no longer in it.

A month later, he died quietly in his sleep. You could call it a peaceful, purposeful suicide. The doctors called it an aneurism. I call it a reunion.

And allegory aside, that's Ben encapsulated and explained. But we're not there yet, are we? Ben has not played his full part. He hasn't earned that reunion. He hasn't recognized or reconciled anything. More to the point, he's got a rather important role to play before we can let him make his exit. For starters, he's going to have to come to terms with the way things ended—so far, he's gotten a free pass to hold tight to the good memories but at some point, he'll have to remember the worst. Celebrating the good times and ignoring the bad makes you weak; it allows your challenges to build up and, eventually, break you.

Of course, it's possible that that's exactly what will happen with Ben. It's hard to say whether he would be better off waking from this dream and dealing with what his life has become or never waking up again. For now, though, that's not his choice to make.

#

The chime of the alarm clock jarred Ben from his sleep and he slapped at it in irritation, groaning as the bell died away into silence. He had no idea how long he'd slept, but he still felt exhausted, as though his dreams had somehow drained him. He propped himself up on an elbow and stared at the other side of the double bed; unmussed and empty. He squeezed his eyes tightly shut, not allowing the tears to come. After a moment, he swung his feet to the floor and let out a sigh.

The bell that had wakened him sounded again and he scowled, glancing first at the silent telephone at his bedside then at the alarm clock beside it, also still. Not the alarm, then ... the doorbell. He could find nothing in his memory to suggest who might be at the door but had similar trouble coming up with a compelling reason not to find out. At this point, even a salesman would make for a refreshing break in the day. And so he eased himself to his feet and set off down the hall.

Ben's legs were tired from the day and it took him time to negotiate the stairs, so he wasn't sure that whomever was ringing the bell would still be there by the time he arrived. When he opened the door, however, there was indeed someone standing there: gray suit, dress shirt, collar unbuttoned ... familiar. Ben squinted at the man, blinking his face into focus; and then his eyes widened as his recent dreams came back to him with breath-taking force.

In his dream, the face of his son had been that of a young boy filled with innocence and hope. The face of the son standing before him now seemed just as it had been the last time they had seen one another and for a moment Ben wondered whether the last two decades of his life had been a figment of his imagination. Perhaps he had only just turned fifty. Perhaps Elle was still alive and he had yet to drive away his only son. Perhaps time had actually made allowances for him.

Ben closed his eyes then reopened them slowly, focusing on the gray at Sam's temples and the lines etched into his face. He studied the wrinkles in the suit, the loose threads at the cuffs, and the way the coat hung loosely on his son's thin frame, and he saw the truth. He swallowed the lump of hope that had begun to rise in him and drew in a deep breath.

"That's a secondhand suit," he said, intending only to confirm what he already knew to be true. To set the time period, establish his son's age and the truth about his life, and to confirm that the Sam standing before him was older than the one who had left. That he was still retired and Elle was still dead and his life was still ending. But the words came out of his mouth sounding stern and reproving—not the way he had intended them.

After a brief hesitation, Sam nodded a confirmation and the world swam in Ben's vision as the billion tiny tragedies and three earthshaking events of the past twenty years happened again in a span of three seconds. Ben forced his gaze to the horizon, fighting off his surging emotions. He no longer had the strength to cry—certainly not in front of his son.

Finally, he was able to bring his eyes back up to meet Sam's and he nearly smiled. "No tie," he mumbled, in way of apology. He studied his son's rumpled suit and scuffed shoes again, and, given the situation, gave a small grunt of approval at the effort. "You look good, though."

He drew a breath and continued. "Your mother is dead." He flinched at the shock in Sam's eyes, his heart breaking for his son, and blinked away another wave of tears, his voice cracking as he continued, "I suppose you'd better come inside."

Inside the house, things grew more tense. The two men sat stiffly on chairs still covered in the plastic that Elle had insisted on, each avoiding the other's gaze and speaking little. Sam's stutter had gotten worse, and the lines etched into his face made Ben feel every second of his seventy years, calling up the past and painting his soul with a patina of guilt.

Minutes ticked by, and with each, Ben wondered why he couldn't simply break the silence with an apology. It was appropriate; even necessary. It was time. But for some reason he couldn't bring the words to his lips. Or, more accurately, he couldn't find a way that "sorry" made his transgression seem less egregious, his errors somehow more understandable. And so, he kept his tongue and studied his son in careful, flickering glances.

The boy had aged, no doubt. He looked older than Ben would have believed, with signs of hard living written on him like faded graffiti. The wrinkles were to be expected after so many years, but there was a hollowness to his cheeks and a hunted, wind-bitten look in his eyes. Taking it in hurt Ben in a way that he'd thought nothing could after Elle's passing.

Without warning, Sam lurched to life, snatching up the bag at his feet with much herk and jerk. He pulled a tattered coat out of the bag and set it carefully, almost reverently, aside, then reached in again and came up with a thin stack of records, which he thrust at Ben.

"Here," he said. "They w ... were sup ... posed to be for Mom."

Ben swallowed the lump that threatened to rise in his throat and tightened his jaw against the emotion that he had hoped to finally be finished with.

"Thanks," he muttered, holding the albums in his lap and flipping idly through them, dimly recognizing the names on the jackets. "Jazz," he continued, hearing the gruffness in his voice but unable to soften it. "She ... um. She would have liked them."

Sam shrugged, then nodded, sinking back into his chair and back into silence, his gaze fixing on a point just over Ben's left shoulder.

Ben watched him for a moment, then broke the silence again. "Sammy," he said, starting as his son flinched at the name.

"Oh," Ben said, surprised at the reaction. "I'm sorry. Well ... son." He sighed. "I know. I understand. I do. I miss her too." Sam turned away at this, but Ben continued, determined to say something relevant before he lost the ability.

"You were closer to her than to me," he continued.

"She understood me," Sam replied clearly, accusingly. "She listened to me. Shhhh ... she let mmm ... me be ... me ..."

"Good," Ben said. "I'm glad." He met Sam's gaze, filled with the conflict between confusion and challenge, and continued. "I'm glad you had someone who was able to—willing to—understand who you were. I know that I wasn't."

"I was going to ask ... " Sam said. "Ask her ... " He stopped, clearly struggling with something, and Ben waited for his son's stutter to ease enough to let him finish. But it didn't seem as though his struggle was with his words but with his intensions.

The phone rang harshly in the other room, and Ben turned, bothered for reasons he couldn't quite explain. A shudder ran through him, and he stared at the receiver until it went silent. After a moment of silence, he turned back to Sam, who was still looking straight through him, chewing the inside of his bottom lip as he had since he was a child. "What was that?" Ben said vaguely. "Ask what?"

Sam sighed. "Nnn ... nothing. Never mmm ... mind." He stared at Ben accusingly. "Are you g ... going to tell mmm. Tell m ... me what happened to h ... her?"

Ben paused, the story spread before him, ready to be told, but he couldn't bring himself to begin. Instead, he laughed.

"You know, it's strange. Right before you came, I had this dream—or maybe a memory—of you as a kid asking me to read to you. Some book that was way too young for you. So, I took you on my lap and told you a story, instead. And that story ... " He trailed off.

"No, dad," Sam said, his voice dead.

"What?" Ben asked, his reverie interrupted.

"Nnn ... no," Sam repeated. "That nnn ... nn ... never happened."

"Are you sure?" Ben asked, somehow already aware of the answer.

"Yeah. You nnn ... never told me any ssss ... Stuhh ... " He sighed and then spoke the words slowly, deliberately, forcing them past his tongue in a voice drained of emotion, the monotone delivery making them land that much more heavily on Ben. "You nnn ... never told mmm ... me stories. We nnn ... never did anything together, rrr ... really. I ww ... wish we had. It would have made you fff ... feel muh ... more like a father."

There was an apology somewhere inside him. Ben could feel it laying down a lyrical counterpoint to the guilty monologue he'd become so accustomed to. But he still could not find a way to begin it. The words swam just out of his reach, tantalizing him with the idea that if he could only lay hands on one, the others would follow. But whether it was a noun or a verb; whether it began with a consonant or a vowel, he couldn't say.

So instead he said, "Well, I am. I am your father, however bad I've been at it. And now you're here and your mother is gone and we're all we've got. You're all I've got left."

Sam simply sat, his eyes boring holes of disgust through Ben for as long as he could hold them in place. Finally, Ben couldn't stand it anymore. "What is it?" he exclaimed, cringing internally as Sam shrank away from the outburst. "Even if I wasn't ... around enough. Even if I wasn't there for you in the way I should have been, please ... " He stared at the boy, who now couldn't seem to bring himself to even return the gaze. Ben sighed. "Sam, please. For the love and memory of your mother ... "

With that, Sam's eyes shot up to meet his with a fire in them that raised a hackle of apprehension in Ben that he hadn't anticipated. For a moment, he was terrified of what his son might do.

But Sam attacked only with words. "What did you do?"

The venom and accusation in the question cut Ben like a razor as the truth behind it tore out his heart. His head sagged until his chin touched his chest. He shook his head slowly. "Nothing. I didn't do anything. That's the ... She just ... faded, and I did nothing."

"Was it your fault?" The voice still cold. No longer accusing, but certain nonetheless.

"Yes," Ben whispered.

Ben heard Sam lurch to his feet and start awkwardly toward the door. "Please, Sammy. Stay, please," he said.

Sam paused the length of a heartbeat and then started for the door again, slower this time but more purposefully.

"You can't go!" Ben cried. "Your mother was so worried about you." He looked up at Sam who was regarding him coldly, and added, belatedly, "I'm worried about you."

"Why?" Sam asked, his eyes holding a question that he didn't seem quite ready to ask.

"Why?" Ben repeated. "I see you. I see you here and I see what you wear and what you have and I ... I know, Sammy. I know what your life is like, and I worry."

"Well, don't," Sam snapped. "Don't www ... worry, because you *don't* really nnn ... know. You know how awful my life is? How muh, mmm ... miserable? My life is no www ... worse than www ... when I was here. It muh ... might be better. I still live alone. The only d ... difference is where I sleep and www ... what I do with chicken bones."

Ben blinked, set back by the venom in his son's voice, but rallied behind his planned peace offering. "Still, I can't imagine you don't need a place to stay. Or some money ... "

Watching the turmoil that raged across Sam's face at that statement nearly stopped Ben's heart as he watched pride battle something much deeper for control. After a moment, the boy seemed to reach a decision; the defiant look sank from his eyes. "Yyy ... yeah," he said softly. "I c ... could use some muh ... mmm ... money."

That admission seemed to sap the fight from him, and he refused to say another word or make eye contact as Ben cobbled together a wad of crumpled twenties and tens that represented all the cash he had on hand.

And as Sam tucked the cash into a hidden pocket of his battered coat, Ben formed what he thought might be the last sentence he would ever speak to his only son, letting the words come as Sam started for the door.

"Whatever you might think, Sam," he said, "your mother and I both loved you. Both of us. She was better at it. She knew how to talk to you. You and I ... we started in different places. You got here earlier than I expected, and it took me time to adjust. And then ... when things fell apart ... I made a decision and it was the wrong one. And I'm sorry. I'm sorry about that. But that doesn't mean that I ever forgot you were my son." Sam did not reply but stood staring at his feet.

"As for your mother ... " Ben continued. "I ... I could have done a better job of being there for her. But she was fading so fast—she was hardly the same person. And it seemed ... better ... to have someone here who could take care of her, because I wasn't good at it and it was only making her hate me more." He laughed, sharply and without humor. "Believe me, toward the end she didn't want me around any more than I wanted to be here. It was just ... We weren't the same people anymore."

Ben paused, waiting for a response or a reaction. "Sam?"

"My name is Puck," Sam replied evenly. "Call me Puck from now on." And he walked out the door, likely for the last time, heading down the front walk, then turning south toward the city. As Ben stood in the doorway, Sam—Puck—paused, taking in the house, and then ambled away, eventually disappearing from view. Ben watched his son until he could no longer see him, then closed the door and moved over to the sofa, scooping up the small collection of old records. Tommy Dorsey, Chick Webb, Artie Shaw: Elle's favorites. For the first time since his wife had died, Ben put music on the stereo. Then he sank into his chair by the foot of the stairs and did not weep.

Cort
Eclipse in 6 hours

Cort stepped out of the shower and into the apartment's steamy closet of a bathroom just after four o'clock on Sunday afternoon, leaving himself plenty of time to grab a bite, swing by the drycleaners to pick up the suit he'd dropped off prior to his adventures at the grocery store, execute a quick change in a gas station bathroom or the back seat of the Jag, and still make it to the Cultural Center long before his dates showed up.

Almost by rote, he worked a fistful of gel into his hair, shaping his dark-brown locks into a pompadour before breaking it down into the artfully unpracticed tangle he preferred.

He cleared a spot on the fogged-over mirror with his forearm and stared at himself for a moment, the tension in his shoulders and the tightness of his mouth showing his anxiety. He locked eyes with his reflection and muttered, "Relax. You know you're more likeable that way." He rallied around that idea, reminding himself that the event had promised a swing band and a hosted bar. He let out a deep breath and closed his eyes, rolling the kinks out of his neck and feeling the tension in his brow loosen. When he reopened his eyes, it was a far calmer version of himself staring back from the mirror. He grinned at his reflection and set about finishing his preparations for the night.

He planned to arrive at the Center no later than seven, an hour before he was due to meet Theresa. Time enough for a drink and, he admitted guiltily, to see if Allison was already there. And if she wasn't, time at least to draw a breath and explore whether the buzz he'd felt with her was magic or mania. Time enough to discover whether an old man in a grocery store had deeper insight into his life than he did himself.

That, at least, was the plan.

At twenty to six, however, just as he was scooping up his coat—a soft, black leather jacket with matching gloves that was the most stylish thing he owned, if far too thin for the cold weather, the phone on his kitchen counter rang. His internal clock suggested, rather sharply, that he ignore it, but the ring had a demanding quality and Cort found himself scooping the wireless handset from its cradle almost against his will. He was greeted by Ryan's voice, picking up their earlier conversation as though it had never been interrupted, his agenda as blindingly obvious as his cajoling tone.

"Hey man, you know what? I was thinking, if it's okay—"

"You want to go to the party," Cort finished, feeling suddenly exhausted, the relaxed demeanor that he'd so carefully crafted evaporating like the fog on his bathroom mirror.

"Well," Ryan paused, clearly thrown by having his gambit anticipated. "Well, yeah. That okay?"

"Not really," Cort replied. "I mean, it'd be cool to have you around, but I've got a lot on my mind—and on my plate—tonight. Having you there will just ... "

"You know," Ryan interrupted, his voice noticeably harder. "I don't actually have to ask you. I got an invitation too."

"I do know," Cort replied, pacing the small kitchen, three strides taking him from wall to wall. "I'm asking you, though. I'm hoping you'll do me a favor. I just want to get there, put in a little face time, and get out again. I'm already wishing I didn't have to go at all, and if you're there ... "

"What?"

Cort sighed. "There's just more pressure, that's all,"

"There doesn't have to be," Ryan replied. "Shit, you'll probably never even see me ... "

"C'mon, we both know that isn't true," Cort interrupted.

"What's that supposed to mean?"

For a moment, Cort hesitated. He looked at the battered faux-leather chair in his living room, knowing that if he was going to open this can of worms he might as well take a seat since it was unlikely to be a short ride. For a moment, he considered letting it go, muttering "never mind" and "go ahead and come" and getting out the door roughly on time.

But he couldn't do it.

He stalked from the kitchen to the living room and dropped into the chair, not bothering to take off his coat. "It means," Cort said, "that you're going to get there, make your grand entrance, and immediately start flashing cash around the room to smooth your way into conversation with whatever girl you happen to set your eye on ... "

"Hey, hey, what the fuck? Why would you say something like that?"

"Because it's what you do, Ry. It's how it works. It's how you operate," Cort replied, adding, somewhat belatedly, "Sorry."

There was silence from the other end of the line, and Cort wondered if he'd gone too far. Then Ryan's voice came over the line again, calm now, and without the joviality that Cort normally associated with him.

"That might be true. You know what? You might be right, Cort. I enjoy myself when I'm out. I like to spend my money. And the people I'm out with? They like it too. I mean, you certainly do, right?"

"Ryan, that's not the point. This is about tonight ... " Cort began.

"But. If you want to call me an attention whore," Ryan continued, "then you're going to want to look in the mirror. Because you do the same thing."

"Bullshit," Cort protested.

"Bullshit!" Ryan repeated, mocking. "Yeah, I guess you're right. It's not the same, is it? Because when you roll into a party like you're the richest, most important guy in the room, it's a lie. You don't have shit."

"I don't have shit yet," Cort added. "And I've never claimed that I do." He sat up, looking around the dim apartment and grimacing at the bent venetian blinds and the threadbare carpet. "I mean, I wouldn't be able to."

"Oh, you never," Ryan spat. "You're going to meet these two women of yours at a party for all the richest people in Chicago. And I'm sure you explained everything to them. That you have an invitation, but that's the end of it. That this party was the only way you'd be able to afford to take them out at all without borrowing money from your best friend."

Cort said nothing.

"Yeah, I didn't think so. Did you tell them any of the stepdad story?"

"It seemed premature," Cort replied weakly. "What does it matter how much I'm supposed to inherit or when I'm supposed to get it?"

"Cort, I'm just going to say this once. I swear: we never have to have this conversation again. But why do you think your old man put a ten-year waiting period on you in the first place?"

"We've talked about this. I have no idea."

"Yeah, we've talked about it. But I've always been nice enough to keep my mouth shut."

"What's that supposed to mean?"

"It means that it's pretty obvious that you're waiting for your money because your dad was smart enough to know that you wouldn't do a damn thing with your life if you got it right away." Ryan sighed. "He didn't want you to turn into me."

"C'mon ... "

"No really. And that's okay. I know who I am. I'm not a genius. I'm not particularly charming. I don't have an interesting story for every situation. You've got a leg up on me in a lot of ways. And it kind of sucks that the fact that I've got some money makes all of that irrelevant. But I hate to break it to you, man: when you finally get your money, it's not going to change anything. That money's not going to change your life."

Cort stood up now, apprehension sending him into anxious pacing. "How can you say that?"

"How much did he leave you?"

"Ryan, I don't want to—" Cort began, but was quickly interrupted.

"Seriously, man. I'm not trying to bum a loan, here. How much do you have coming?"

"I don't know, it depends on interest, and a bunch of other ..."

"Uh-huh. Yeah, I get it. How much?"

Cort sighed. "About a million, million and a quarter."

"That's what I thought," Ryan replied.

"So? What difference does it make?"

"Trust me, it does. Because ... you're not going to be rich, Cort. Your old man left you money, but not crazy money. If you try to go toe-to-toe with the people you're hanging around with right now, myself included, you'll burn through it in a year. Maybe two."

Cort opened his mouth to reply, but Ryan pressed on, his words coming quicker, and Cort sensed that, though this was the first time he was hearing it, this speech had been on Ryan's mind for years. He felt sick.

"No," Ryan was saying, "if you're smart, it's mostly just going to sit somewhere, locked away, and you're going to live on the interest at a 'normal person' level. Fifty, sixty grand a year if you're lucky. You might have a little more free time than most people, but you are not going to be "special." Shit, you'll probably have to get a job. Never thought of that, did you? That's why your stepdad did the right thing by making sure that you didn't tear through it like a moron, even though I'm guessing he was assuming you would have a lot more figured out by now."

Cort said nothing.

"Anyway," Ryan continued, "I'm really just calling to tell you that I'm coming to the party tonight. I'll see you there. Feel free to come over to talk about this if you want. Or we don't ever have to mention it again."

Cort continued to listen, but only silence came through the receiver. After a long moment, he began to wonder if he'd missed Ryan hanging up.

"Ryan?"

"Yeah?"

The reply surprised him, and he searched for something to say.

"Why do you think people like me, then?"

"What makes you so sure they do?" Ryan replied bluntly.

Cort paused. "I don't know ... " he said, the honesty of the statement feeling foreign to him. "I guess I never really thought about it."

"Yeah," said Ryan. "And that's why. I'll see you at the party."

There was a click as Ryan broke the connection, but Cort sat holding the phone for a few seconds longer, his gaze finding soft focus on his keys, still resting on the kitchen counter. After a moment he walked over to set the phone back on its cradle. He glanced quickly at his watch to make sure he was still on schedule, then swore and ran for the door.

He hurried out to the Jag and leapt in. But the car refused to start at the first twist of the key. And the second. And the third and fourth, the old engine sputtering indignantly at being pressed into service twice in the same day. By the time it had shaken itself awake, Cort had lost another ten minutes—just enough to make him three minutes late to the dry cleaners, and all his pounding on the frosted window couldn't spin the closed sign around. Instead, he spent nearly an hour finding a store that was still open and another thirty minutes picking out a pair of cream-colored slacks and a deep blue shirt and tie that he couldn't afford as a replacement for the suit he'd had to leave behind, all the while cursing Ryan under his breath and drawing shocked looks from his fellow customers.

He finally stepped into the Cultural Center just after eight-thirty, having missed his chance to connect with Allison, already running behind for his date with Theresa, and practically trembling from a backlog of frustration and anger.

He took a moment in the mirror-lined foyer to collect himself, recognizing the rage in his eyes as "unfit for public consumption." To counteract the anxiety roiling within him, he forced himself into routine, checking his coat and gloves and then, standing alone in the center of the lobby, staring himself down in the surrounding mirrors until the frustration reflecting back at him died away. His watch beeped the quarter hour, but he ignored it, just as he ignored the festive clamor on the other side of the doors. Instead, he studied his own reflection, willing the tension out of his shoulders, the sweat off his brow, and the jaunty grin back onto his face, all the while nodding his head to the muffled sounds of swing music pulsing through the doors.

After a few minutes he was able to meet his gaze in the mirror and be satisfied with what he saw, his maddening conversation with Ryan invisible on his face. He glanced around the room one final time, nodded cordially at the multitude of placid Corts that now surrounded him, then took a deep breath and opened up the doors.

Cort fell into the ballroom crowd with a delicate but precise impact, a puzzle piece searching for its niche. After the eye-of-the-storm calm of the foyer, the assault that greeted him inside knocked him back a step, the shifting patterns of people interrupting his inertia, wrapping delight up in disorientation and dropping it in his lap with an expectant smile.

He moved carefully past dancing couples and board presidents hard-selling bored millionaires. The typical non-profit social paradox: people desperate for money begging from people desperate for significance. From time to time, he caught a flash of long blonde hair that would grab his gaze before the sight of a sharp nose, a weak chin or a moustache forced him to release it again. None of them Allison.

Finally, as he neared the bar, he found a face that he recognized. Round and genial, topped with an immaculate blonde coiffe and "out of place" in casual-ware that was clearly worth more than most of the tuxedos surrounding him, all the while grinning with an idiot's bravado: Ryan, leaning on the bar and tossing peanuts into his mouth with a casual flick that Cort happened to know he'd spent multiple days practicing. He wondered if his friend hadn't called him from that very bar stool two hours earlier to ask permission to attend a party he was already at.

Cort sighed, and started to sift his way through the crowd, at once perturbed by Ryan's presence and thankful for a familiar face.

A couple of steps later his demeanor swung dramatically as he recognized Allison on the stool next to Ryan's. Cort's jaw hung slack, and for what may have been the first time in his life he found himself tongue-tied. Yanked from the water to flop and flounder helplessly on the sandy beach of disbelief.

Twice he started forward to interrupt what he recognized as one of Ryan's standard opening lines ("You know, being a multimillionaire just doesn't mean as much when you have a weak heart ... ") then cut himself off as he realized that he had no idea what he would say.

"Excuse me, bud. You're talking to one of the two women I was hoping to choose between tonight."

Or, "Hi, Allison. You shouldn't talk to this guy. He's a real player—and I should know!"

Or, "Oh Christ, I hope you two aren't talking about me ... "

But instead ...

"So ... this is the second time."

The voice at his ear surprised Cort enough to make him start, and he jerked his gaze away from the mesmerizing couple. He spun around to see Theresa standing before him, her arms crossed, her eyes narrowed to slits and flashing suspicion at him. She looked, even in anger, more attractive than he had remembered. The smooth amber of her bare shoulders was emphasized by the deep green of a strapless dress, her sharp features softening in the dim light. But she didn't give him a chance to linger over her appearance.

"Second time for that reaction, too ... "

Already off-balance from the shock of the past few minutes and the turmoil of the past two days, the only words that Cort could bring to his lips were, "What? You ... what? Second what?"

Theresa's mouth tugged up into a sardonic grin and she gave a snort of derision. "Eloquent."

She stared at him a moment and when he didn't respond she continued. "That's the second time I caught you staring at that exact woman and the second time you jumped out of your skin at being caught," she said, ticking off the indiscretions on her fingers.

But that moment had been all that Cort needed to collect himself. He smiled easily and looked at Theresa from under his eyebrows. "Okay, you got me. I was staring. But it's not what you think."

"No?" she replied, her voice sharp with skepticism.

"No," Cort answered. He glanced quickly from side to side, then returned his gaze to her. "That woman's name is Allison," he began, lowering his voice and smiling to himself as she leaned closer to hear him over the noise of the crowd, just as he had intended. "The guy next to her," he continued, "is a good friend of mine—Ryan Dotson. I've been trying to get the two of them together for a while now, but they're both too proud to be set up, so I had to arrange a 'chance meeting' to see if things would click. This little shindig seemed like the perfect chance." He made a show of glancing at his watch before continuing. "Unfortunately, I got so caught up in their romance that I forgot about mine, and now I'm sure you must think that I was both late and rude. I hope you didn't think I was standing you up?"

"Eh, not really," Theresa replied dismissively, her eyes flicking back and forth between Cort and the couple at the bar. "I just wondered what the hell was going on."

Cort fought the urge to follow her gaze over his shoulder, managing to subdue his desire both to steal another glimpse of Allison and to verify for himself that Ryan was living up to expectations and completely fucking things up with her. "Well, now you know," he replied brightly. "What do you say we forget about them?"

Theresa nodded, her smirk still riding the corner of her mouth up toward the glint in her eye. "Yeah, sure. You can buy me a drink."

"You got it," Cort agreed, covering his sigh of relief. "But not at that bar. Let's leave the lovebirds alone and find some privacy."

"Perfect."

He smiled. "So, I'm forgiven then?"

Theresa's smirk widened. "We'll see. Let's just say you're doing better than your friend."

Cort finally allowed himself a look back across the room, just in time to see Ryan slip away into the crowd, leaving Allison sitting alone. He turned to watch as Theresa walked away from him toward the bar, admiring the curve of her hip in her snug green dress but feeling somehow detached; bumped out of the room. He allowed his gaze to shift back to Allison and felt immediately tugged in her direction, and that tug resolved things. He would be up front and honest. He would say to Theresa, "Hey, you know what? I don't think this is going to work out," and then cross the room to the bar and make his latecomer apologies to the woman he'd met first. Perhaps the penciled addition of the word "smitten" to his personal dictionary deserved to be gone over in pen. Perhaps there was something different about her; something enduring. Perhaps, for once, he was meant to play the longshot instead of the sure thing.

But now he could see that she was talking to someone else: a businessman sitting beside her at the bar, absurdly thin, practically skeletal. Allison seemed well out of his class, but for some reason the idea of interrupting their conversation with his belated come-ons made Cort feel as though every person in the room had moved a step closer; that they were all staring at him—breathing his air. His gaze blurred and the figures at the bar swam in his vision. "Let it go," he muttered. "He's got no shot. Besides, what'd you think it was, true love?"

"I know. Not so much." Theresa's voice pierced his reverie and he started, turning to see her eyes flashing with cool, detached mirth. "Too bad for him, huh?" she finished, the sympathy in her voice conspicuous by its absence. "Come on, buy me that drink."

Cort opened his mouth to explain that he couldn't, but found that he couldn't articulate a single good reason why not. And so he found himself stammering, "On my way," and following Theresa to the bar, fighting the urge to glance over his shoulder at the woman he was possibly (but probably not) fated to be with.

Cort was still cursing under his breath as he caught up with Theresa, his jumbled soliloquy of bad judgment, worse luck, and a so-called friend's betrayal leaving him just attentive enough to nod along without having the slightest idea of what Theresa was talking about.

And then, suddenly, the sound of her voice was gone and she was turning to face him, eyebrows raised in question.

Cort gaped at her for a moment, mind whirling, grabbing at the half-heard, mostly disregarded threads of conversation that had been flowing past him before finally giving up. "Sorry, what was that?"

Theresa sighed heavily. "I said, 'Lucky, huh?'"

Cort nodded, grinning. "What was lucky?"

"Seriously?" Her eyebrows arched to avoid being scorched by her glare. "Haven't you been listening?"

"No, no," Cort protested. "I'm listening. It's just loud in here." He smiled again, moving closer to her as they reached the front of the line. "I am listening," he repeated. "Honestly."

"Okay," Theresa replied, skepticism in her voice and eyes.

Cort laughed. "Don't look at me like that. You'll make me cry!" He watched her out of the corner of his eye as he signaled to the bartender, smiling to himself as he saw her suspicion fade and her lips twist upward in a tentative smile. "Here," he said, "let me get you a drink." He turned to the curly-haired college student behind the bar. "Let me get a light beer and a ... "

"Cosmo," Theresa finished. "Thanks."

"No problem." Cort bit back yet another curse. While the bar offered a full range of drinks, only the beer and wine were hosted, and the clothes on his back had maxed out his credit card. "Light beer and a Cosmo," he repeated. What the hell, the charge wouldn't go through until the following week anyway. He leaned on the bar and grinned at Theresa, his confidence rising at the visible effect that his smile had on her. "Now really, what was lucky?"

Theresa's eyes found her shoes as she turned surprisingly shy. "You were."

"Me? How?" Cort allowed his focus to leave her for a moment as the bartender returned with their drinks. Cort passed him a Visa card in exchange, with the profoundly optimistic instruction to "keep it open." "For you," he said, passing Theresa her drink. "So, how am I lucky, apart from the obvious?"

Theresa blushed and took a swig of her drink, the violence of her gulp at severe odds with the delicacy of the glass. "Well," she continued, "there were three separate times when tonight almost didn't happen."

"Three?"

"Yeah. I normally don't talk to guys who come on to me out of nowhere. That's a creep move, you know?" Another pull from her Cosmo left her glass slightly less than half full. "So I almost turned you down right off the bat. Then, after I said yes, I started thinking about it and almost talked myself into not showing. And then, when you were late ... " she finished, anger at the memory tightening her jaw.

"You almost left," Cort said, sipping his beer.

"Yeah. And then I saw you staring at that blonde again, and I was like, 'This is too much ... This is Tom all over again.'"

"So actually, that's four," Cort interrupted.

"What?"

"Four times you almost bailed on me."

Theresa paused, then laughed and took another gulp of her drink, the remains of the pink liquid rapidly disappearing. "I guess you're right! Lucky boy."

"It's not luck," Cort replied with mock seriousness.

"No?"

"Nope. I'm just a romantic cat." He smiled.

Theresa smirked in reply. "Are you? And what does that mean?"

"It means I've got nine lives. Nine chances, in this case. So, I've still got five left to burn."

She laughed, the sound a machine gun stutter that caught him by surprise, out of place coming from her small frame. "Nice. But don't count on it. I tamed my Tom Cat, and I can break you, too."

She paused, and Cort sighed, knowing what he was meant to ask next and dreading the consequences. But as the pause built toward awkward, he was forced to fill it. And so ...

"Tom?"

"My ex. Asshole. My asshole ex, I mean." With that, she polished off her drink, setting the empty glass on the bar.

Cort nodded a tired reply, signaling to the bartender for a refill even as he kept his gaze on Theresa as she rattled through a string of condemnations, many that Cort found remarkably familiar.

He passed Theresa her new drink, which she took without seeming to notice, and let his mind wander, his rootless backchanneling guided by snatched tidbits of complaint about the manipulative, commitment-phobic, and probably impotent Tom.

Author's Note: For the record, Tom is not a part of this story. He's not a main character or even a secondary player—he's barely third chair. He's Aaronson or Jones or Rutherford to my Goldstein. He has no impact on what's happened and no bearing on what's to come. That said, he's not entirely irrelevant—though I'll let you decide just how much to extract from his story.

For fun, let's see who tells it better, Theresa or me... I'll go first:

Tom is one of those people who seems dedicated to the idea that their life would be "so much easier" if only they could be someone—anyone—else. He's the guy who is so obsessed by the cracks in his driveway that he doesn't notice that the neighbor's house is on fire. And, like most of his type, he's completely full of shit—on several levels.

He's not unattractive, with dark hair and eyes and what romance novelists might call "chiseled" features—but he can't seem to get past the fact that his dark eyebrows are a bit bushier than he'd like or that his angular nose is just a bit too large.

He's an intelligent guy, but he's often too intimidated by the crowd to participate in conversation and must be constantly re-engaged—coaxed into offering his opinion. When that opinion is contradicted, however, he takes it as a personal insult and becomes (at best) defensive or (at worst) dismissive.

He can be a pleasant man with a self-deprecating sense of humor, but in social situations he has the tendency to either avoid the pressure of attention or consciously seek it out—at times shutting down entirely (thereby earning himself concern and sympathy) and at others being consciously disagreeable (so that he can later claim that any awkwardness was intentional).

In short, he has adjusted to the fact that, while he is attractive, intelligent, and engaging, fragility ultimately earns him more attention than any of those more common qualities. At the same time, he has discovered that it is easier to control people through subtle nudges than by going too quickly to the whip.

When people sense this about him it tends to put them off. Or at least that's my not-completely-objective view. But let's hear what Theresa has to say ...

"Honestly, he was the biggest asshole," Theresa said, gesturing with her drink, not seeming to notice as some of it sloshed to the floor. "I didn't realize at first, but I mean, seriously, what kind of guy cries every time you go down on him and then won't even talk to you when it's over? He used to tell me all the time how pretty I was, which sounds nice, but he'd do it over and over until the words all blended together. 'Yersopredyersopredyersopredy!' And when I asked him what the fuck he was doing, he'd tell me it was a joke and then get all moody when I didn't get it. Well, I *don't* get it. There's something wrong there, you know?"

Cort nodded sympathetically. "Yeah, the guy sounds a little off ... "

But she pushed on. "It's like he tricked me into falling for him. Like he wasn't even interested, he just needed me to prop him up, to keep him from self-destructing, you know? And then he used that to manipulate me into doing whatever the fuck he wanted. 'Oooh, I'm so depressed, will *you* clean the apartment? I don't wanna move.' And then after all of that bullshit, *he* cheats on *me*! I mean, can you believe it?"

Author's Note: To be fair, we should probably include Theresa's initial take on Tom—before things went sour— just to present a more complete picture. Let's try again, a few months earlier, with Theresa talking to her friend, Marla, near the end of October.

"I'm telling you, he's so sweet! It's like he has no idea how cute he is. I mean, the flowers he brought were torn to hell and probably dead, and he looked like he'd found them in the dumpster he'd woken up in ... But he's standing there on the doorstep, holding them out like they were the most expensive bouquet in the store and looking at me with those eyes ... You can't be mad at someone like that, even if he is three hours late. So anyway, I guess he just broke up with his girlfriend, or she threw him out or something, so he's going to stay with me until he can find a place. Isn't that exciting?"

Author's Note: And there's the problem. When you commit too soon, you're tying a blindfold on yourself. And when you do it for the wrong reasons, whether it's because they're ten times more attractive than anyone you've ever met or ten times as needy, you're signing your name to a duty roster. And it doesn't take a genius to know that signing your name to anything while blindfolded is a bad idea.

When you love someone who is out of your league, you give them power; you promise them that you'll let them get away with anything. When you label someone The One, you commit to twisting yourself into knots to make yourself into their The One—only to have to struggle to unknot yourself later, once you've realized that thinking of anyone as The One is like hooking The Fish or cooling your drink with The Ice Cube.

And should you commit yourself to someone because they need you—when you agree to play nurse to a wounded bird—you are offering your attention, affection, and care with no hope of reciprocation. Weakness is dangerous—it will draw you in, win your heart, and sap your energy. But the weak do not deserve your pity, your compassion, or your sacrifice, because they can never give back. No matter how much you love, no matter how devoted you may be, a bird with a broken wing is never going to thank you or find a way to make things square. All it will do is whimper about how much its wing hurts and shit on your curtains. And by the time that wing doesn't hurt anymore, it's ready to fly away. If the wing never heals ... well, eventually you get tired of changing bandages and curtains and listening to pained chirps.

To pull us out of this extended metaphor: graduating a relationship from casual to serious, from "a possibility" to "a certainty" plants a stake in the ground that you'll be tethered to for the foreseeable future. Be sure that you like the spot you've chosen, because if you don't, it is only a matter of time before you begin to resent your partner for pinning you there. And ultimately, that resentment will taste a lot like failure.

"The biggest problem was that he was so self-centered. It's like he thought the whole world revolved around him. I mean, you couldn't tell at first because he always acted so impressed by other people. Everyone was smarter than him, everyone was better looking than him, everyone was ... just better than him. But then he'd be sure to get his little digs in. He'd be telling me how smart I was, but then he'd jump on some little thing I said or the way that I pronounced a word and mock me about it endlessly."

"So you don't like being teased, then?" Cort smiled. "Duly noted."

"It's not that!" she demanded. "It wasn't even teasing, it was ... I don't know ... mean."

Cort held up his hands. "I know, I know. See? I was teasing."

She didn't seem to notice the joke. "Whatever. The thing is, he would always get around to belittling you, eventually. Like you'd tried to pass yourself off as better than him and he needed to tear you back down. Prove that he was superior. If we went too long without talking about him, he'd start sulking and tune me out completely. I'd have to beg to get him to even come to bed. Eventually, I was apologizing for pissing him off more often than we were actually on good terms, and I just didn't have the energy anymore, you know?"

> **Author's Note:** An excellent point. God forbid the needed ever abandon their role as caretaker. Even if you don't expect your wounded bird to show you gratitude for helping shepherd it through life, God forbid you allow the relationship to move toward that of equals. Nurse and patient were never meant to share responsibilities any more than

CEO and Wage Slave, or Sergeant and Private, or God and disciple (although that's closer). Start down that road and you are handing over the asylum keys without a struggle. When the weak are given power, one of two things can happen: either they have no idea what to do with it and end up inadvertently hurting you, or they quickly learn exactly what to do with it and hurt you intentionally. Either way, the result is not difficult to predict.

"Anyway, that's when I caught him cheating on me." She paused, looking at Cort expectantly.

"Seriously? What a prick!" he interjected, hoping that he hadn't missed his cue.

"Yeah. I'm not stupid. I could see what was happening. He started getting phone calls that he didn't want me in the room for, and then he'd disappear and be gone for hours. After a week or so of that kind of thing, I followed him."

"What, like to a hotel or something?" Cort asked. "Someone's apartment?"

"No, he was at a restaurant with some random girl. They were just talking, but it was all the stuff he used to say to me! I mean, he even did the 'yersopredyersopredy' thing and she laughed like it was the funniest thing she'd ever heard. And then when they left, she kissed him on the cheek and he hugged her like she was the most important person in his life. It made me so mad. After everything I'd given up for this guy, and he just moves on! I kicked him out that day; left all his shit sitting on the curb outside the apartment, and I haven't seen him since. And I don't regret it at all. Not even a little."

Cort smiled tightly in what he felt was a sympathetic way but which he really intended to mean, "Um, as far as I'm concerned, that's a little thin. You should talk to my friend Ryan if you want to hear a legit description of cheating ... "

Author's Note: Actually, it's unfortunate that Cort and Tom will never meet. There's a lot that Cort could teach him—about confidence and self-assurance, about charisma and conversation. I feel as though I've learned a lot even in the brief time we've been following him. But as much as he could have taught, there's just as much that Cort could have learned. Tom had come to understand that delaying your decisions too long ultimately makes those decisions irrelevant. He'd felt the sting of waiting to let go of a relationship that is, ultimately, destined to fail, and he had learned to recognize the difference between what you have and what you want—a bird in the hand will die if you hold onto it too tightly. But Cort will not have time for those lessons to sink in before he misses his moment of tuning. And, frankly, for the momentum of the story, the timing really couldn't be any better for us.

In other words: things are about to get interesting.

"So anyway, you better watch your step or you'll end up like my Tom Cat," Theresa finished.

"Right," Cort replied. "Declawed. I get it." Adding, silently, "and probably living with some woman who's actually willing to listen to him every once in a while."

He smiled at Theresa, wondering how to escape the conversation before it crept around (as all ex-boyfriend conversations invariably did) to his own dating history or before she decided to test his ability to regurgitate facts from her rambling diatribe. "Hey, do you want to dance?" he asked abruptly.

"What?" Theresa replied, her stream of chatter faltering as she tripped awkwardly over the change in topic and the thickness of a tongue steeped in three Cosmos.

"Dance," Cort said. "With me. Do you want to?" He did a quick side to side shuffle, then mimed a dip and looked up at her expectantly.

"Oh. Well, I don't really dance ... I mean ... "

"Come on," Cort grinned. "The band is finally playing some good music. It's easy. All you have to do is follow me." He watched her, wondering whether it would be the smile, the mimed dip, or the third Cosmo that would eventually make her give in.

"Okay, fine," she said finally. "But don't expect much. I'm really bad."

"It is my experience," Cort replied as he led her to the dance floor, "that no one is as good as they think they are. Or as bad."

But she was.

After only a few minutes on the floor, Cort was ready to pack it in. It wasn't just that she couldn't dance, it was how she managed to combine so many different aspects of bad, fusing them into an astonishing amalgam of catastrophe. It took Cort's breath away (even as it crushed his toes under high heels and bruised his ribs with sharp elbows).

She refused to follow his lead, at times staggering in response to his guiding hands and then jerking him roughly toward her as she fought for control, at others letting her arms hang loosely, flopping between them like overcooked pasta. Their introduction to the dance floor made it feel like a midway carousel that has thrown a piston, sending one horse off to charge wildly up and down, oblivious to the tempo and rhythm of the tinkling music or the patiently amused looks surrounding the cacophony.

By the time it became obvious to Cort that, in addition to all of this, his dance partner possessed a sense of rhythm that could best be described as "missing" or, for that matter, "possessed," every other couple on the floor was counting the seconds until the tempest that had exploded into their midst would be led quietly away from the dance floor for a nice glass of punch. After a few minutes, Cort was more than happy to oblige.

"I told you!" Theresa dropped into a chair, snatching a cocktail napkin from the table in front of her to blot roughly at her brow.

"You did indeed," Cort replied, forcing a laugh. "But hey, the best we can do is the best we can do, right? Besides, you weren't awful ... "

"You're just saying that," she said, crumpling the sweat soaked napkin and dropping it onto the table.

"Absolutely not," Cort insisted, fighting to keep from staring at the tiny shreds of napkin now clinging to her still damp forehead. "You definitely were not awful. (You were much worse than that," he finished silently.)

"Okay. Thanks," Theresa said, mollified.

"No problem." Cort dropped into the seat across from her.

Theresa smiled at him, but in her post dance state, her hair in disarray and her sweaty face dotted with scraps of napkin, she bore little resemblance to the polished, alluring woman that Cort had found so attractive such a short time ago.

"I'll be right back," Theresa said, resting a hand on his shoulder as she stood. "I'm just going to go to the ladies' room to get cleaned up."

"Okay," Cort replied. "I'll nip over to the bar and refresh our drinks and then meet you back here."

"Sounds good. See you soon." She let her hand trail across the back of his neck as she crossed away from him, the light brush of her fingers less flirtatious than irritating, the damp-fingertips version of nails on a chalkboard.

Cort let out a breath that he hadn't realized he'd been holding and felt all of the false energy he'd propped himself up with go with it, leaving him drained. He shook his head, half in disbelief at what had just happened and half in dread at the fact that he was in for even more.

As he reached the bar and took his place in line, the music started up again, and he turned to look back at the dance floor, watching as the couples began to weave their moving tapestry. The music changed, somehow feeling at once deeper and more innocent. More free. Without thinking of it, and nearly against his will, he pictured himself back on the floor, this time with Allison, she moving lightly in his arms, a sharp contrast to the sharp-elbowed dervish that Theresa had been. The thought made Cort himself feel lighter, as though in this version of the dance every muscle in his body could move in harmony, inspired by the grace of his partner.

And so, when the song came to an end and he found himself still standing in line at the bar, it was more a suspension of a dream than the end of anything. And, as in waking from a dream he felt confused and disoriented, unsure of what, exactly, was real. He signaled to the bartender for another round, hoping that it would, at least, help the night to go by more quickly.

The bartender passed him a beer, wordlessly, from which Cort took a large gulp, the carbonation burning pleasantly against the back of his throat. He caught his breath, then tilted the bottle up again, chugging the golden liquid as though it could stop time or somehow trap Theresa in the bathroom. He finished the beer quickly and was preparing to start on a second when he felt a soft hand on his shoulder.

"Whoa, slow down, killer!"

Cort jerked involuntarily at the unexpected touch, his body's spasm rattling the bottle painfully against his teeth and sloshing beer against his neck like an icy splash of cologne. The chill of it migrated immediately throughout his body and he snatched a fistful of napkins to blot away the liquid, praying that he had been mistaken in his recognition of the voice that had prompted his alcoholic seizure.

"Well, that was even more of a reaction than I was hoping for ... "

He winced, stunned by the rapid succession of bad-luck moments that seemed to be piling up on him, then pasted on a smile as he turned to face a grinning Allison.

Seeing her again, Cort found himself unexpectedly stuttering and bashful. It wasn't the way that her blonde hair caught the ambient light of the room, using it to throw gold at him; it wasn't the piercing blue of her eyes or the (admittedly stunning) cut of her soft blue dress. All he could be sure of was the warmth that washed over him in that moment, which seemed only partially due to the several Michelobs he'd polished off. For some reason, though, his stunned moment started him chuckling, and soon he was laughing out loud, shoulders shaking and tears rolling down his cheeks. Allison stared at him bemusedly for a moment before his mirth crossed the few inches between them and coaxed her into her own tremors. Before long, both were laughing.

"And you know," Allison said finally, wiping tears from her eyes, "I don't have the slightest idea what's funny ... "

Cort's laughter subsided and he opened his mouth to explain just how improbable it seemed that he could be standing there with her, after all of the obstacles and mishaps that had threatened to derail him—from Ryan's interruptions to Theresa's presence; from his car to his dry cleaners and back to Ryan again. Even his spilled drink seemed a part of the night's inevitable disaster. He started to tell her about all of it and about how buoyant it made him feel now that the wind had shifted and good luck was blowing in his direction again. He started to explain that she was somehow special, if only for the fact that she could change his mood, his luck, and his life just by her presence. But with that monologue poised on his tongue, he hesitated, the liquor in his bloodstream running counter to its traditional effects and trapping his words inside. He could feel them on his knotted tongue, poetic and gallant and poised to strike. He could feel charismatic patter ready to spring to his lips, but he wanted nothing to do with it. It seemed to him that retreating to the safety of a practiced line or slipping into banter would taint the moment, and that feeling was confirmed by the spark in Allison's eyes as her amusement slow danced with candor and sincerity.

So, instead, he smiled, nodding an insufficient reply until their laughter had died out, and then a moment longer. He shook his head ruefully and looked down at her. "I don't know, but it was funny. Just life, I guess."

Allison raised her glass, toasting him. "Perfect. Here's to life, with all of its complexities, implausibilities, and accidentallys."

Cort nodded, holding up his nearly empty bottle in return as she continued.

"You know, I thought we might never actually connect, especially when I didn't see you earlier."

Cort winced. "Yeah, I'm sorry about that. A million things made me late and then one thing ... well, one person, hung me up."

Allison grinned at him. "Your date. I know, I saw you dancing."

His wince deepened. "Even better. I bet we looked like a couple of drunk wrestlers."

She nodded. "On a patch of ice, sorry to say ... "

Cort burst out laughing again. "Awesome. Just goes to show you that what's first isn't always what's right. This time I might have been better off just changing my mind and suffering the consequences."

"Even if "the other option" thinks less of you for making the change?"

He shrugged, still smiling.

"It's going that badly, huh?" she said, her tone a blend of sympathy and amusement.

"No, no," Cort replied. "She's very ... nice."

"Is she?" Allison asked.

"Not really." He laughed. "Sorry. That's mean. I think we just aren't quite a match."

"But you never know until you give it a try, right?"

Cort thought a moment. "I don't know. A few days ago I would have agreed, but I'm starting to wonder ... Sometimes, maybe you know."

She blushed again, and he hurried on to break the sudden awkward tension. "Anyway, sorry for leaving you high and dry—but your night's probably better for not having to deal with me on the dance floor anyway."

"You weren't that terrible," Allison protested, her laugh blending with his. "And it takes two to tango ... however badly. Don't worry about me—I can amuse myself. I made friends at the bar while I was waiting for you."

At the reminder, Cort felt a brief surge of jealousy and a stab of anger at Ryan but buried it. "I know," he said. "I saw. I actually thought about coming over, but I didn't want to interrupt you and Ryan ... "

Her eyebrows quirked at the name. "Ryan? I don't think I talked to a Ryan ... "

"Really?" Cort cocked his head. "Blond guy. Athletic. Leather jacket, chinos, and loafers with no socks. Looks like ... well, like a rich model, I guess."

Allison laughed. "I stand corrected. Apparently I did talk to Ryan. He was somewhat ... less than a delight? And not particularly good with a hint." She paused. "Do you know him? I don't mean to be insulting ... "

"He's a very good friend and your description is perfect," Cort said honestly. He took a drink from his beer. "So," he continued, "someone else then."

"Yep," she replied brightly. "The second guy was quite the opposite of your friend. Very respectful was Mr. Love."

Cort rolled his eyes. "Mr. Love? Come on. That was a line."

"It wasn't!" she insisted. "Robin Love. Honestly. I was as skeptical as you until he showed me his driver's license."

"Robin Love." Cort shook his head. "That doesn't bode well for me, does it? Looks like you have your choice between Love and Jamison."

She laughed. "I guess so."

"So?" Cort asked. "Should I be worried?"

Allison lowered her eyes, smiling slightly. "Nothing like that. He was just ... an interesting human. A combination of awkward and amusing."

"That doesn't sound bad."

"Nope," she replied cheerfully. "Not bad at all. And I should say that I love Jamison. Besides, you're the one who's on a date. Maybe it's me who should be worried ... Should I be?" She read his expression and laughed, her hand finding his elbow and resting there even as his awareness of her touch found a place to rest at the forefront of his thoughts. Improbably, that overriding awareness increased as she pulled him toward her, lowering her voice to a mock whisper. "At least I'll have a chance to get even ... "

Cort's eyes met hers. "Oh?"

She nodded. "I promised Mr. Love a dance and I need to make good. Hopefully I can handle his cologne." She grinned. "I think he went a little overboard preparing for the party tonight."

That hit close to home. "A little much, huh?" Cort replied. "What kind?"

She frowned. "I don't know. Potpourri?"

"Elegant," Cort said.

She slapped him on the arm. "Be nice. Or you won't get a chance to redeem yourself."

He raised his hands in surrender, smiling at her.

"Anyway," she sighed, "I should go. It's my turn to make a mockery of the dance floor."

Cort felt laughter bubbling out of him for what seemed like the hundredth time. "Fair's fair."

They stood in silence for a moment, the hush between them not feeling awkward but full of possibility. As the crowd of dancers came to life again, Allison seemed to come to a realization of place, becoming aware of the music and commotion of the people around them. Her escape from their shared moment broke Cort out as well, and both pitched desperate words into the conversational void they'd created.

"I hate to ... "

"Well, I guess ... "

Allison smiled. "You?"

Cort smiled in return and shook his head. "Nope. You go ahead."

She drew in a long breath and released it, contemplative, and then went on. "I was going to say that I hate to leave you, but I'm feeling guilty. I should check in on my new friend."

"And I should get back, too. I don't want *my* friend to think I ditched her, even if that's feeling like an attractive option."

"Don't you dare!"

He laughed. "I was kidding ... "

"You better be," she replied with mock severity. Take care of her. Make sure she gets home okay. How you treat this girl will do more for my impression of you than anything else."

Cort took a moment to breathe and think. Allison watched him curiously, as though trying to predict the end of a mystery; to guess who might be the killer and who the hero. The image amused him, and he spent a moment twirling it around in his head as he studied his shoes before returning his gaze to her, still watching him inquiringly.

"Star-crossed, aren't we?" he said.

"I don't think so," she replied seriously. "I think it's just that tonight isn't the night. We'll get there. This city is smaller than people give it credit for."

He nodded, warmth and happiness spreading through him as she squeezed his hand and turned to go. "Or," he said spontaneously, "we could guarantee it and you could give me your number."

This earned him another light burst of laughter. "I wondered when you were going to get to that. Got paper?"

He reached into his pocket and his fingers brushed a small square of light cardboard. He pulled it out to reveal his coat check claim ticket. He held it up triumphantly.

"That'll work, I guess," she said, taking it from him and cupping it in her right hand as she scribbled a number on it with her left. "I probably shouldn't tell you this, but I wrote it down after I walked away the other day in the grocery store thinking that you might ask for it, but you never did. And I definitely shouldn't have said that, right?"

"Honestly?" Cort replied. "For some reason it didn't even occur to me to ask. And every time it did, it went right out of my head as soon as I saw you again. Maybe I just knew it would come in due time. Inevitable, you know?"

"Well," she said, handing him the paper back, "now it has."

"It has," Cort smiled.

"And?" Allison said, arching an eyebrow and looking at him expectantly.

"And what?" he replied, doubt creeping into his voice.

"You don't think I'm going to give you something for nothing, do you? You're buying my phone number from me. The price is your number. Straight trade or no deal."

Cort grinned as he took the pen from her. "Okay, then. Fair is fair." He jotted his number onto a cocktail napkin from a nearby table, adding spontaneously, "Implausibly, accidentally, and secondly yours, Cort."

Allison glanced at the napkin, her lips quirking at the addendum, then folded it in half and tucked it into her purse. "Until next time," she said.

"Next time," he replied. But as she turned to go, he found Ryan's voice buzzing in the back of his mind, "*I'm sure you explained everything to your two dates. Have you even told them the stepdad story?*" and he heard himself blurt out, "Hold on one second."

She turned, looking at him quizzically.

"Only," he started awkwardly, finding the words of the story for the first time he could remember. "You don't know anything about me, and I don't want to give you the wrong impression. I'm not necessarily ... I mean, I'm not actually ... "

Allison held up a hand. "Ah ah. Not yet." She took a step toward him and rested her hand lightly on his chest. "I like you. That's the important part. We can fill in the details later."

Cort smiled. "Hard to argue with that. I've got some very juicy details for you, but if you want, they can wait until next time."

She nodded at him, still grinning, and as she walked away, Cort felt the rhythmic stutter of his heart surge, hammering against his ribcage, its intensity increasing as he watched her disappear into the crowd.

Cort closed his eyes for a moment, listening to the sound of the crush of people surrounding him. A few moments later he was feeling more in control. More like himself, however unsure he was that that was a good thing. And so it was that he opened his eyes again just in time to see Theresa stepping back into the room, holding another full Cosmo, her eyes scanning the crowd.

Surprisingly, he was pleased to see her. Far from resignation or despair, he felt refreshed. He watched her searching for him and he began to smile, putting aside her awful dancing and ex-boyfriend diatribes to focus on her unusually endearing mix of anxiety and petulance. She was absolutely charming, in her own way. Cort watched her move through the crowd, her skin glowing in the dim light, and decided, spontaneously, that Theresa would be the challenge he needed. Not to see whether he could get her into bed, of course. Instead, he decided to see whether he could execute the disentanglement he'd advised Ryan on so recently. He waved at Theresa, who smiled when she saw him and began to fight her way across the crowded room in his direction.

"Sorry that took so long. Why didn't you tell me I was such a mess?" she demanded as she drew closer.

"Honestly, I didn't even notice." he replied.

"You're a liar," she said flatly, but with a trace of gratification. "A nice liar, but still a liar."

"Not at all," Cort replied, "you look great." He drew in a breath, intending to continue the sentence with a "but, you know ... " and then paused, unsure how to proceed. How best to suggest that, attractive or not, it wasn't going to work out between them without igniting her explosive temper?

"Whatever," Theresa broke in, her false impatience failing to completely cover the pleasure in her voice. "Anyway," she continued through a pasted-on look of innocence, "were you able to keep yourself busy while I was gone?"

Translation, Cort thought to himself, *Have you been a good boy or should I be clawing someone's eyes out?* And with that his mind was made up: he'd try to make the transition from potential hookup to good buddy. He'd let this woman off the hook so slowly she'd never even taste the metal. He smiled. "Absolutely. I bumped into one of the two friends I was trying to set up and had a chat about why it wasn't working out."

Theresa's eyes narrowed almost imperceptibly. "The man or the woman?"

"The woman," Cort replied. "Allison. And apparently Ryan has been an ass tonight. Again. She wants nothing to do with him."

Theresa smirked, her eyes moving to a point just over Cort's shoulder. "She has a weird way of showing it. She's dancing with him."

Cort made a show of glancing carelessly over his shoulder, as he cursed Ryan, wondering what he'd done to win his way back into Allison's good graces. "Probably just being polite," he ad libbed. "Ryan tends to pull that 'kicked puppy dog' thing as a last resort when he knows he's striking out."

But now Theresa was frowning, still focused on the action behind Cort. "No. Actually that's not your friend she's dancing with, I don't think."

"Either way," Cort interrupted, his impatience to move the conversation away from Allison making his voice sharper than he intended. "Let's talk about something else." He noticed the surprised look on her face and pressed on hurriedly. "Let's take a walk. There's supposed to be an eclipse later tonight. Do you want to see if we can see it yet?"

"Outside?" she said, looking at him as though he'd suggested they make their exit through the nearest window. "It's freezing!"

He sighed, casting another quick glance over his shoulder for Allison but failing, this time, to find her in the crowd. "Well then, why don't we find somewhere to sit and talk?"

She looked at him skeptically.

"I just want to get away from the crowd," he explained somewhat desperately. "You want to get to know me? Here's your chance. I promise: I'll answer any questions you want."

Theresa seemed to consider the suggestion for a moment before a sly smile crept slowly over her face. "Okay," she said finally. "But I'm going to hold you to that."

"Fine, hold me in whatever way you want to," Cort said, relief sliding into him. "I swear I am an open book."

They found a place to sit in a small alcove just off the larger foyer, empty except for a few stray members of the waitstaff talking softly in a corner. They curled into facing leather armchairs, each clutching a half-full drink and finding that the quiet that surrounded them once they'd left the main room had made Theresa shy and Cort nervous. He absentmindedly peeled the label off of his beer as he flipped through a mental rolodex of conversation starters, none seeming appropriate to the situation. He found a solution to that problem when he felt her eyes move to him and then away again.

He leaned back in his chair and crossed his legs, feeling his lopsided grin creep back as he laced his hands behind his head. "So," he said, "you were saying that you don't know me that well."

"Well," she stammered, her eyes struggling to decide whether it was all right to lock with his or whether they were better off roaming the small room. "Well, I mean, no." She took a long sip from her drink, then narrowed her eyes and fixed her focus on him at last. "No. Of course not. I just met you yesterday."

"Okay," Cort laughed. "I agree. I'm just checking. So what do you want to know?"

"What?" Theresa blinked, and her eyes threatened to do another tour of the room. "What do I ... "

"What do you want to know?" Cort repeated. "Anything. Like I said, I'm an open book."

"Okay," she replied, doubt still floating in the undercurrents of her voice. She cocked her head and stared at him, eyes still narrowed but with the prospect of trust present behind the surface of suspicion. Cort, for his part, kept his eyes locked on hers, smiling slightly and wondering what she would ask, confident in his ability to answer with the interesting truth or a fascinating lie. After a moment, she straightened and tried to take a gulp from her drink but found it empty.

"Uh-oh," Cort grinned. "Tragedy. You need a refill." He turned over his shoulder, signaling to get the attention of one of the waiters, a gangly kid with straw-colored hair who would have looked fourteen if it hadn't been for his patchy goatee.

"Yes sir?" Goatee asked, sauntering over.

"We need another Cosmo here, if that's okay," Cort said. "And I'll take another Michelob. I have a tab at the bar."

"Sorry," the kid replied. "I can't add things to your tab. You'd have to pay cash."

Cort sighed, and was about to take it as a sign to wrap the night up, but he caught Theresa's eye and found a glint there. She had a question poised on the tip of her tongue, and for reasons he couldn't quite name, he wanted to know what it was. And so he dug out his wallet, slid his thumb in between his ATM card (currently useless) and the blue laminated paper that still marked him as a valued member of Blockbuster, and pulled out a folded bill, which he unfolded to reveal Ben Franklin smirking up at him. He passed the bill—and with it his only remaining safety net—to the goateed waiter and said, "Hold onto this. You can give me my change when we're done for the night."

"Yes sir," the kid replied, striking off for the bar.

Cort turned back to Theresa again, amused to find that the eagerness of her gaze had intensified. He had a flash of realization of what it must feel like to be Ryan. Funny, since now he was, quite literally, broke. "So?" he prompted, doing his best to bury the thought.

Theresa cocked her head at him, her eyes still alight. "Anything, huh?" she said.

"Anything."

"Okay." She shifted in her seat, her smirk telling him that she'd thought of a stumper; she thought she was winning. The idea tickled him, and while a part of his mind whispered that he ought to be worried, he smothered it with beer and bravado.

"Tell me," Theresa continued. "How did you meet these friends of yours that you've been trying to set up tonight?"

"Ryan and Allison?" Cort said easily. "Sure. Why not?"

Internally, however, he winced. He'd been looking forward to the chance to play with honesty for a little while, if only to be sure that he still could. But there was simply no good answer to either side of that question. So he opened his mouth to let the lies come out.

And even as he was replying, he was selecting and rejecting storylines. Setting aside the outlandish or unbelievable, eliminating those whose debauchery made him look less than dignified and burying anything even remotely resembling the truth. Though it might make a good story, he couldn't tell this woman that he and Ryan had met as a result of an evening spent hitting on the same woman, a circumstance that had repeated itself multiple times since (including, in a coincidence that might have been amusing if it weren't so depressing, that very night).

And Allison! A glance at Theresa's now suspiciously furrowed brow told him that she wouldn't be pleased to hear that he'd met Allison in the grocery store moments before he had been challenged to ask Theresa out or that he had been trying to backtrack ever since.

Instead, he made up his mind to punt; to tell her that the stories were too boring to relate or simply beg off with an "I work with them" abdication. But then he found the word "Thermopylae" sitting unexpectedly on his tongue, as though waiting for him to catch up, and frankly, that seemed like more fun. From time to time, it felt good to take a risk just for the joy of it; consequences be damned. With an internal throw of the dice, he let the story come, thanking God for the gift of invention.

"I met Ryan," he began, "in a bar, naturally enough. I was alone; just there to relax and do some writing, so I was tucked back in a corner by the kitchen, where I could get some privacy. Ryan was playing pool with some other guys, but he didn't look like he'd come in with them." He paused.

"What do you mean?" Theresa asked.

"Well," Cort replied, smiling to himself as the story laid itself out, staying just ahead of him as he let the words flow. "I remember thinking that he didn't look like the biker type, in his three-piece suit and wingtips."

He took a moment to savor her surprised laughter, then pressed on. "So, I'm looking at all these Hell's Angels types surrounding this guy in an accountant costume and I don't know what to think: Is he their banker? Their business manager? Their defense attorney? Turns out it was a little sketchier than that ... "

He watched with pleasure as Theresa leaned toward him, drawn in by the story. He wondered idly to himself how far he could push it. Savoring the danger, he made the coin-flip decision to allow the story to spin itself out. He curled his left hand into a fist and used his thumb to crack each of his fingers in turn, then did the same with his right hand, waiting for that instinctive sign to continue.

"Sketchier in what way?" Theresa asked, right on cue, her curiosity shattering his contemplation and freeing the story. Smiling, Cort laced his hands behind his head and let the story run.

"Sketchy because he was hustling them," he replied, feeling a small thrill at the widening of her eyes. "See," he continued, "what I didn't know then is that Ryan is a master of useless skills; a collector, almost. He grew up rich and never really had to work, so he had a lot of hours to fill. He got pretty good at a lot of worthless time wasters. Pool, darts, card tossing, slight-of hand, and a million other things. And that's fine. But sometimes he gets bored and tries to make his useless talents useful, and that can get him in trouble. Like it did that night."

Cort took a moment to glance around, as though making sure no one was listening, then leaned forward, chiding himself for the drama, but enjoying it nonetheless. "So," he continued. "Ryan took about five thousand off of them before they caught on, but when they did, they were not pleased. So, next thing I know, I'm watching him get a pool cue cracked across his back. He went down hard, too.

"Why didn't you do something?" Theresa interrupted.

"Hold on, hold on ... " Cort replied, raising his hands. "I did do something. I went over and talked to them. I got them to back off and then got Ryan, who I'd never even met before, on his feet and back to my table. It wasn't easy, either. But that's not where it ended.

"I remember watching Ryan drop into a seat at my table, wiping blood off his face and swearing under his breath. Next thing I know, he's throwing beer bottles at the bikers and yelling something about Attica. Which didn't even make sense, come to think of it."

"Oh my God," Theresa breathed, eyes wide.

"Exactly. Not a good situation."

"So what happened?"

"Well," Cort said, stalling, not willing yet to let go of the euphoria but knowing that he had to wind it down. He took a breath and settled in for the home stretch. "Well," he said again, "they came after us, of course, in a swarm. And even though this is the part where I'm supposed to exaggerate how many there were or how big they all were, I'm not exaggerating when I say that we had at least a ton of pissed off biker bearing down on us. Scary.

"So anyway, I pulled Ryan up from the table and into the little hallway that led to the kitchen and bathrooms. And then ... " He paused.

"And then? What?" Theresa pressed.

"Well, then we held them off until the police got there and arrested everyone," Cort said, allowing the simple absurdity of the statement make it true.

Theresa stared at him for a few seconds, and he could see the doubt spreading slowly through her thoughts, then trickling down to register in her eyes and in the tightening of her mouth. "And that's it?" she burst out finally. "Just like that? That's bullshit!"

"What?" Cort replied, laughing.

"You did not," Theresa said, "beat up a group of bikers all by yourself."

"You're right," Cort said seriously. "Ryan helped."

"Bullshit."

"Okay. Hold on ... " Cort said, laughing again. "I didn't say that we beat them up, just held them off. I know it sounds far-fetched, but bear in mind, in that tiny little hallway we were really only facing a couple at a time. It was like our own mini-Thermopylae ... "

"Mini-what?"

"Thermopylae? Where a couple hundred Spartan soldiers held off two-hundred thousand Persian troops ... "

Theresa's face was blank. "Never heard of them."

"It's not important. The point is that they got set in a narrow passage and held out against major numbers because they had position. And determination."

"And you're saying that you—"

"I also had determination," Cort interrupted. "I was determined not to get killed by bikers. And I had a pool cue, so ... "

Theresa laughed. "And with determination and a pool cue, you and the Spartans won."

"Well, no," Cort admitted. "That's where it all falls apart. Someone turned traitor and ratted the Spartans out and they got overrun. And they probably had zero pool cues. But Ryan and I did hold strong until the police got there. No traitors to screw us over.

"Anyway, we've been friends ever since. It's not easy to come through something like that and not end up with a bond, you know?"

He stood as the goateed waiter returned with their drinks, passing Theresa hers and then sinking back into his chair to take a long and, he thought, well-deserved tug from his beer.

"How in the hell do you know all that?" Theresa asked abruptly.

"What do you mean? I was there," Cort protested, fully aware what she meant.

"No, I mean about Therma-play and Persians and all that ... "

"Oh," Cort said, feigning surprise. "I don't know. I read a lot. Watch a lot of History Channel. Some things just stick with you."

"Not me," she replied, draining half of her new Cosmo in one gulp. "I never heard of any of it."

Cort nodded, unsure whether she was looking for a more concrete answer about where he'd come up with the information. Silence, or possibly one of Ben's moments of tuning, settled over them and Cort took that moment to breathe. *Not bad, all things considered*, he thought.

And the best part was: it could have been true. That it was a complete fabrication couldn't take away from its core of plausibility. With luck, the lie had even been enough to make Theresa forget that she'd also requested the history of Allison. But as he watched, her eyes took on the piercing, suspicious look that had become so recognizable.

"So," she said, knocking back the rest of her drink. "What about the woman?"

"Allison." Cort forced a laugh. "Honestly, that's a bit trickier."

Jesus, was it ever! Beneath his smile he cast about for a snatch of story or snippet of information that he could mash into an explanation that she would accept.

"What do you mean, trickier?" she demanded, her voice cutting into his thoughts.

Ironically, though, the interruption had given him a path for the story. Once under attack, he had to scramble and a strategy came naturally. Surrender and parlay.

"Trickier because I initially met Allison because I was asking her out." He saw the flash in Theresa's eyes as they narrowed to an almost cartoonish pair of lines under a V of eyebrows. He rushed on.

"It only took one date to realize that we'd be better as friends than in any kind of romance, but that's not the part you want to hear," he said (silently adding *or anything that I want to think about*), wincing at the necessity to end his potential romance with Allison, however fictionally. He pushed the thought aside and continued.

"But if you want to hear about how we met ... " He paused, then grinned. "I guess you could say it was because of Lincoln."

Theresa blinked at him. "Wait? Because of what?"

"Lincoln," Cort said seriously. "Abraham? Sixteenth president? Have you ever heard the superstition about picking up pennies on the street?"

Theresa shook her head.

"Pretty simple. Heads up, it's good luck, so you can pick it up. Heads down draws a frown, so you want to leave it there."

"Okayfine," Theresa said, her words starting to slur together. "I get it. But what does that have to do with ... "

"I'm getting there," Cort interrupted. "I've had that stupid little rhyme in my head since I was a kid. As dumb as it sounds, I actually still follow it. Heads up, good luck; heads down, draws a frown. So I only pick up a penny when I can make eye contact with Abe.

"Well, I'm walking down the street one day and I see this attractive blonde woman stoop down to pick up a penny. And I'm thinking to myself, 'Hope it was face up or she's asking for trouble.' But then, instead of standing up, she puts the penny back down and walks away.

"Once she's gone, I walk over to look. Sure enough, there's Lincoln staring at me like he's wondering what I'm going to do. So I scoop it up and move down the street after her."

"You followed her?" Theresa asked.

"Only kind of," Cort replied. "I was going that direction anyway, but I'll admit I was curious. It seemed odd, you know? I couldn't shake the rhyme out of my head and I wanted to figure out what she was up to.

"Well, after a block or two, the whole thing happened again. She bent down, picked up a penny, looked at it, and put it back down again. So this time, I caught up with her and asked her if she'd dropped it. She looked embarrassed and said that she hadn't. I must have given her an odd look, because she asked if I'd ever heard the kid's rhyme, 'Head's up, good luck.' When I said that I had, she shrugged and said that she'd had plenty of good luck and wanted to share it with people who needed it. So she was picking up face-down pennies and flipping them face up; creating luck for other people to find."

"Weird," Theresa said.

"Maybe a little," Cort replied, too caught up to notice the jealousy in her voice. "But endearing and cute, too. And being the wit that I am, I cobbled together a pickup line and asked her out."

"Oh really? And what was that?"

Cort blinked, momentarily disoriented. The story, as phony and spur-of-the-moment as it had been, had rekindled his interest in Allison and left him unprepared for the voice and visage of another woman. To his credit, he recovered well.

"Here," he said. "I'll show you. Got a penny?"

Theresa eyed him for a moment, then gave a heavy sigh and reached down for the purse at her feet, nearly sliding to the floor in the process. With a mumbled "oops," she hoisted herself back into her chair and pulled out a fistful of change. "Here," she said, her palm full of coins thrust between them in challenge. "Pick me up."

"You scoff, but you have no idea how closely this penny relates to you," Cort said, selecting a copper coin from the small pile in her hand.

"Like how?"

Cort stood and walked over to kneel beside her, holding his palm out in front of them. "You see this? 'E Pluribus Unum?' That's about you. It's Latin for 'one out of many.' Which you are. Of all the many women here tonight," he said, looking into her eyes even as he bit his tongue at the ungainliness of the line, "you are the one that I've chosen to be with."

Theresa wrinkled her nose. "Smooth," she said.

"I know. Corny, huh? I can't believe I thought it would work."

She smiled, despite herself, then ruined the moment with a small hiccup. "But it did?"

"Nope!" Cort replied cheerfully. "She did what you just did, laughed at me. So I bet her dinner that I could tell her where her penny came from."

"How hard is that?" Theresa said. "Washington, D.C."

"Actually, no," Cort replied, glancing at the coin in his hand again. "As luck would have it, both that one and this one came from Denver."

"Denver? How can you tell that?" Theresa asked, peering over his shoulder at the small coin.

Cort moved his hand slightly, grinning to himself as she unconsciously leaned closer, then fighting to keep from rolling his eyes as her lean carried her into him. Knowing that you had captured someone with a story was one thing; stealing their interest by getting them drunk was another. He decided to end the conversation, and the night, before things got out of hand. "If you look right next to the date," he said, "you'll usually see a letter that tells you where the coin was minted. D means Denver. CC means Carson City. If there's no letter, that means Philadelphia. It's easy, as long as you know where to look."

He stood and was surprised to find the goateed waiter behind him, holding yet another Cosmo.

"Wow, dude. I had no idea. That's really cool," Goatee drawled.

"Is that from me? I mean for. Is that for me?" Theresa asked, gesturing in the general direction of the drink.

"Oh. Yeah." The waiter handed it to her before Cort could manage a "maybe we should slow down" or a "I didn't order another round." Instead, he was left to lamely toss a "Could you just bring me my change?" after the retreating waiter.

"Change?" Theresa whined, and Cort was dismayed to see that, once again, she had polished off nearly half of her drink with a single gulp. "Are you leaving?"

"Yeah," Cort replied, feigning disappointment. "I think so. It's getting to be that time. The party's probably dying down. I should head out ... "

"Why don't you come over and sit by me for a second instead," Theresa said, patting the seat beside her.

Cort stared at her. She was sitting on a leather armchair not nearly large enough for two people. "Sit there with you?" he asked.

"Sure," she slurred. "I'll make room for you."

"I'm not sure that's the best idea."

"Hey!" she said with mock severity. "Hey. Guess what? I like you. I like you and," she leveled a finger at him, "and I don't like very many people. So. You're lucky. And you're rich. So I like you and you can sit by me."

Cort allowed himself to wonder briefly how he'd let things get this far. It was time to bring this particular chapter to a close. "Actually," he said. "I'm not rich."

Theresa scoffed. "Okay. You're not rich. That's fine. That's why you come to a party like this wearing all new clothes and buying drinks with hundred dollar bills. But okay." She tilted her head toward him and winked deliberately with both eyes at once. "It's a secret."

"Whatever you say," he replied.

"Hey!" Theresa repeated, once again gesturing at him, this time with her half-full drink, the pinkish liquid sloshing out onto his lap. "Oh shit!" she cried as he jumped to his feet, brushing at the spreading wet stain. "Oh shit, I'm sorry!"

Cort sighed. "Don't worry about it," he said. "They weren't expensive."

"I'm so sorry," she repeated, struggling to her feet. "Maybe we should just leave. You could drive me home?" With this, she leaned toward him, overbalancing into his arms.

He caught her, surprised at how light she was, casting anxious looks around the lobby as he set her on her feet. "You know," he said, "let's just take a little walk first." She looked at him quizzically. "Get you some air?" he finished lamely. After a moment's consideration, she nodded and they moved off down the hall.

They'd reached the top of the stairs before he questioned the wisdom of taking a drunk woman for a walk; movement seemed to have somehow quickened both her absorption of alcohol and her determination to bring him home with her. She clung to him with a fierceness that suggested both desire and instability.

"I know I can trust you," she said as he hesitated at the top of the first step. "You can sleep on my couch if you can't drive home. I don't mind."

He tried to ignore the logic that made it all right for him to drive as far as her home but no further. "I'm not sure that's a good idea either ... "

"Well," she said brightly. "Then you can have the bed and I'll sleep on the couch. Or not." And with that she started down the stairs.

Shortly after college, Cort had moved himself into a second-floor apartment on the north side of Chicago. He hadn't been able to find anyone to help him move, which hadn't mattered much, as he really hadn't owned much more than a broken futon frame and a kegerator. The only thing that had given him trouble was a large wooden bookshelf that he'd inherited from his former roommate. He was able to get it off the ground by himself, but after that actually moving it in any direction posed challenges. He'd managed by humping the thing up each individual step, resting after each expulsion of effort. Eventually, he'd made it—long after he'd lost feeling in his arms and possibly separated both of his shoulders.

This was worse. This was moving that same bookshelf back down the stairs if it had been made out of jello and had an agenda.

He dimly remembered marveling at how light she'd seemed just minutes earlier and wondered what he'd been smoking at the time.

By the time they reached the landing that signaled the halfway point, Cort was questioning nearly everything. Why had he come to this party? Why had he continued talking to this woman after he knew he wasn't interested? Why had he bought her so many goddamned drinks and why had the waiter decided to bring even more?

As they sagged against the wall, he catching his breath and she presumably trying to hold down a half-dozen drinks, Cort had a flash of insight: the Kiss of Death. Ryan might scoff, but if he could turn this woman off with one kiss, it would be well worth it.

Theresa was resting her head on his shoulder, her eyes at half-mast. The time to act was now.

He straightened up, jostling her to her feet as he turned to face her. "What?" she mumbled, sleepily, and before she could react, he grabbed her by the shoulders, pulled her forward, and laid his best dead fish on her.

It was awful. His mouth hung open and flaccid, his tongue flopped loosely forward, not so much probing hers as draping over it like a wet, woolen blanket. He let out a long, slow breath and then slowly released her shoulders, expecting her to recoil.

But he had underestimated the power of Gray Goose. At the touch of his lips she had tightened. As his tongue had wilted onto hers she had pulled back. But after a moment's adjustment, she rallied, throwing herself at him and wrapping both arms tightly around his neck, driving him backward into the wall, where he cracked the back of his head against the wooden molding. The shock of it made him see stars, and he jerked forward, bringing their foreheads together with a thud and driving his jaw shut, his teeth closing on both of their tongues.

Theresa's arms, which had been clinging to him tightly, went slack as she finally released her grasp on consciousness and slumped, catching her head a ringing crack against the paneled wall before sprawling to the floor.

He staggered but managed to stay on his feet, his head swimming and his mouth full of blood that he hoped was his own. He felt a wetness on his face and wiped his chin with his hand, baffled when it came away red, before he realized that his nose and lips were also bleeding.

Stunned, he knelt over Theresa as he tried to staunch his gushing nose, his mouth tasting of rust.

She was breathing evenly and not bleeding as badly as he, and he guessed that her unconsciousness was due as much to alcohol as to their collision. Still, she was resting awkwardly against the wall and so, with one hand plugging his nose, he eased her down to the floor until she lay flat. He stared at her for a moment, wondering how things could possibly get any worse.

It didn't take long.

"Hey you! What are you doing to that woman?"

Cort looked up at the small man at the top of the stairs staring down at him through round, wire-framed glasses and, for one sinking moment, saw himself from the other man's point of view: saw his face and shirt smeared with blood; saw himself crouched over an unconscious woman. And he couldn't blame the man at all when, after taking only a second or two to gape at the scene, he fled, calling loudly for help.

    Less than five minutes later, Cort was wearing a pair of handcuffs and wondering, again, how things had gotten to this point—a question that was quickly taking on hobby status for him. His nose had finally stopped bleeding, his new shirt soaking up most of the blood just as his new pants had accommodated the majority of that last cosmo. But his tongue still throbbed angrily, and he felt the constant need to spit, knowing that it would be bright red even before he saw it hit the snow outside. Theresa was awake, and he briefly considered trying to convince the rent-a-cop who was holding him to ask her about the alleged assault. But the half-groggy, half-drunk look in her eye told him it would be a crap shoot at best. Instead, he let himself be led to the front door of the Cultural Center, his eyes fixed on the bespectacled man who had reported him, wondering idly why the damn man was waggling two fingers at him in an odd, fluttering peace sign and, more to the point, why he was smiling so broadly.

Ben

Eclipse in 2 hours

Author's Note: And now, finally, we reach the eclipse I promised so long ago. My apologies for the delay, but a lunar eclipse can be a mysterious and portentous phenomenon; its meaning can change with the slightest variant in culture—each shift in the breeze that is mythology and religion—and its impact on our players will be profound and diverse. So, it's important to treat it with care. To start, let's be clear on a few facts— lay down some ground rules, if you will.

Despite its foreboding, the power of an eclipse is ethereal. The fact that such a beautiful, celestial body can, in a blink, go bloody and savage makes what should be familiar feel indescribably foreign. And so we force ourselves to overcome our irrational fears of a rational phenomenon. We fast to starve out the spirits of the dead, beat mirrors to force the great dragon to cough the moon back into the sky, and cry to the heavens for a way to remove the arrow that has wounded her. We struggle to set right a world that never went wrong—or, at least, one that we could never hope to fix.

And then, for some—for the ambitious—the goal is to touch the moon while she is in shadow—steal some of her power, gain some of her insight. Borne, perhaps, on the smoke of a funeral pyre or on the back of a kite, riding the smoke or the paper and wood to dance around her bloodshot eye. There is joy in that dance—the controlled unpredictability, the restrained freedom; there is an omnipotence. From that vantage, you see the world below. You can anticipate the future. There is a power there.

Aspire to too great heights, however—dance too long in the sharp-edged winter breeze—and your string may snap, your dance growing wild and frantic as you lose yourself to the random whims of the air. And once your string is broken, it is impossible to reconnect.

And so we return to Ben.

Ben has been around longer than he would care to admit—he has read his fair share of books and visited any number of countries. He knows about the great dragon of China, the archer of the Ge, and about the never-ending battle between the sun and moon. I feel sure that he would read portent in this eclipse if he were in full possession of his faculties. Unfortunately, he has been adrift for eighteen days now, so he's unlikely to be very dependable. Still, with the laws of cause and effect, with the interplay of augury and consummation, there's no telling what might happen.

So, watch with me as he watches the moon slowly turn the rusty red of fresh blood, and then has his attention seized by a shadow drifting across the snowy lawn next door. Follow along with him as his eyes track a large, dark form moving toward the house next to his, climbing the stairs to the porch, and then hesitating. Look back at the moon and allow her warning to pull at you, and then tell me that you wouldn't do as Ben did—that you wouldn't fumble for the telephone and dial quickly without taking your eyes off of the scene unfolding before you. That when the mechanical voice asked you your emergency you wouldn't mumble, "I'd like to report a crime at the house next door," then give your address and hang up, wondering what will happen next. An eclipse is, after all, a motivating thing. And it will inspire all of our five men—even if it takes an extra nudge to set some of them in motion.

So let us dance with Ben on the end of a kite string. See if you recognize the moment when that string snaps.

#

Ben woke in his chair, the record player beside him halfway through its playlist. He listened as it scratched its way through The Complete Helen Forrest with Harry James Orchestra, scowling when the song didn't match the tune in his head.

All our friends keep knocking at the door
They've asked me out a hundred times or more
But all I say is, 'Leave me in the gloom'
And here I stay within my lonely room, 'cause

I don't want to walk without you, Baby

Walk without my arm about you, Ba ...

... day you left ... thought I'd take a ...

... get you right off my ...

I don't want to walk ... don't want to walk ... don't want to walk ... don't want to walk ... don't want to walk ...

"Elle? The stereo's skipping ... "

Ben hoisted himself to his feet, unconcerned by the lack of response and trying to remember whether his wife had told him that she was going out, then moved over to shut off the music. He listened to the record player labor through another couple of rounds of " ... don't want to walk ... don't want to walk ... don't want to walk ... " before reaching down to snap off the power, flinching as the telephone behind him immediately blared, cutting through the new silence. Almost without thinking, he crossed to the kitchen and scooped the phone off its cradle.

"Yes?"

"Ben Dawes?" The voice on the other end was quiet but sharp. Whispering knives at him. Ben winced.

"Yes," he repeated, marveling at the exhaustion in his own voice.

"I'm surprised you're still there," the voice replied. "You must like being alone."

Ben didn't reply, and a moment passed in silence.

Finally, the voice continued. "You should know, Ben," it said, "that this is your time. This is your tuning. Your time to decide."

"Elle," Ben whispered.

"And?"

"And Sam."

"What about them?" the voice prompted.

But Ben ignored the question. "Have you called here before?" he asked, his voice hoarse.

"Every day," came the reply. "Why?"

"I don't know," Ben whispered, clutching the phone with both hands.

"That's right," the voice said. "You don't. But the moon will tell you. Look to her for answers." But now Ben was crying softly and could not bring himself to answer. There were a few seconds of silence, and then the thin voice spoke again, this time with the barest trace of ... what? Compassion? Regret? Urgency? "We're almost done, Ben. I need you to look out the window now."

Ben wiped his eyes and shuffled over to the window to stare out at the snow-muffled night.

"What do you see?" the voice prompted.

"Neighborhood," Ben replied. "It's night. Quiet."

"And next door?"

Ben squinted. There was a shadow stalking across the porch of the big brick house next door—what was their name—Moran?

Masters? Didn't matter. "Someone looking in the window," he said, concern in his voice. "Someone should tell them. Call the police."

"Don't worry," the voice said. "You already did that. But here's the thing: the police don't know enough … yet."

Ben frowned. "I don't remember … "

"It doesn't matter!" the voice hissed. Then, calmer, "Listen. Sometimes, when you need something done, you need to push a little harder. Be more firm. You know that. Elle knew that too, didn't she?"

Ben nodded, forgetting that this disembodied voice couldn't see him. But apparently it could, because it went on. "That's right, she did. She knew how and when to push. And you need to give the police a little push, right now. So we're going to hang up, and then you're going to call 9-1-1 again, okay?"

Ben's frown had deepened, and now his eyes were nearly closed. "I don't know," he muttered.

"Yes, you do," the voice snapped. "I know you can't remember sometimes, Ben. And that's fine, but remember this: when I hang up, you're going to call the police and tell them that you recognized the man breaking into your neighbor's house and that man is Reggie Webb. You got that?"

Ben was silent, staring out the window.

"Ben? You got that?"

"Yeah," he replied softly. "Reggie Webb."

"Good," the voice said sharply. "Don't mess up your moment of tuning, Ben." And the line went dead.

Ben pulled his gaze away from the window and sank into his chair, allowing his eyes to close. As he did, memories came flooding back: the day he'd demanded that Sam leave home, the hardness of Elle's face; the sharpness of her tongue. Bad memories. In his mind, he allowed the disquieting pictures to blur and go blank, replaced by a soothing, numbing grayness that felt almost like sleep. He allowed it to flow over him, washing away everything but the present.

Finally, he opened his eyes and realized that he could once again hear music playing. And that he was still holding the telephone, which was now emitting a startled, pulsing beep.

He hung up the phone, smiling through his confusion, then wiped moisture from his cheeks and listened, wondering what the game was. Whether Elle and Sam were joking with him.

This new music felt odd to Ben—bright and frenetic, as though it was playing too fast. A 78 running at 45 speed. It was shrill and young and jarred Ben's rhythms. He rested a hand on the phonograph as though to still it, as if it could produce sound without motion.

He put an ear to the speaker, but the velvet box was still, and so he turned to survey the room. The television was dark, the radio silent, the record player quiet.

The front door, however, was ajar.

Ben moved to the door, every movement feeling strange, as though he had been set on a course from which he could not deviate. "It's only music," he muttered, reaching for the doorknob. "Chaotic music, but still ... "

He opened the door and stepped into the night. The sky above showed only a few wisps of scattered clouds, but flashes of lightning far up in the atmosphere gave the night an element of surprise. Standing on the doorstep, Ben felt the cold immediately start to seep into him and he turned to go back inside to his fireplace, but found that his legs refused to move. He felt pulled in a direction that he had not chosen, placed in a story that he did not fully recognize and that did not feel like his own.

The neighborhood around him felt wrong. He had stepped out of his house on Richmond Street only seconds ago—that wonderful house; his first house, the one he'd bought just after he and Elle had gotten married. He'd gotten out of his chair next to the bookshelves, across from the door to the tiny kitchen; everything exactly where it was supposed to be. He belonged in that Richmond Street house, along with the trove of good memories. But now he found himself facing Eastwood Avenue, and he had memories of that house, too. Strange, hazy images of Sam leaving and a different, challenging version of Elle. Not as good, those Eastwood Avenue memories.

Ben looked over his shoulder at his front room, his chair practically calling to him to return. He stared for a moment, feeling the pull—the warmth of the house, Elle moving through the kitchen just out of sight, and then he turned back to face the strangely familiar street before him. He listened to the manic tincture of the music that had lured him out in the first place, now punctuated with laughter, and he wondered what story he had allowed himself into, what mythology he was living in. He could feel the chill on his cheeks, could hear music and the crunch of old snow under his shoes. It all whispered "real" to him. Moreover, he could sense the moon above waiting patiently for him to come out; waiting to go blind so that she could finally pass impartial judgment on him.

As a sort of test, Ben locked gazes with the moon, staring her down and offering a challenge, demanding that she finally carry him away with her. But the clear light proved too much for him, and he closed first one eye then the other, blocking out the empty promises and the reminders of the past that each shaft of light carried with it.

Strangely, with his eyes closed, things became clearer. There was a taste of iron on his tongue and the cold night air turned warmer and moist. There was a texture to the breeze that made it feel as though the night was breathing. The ferric taste intensified, and he wondered whether he might be dying. Or perhaps it was simply time, finally, for him to be born, and all of his memories were fetal dreams of what life would bring. Elle, the birth of his son, the tragedies that both of those joys evolved into all just tremors in the blood.

The music grew louder, mixing with childish laughter and then fading again before being cut off by a rough voice.

"Hey man, you okay?"

Ben opened his eyes, the reflection of the moon on the snow making him squint to see the shadowed figure on the porch of the house next door.

"Yes," he replied, adding, "I'm either asleep, or dead, or fine ... "

"Alright," the figure laughed. "Well, you're going to want to close your door, or your house is going to be a freezer ... "

Ben glanced over his shoulder. The well-lit room felt dim and cold; far-off and unwelcoming.

"It's not my house," he called out, pulling the door closed behind him anyway.

"Sure, whatever. You can come over here if you want to. There's a fire inside if you can handle the noise. Otherwise, you can sit here and watch the eclipse."

"Eclipse," Ben repeated.

"Uh-huh. Look up."

But his eyes had already slid upward, taking in the moon, one edge now a cloudy, deep red. Foreboding. Ben bit his lower lip, hard enough to draw blood, then shuffled slowly across the lawn, wondering who was going to die.

Climbing the three low stairs to the porch, Ben took the opportunity to steal a closer look at the bulky shadow that had spoken to him from the darkness. Closer up, the shape was more distinct. Dark pants and a leather jacket that flapped open in the breeze. But proximity did not lighten the hue of the shadow. If anything, the man grew darker the closer Ben got. He stopped on the steps. "You ... " he said, faltering. "You're a Black, right?"

"Uh ... yeah," the shadow returned. "Good eye. That a problem?"

The porch was dimly lit by the amber glow of a small space-heater in the corner, and in the scant light Ben could just make out the smile on the man's face. Not until he was a few steps away did Ben realize that the man was a head and a half taller than he and twice as thick, a fact he was surprised to find didn't concern him at all. He jerked to a halt, arms continuing to swing as though he were still walking. "Nah," he replied. "Just funny seeing one of you in this neighborhood. But I'm not prejudiced," he finished stupidly, adding "My barber's a Black too ... ... " before trailing off.

The man let out a grunt of laughter, then gestured him up onto the porch. "Well, that's great. Bet you got the best cut of all the old white men in the neighborhood. Take a seat if you want." His voice was higher than Ben had expected, sounding almost artificially sped up, reminding Ben of the music that had been playing in his small house. "It's a little warmer over by the heater. Not a lot ... but it's something."

Ben nodded his gratitude, crossing the porch to sink into a folding chair set beside the glowing space heater, relishing the scant warmth that it offered. He rubbed his hands together, imagining that he could feel his blood start moving again. Then he glanced up and caught the other man looking at him.

"Thanks," he murmured. Then, louder, "Name's Ben Dawes."

"Reggie," the big man replied. "Webb. Lots of people call me Spider."

"Nice to meet you," Ben replied automatically, adding, "I don't think I've seen you before. I thought I knew everyone on the block. You move in recently?"

"I thought you didn't live over there," Spider said, nodding at Ben's house. "You live in this neighborhood or not?"

Ben stared across the lawn. "I'm not sure," he said finally. His brain danced backward over the past fifteen minutes, but slipped and slid on the ice, finding no solid purchase. "I ... I'm sorry ... "

The other man's gaze softened. "Hey man, that's okay. Don't worry about it. I'm just making conversation." He shuffled his feet. "So, um, you got family?"

"Spider." Ben said. "That's clever. Spider Webb."

Spider laughed again, a deep, resonant laugh that laid a bass line under the tenor of his speaking voice. "So they tell me," he said. "So they are always telling me. Truthfully, I prefer Reggie, but for every one of my old friends that I get to stop calling me Spider, someone new tags me with it again and it all starts over. Maybe I should change my last name next time around ... You're lucky you don't have that problem, Ben."

Ben nodded seriously. "Lately, I've been having serious issues with time."

Spider's laugh dried up, but he maintained his face-splitting smile. "Yeah, well. I can understand that, man. There's not enough hours in the day to do what needs doing. I don't know how God manages."

Ben restrained himself from shaking his head. It wasn't what he'd meant, but how could this man know that? "You don't live around here."

The observation pushed Spider's eyebrows up. "No, we don't. We live on the south side. Got a little apartment in Roseland. We're just here for the birthday party," he added, nodding at the house.

"Ah," Ben replied. "Birthday." Which, of course, explained everything, from the music to the presence of a stranger on the porch. "Whose?" he added.

"My daughter," Spider replied. "Cate. She's five. We're ... well, we're not ... One of her school friend's folks offered to throw her a party, and I'm not one to turn down an invite like that, so ... " He drifted off, letting his sentence finish itself, then broke his own silence. "Truth: I should be inside right now. I just couldn't hack the, uh ... music. Ducked out to get some air, grab a smoke. and catch some of the eclipse."

Once again, the word forced Ben's eyes skyward, where they found that the face of the moon was now more than half mottled, as if caught mid blush, the reddish tint calling the taste of blood back to Ben's tongue.

Ben's train of thought was broken by the slap of the screen door against its frame and the sight of a tiny blonde girl momentarily backlit by the bright light of the kitchen. The unexpected sound and the angelic sight were enough to jar Ben's grip on his thoughts loose, and he wandered momentarily across the floor of a gymnasium and down the aisle of a grocery store.

The door swung closed, cutting off the light so that the porch was lit only by the space heater, the burr of Spider's cigarette and the girl's halo of golden curls.

"Elle?" Ben whispered. But as the words left his lips he knew them to be wrong. Not Elle then. So ... perhaps Allison? Or someone new ...

"Cate? What are you doing out here?"

The little girl shrugged, committing fully to the gesture in the manner of a young child, her shoulders nearly touching her ears.

"Getting tired?" Spider continued.

A shake of the blonde head.

"No? Just bored then?" Spider stood from where he'd been leaning against the porch railing, not waiting for an answer this time. "Come over here, sweetie. I want you to meet someone."

The girl moved slowly forward, her desire to be there trailing behind her.

Spider laid a large hand on her shoulder and turned her to face Ben. "Cate, this is my new friend Ben. Can you say 'Hi'?"

Ben struggled to his feet and tried to smile at the girl, but her face was changing before his eyes: a young Elle one moment, then the girl Allison, and then his young dance partner from the museum, each face seeming ridiculous on the little girl's tiny body. He blinked owlishly at her.

Cate stared at Ben for a moment and then turned away. Spider smiled apologetically. "Sorry, she's usually very outgoing. Can't get her to shut up most of the time. Probably just getting tired. It's been a long day."

Ben nodded. "For me too." His eyes climbed toward the sky again. "Or maybe it's the eclipse."

Maybe she's just like me, he continued in his mind. *Afraid of what it means and wondering who's going to die.* He kept the thought tightly in his grasp, not allowing it near his mouth. Instead, he turned his eyes away from the moon's bloodshot eye and back toward the tiny girl, who now stood behind her father, hugging one of his legs, her eyes fixed on the sky. Ben heard himself say, "It's very nice to meet you, Cate. I understand it's your birthday. How old are you today?"

He'd half expected her to ignore the question or hold up her fingers in infantile reply and was pleasantly surprised when instead she said simply, "Five."

Her voice had the pitch and tenor of a child but carried its own gravity. Even such a short speech reminded Ben not to expect the annoying chirp of a toddler but the wisdom and grace of a girl. He pressed on, raising his mental estimation. "And how do you like being five?" he asked. "Is it better than four so far?"

Again, her response caught him by surprise, this time for its non-sequitur, and for its import.

"Why is the moon bleeding?"

Ben's thoughts spun again, like the wheels on a slot machine, and he watched the images flash before his eyes with no idea whether they would finally come up blanks or skull and crossbones, or triple cherry. Each, it seemed, had an equal chance and each, he felt, carried its own, predetermined ending.

"It's an eclipse, sweetie," Spider said. "Right now, the Earth is between the sun and the moon and that makes the moon look darker. I don't know why it turns red, but it's not bleeding. It's just hiding in our shadow." He glanced over at Ben. "Weird the stuff you pick up, huh?"

But Ben's wheels were still spinning loosely, as though the gears had been removed and the axels greased. He closed his eyes as the world moved around him. He felt drunk, felt his gorge rise, and forced his eyes open to fight the surge of vertigo. He shuddered violently then croaked, "That's not true."

An awkward silence swept the small porch, but Ben did not notice, pressing on. "She is bleeding. It's a sign. The moon got 'bit bear'—or she's been shot. I can never remember. But it's bad luck. Someone is going to die."

"Hey man, knock it off." Ben blinked and saw Spider's face come into focus in front of him, voice filled with hushed anger.

"I'm sorry," Ben whispered. "But I'm right."

"Whatever," Spider replied. "There's no need to scare the kid. Keep your crazy to yourself." He turned to the small girl, kneeling beside her and whispering in her ear.

Ben sagged against the wall. He couldn't call to mind exactly what he'd said to make the man angry, but he knew that it had been true. Something ominous was in the air. There was a high whine building that was growing in pitch and intensity. He wondered whether anything could be done to change the future. He wondered whether the gods would demand a sacrifice and whether it would be him or whether it had been Elle. He wondered how loud the see-sawing whine would get before it split his head in two. He clenched his eyes shut, gritting his teeth, trying to keep the sound inside, not wanting the little girl to hear it. But now she and her father were looking around as though they were hearing the same noise.

Ben followed their gaze and saw a strobe of red light playing off the houses on the corner, their color harsh and threatening, mimicking the moon that now hung low and blood-red above them. Moments later, a police car turned the corner, crawling slowly down the block, lights still flashing, even though its siren had gone silent.

"Cate, you go inside. Right now." Spider stood up, eyes locked on the car. His daughter clung tightly to his leg and Ben watched as the large man struggled to pry her loose, kneeling before her again. "Sweetie, it's okay. I want you to go inside and get warm now, okay? I'll come in pretty soon."

There was a moment of potential protest, and then the girl nodded and stepped back into the house, her father closing the door behind her. "Now what do you think these bastards want?" he muttered.

Ben was still propped against the wall, but the flashing lights made the world swim in front of him and chaotic memories rose up in his mind like bile—bitter and poisonous, their bite choking off his reply. He could feel the other man's eyes on him but could barely bring himself to look at him: disheveled and unkempt, just as he remembered. Remorse flooded Ben as he stared at the blurred memory of his son standing before him again, larger than he remembered, but shifting side to side and mumbling in his distinctive stutter, "Ah shit. Don't stop. Don't stop here ... " The colored lights flashed painfully in Ben's eyes and the deafening siren gave a final, threatening whoop then left them in an ominous silence that he felt the desperate need to fill, fighting himself to say what he'd known was necessary for over a decade.

"I'm sorry," he finally managed, the long-due apology sapping his strength and leaving him sagging against the wall of the house.

"Hey ... whoa. You okay? What's the matter?" His son's concerned voice sounded stronger, more sure of itself than Ben remembered. But he no longer trusted his memory. He pressed on, knowing that if he wavered even a moment he would grind to a halt.

"It's my fault ... I'm so sorry." Ben shook his head, unable now to bring himself to even look up.

"What do you mean? What's your fault?" came the reply.

"I called them. It's my fault."

Ben felt hands on his arms, felt himself physically moved, nearly falling as he was shoved roughly against the wall with a force that took his breath away, both from the impact and the surprise.

"You what? Why the fuck would you do that?"

Ben was weeping now, uncontrollably. "I called them on you. I'm so sorry, Sammy. I know you didn't do it, but I didn't know it then ... It's my fault. I should have trusted you."

"Jesus." The voice was tinged with disgust now. "You really are nuts, man. Who do you think you're talking to?"

The light around them intensified painfully and Ben winced against the unexpected glare as the night was cut through by shouts. "You! Move away from that man!"

The large, heavy hands released him, but Ben's memories had been sprung and the words came uncontrollably now, fast and hot, demanding that they be said even if they were no longer being heard.

"It would have meant my job. When the money disappeared I had to do something. You were the only one there ... " Ben could hear the pleading tone in his voice and drew a deep breath to steady himself. "I told your mother that I had no choice. But I had already called them before I even talked to you. But then, we never talked, did we? That's my fault. I'm sorry. I'm so sorry, Sammy. Can you forgive me?"

"Okay, okay. Chill out. I didn't do anything."

The response felt disconnected, and didn't give Ben the resolution he needed, and he clutched at his son's coat. "Sammy, can you ever forgive me?" he cried.

"Yeah, yeah. Whatever, man. You're good."

Ben collapsed against the wall, letting out a huge, quavering breath as relief overcame him, washing away his pain and his grief and his guilt ... and his memories, a side effect of his catharsis that left him empty, as if some unnamed force had passed a magnet over him, wiping him clean. Leaving him drained and confused and utterly blank.

In the background, strange voices carried on their shouted conversation.

"Kneel on the ground, hands behind your head."

"Alright, alright. Don't shoot me, man. My hands are up ... "

There was a creak of boards as the voice nearest him complied. Ben realized that he was still leaning against the wall and straightened up, squinting at the bright lights that cut at him from the top of the police car. A pair of cops had emerged from the car and were moving up the walk, and for a moment Ben smiled. They looked like an old vaudeville team, though he couldn't quite remember the men's names—they had been funny though. The one in front was tall and angular, moving toward him with one hand held at his side as he continued to shout at them. His partner trailed behind, short and squat, almost rotund, seeming much more hesitant. Ben shivered, wondering idly why they were all out in the cold so late at night.

A voice in front of him rose up, complaining, and Ben glanced curiously at the large black man kneeling near him and raising his voice in complaint. "Hey, not to be a pain, but can you at least tell me what's going on?"

The tall cop had reached the porch now, and Ben could see that he did not resemble the comedian that Ben had initially imagined, but was blond and hawkish instead, an Aryan Bud Abbot. His voice had the same authoritative tone, even if his material seemed, to Ben, profoundly unfunny.

"None of your business," he said. "Just stay where you are." Then, to Ben, "Sir, are you okay?" Ben let his gaze drift to the other cop, now close behind his partner at the top of the stairs, his belly keeping him from getting closer. Like Aryan Abbot, he too had become less familiar as he grew closer, morphing into a Hispanic version of Oliver Hardy. "Sir, are you the gentleman who called us?" he asked, his voice much softer than his partner's.

For reasons he could not name, the question made Ben feel nervous—threatened and guilty—defensive for reasons that he couldn't explain.

"No. No, I didn't call you. That's not something I would do." Without thinking, he continued. "I wouldn't. That would ruin everything."

"Excuse me?" the tall cop replied.

"I mean, I didn't do it. Did I?" Ben squinted, fighting to match his side of the conversation up to reality.

"Don't read too much into it," the black man cut in, shifting to face them. "I think he's a little out there."

"I need you to be quiet!" Aryan Abbot barked. Then he turned back to Ben. "You're sure that you didn't call us, sir?"

Ben shook his head. "No. Nope, not sure. Not me."

Abbot grimaced then turned his attention back to the kneeling man. "All right, then. Who are you and what are you doing out here?"

The black man grinned up at him. "Reggie Webb. I'm here for the party."

"Party?" the cop repeated.

"Yeah. The birthday party inside. Can I get up now? I didn't do anything."

"Hold on," the shorter cop broke in. "Reggie Webb?"

"Yeah ... "

"Reginald John Webb?"

The black man twisted again, turning to face Hispanic Hardy. "Yeah. Wait, how'd you know that?"

The two cops exchanged a glance. "Let me see some ID," Abbot snapped after a moment.

Reggie took his hands from behind his head and reached for his pocket.

"Slowly," Abbot said, drawing his gun.

The kneeling man dipped awkwardly into his front pocket and pulled out a battered wallet, passing it to Hispanic Hardy, who flipped it open to study the driver's license there. Aryan Abbot moved over to join him, Reggie craning his neck to follow them.

Silence settled over the small porch, no one moving but Ben as he shifted his focus back and forth between the three men in front of him. With each shift, he lost traction with what was happening; grew more and more suspicious of the black man kneeling on the ground. Why were either of them here? Why was the man being arrested? What had he done, and to whom? What was he even doing in the neighborhood?

As Ben stared at the man, his eyes seemed to sink into his skull, his brow lowering and his jaw jutting out as his worried grin turned into a sneer. He looked dangerous. He looked like a criminal. Ben glared at him.

Abbot's voice broke the silence. "Put your hands behind your back for me, please."

At this, Reggie seemed to deflate. "Ah shit. No, man, c'mon ..."

"Do it now!"

"Man, I've been out for five years. I didn't *do* anything."

The hammer of the policeman's gun clicked into place. "I'm not going to ask you again."

Letting out a great sigh, Reggie complied, but he didn't stop talking as Hardy snapped handcuffs on him. "You have to tell me what I did, don't you? That's the law? C'mon, what's this about?"

Abbot grabbed the front of his jacket and stood him up. "How about you see if you can guess?"

"Man, I wish I could! Let's just talk about this."

Abbot held up a hand. "Do you own a gun, Reggie?"

For the second time in less than a minute, Reggie seemed to deflate. "Oh… Oh no. No, no, no you ... you son of a bitch."

"So you do?"

Reggie said nothing.

"Yes? No?"

"No," Reggie spat. "I sold it. This morning."

"Interesting," Abbot replied. "You should tell us more about that. Come on."

The three moved away, seeming to have forgotten about Ben, but he watched as they walked down the stairs to the sidewalk, the black man stunned into submission.

The sound of the snow under his feet seemed to wake Reggie up, however, and he surged to life. "Wait, wait. Hold on. Cate!"

The two cops strained to hold him, their angry cries unheard by the struggling man. Amid the turmoil, Reggie's eyes found Ben's and his face brightened. "Hey man, you remember me, right? You're not that crazy. You can tell these guys I've been here for a while? You can tell them my daughter is inside. Please!" He stopped fighting and turned to face Hispanic Hardy. "Please, he'll tell you. My daughter's in there ... "

Abbot and Hardy turned to face Ben, and he found himself confronted by a trio of stares, their gazes mocking him, his washed-out memories tormenting him with the knowledge that he had lost everything he ever knew and any sense of where he belonged. At the same time, they demanded answers that he didn't have. Embarrassed, he gave a slight shrug and turned away.

"Fuck you!" the black man bellowed. "You crazy son of a bitch!" Ben did not turn to look but heard the man continue behind him, his voice soft and earnest now. "Seriously, my girl's in there. She's five years old. I'm all she's got. Please ... "

"Her mother ... ?" the taller cop asked softly.

"Gone," Reggie replied. "Minneapolis, last I heard, but I'm not even sure of that."

A moment passed, and then tall cop spoke again, this time more firmly. "I got him. You take care of the girl." Footsteps crunched back toward Ben, and he turned to see the fat cop walking toward him again, the other leading the handcuffed man toward the squad car.

The fat cop shot an odd look at Ben as he passed, and Ben tore his eyes away from the scene of an innocent man being loaded into a police car, looking instead in the front window of the house, where a small blonde girl stood, pressed against the glass, her cries muffled by the thin barrier of glass between them and the thin music still streaming from inside the house.

The fat cop had stopped at the door and now turned back toward the car. "Hey, what do I do with her?"

"Stay with her for now," the tall cop called back. "I'll call Child Services to come and get her."

At this, the black man's head snapped up in surprise, but the door had already been slammed shut on him, and his thrashing struggle didn't do more than make Ben uncomfortable again. He turned away as the man threw himself against the squad car door to no effect, shouting curses that Ben couldn't hear.

Instead, he stared back in the front window, his gaze drawn again to the blonde girl, her image magnified by the frosted glass between them. Her worry radiated through the window, penetrating Ben, but though the feelings permeated him, he could not connect them to any memories, nor could he offer apologies or explanations or even begin to make amends.

And so he focused on the girl, drowning himself in her tears, allowing them to wash over him like Lethe until he was merely numb from the cold, gawking at a police car as it pulled away from the curb, its captive slumped against the window, gaze fixed on the house.

Ben wiped his eyes, surprised to find some tears still there, and wondered where they had come from; or whether they were simply a product of the wind. He looked around the unfamiliar porch and his gaze found its way up to the sky, where a rust-red moon stared down at him balefully. Ben yawned, jaw cracking, then walked slowly across the lawn to his front door, wondering whether he would find his wife and son there waiting for him. In the distance, he could hear the telephone ringing.

> **Author's Note:** Well, it's about time. I find it fascinating that Ben has finally crawled out of his delirium—escaped his own head long enough to actually pass on some information.

Particularly ironic (and timely), since it's the last chance he'll have to do so. Of course, he's done a predictably good job of confusing things. Lest you hit blank pages before reality sinks in, here's the gist:

You've probably gathered that Ben got his son (Sam, Puck—whatever you're comfortable with) a job at the factory where he worked. A low-level office job, to be sure, but one that Puck had seemed perfectly suited for, his dexterity and his knack for repetitive motion having manifested itself at Ino's barbershop so many years earlier.

You may also have gathered—though Ben was less than clear on this point—that the company's payroll had gone missing on Ben's watch, and that files that would have helped locate it had disappeared through Puck's fast fingers.

Ben's decision to report the crime, and his son as a suspect, had not been a rash one—he'd examined the situation, explored the possibilities thoroughly, and had found himself unable to find any other logical solution, and so he had made his decision, confident that if his son was innocent, it would be proven out in any subsequent investigation. He hadn't anticipated the degree to which that the process would break Sam, or their relationship, or his marriage.

By the time Sam was exonerated it was far too late. He had left the company and his father's house, not realizing how difficult it would be to find another job or to survive on his own. By the time the files (and, shortly thereafter, the money) were located some weeks later, Sam was long gone and Ben and Elle had begun their downward spiral.

And so they were left mired in mistrust, loneliness, antipathy, homelessness, strife, guilt, and regret. All because of one bad decision—one refusal to take the time to ask the right questions. All in a time of tuning.

Like father like son.

And now that this memory has finally seen the light, we can consider Ben spent. He has purged himself of memories—we have seen the history of his relationship with Elle, the story of the birth, alienation, betrayal, and banishment of his son, and listened to his theories of life, love, and relationships.

Now, he has nothing left to bind him to reality or to this earth. He has done everything he can for us. And his contributions will not go unrecognized. When he gets home, he'll be pleasantly surprised to find a bottle of bourbon standing on his stoop—enough to purge the foul taste of Elle's last few years from his memory for a little while longer. Or forever, should he pair it with the various painkillers in his medicine cabinet. He's earned that choice. He deserves that peace.

That's not to suggest that he's ready to die. Suffice it to say that he'll be able to untether himself at last. Tonight or tomorrow or a week from now, he'll drift into a dangerous channel and that will be the end—he and Elle will finally be reunited. For us, though, he's no longer worth watching—this story doesn't need him anymore.

Tomorrow, perhaps he'll open the paper and read of a young woman being attacked at the Cultural Center and another gunned down on the cold Chicago streets and no names will spring to his lips. He will not even have enough memory left to worry about Elle or Allison. He won't recognize the names of Cort and Spider. He'll feel an odd sense of remorse then turn the page to read a story about Kosovo or the Chicago Bulls.

And so let's turn the page on him as well. He's played his part, and he won't notice the time passing. I would guess that he's even stopped wondering who's going to die.

Spider

Eclipse in 4 hours

Author's Note: Before we go any further, I should make a confession: I haven't been completely honest.

In life, there is a tendency to see things in absolutes. To say that this politician is selfless and moral, while that one is power-hungry and corrupt. That Democracy is good and Communism is evil—or vice versa. Faced with a difficult choice, there's an innate need to label one decision as right and the other wrong.

But that's an oversimplification, and one that I take issue with, even as I'm guilty of it myself.

How can we pretend to fairly judge someone's actions, however heinous they may seem, without knowing the full context—the surrounding history and extenuating circumstances? How can we play arbiter without learning what prompted the decision or give a thumbs-up or down before we've seen its impact? I don't mean to imply that it's impossible to toss off a casual "well, sometimes good people do bad things" (or its far more fascinating B-side.) I'm just suggesting that it may be narrow-minded to guess whether this "good" person did something noble or wicked before you've seen how it plays out. Let us not attempt to estimate the beauty of the Sistine Chapel by studying the right thumbnail of God. Good people doing bad things, bad people doing good things—ultimately, it all comes out in the flood.

Here's the point: people do things. Sometimes they turn out well, sometimes not. Sometimes, even when the motive is selfish, the benefit is greater than the cost. Sometimes, the bad thing that the bad person did has a grander, more important purpose. Sometimes, it's best to simply watch as events transpire and save your judgments for the afterparty.

Take Spider, for example.

Considering the man as I've shown him, you could say that his is a story of redemption. The flawed man who overcame the odds and reshaped himself as a champion. But that's a shallow and clichéd version of the truth. Spider almost certainly had moments of generosity during his dark days, and I can promise that he has not been without sin since his deliverance. From our vantage point, his life consists of two books—the evil years and the good years. But holding his story to those standards means ripping out pages from each, to the point that reading them would be an exercise in frustration—an incomplete film that jumps frames every time it hits something that doesn't fit its context.

Just know: for better or worse, there are pieces of this story—of all of these stories—that you haven't seen. You haven't seen them because that's not what I've chosen to show you. Please try not to pass judgment until the story has played itself out and you can see the results. Then we'll decide whether it was worth it—whether the story we've crafted is the one we'd hoped for and whether the choices were ultimately good or bad. Until then, try to forgive me when we must jump frames.

#

"Goddamn it!" Spider slammed a fist down on the bar, drawing a cold stare from the bartender and momentary glimmers of interest from the few patrons scattered throughout the room.

"Calm down." Jamie looked at him calmly from the barstool beside his, exhaustion already etched onto her face after only four hours on shift. "You're not impressing anybody, just making enemies." She lowered her voice. "I told you: they count our drawer after every shift. Sometimes they even swap out in the middle to make sure we're not skimming. No way am I dipping in and losing my job for this."

"And I told you," Spider began, his voice rising again until he noticed the stares finding their way back toward him. "And I told you," he began again, his voice hushed this time, "that I'd find a way to have it back tonight. I swear: no one's going to know."

"Uh-huh," she replied, unimpressed. "We have a customer fifteen feet away and two other employees in the place—all of them staring at us now because you're making a scene, but they're not going to notice me grabbing fifty bucks out of the register."

Spider turned to look. "That creepy motherfucker? That's the judgmental asshole that was on the train with us. You don't owe him shit."

"Why, what'd he say?"

Spider paused. "Nothing much," he replied awkwardly. "It's the way he looks at me. At us ... "

Jamie rolled her eyes. "You're amazing, you know that?"

"Come on, babe. Forget that guy, the store closes in half an hour. You want Cate to have a good birthday, don't you?"

"Yeah, I do," she replied. "But I also want to keep my job. I'm not sure me getting shitcanned guarantees your baby girl the perfect birthday." She sighed. "I'm sorry, Reg, really. I know you think this is important, but there's nothing I can do. I thought you said you were going to sell your ... "

Spider cut her off with a wave of his hand. "I was. I just ... haven't collected yet. And it's not a sure thing anyway. I'm not even sure it's a good idea ... "

He swirled ice around the bottom of his glass, its path smoothed by the quarter inch of Coke still remaining. He could feel her eyes on him but refused to look up at her, instead tipping the last few drops of soda into his mouth and setting the glass back down harder than necessary.

"Here," she said, standing up. "Take this." She pulled a battered bill out of the pocket of her jeans and held it out to him. "I can buy dinner with my tips later on."

He took the bill skeptically and flattened it on the bar, then turned on her. "Jesus, Jamie! Ten bucks? That's barely enough for the train."

She shrugged. "That's what I got. Take it or leave it. I'm done thinking about this. Tell Catey 'Happy Birthday' for me."

She sauntered away, pushing through the swinging door to the back room. Spider watched her go, clutching the crumpled ten and feeling deflated. He stuffed the bill into his front pocket and stood, his barstool scraping loudly on the linoleum floor, drawing more curious stares. He made eye contact with the man from the train and sneered at him. "See anything interesting?" he called. "Why don't you take a picture?" He'd expected to see the little man's eyes shoot back to whatever he was working on. He'd expected him to be cowed, as he had been the first time, and was surprised when he held Spider's gaze, his lips pressed tightly together. The look made Spider feel like he was on the inside of the monkey cages at the zoo. It gave him the chills, and he broke his gaze away. "Whatever," he muttered. "Mind your own business and stay out of mine, asshole."

He walked slowly over to the front door and stood staring at it for a moment, wanting to turn and look again to see whether the creepy dude was still watching him, but he stepped out through the door instead, wondering where he could possibly find the money for a reasonable birthday present and feeling the man's eyes on him even after he was blocks down the street.

#

Spider shouldered his way down the crowded sidewalk, the stream of bodies all seeming to press in the opposite direction as though everyone in the city wanted to be in whatever spot he'd just stepped out of or walk in his footsteps awhile. He wished that he could take some of them up on it, let them feel what it was like to struggle for every dollar to where you had to take your girlfriend's dinner money to afford the train, all while fighting the urge to pick a pocket or snatch a purse, knock a businessman down or an old woman into the slush at the side of the street, knowing that it'd be the end of your life if you ever gave in to the urge and got caught.

He stepped into the mouth of an alley for a moment to escape the crush, tracking success stories as they flowed past him and casually categorizing them by their pants: Khaki meant low-level—data entry or maybe a temp. Light gray was for management, but not too high up. Probably wearing a short sleeve button up under the winter coat. Black meant executive, except when it meant waiter, but it wasn't hard to tell one from the other just by looking at hairstyle. Jeans were surprisingly hard to call. The owner could be anything from billionaire to broke. Spider couldn't tell the difference between high-end and bargain-basement denim and didn't care to. Dark gray was almost as tough. People who wore dark gray slacks were usually pretending to be someone they weren't.

He looked down at his own pants, black jeans worn at the thigh just enough to show the residual dirt he could never seem to get out. No mistaking the message they put out. He let out a sigh, then stepped back out into the throng, wondering what he could turn ten dollars into that would approximate a present, if he even made it to the store before it closed.

Lost in his thoughts, it took him several moments to notice that the crowd was dodging around him, throwing dirty looks in his direction as they did so. Finally, as he reached a pocket of the sidewalk empty of people, he felt hands plucking lightly at his jacket and heard the murmured "W ... wait. Please."

Spider stopped abruptly, and the man who had been pacing him nearly walked up his back.

"Jesus," Spider said, startled partly from the near impact and partly from at the shock of seeing the man standing before him. If it hadn't been for the stutter and the heavy patchwork coat, Spider might not have recognized him. The grime had been scrubbed from his cheeks and he was wearing a light gray suit ("middle management," Spider thought) that looked out of place on his thin, stooped shoulders.

After a moment's discombobulation, Spider recovered, pulling the man forward by the elbow until they reached another alley, stepping into its nominal privacy.

"You scared the shit out of me," he hissed, quickly scanning the alley to ensure that they were alone. "I wasn't sure I'd even see you again." He hesitated a moment then thought of his daughter at a Richie-Rich birthday party in the suburbs and the decision was made. "Did you get the money?" he asked, gritting his teeth.

The man started to speak but then nodded instead, pulling a dirty fistful of bills from the pocket of his slacks.

"All right, all right," Spider muttered. "You don't have to flash the world." His eyes roamed the empty alley again and then darted to the street where the occasional businessman or woman popped into view and then out again just as quickly, showing no apparent interest in the transaction taking place just far enough away to fall completely outside of their world.

He rifled quickly through the bills and then stuffed them into the pocket of his jeans and reached into his jacket for the chamois-wrapped bundle. Now he could actually feel the eyes on him: curious, studious; judging him, evaluating him and wondering exactly what he was going to do, and he entertained the brief, crazy idea that the rest of his life hung on this one moment. He met the eyes of the man standing in front of him and saw the need that he felt reflected back at him a thousand-fold. They might have different desires but they were clearly living in the same story. Spider swallowed and then thrust the bundle out to the ragged man, his station in life not at all disguised by his suit, and watched it disappear into one of the many pockets of the man's coat.

"It's not loaded, so don't get any ideas about taking your money back off of me when I turn my back," he said, glowering at the man, second thoughts gnawing anxiously at him, his stomach rolling with trepidation and foreboding. But the shock evident in the man's wide, innocent eyes told him that he was in no danger. Probably no one else was, either. Most likely the poor guy just wanted some protection.

"So, okay then," he muttered. "There's a box of ammo in there too, but there's not much left. Sorry 'bout that." The two regarded each other for a moment, and then the man nodded at him and stepped backward into the sidewalk traffic.

"Hey!" Spider called after him. "You be careful with that!" But the man had disappeared, borne away by the crowd, his cheap suit the perfect camouflage for the terrain.

"Shit," Spider said to himself. Then, "I wonder what he wants it for? God help us."

He let out a sigh and slipped into the crowd himself, wondering idly how long it would take him to decide whether what he'd just done had been a good of bad decision.

#

At five minutes until six, he was the only person rushing into FAO as the few other customers finished up their purchases and stepped out. He didn't waste time but stalked through the aisles as quickly as possible, his eyes sweeping the crowded shelves. He made a full circuit of the store without interruption before turning a corner and coming face to face with two red-poloed employees, one looking nervous and the other suspicious, disguising it with an "Excuse me, but we're closing" smile.

"Can I help you find something?" Suspicious said, breaking the stalemate.

"Yeah," Spider replied. "You can. I need to get a ... a Furby?" He flushed slightly, the request feeling ridiculous, jarring at his history in a way that left him flat-footed, but he rallied, glaring at the clerks as though daring them to call attention to his dirty jeans and bristling beard.

Nervous laughed. "You and everyone else." Spider's glare deepened, and the clerk's laugh squeaked a bit. "I just mean that we're sold out. We have been since a month before Christmas. There's a wait list."

"Wait list? What? Are you shitting me?" Spider watched as the two exchanged glances. "No, hold on. Never mind. Just give me a second. I'll find something else."

Suspicious opened his mouth to speak, but Spider's expression seemed to change his mind. "Of course," he said. "If you'd try to hurry, though, sir. We have to close in just a minute or two."

The "sir" sounded as though it didn't fully jibe with the clerk's perception of Spider and only merited inclusion for safety's sake, but the man was now gesturing down the aisle and toward the front of the store where two security guards were in the process of locking up, and so Spider nodded, muttering insincere thanks.

He turned to survey the store, questing for anything that would make a reasonable present, no longer concerned about price or propriety, only speed. He paced through rows of dolls and stacks of board games, but nothing felt even remotely right. Until he saw a scale model of a motorcycle; a Harley no less. Spider picked up the box and turned it over in his hands, smiling, then strode quickly to the front of the store.

The nervous clerk took the box from him, scanned it, and murmured, "seventy-four sixty-three, please."

Spider winced. He'd neglected to look at the price, but at this point there was no turning back. He pulled four of the five twenties out of his wallet and passed them over to the clerk, who still hadn't made eye contact. "Hard to believe it's so expensive, huh?" he said, smiling in the hopes that it would put the kid at ease. "I bought my first bike for two hundred. It was a piece of shit, but still ... "

"Don't worry, sir," the kid replied. "Your son will love it."

Spider stared at him a moment then let his eyes drop to the cycle. "It's for my daughter," he muttered, and then sighed, wondering what the hell he was thinking. A model motorcycle for a five-year-old girl? But she did love to ride with him, despite her mother's paranoid demands that he keep her off the bike. His eyes found their way to a stack of Barbie dolls beside the register, and on a whim he snagged one: a stick-thin black girl with a rack that, in real life, would have had her swimming in free drinks. He stared at it for a moment and then held it up. "You got any of these with blonde hair?" he asked.

The clerk stared at him. "Um ... most of them have blonde hair," he began.

"No, man," Spider interrupted. "Black girls with blonde hair." He saw the clerk's expression and shook his head. "Never mind. I'll take this, too," he said, passing over his last twenty.

#

Thirty minutes later, he stood in front of a large brick house, new construction on a block of older, weathered bungalows, clutching a plastic shopping bag and running through his options. Through the thinly curtained front window he could just make out the interplay of shapes; the mix of shadow and motion and colored light that suggested a party. But the scale of the brick building intimidated him for some reason, stretching out to cover every available inch of the lot, jutting into the sky as if to say, "I need all the space I can get and I don't care what you think, I will have it."

Ordinarily, Spider did not think of himself as easily cowed. He'd been in situations in which he'd had legitimate reason to feel threatened. He'd been jumped, beaten until he could barely stand, and on the run from one thing or another for too much of his life.

For some reason, though, the parents of Cate's classmates at the private school that her grandfather had insisted on (and, to be fair, continued to pay for) were more daunting than any of it. To this point, he had avoided coming face-to-face with any of them, dropping Cate off at school early, before anyone but the half-blind Mexican janitor had arrived; begging off parent-teacher meetings and making apologies when any social opportunities presented themselves. Staring at the house, he wished he'd decided to maintain that spotless record. When he'd gotten the call inviting Cate to a party for all the winter birthdays in the class, he'd recognized it as the only way his daughter would get a legitimate party at all. What had possessed him, on the spur of the moment, to attend the damn thing himself, however, was another question entirely.

He crossed the street and grudgingly picked his way up the path to the small porch, where a glowing space heater made his time standing in front of the large, intimidating door somewhat warmer, if no less awkward.

After several moments of indecision, he pressed the bell, letting the deep, resonant chimes from inside remind him that the people who lived here were out of his class, even if his daughter had somehow measured up.

On the phone, the woman planning the party, Janine Morgan ("Call me Ginny," he remembered), had sounded warm and friendly, laughing when he suggested that he probably shouldn't come, that he might not fit in with the crowd. She'd sounded sincere, and he'd hung up believing that she truly wanted them, both of them, in her home. That she was honestly disappointed that he was sending Cate on her own. That feeling lasted right up until she answered the door.

The look on the woman's face, however carefully masked, made him take a half step back, wishing he'd given himself time to get cleaned up—at least changed his jeans or trimmed his beard that had a tendency to twist itself off in every direction like an overused paintbrush. Instead, he tugged ineffectively at the front of his jacket with one hand, smiling nervously as he waited for her to break the awkward silence.

"Can I help you?"

It wasn't what he had expected, and the question threw him, perhaps more than it should have.

"Um, yeah," he muttered. Then, a bit more solidly, "Yeah, I'm here for the party?"

She didn't move from the doorway, but merely waited for him to go on, as though his first attempt had made so little sense that he would have to begin again. She looked as though she couldn't understand why he hadn't just gone around to the servant's entrance. With effort, he swallowed his indignation.

"I ... I'm Reggie," he explained, barely stopping himself from saying "Spider" in his anxiety. "Cate's dad?"

Now the woman reacted with something closer to friendliness, a smile emerging—looking a little forced, but there all the same. "Of course! I'm so sorry, I didn't expect ... " Her eyes travelled from his scuffed motorcycle boots to the bristle of his beard and back again, and her words trailed off, momentarily, before she rallied, smiling falsely. "That is, I didn't see you when you dropped Cate off and I didn't realize that you were coming back so soon. Please, come in."

Spider nodded, flashed a quick, just as phony smile back, and followed her through the front door.

Inside the house, things only got worse. Spider stood awkwardly in the front hall, his boots leaking dirty water and balls of icy slush onto the polished floorboards.

"Can I take your coat?" Ginny was saying.

"Um, no. No thanks," he replied, adding "I might duck out for a smoke in just a second. Probably better to hold on to it." Figuring that sounded better than "I don't remember what shirt I'm wearing, and I can't promise that it doesn't have any holes. Or that it does have sleeves, for that matter."

"If there are presents for the birthday kids," she said, gesturing at his bag, "you can leave them on the gift table. We're all in the downstairs den playing Pin the Tail on the Donkey."

Spider stared at the table laden with brightly wrapped boxes and then down at his plastic bag and the two small, unwrapped packages it contained. "Yeah, okay," he said. "Hey, could you send Cate up for a second?"

She blinked at him. "Oh," she said with forced brightness. "Of course." Her eyes made a circuit of the room, and Spider imagined her doing a quick assessment of the various knickknacks on the shelves and end tables, calculating value versus weight and trying to determine how much he could steal in the time it took her to locate his daughter.

"I'll just run downstairs and find her," she was saying. "It won't take more than a few seconds, okay?"

Spider nodded.

"Okay then," she repeated, smiling widely, though Spider could see panic in her eyes. She stared at him a moment longer and then turned quickly on her high heels and disappeared through a convenient doorway.

Spider let out a breath he hadn't realized he'd been holding and slumped a bit, suddenly exhausted. The air inside the house seemed to have gotten stuffier in the four minutes he'd been inside, and the weight of the gift bag in his hand dragged at his shoulder. He hefted it, glancing inside, half-heartedly hoping that the toy store clerks had gift-wrapped his purchases and he'd simply failed to notice. No such luck.

Looking at the side table packed with brightly wrapped boxes only made his mood sink further. *If you've got presents for the birthday kids*, Ginny had said. Kids plural. Was he supposed to have brought gifts for all of them, not just his own daughter?

He wandered over to the table and sifted idly through the boxes stacked there. Sure enough, there were five or six with Cate's name on them from the various parents who were, even now, downstairs sticking pins into an ass's ass. Staring at the gifts, Spider felt anger building in him and, for a moment, he considered moving the charity gifts for his daughter from the table to the trash. Hadn't he spent almost a hundred dollars on the girl? Shouldn't that be enough? And how dare they try to compensate for him, presuming that he couldn't give his child a birthday party on his own?

A moment later the feeling had passed. He let the anger drain out of him, clutching the table with both hands, the plastic gift bag still curled into his right. But now he felt eyes on him. He felt watched.

He turned, casually, as though the motion were part of a larger goal; to go downstairs to check on Cate, perhaps, or to see if he couldn't be the best donkey-tail pinner in the house. In doing so, he let his eyes explore the room. They quickly found their way to the stairway leading to the second floor. The posture of the man standing halfway up then stairs, leaning on the railing with one hand, marked him instantly as the owner of the house just as surely as his rigid side part and brightly colored sweater marked him as an asshole. Probably a Sean or a Kurt.

Spider offered him a cautious nod and received a curt (or possibly a Kurt) one in return; a nod that said, "I'm not racist, and I'm not accusing you of anything, but I'm going to stand right here until you leave my house."

The subtext of that nod brought Spider's anger boiling back to the surface, and he was about to cross the room to ask Kurt just what his problem was when the basement door swung back open and Cate emerged like a sprung jack-in-the-box. She took a second at the top of the stairs to locate him and then exploded into his legs, spewing excited stories about games and cake and something called "Pokèmon."

Still feeling the eyes on him, Spider stooped to awkwardly pat her on the head (*like a dog,* he thought. *Wonder what these holiers will whisper to each other about that after we've left?*) He snorted and then knelt beside his daughter to give her a proper hug. After a moment, he pulled away, holding her at arm's length to look into her eyes, which were shining with five-year-old enthusiasm.

"Are you having fun, Sweets?" Spider asked stupidly.

She nodded, her young eyes telling him that of course she was having fun.

"I got you a present," he continued. "Well two, actually—"

But she cut him off, throwing herself into his arms and hugging him fiercely. "Thank you!" she squealed. "I love you, daddy!"

The eyes fixed on Spider were growing in number. He could feel it. He straightened.

"Well my ... goodness," he managed, the words feeling odd and phony. Not him. But he pressed on. "Here. At least look and see what it is ... "

He reached into the bag and pulled out the model Harley, passing it to her with a sheepish, *I-have-no-idea-if-you'll-like-this-and-I-can't-believe-I didn't-have-them-wrap-it-but-it's-what-I've-got* grin.

As he watched her turn it over in her hands, his heart caught in his throat. Finally he blurted, "It's the same model as ... Hey, Sweetie, if you don't like it we can—"

But again she interrupted him. "It looks like the one I can't tell momma I get to ride on," she said, her voice filled with wonder. "It looks like ours!" She hugged the bike to her chest and then turned, bolting for the basement door. "I have to show everyone!" she cried before disappearing down the stairs.

Spider sat on his heels, stunned, his fingers still wrapped around the Barbie box, ready to pull it out in the event she'd hated the bike. Gradually, he allowed his somewhat sheepish gaze to creep up to meet that of the parents who had come up to observe the commotion. He had expected to find amusement in their eyes and was not disappointed. However, he had not anticipated the looks of understanding and commiseration and possibly even ... respect? They nodded smiles at him as they drifted back downstairs to the party, their shared status as parents apparently enough to overcome their disparate socio-economic (not to mention racial and criminal) status, at least for a night.

Ginny was the last to leave, smiling what looked like an honest smile at him. "Are you sure you won't come downstairs with us?" she asked. "There's cake ... "

Spider smiled. "Maybe in a while," he said. "After all of that, I need a smoke. But I'll come down after, I swear."

She smiled at him again as he set the FAO bag on the gift table. Let some other kid have the Barbie. Maybe she could wash their pink Corvettes or clean their Malibu mansions. He smirked, then shook his head and headed for the door.

He was surprised to find that he was somewhat ashamed of himself, if not for the way that he'd acted, then for the expectations he'd created for the evening. He'd anticipated that the parents of his daughter's classmates would be judgmental, disdainful, and bigoted. He was almost shocked that they'd treated him kindly. It just went to show that you could never be sure what to expect, even when you were sure you had someone pegged.

He crossed to the door, the still-smiling Ginny trailing behind him, and stepped out onto the porch, where he was greeted by a sharp gust of wind and the rust-colored beginnings of an eclipse. Eyes on the sky, he retrieved his cigarettes from his jacket pocket and tapped one into his fingers. He was just lighting up and thinking how unfair he'd been to these people who had been nice enough to throw his daughter a party when he heard the front door's lock turn behind him and Ginny's high heels clicking away toward the basement door. He stared at the door, stunned, and wondered idly how he was expected to get back into the house before realizing that he wasn't.

Anger surged through him, threatening to boil over and spill into the night, where it would have caused who knows what kind of chaos. But the chill of the wind dulled his edge, cooled his fire, and he found himself filled instead by a grudging forgiveness of the small-minded, large-pocketed families who'd taken his Cate under a cumulative wing that he himself could never fit beneath. *Shit,* he thought, flicking a glowing ember into a drift of snow and relishing the small, pained sizzle it made on contact, *maybe I should count myself lucky that they didn't think I was trying to break in and have me thrown in jail.* That, at least, was one tragic end he had managed to avoid. Best to thank God for small favors. To count himself lucky and wait for Cate to finish with the party and then take her home. Suddenly, Spider couldn't wait to get back to a place where he actually felt like he belonged.

#

The back seat of the squad car felt nauseatingly familiar. Spider sat slumped, leaning against the door to keep the handcuffs from biting into his wrists, which were crossed awkwardly behind his back. Despite the pain, he could feel his rage draining away, replaced by trepidation and despondency. The taller of the two cops sat in the front seat, alternating squawks with the radio as he called in Spider's arrest. Over the bursts of static, Spider could just make out the words "suspect," "witnesses," "resisting," and "apprehended."

"Hey man," he broke in. "I wasn't resisting. Don't say that ... " But the cop ignored him. He shot a glance over at the house, where the fat cop stood in the doorway talking to Ginny. Behind her, framed by the doorway and visible through the curtained window, Spider could see the rest of the parents, their curious stares biting into him more deeply than the cold metal of the handcuffs. He could no longer pick Cate out through the window, which he was grateful for, both to spare her the scene and to spare himself the reminder of how much he'd let her down. He dragged his eyes away from the house and back to the tall cop's neck, willing himself to hate the man, and surprised to find that he couldn't.

Just as the thought went through his head, the cop put down the radio handset and, as though he could feel Spider's eyes on him, twisted in his seat, making eye contact for the first time. Several moments passed as the two men stared at each other until finally the cop spoke.

"What?" he said simply.

"Hey," Spider replied, his voice softened by the helplessness of the situation. "Hey man, I just want to know what's going on."

The cop snorted, but Spider continued. "I know you don't believe me, and there's nothing I can do about that. But I swear I don't know what happened or what I'm supposed to have done. I just want to be sure that my daughter's going to be okay. I just want to ask that woman if Cate can spend the night here until we can get all this figured out and I can come back and get her. Please, just don't call Child Services right away. You do that and I'll never get her back." He was careful to omit his worry that, if they'd found his gun and somehow already traced it back to him, that possession alone could cause him some serious problems. While he didn't really believe that the fragile, stuttering homeless guy who'd bought the piece off of him could have done anything stupid with it, if he'd even gotten picked up and the gun had been found on him ... that was trouble enough.

"Honestly," the cop was saying, "I don't think where your daughter spends the night is going to be your biggest problem." He turned away as the passenger door opened and the fat cop eased himself into the passenger's seat.

"All set?" the tall cop asked.

Fatty nodded. "Till tomorrow. Then a shitload of paperwork."

"Hey," Spider insisted, his eyes fixed once more on the tall cop's neck. "Hey, hold on. What do you mean?"

The tall cop had already shifted the car into gear, but he slammed it back into park and swiveled in his seat to stare through the plexiglass partition. "We found your gun, Reggie," he said.

Spider sighed. "Yeah. I know. I mean, I figured. I should have just turned it in, I guess, instead of selling it, but ... "

"We found it at the scene of a crime."

Spider stopped. He could feel both cops' eyes on him, the tall one's look stern, the fat one's closer to pitying. The pity scared him more than anything so far. "What crime? What did that fucker do?" Neither cop responded immediately, so he pressed on. "Whatever it was, it wasn't me. I didn't do it. I've been here all night!" he added desperately, cringing as the obviousness of the lie rang in his ears.

The tall cop hadn't stopped looking at him throughout his speech. He seemed to be weighing his options; trying to decide which way to go. After a moment, he spoke again. "Did you know a girl named Jamie Hawkins?"

Spider felt his insides clench. "What do you mean did I?" he murmured. The phrase "What happened to her?" sat heavily on his tongue, but he could find no point in saying it. He already knew the answer.

The tall cop watched him a few seconds more then turned to his partner. "I think you can read him his rights now," he said, and shifted the car back into gear, pulling away from the curb.

As the fat cop's voice started in on the Miranda warning Spider stared dumbly out the window, watching as the house slid slowly away behind him. Ben was still standing on the porch, looking around as though unsure where he was supposed to go now that the drama of the evening seemed to be over. As Spider watched, he stepped delicately down the stairs and wandered back toward his own home. On the way, he passed another man that Spider hadn't noticed. Small and lean and stunningly familiar, wearing a long gray coat, the light from the streetlights reflecting off of his circular glasses—two full moons obscuring his eyes, cut through by the flashing red of the squad car's lights.

The man, who had been watching Ben make his way home, turned to face Spider and gave a small wave. Then, to Spider's astonishment, he formed a gun with his finger and thumb and mimed two shots in Spider's direction. As the car started to pull away, he pulled a small notebook from his coat pocket and began to write in it, his gaze flicking back and forth between the car and whatever he was writing. Spider twisted in his seat to stare out the back window, but as the distance between them grew greater, the man seemed to disappear into the night.

One of the first things Spider had done after he had first gotten out of prison was to get a new tattoo. His first tattoo as a newly free man had been simple: a necklace of gothic letters that ran across his collarbone spelling out his new agenda: Dream Big.

Finding out that he had a daughter and having her put into his care had only amplified those dreams, and whether he'd been able to accomplish what was necessary on a day-to-day basis or not, the dreams had never faded. Since that day he'd been proud to have a goal. Proud to be able to dream of a day when things would be better for him and for Cate. Now, as his hands went slowly numb from the pressure of the cuffs as he sat stunned and unfeeling in the back seat of a Chicago Police Department squad car, he was forced to admit that his big dreams had been nothing more than that—dreams. And now, thanks to the little fucking demon in the gray coat and the moon glasses, he could see no reason to ever dream again.

Author's Note: Technically, what just happened is impossible. There's no way, no matter how urgent the need, no matter how important the crime, that the Chicago Police Department could possibly trace a gun that fast, much less find the location of the owner, particularly when he's at a party with people he's never met in a neighborhood he's never been to.

First of all, owning a handgun is illegal inside the city limits unless you've been grandfathered in (and, let's be honest, the odds of them making an exception for a former gang member recently released from prison are slim). But even when someone has brought a gun into the city illegally, when it is found at the scene of a crime, they still have to bring it in, run a trace, dig up the information on the person who comes back as a result of that trace, and then go through the painstaking steps of tracking that person down. And that's if the gun has been legally sold from person to person.

So, yes. Basically, what has just happened is impossible.

But when confronted with the impossible, my job is to find a way to make it possible—whatever it takes. For example: what would it take to get a romantic rival to leave the object of your affection alone? Is it enough to have a conversation with that rival, laying out the reasons why you make a better match and hope that he comes around to your way of thinking? Or should you make your case to your shared love interest and hope that she finds you more appealing than the alternative? Or would it not be more effective to simply distract your adversary and then nudge him out of the way—a pretty girl, a few drinks, a convenient flight of stairs? You see my point.

Or consider the case of a father and daughter. What would it take to make an otherwise confident, self-assured man begin to doubt the love of his child enough that he is willing to drift back toward old habits in order to win the affection of a little girl whose love has never been in question. As it turns out, it wouldn't take all that much.

By the same token, sometimes the police need a helping hand—a nudge in the right direction, you might say. It's amazing how large an impact a simple phone call can have, particularly when it provides answers before they know they're looking for them. A simple statement of worry by a concerned citizen that an argument in the alley behind a bar ended with a woman screaming the name "Reggie" and what sounded like a gunshot. Or a telephone call warning that a neighbor's house is being broken into and a second call that drops an interesting name into the mix.

Little pieces add up, bit by bit. Ultimately, you find the right mix of ingredients and things start to come together. After that, it doesn't take much to finish things off.

Puck

Eclipse in 1 hour

There is a pace, now. A measure of time that allows the pock-pock of footsteps to find niches in the music of the street and nestle there. Life has a tempo again, and Puck has a new purpose. Cash in hand has made his life and his plans significantly easier. Though he'd been mostly sober for the past several months, it had been by necessity more than by choice. Now, cash in hand has allowed for some changes. His belly warm, Puck moves easily down the sidewalk, most of a fifth of Gilby's Dry Gin having chased away his anxiety and his butterfly ticks, at least for the time being. The slow-motion fuzz in his limbs feels comfortingly familiar, and although he knows that it is a temporary respite, he savors the release that it provides.

He waits for the light to change and then hops off the curb and crosses the street in a half dozen strides, marveling at the ease with which he can move, slightly in awe of himself and of the bouncing, floating sensation that steers him down the street.

When he'd left the old man—his father—Puck's pockets had been laden with troubles. Heavy with history and unwanted knowledge, with gratitude and with guilt. He'd stumbled down the front walk on feet that felt thick, shoulders hunched under some invisible load, the weight of his eyebrows pulling his face into a painful grimace. Heavy steps, heavy thoughts, heavy heart.

Now, only his coat feels heavy. Puck smiles softly to himself and pats his pocket, his fingers fluttering along the outline of the reassuring weight that means that his burden will soon be lightening. The last trade that has given him the power to put things right. To ensure that Jamie will finally be safe.

He turns the corner into his alley and, although he is expecting it this time, he cannot bite back the panic that buffets him when he sees his body double curled up as he'd left it, beside the heating grate, feigning designs on his nest. Unbidden, his lips shape the words, "Can't, can't ... can't lose it," and then he hurries down the alley, anxious to reclaim his home and uneasy at the thought of even the hastily assembled doppelganger occupying his space for a moment longer than is necessary.

When he reaches the imposter, however, he finds himself unable to go any further. He cannot bring himself to bend down and lay his hands on the cold pile of trash bags and newspaper, much less break it apart. Instead, he watches it lay motionless, defending his nest with single-minded purpose. He stares for so long and with such intensity that he begins to imagine that he can see the "body" breathing.

Puck shakes his head in scorn. "Sss ... stupid," he snorts, derision nudging him back to life. He kneels over the motionless form and rests a hand on the ball of newspaper that makes up its right shoulder, muttering "Time to disap ... pear, fff ... friend" as he pulls it apart.

But the body jerks away from his hands. "What the fuck are you doing?" it rasps in a voice thick with sleep.

Puck springs to his feet, pressing his back against the wall, a scream caught in his throat. As he watches, what Puck had taken for a pile of trash seems to contract in on itself, amoeba-like, reforming into a man built like a collection of bent wire and hard anger leaning against the wall across from him, his coat the shiny charcoal of plastic garbage bags, his face and hands hidden in shadows.

"Well?" the man rasps. "What do you want?"

Puck's tongue feels swollen, and he struggles to speak around it. "Y ... you. You're in m ... my spot," he manages to say.

The usurper's laugh reminds Puck of radio static. "Seems to me," he says, coughing punctuation—a semicolon—into the sentence; "It seems to me that this is not your spot anymore."

Puck fumbles with his thoughts like a pair of wet gloves, struggling to form rough expressions of anger and outrage. He searches for words that will convey his loss and that will explain to this thief exactly what he has stolen and why he must return it. But shot glasses full of assurance are quickly emptied, and Puck's tongue feels thick and heavy. He writes furious poems in his head but can vocalize only "Can't. Can'tcan't. Can't! Can'tloseit, loseitno ... nnno ... no ... "

"Cah! Cah! Cah!" the other man mocks. "Speak English, if you can. This is my spot now."

Words scatter and disappear, escaping Puck with each violent shake of his head.

"No?" the other man says. "Why not? What's the big deal? It's just a piece of wall ... "

Again Puck shakes his head, a thousand words at his lips. How to explain that this three-foot stretch of alley is so much more than that? That it provides him warmth and safety. That it gives him shelter and camouflage. That it is the only spot in the city that allows him to keep track of the time and temperature and simultaneously ensure that Jamie will pass by him every night. How can he explain that this is all the home he has? Impossible.

But somehow the usurper seems to see it in his eyes.

"It's important, isn't it?" he asks. "Why? It's not really secure or warm here. This spot doesn't give you any real protection—although that's closer ... So what is it?"

Puck's only answer is a bouncing series of nods. But the man's voice hardens. "Yeah? Well, tough shit. How bad do you want it and what do you have to trade?"

Puck's hand snakes into his jacket pocket to stroke the chamois-wrapped bundle, fingering the cold metal of the black man's gun. In his mind, he barks a sharp retort: "Get the fuck away from here. This is my home, my nest. Mine. And if you don't leave me alone, I will kill you." It sounded good in his head. The fact that there was no stutter making it even better. It would be so easy, but the idea of threatening the man makes Puck feel small, somehow.

Like young Sam in the barbershop not understanding the laughter. He leaves the gun bundled in his pocket.

"No. Nnn ... nothing," he says, defeated. "Sss ... sorry." The word seems to draw all the air from his lungs. He turns to go.

"Hold on there, guy," the gravel voice says. "What about that coat?"

Puck stops, half-turning to face his usurper. "Mm ... my coat?"

"Yeah. Looks warm," the man replies. "I'll swap you that coat for this cherry spot. That's a deal and a half."

Despite his hurry, it takes Puck several minutes to take off his coat. It keeps catching on him. Not because loose threads snag the buttons of his shirt or because his hands get caught in the lining—he's stitched it together too well for that. It is the coat as a whole that keeps catching on Puck's memories. It has been with him for his entire life—his real life, at any rate. It has kept him safe for years. It feels as much like home as anything ever has. But he manages to peel it off, nonetheless. There are times when the past must be eliminated.

"Everything depends on right now," he reminds himself. "The present is fleeting. The past you can never get back. The future is not yours to bargain with."

He lets the coat slide down his arms, dropping it into a depressed pile on the ground. He wonders if this is how snakes feel—their skin shedding off of them as they think "well, that was anticlimactic ... " He stands numbly beside the coat, feeling newly amputated. As though there's an itch he can't scratch because the itchy patch doesn't belong to him anymore. Phantom limb syndrome. The coat looks wrong, lying on the dirty pavement, so Puck scoops it up, clutching it in his hands for a few final moments. Finally, he pulls the chamois bundle from the pocket and extends his arm, offering the coat to the other man, who has risen to his feet.

Seeming to recognize the importance of the moment, the usurper accepts the offering with solemnity. And not until the coat has left his grasp does Puck feel the cold of the night fall upon him, stealing the warmth from his blood and the breath from his body.

Puck feels himself contract under the weight of the chill, too dizzy to notice the world going on around him, to hear the muttered, "Nice doing business with you, Pucky-Puck. You won't live to regret it. Believe," as the stranger turns to leave. If Puck did notice these things, he would recognize them, and that would change everything, but he is too preoccupied with the cold to notice the man slip on a pair of thin glasses or the circles of reflected light that they create beneath the bill of the black cap that he wears. He does not smell the waft of floral perfume before it is carried away by the swirling wind. Instead, he staggers over to his nest, collapsing against the brick wall and slumping to the ground to lean against the restaurant grate, his body craving its onion-scented heat.

Somehow, even the warm air washing over him from the restaurant's duct feels insubstantial, and panicked thoughts begin to build within him, demanding to know why he is so cold; whether it was the overstuffed coat that kept him warm all this time and not his nest. Puck pulls his light gray suit coat tighter around himself, remembering the warmth of flannel and fleece and cashmere, of oven-heated air, of the summer sun, and of his mother's arms. He strokes the inside of his lapel compulsively, his mind turning the thin cotton into cashmere, the biting cold into security. Even as the memories toss in the waves of his mind, his eyes steal up to the clock across the way, waiting for the time as he wonders whether he has finally managed to catch up.

    10:09 p.m ... . 2 degrees ...

    Puck smiles to himself, his teeth automatically finding the grooves in his lower lip and coasting smoothly along them. Plenty of time. He settles back against the grate and its marginal warmth, puffing his chest up as a barrier to the chill as he waits. This time he will not fall asleep. This time he is ready.

    He can still sense the nearness of his dreams and of the demon. He can feel its evil eyes on him, but Puck has confidence now; he has a newfound sense of power, purchased from a gruff black man in a motorcycle jacket with money Puck had begged from the old man that his father had become.

    Puck unwraps the gun and holds it in his right hand, feeling the warmth that it brings to his entire body, even through the biting cold of the steel against his palm. He has never felt safer.

    Still, he can sense the demon watching him, waiting for him to make some mistake, and that gaze brings back some of Puck's chill.

He glances furtively around the alley, hoping to catch some slight movement in one of the shadows that will allow him to put his new protection to use. But there is only stillness among the trash bags and cardboard boxes and the occasional drift of snow at the mouth of the alley. Puck glances up again at the bank clock, and that's when he sees it: the large, baleful eye of the demon, blood red against the velvety black of the night sky, hanging just over the horizon and the jeweled lights of the sleeping city. Puck's eyes lock with that bloody, cycloptic orb, the moon reflecting degradation and disdain back at him from beneath its low black cap, and his bowels turn to water. Despite his best intentions, that world begins to spin around him, a drunk's carousel that he cannot seem to exit. His stomach rolls, the warmth that he so relished having turned into a strange but familiar sickness.

Finally, Puck can stand it no longer. He whips the pistol from his side and staggers to his feet, aiming right at the heart of the taunting, bloody eye. "L ... leave her ... alone," he whispers through cracked lips. "Or I'll kill you."

The deliverance of the threat saps the last of Puck's strength and he drops his arm, slumping back to the ground and cradling the gun to his chest as his eyes drift shut, confident that he has made his point. Jamie will be safe. The demon will have to find a new target. One without a protector willing to sacrifice everything. Puck smiles triumphantly.

He pulls the bottle of gin from the front pocket of his slacks and drains the last of it, savoring the burn that simultaneously warms him and quells the turmoil in his belly. Eyes closed, Puck smiles again, his face hard and stiff from the cold. He lets out a long, deep breath, feeling a strange calm settle over him.

Once again, Puck finds himself standing on the front lawn of the small off-white house, this time beside his father, watching out of the corner of his eye as the old man pats the air, molding and shaping the wind or looking for something that Puck still can't comprehend.

Just as before, his father gives up and disappears into the house, leaving Puck alone to continue on his own. And once again Puck takes up the hunt, searching first simply for the knowledge of what he is meant to be looking for and second for the something itself. Holding both of his hands before him, he pats the air, unanswered questions on his fingertips. He is mildly surprised to find that his hands are empty and wonders briefly where his gun has disappeared to; whether he is meant to be looking for a new protection or perhaps for the end of his quest. After a moment, however, he abandons the thought. Because he has begun to find ... something.

As his fingers shape the nothing in front of him, the world drops out of focus. Puck's heart, already dulled by the deep chill of winter and the heavy peace of sleep, slows further. His thoughts, so accustomed to dancing a tap dance to the variable rhythm of life, find a slipstream into the slow drift of a waltz. At this slower pace Puck can see so much more clearly. He begins to caress the air with greater determination, gradually coming to understand what he is actually looking for. He is looking for warmth in a time where there is none and in a place that will not allow it.

He is looking for safety, even as he realizes that he has willingly given it away.

He is looking for love, not realizing that even the idea is self-delusion.

Puck is looking for a home, even though he has long known what home entails and has chosen homelessness instead.

And suddenly, the wanting of these things is not enough. Life demands that he have them. If he can protect Jamie from his nest beside a dumpster in an abandoned alley, then he can imagine her safely in his father's house, the three of them creating the home that was never complete the first time around. It took losing his coat—his greatest source of protection—for him to realize it, but Puck is finally ready to stand up for himself; to the demon, to Jamie, and to his father. Warmed by the thought, he tries to open his eyes but finds to his horror that he cannot. Panicked, he jerks the gun up again, intending to shoot the moon, or the world, or himself if it will put everything right, but his arm will not move. He jumps to his feet but remains slumped on the ground. He cries out silently, even his spastic tongue betraying him with its stillness.

And that is when the truth sinks in. He has failed. Puck will not be able to protect Jamie from the demon or anything else. He feels his heart slowing further with every passing second, every " ... " on the clock tower that he can't open his eyes to see, and he knows that, somehow, he has been beaten. Lying helpless in a corner of a random alley, Puck cries tears that will not come, beating his fists against the walls of the prison that his body has become.

Author's Note: And this is where we leave him. Curled up among the boxes and trash, his face pressed against the cold metal of the heating duct of the Taqueria Mexican Restaurant, his left hand cradling his right, which now stiffly clutches nothing—as if whatever protection it held has been pried from his frozen grasp. Up close, you can see his raw, clean-shaven and wind-chapped cheeks, unaccustomed to the winter cold. Pull back just a bit, and what you notice most is his missing coat. He looks naked without it. He doesn't look like himself—doesn't belong here at all, now. He is an oxymoron, sprawled in the alley dust with dirty snow staining his thin, gray suit.

Take another few steps back and his humanity disappears, vanishing, as so many street people do, into the detritus of the alley. Just another pile of discarded clothes and empty packaging.

Three more steps back and he's gone, the world around his alley driving him from memory: the commotion from a bar down the street, the blood red moon now half-covered by the earth's shadow (or perhaps half-closed in a seductive wink). From here, you can read the hand-lettered sign that hangs in the window of the taqueria. "Closed January 19th through February 13th for renovations."

Puck is gone. And it's not because of Spider's gun, or the winter chill, or the distraction of a bloody moon (although that's closer). Even if his presence has permanently stained these pages, he lost his hold on the direction of the story—and it's the best thing that could have happened to him. His long battle with the world is over. Puck is gone. Make your peace and let's move on. He never really belonged here anyway.

Cort
Morning

Cort stood in line, impatience pushing him from one foot to the other and then back again, his eyes climbing the marble walls, taking in the shafts of late-day sun that found their way through the tall, barred windows and following them back down to the tiled floor, where he studied the heels of the man standing in front of him: shiny black leather under olive slacks.

He shifted his weight again, smoothing the small scrap of paper against his chest, the sweat there smearing the ink and blurring the writing. He grimaced.

"Next?"

The line moved forward and the old man in the olive slacks shuffled over to an open window. Cort found himself at the front of the line, confronted by an unexpected question: What the hell was he doing here?

He searched his memory for an answer but could find nothing to grab onto. In fact, he had no memory of the recent past. Just hazy images, blurred by sweaty hands and further obscured by a blinding headache that he attributed to too much alcohol the previous night.

Headache be damned, Cort thought. *I should have some idea why I'm standing in a bank that could pass for a cathedral.* But even as he turned his memory over once more, surprised but strangely unbothered by the fact that his life's history seemed to have disappeared as if from a blow to the head, the call of "Next?" pulled him from his daydreaming and toward the empty window before him.

The teller on the other side of the bars was familiar, if unremarkable. Dark eyes, dark hair styled in a painfully non-impish pixie cut, and an unfriendly expression that said, "I already know that you're trouble."

Cort smiled, hoping that a little charm might melt the woman's icy glare, but the movement magnified his headache a hundredfold, and he abandoned the effort, settling for a meek shrug as he pushed his smudged withdrawal slip across the counter.

The girl stared at the paper, then picked it up and held it in front of her, squinting, and Cort found himself staring at her forehead, where several small pieces of paper were stuck, clinging to her brow from old sweat. For some reason, the sight of them made him nervous.

"Sir?"

Cort blinked. "I'm sorry, what?"

She sighed. "Weren't you listening? I said I can't read this. What is it you want?"

Cort stared at her, fighting to keep his eyes from drifting up to the paper stuck to her forehead, not sure how to explain that he had no idea what he wanted. That that was the problem. He shrugged.

The girl opened her mouth as if to berate him for wasting her time and then stopped mid-chastisement. Her eyes flicked to the right, briefly, then returned to Cort. "He wants to see you," she said simply.

Cort nodded. "Okay. Who does?"

She rolled her eyes then jerked her head in the direction her eyes had gone. "Over there." And then she seemed to forget that he had ever existed, looking through him as she called, "Next?"

Cort moved away, following her eyes and head, but hit a patch of rough air and found himself drifting into no-man's-land, caught between the teller station and the dark collection of desks on the far side of the room. He turned in one complete circle, as though preparing for a game of Blind Man's Bluff, and then walked toward one of the desks at random, borne by nothing more than a dimly felt tug in that direction.

The man behind the desk justified Cort's unfounded confidence with a thin smile and a "Hello, Mr. Jamison. Please, have a seat," and Cort dropped onto the surprisingly hard chair facing the desk. The man before him was every inch a banker, Cort thought. Small and thin and pale, his skin nearly as gray as his suit—clearly accustomed to life indoors. The man's round, wire-frame glasses reflected a stray shaft of sun, obscuring his eyes and then, as Cort watched, darkening into sunglasses so heavily tinted they looked nearly black—a pair of yawning, bottomless holes. Cort shivered.

"Mr. Jamison?" the man was saying. Cort realized that he'd turned away in horror and let his gaze creep back to the glasses—which now were perfectly normal sunglasses. "How can I help you today," the man said pleasantly.

"Um," Cort began, "I'm not sure. There seemed to be a problem reading my withdrawal slip, but I could have just filled out a new one ... "

"Could I take a look at it?" The banker smiled again—a tight lipped smile that seemed to indicate a willingness to help and a reluctance to make any promises. Cort pushed the scrap of paper across the desk, noticing as he did so that the ink was now completely illegible, so that even he had to struggle to decipher the scrawlings. "You know, I should probably just rewrite that ... " he began.

"No need," the banker interrupted. "It says here you're looking to make an initial withdrawal of one hundred dollars and a second withdrawal of one point five million dollars. Is that correct?"

"I guess so," Cort answered, staring at the paper in the man's hand.

"Are you sure that'll be enough?" the banker said, smiling his tight smile again. He held up a hand before Cort could reply. "I'm joking, of course. Just give me a second." He dropped the paper back onto the desk, tapped a few keys on his keyboard, and then leaned in to peer at the computer screen. As he did, Cort found himself leaning the other way—both out of a desire to be further away from the man (and to escape the cloud of floral cologne he seemed to have showered in) and even more so to see around the man's glasses, which continued to alternate between flashing mirrors and black shields—neither allowing a glimpse of the eyes behind them. By leaning almost far enough to fall out of his chair, Cort could just make out the twitch of an eyelid, but he could not quite see ...

"Well, here's the problem," the other man snapped, sitting up with an abruptness that nearly sent Cort to the floor. "You don't have the funds to cover that kind of a withdrawal, Mr. Jamison. In fact, your account is practically barren."

Odd choice of words, Cort thought. But he said, "Really? That's odd." The man simply stared at him, his thin smile frozen on his lips. Cort stood. "Well, I'll have to look into that, I guess," he stammered. "I'm sorry to have wasted your time."

He turned to leave, but the man's voice stopped him. "I'm afraid you don't understand. Your first request is not a problem—even if your account doesn't cover the funds, it would be a basic overdraft." He leaned back in his chair, the pinpoints of light at the center of his glasses fixed on Cort.

"No, what I take issue with is the transaction that you've got coming in second. This one is a problem, and one that we're going to have to deal with rather severely. What you've just done—or what you've just tried to do—is attempted robbery. And you can't steal from me."

Cort stared, watching as the banker's glasses shifted from black to bright again, throwing reflected sunlight at Cort, lancing into his brain and reactivating his headache. The small man behind the desk regarded him impassively, his thin lips pressed into a line of disapproval.

"No," Cort stammered. "That's not right. I mean, I wasn't trying to ... That money should be there. I should have it. I'm supposed to have it. I don't know what's going on, but it's only a mistake."

The light from the other man's glasses had grown so bright now that it felt hot, threatening to burn through Cort where he stood. He could no longer see the man's face at all through the glare, but he could hear the smile in his voice, amusement dripping from every word. "Why do you need all that money anyway, Cort?"

"I don't know," Cort muttered. "It's supposed to be mine. I've got it coming to me."

"Perhaps you do," the banker purred. "But for what use? To buy yourself a celebratory drink at Lonnie's? Or to post bail?"

Cort could only shrug, wincing as he did so, the top of his head threatening to peel back from the growing heat, his eyes slitted in pain and a futile attempt to block out the glare.

As though he'd noticed Cort's distress, the banker reached up and removed his glasses, the glare immediately disappearing, leaving Cort to blink the spots out of his vision. He closed his eyes, reveling in the cool breeze playing over his face, trying now to simply subdue the throbbing in his head and jaw.

"You can't have the money, Cort. You can never have the money. You don't have the right. But I'll tell you what. I'll get you out of jail, if it comes to that. How does that sound?"

Cort opened his eyes and met the other man's gaze for the first time. For a moment, he thought that the man had put his glasses back on, this time in tinted form, but was horrified to realize that the large dark circles were actually holes—bottomless, yawning holes in the man's face that seemed to suck the light out of the room and Cort's breath from his lungs.

"Now. That's settled," Robin Love said. "So you get out of here. I don't want to ever see you again. You just leave her alone. You may have seen her first, but you're better off sticking to second. It suits you better." He waggled two fingers at Cort—a fluttering peace sign that forced Cort a stunned step backward, his chair catching him just at the knees and dropping him onto it hard enough to rattle his teeth. He cracked his head on the back of the chair and stars swam in front of him for a moment, but through them he saw the man smiling at him, a set of crooked, broken teeth flashing between his thin lips—and for a moment, Cort thought he could see ... something in the yawning pits of the man's eyes, though he couldn't make out what it was. Before he could reach a conclusion, however, his headache crested, and he found the black of unconsciousness washing over him.

#

The world on the inside of Cort's eyelids turned just as steadily as the world outside, and as he found his way back to wakefulness, he had to fight to keep his balance and maintain control of his equilibrium. A few minutes of steady, measured breathing brought him a small sense of composure, despite the continued lancing pain behind his eyes. But a loud, unexpected metallic slam made the world lurch again and Cort was fighting his rising gorge, struggling to hold down his dinner, the liquor mixed into it stinging his throat and his sinuses. He swallowed hard, wincing against the burn, and coughed, then spat, his eyes still closed but no longer caring where he was or who was watching.

There was a grunt from somewhere in front of him, and Cort set about convincing his eyes to open. Weak gray light fought past his slitted lids and despite the dimness of the room, Cort had to struggle to adjust to the intensity —a blind man finding his sight in heaven ... or somewhere less desirable. Eventually, through the glare, shapes began to emerge.

He was in a small room, sparsely furnished with squat, stone walls on three sides and, to Cort's dismay, a wall of bars making up the fourth. Nothing much more to distinguish it except ...

"You alright?"

The voice was gruff but concerned, emerging from a corner of the room that Cort had taken to be a collection of rags and shadows. Looking closer, he could make out the slumped bulk of a man, his dark skin glowing in the dim light. Though his face was in shadows, Cort could sense the man's eyes studying him intently.

Evaluating. Judging. It reminded him of his dream of the bank, which is to say: it made him ill at ease.

And still the man's eyes bored into him. Finally, for lack of anything better to do, he answered. "Fine. I'm fine. What's it to you?"

"Nothin' man," the man replied, his voice an odd mix of geniality, apology, and regret. "You look like I feel, is all. No offense."

"It's okay," Cort heard himself say. "None taken."

"Yeah, I bet." The other man shifted in his seat, leaning forward to rest his chin in his hands, his elbows on his knees. "What'd he do to you?"

Though the question made an odd sort of sense, Cort's mind refused to cooperate with his mouth, and he stammered, "What? Who?"

The man regarded him silently for a moment, his gaze chiding. "Either you know or you don't," he said.

Cort shrugged. "Fine. Then let's assume that I don't. Right now, I don't even know how I got here. Last I remember I was sacrificing my night to get someone home safely, even though she was determined to drink the world. Next thing I know I'm fielding cryptic questions from some random guy in the drunk tank. So forgive me if I'm not automatically up for finding shared interests." As the vitriol bubbled over, it took much of Cort's energy with it, leaving him drained and painfully aware that he had just intentionally insulted the rather large man that he was locked in a cell with.

Luckily, the large man only laughed. "Alright," he said. "Only you need to know that this is no drunk tank." He looked at Cort knowingly, and when he didn't respond, continued. "You and me are in deeper than you know. This is a holding cell. Eventually, we're probably both headed away for a long while."

Cort gaped at him. "What? Why? How do you know that?"

"Couple of dangerous guys like us? What else could they do?" he replied. "Seriously. They're going to do me for murder, so they won't be keen on letting me slide out of here. And from what they were saying when they dragged you in, you're fixing to go down for assault and attempted rape."

A million denials flung themselves at Cort's lips, but none made it, leaving him to stare dumbly through the bars.

"To be honest," the other man continued. "You waking up is the high point of my day so far. Shit, maybe my week." He seemed to notice Cort's stunned look. "I mean, you snore something fierce, man. I think your nose might be broke."

Cort reached up and gingerly touched his still-throbbing nose, sending a fresh bolt of pain through him, starting between his eyes and spreading like liquid fire that pooled at the base of his skull and then sank into his spine. All of this in less than a second.

He let out a long, exhausted sigh, realizing after a moment that he was not sighing, he was moaning. A low keen that seemed to emanate from the center of his chest. He closed his eyes and allowed the pain to wash over him. After a moment, he became aware of his cellmate's gaze and reopened his eyes, letting the moan turn itself back into a sigh. The other man had shifted position and now sat facing Cort, his back against the wall and his considerable frame twisted into a lazy lotus position. He was staring at Cort curiously.

"Sorry," Cort muttered, not sure what he was apologizing for, but his embarrassment at the situation filling him with an odd sense of contrition.

"Don't sweat it," the big man replied. "I feel pretty much the same way."

Cort nodded. "Thanks ... um ... "

"Reggie," the other man supplied. "But I suppose you might as well call me Spider."

Cort nodded an understanding that he didn't feel and continued. "Okay, Spider. It's just ... I think I might have just given my life away. For nothing."

Now Spider was nodding. "I hear that. I definitely hear that. I'd say I did the very same thing tonight. Did it, or had it done to me. Same either way."

"How so?" Cort asked.

Spider let out a deep burst of laughter, his teeth flashing. He stretched his arms up toward the ceiling, his shoulder muscles rippling. "You kidding?" he asked. "Being taken in for murder can put a crimp in your lifestyle whether you did it or not."

"And did you?" Cort blurted without thinking.

Spider's mouth twitched at that. "What kind of question is that to ask a man, detective?" he asked, smiling. "I assumed we were both as pure as the driven snow."

"Sorry," Cort muttered again.

"Never mind, man. I'm fucking with you. I've got a couple priors, and I've been to prison, and I deserved all that. But this here? This is bullshit, and I'm pretty sure it's going to put me back inside even though I've been straight for five years."

"Damn," Cort replied. "That ... I mean, that sucks. But if you're innocent ... "

"Innocent." Spider scoffed. "Shit, none of us are innocent, really. You can't be innocent and survive in this world."

Here, Spider's sense of sardonic humor seemed to drop away, and for a moment, Cort could see the hurt that it had been covering reflected in the man's eyes. He wondered whether to ask what the worst part was, not anxious to put his foot in his mouth again. As it turned out, the question wasn't necessary.

"Anyway, whether I get out of this or not, whether they believe a single goddamned thing I say, doesn't matter. Just getting taken in is going to cost me my daughter. No way around that. Even if I get out of this, they'll never let me see her again. Count on that."

Cort sat in silence, unsure what to say—a feeling that had become too familiar to him over the past twenty-four hours.

The other man managed to manufacture a smile. "So, what about you?" he asked.

"Me?" Cort replied, still fumbling with the overload of information. "Um. No, I don't have any kids," he finished stupidly.

Spider's bark of laughter echoed through the cell again. "Yeah, okay. But I'm asking how you managed to ruin your life?"

Cort felt a flush of embarrassment creep up his neck and he shrugged it away, forcing casualness into his voice. "Oh," he said, his voice intentionally light. "Well, you know. That's kind of a long story ... "

Spider snorted, spreading his arms wide and glancing around the small, heavily barred room. "And?"

Cort laughed. "Yeah, I suppose that's true." He cracked his knuckles, studying them closely for a long moment. "It's funny," he said finally. "It's been a really long time since I told anyone about this. The truth about it, anyway."

"I get that," Spider replied. "You get in the habit of lying about something that don't need it."

"No," Cort said, turning the comment over in his mind. Then, "Okay, maybe. But there's something else, too. Maybe I thought I could create a different truth if I worked at it hard enough. Either way." He paused, allowing the story to gather momentum and, when it refused to do so, thrusting words into the void, desperate to fill the silence.

"So anyway," he began, talking quickly. "I never knew my dad. Grew up with my mom. We didn't have much, but we got by." He laughed. "Jesus. This is why I don't tell people this. It sounds so cliché. Chicago's own After School Special."

"Is it true?" Spider asked.

"Yeah," Cort replied.

"Well, then relax. Just talk."

Cort sighed. "Okay. So me and my mom, on our own all my life. She died when I was seventeen." He paused, waiting for the requisite "Oh, I'm so sorry." To which he would reply with an automatic, if insincere, "That's okay, it was a long time ago." But Spider just sat watching him, elbows resting on his knees, stone-still.

"Anyway," Cort stammered. "I was going through her things, getting ready for the funeral and all of that, figuring out what to keep and what to get rid of. She was a real pack rat. We had a room that was full of boxes for as long as I can remember. Boxes of old newspapers. Boxes of records she never played. Boxes of empty plastic bags, for Christ's sake. Anyway, I was working my way through all that shit and I found these letters."

"From your father?"

Cort blinked at the interruption, then laughed. "Are you kidding?" he said. "Never. No, these were letters *to* my father. Stuff she'd written to him but apparently never sent. Telling him what was going on with us, what our lives were like, what I was doing and how I was growing up. Asking for help, sometimes, which had to have eaten her up, but then maybe that's why she didn't end up mailing them. Or maybe she did send some ... Either way, those letters never got her any help. But they did tell me who my father was."

He glanced up at Spider again, waiting for him to fill in his part—to ask "Who?" in a breathless, eager voice. But the big man continued to simply watch him, waiting.

And for some reason, Cort couldn't bring himself to drop the bomb. The story needed a segue, a buffer of some kind. A breath. That's the way stories were meant to work—the layering and the pacing as important as the facts. The timing needed to be right. And so instead of naming names, he said, "You know that building downtown, all glass. Lights up like a beacon at night?"

Spider frowned. "I guess ... There's about a half dozen that look like that."

"Yeah," Cort replied. "Exactly. They're all built and owned by Victor Carlsbad. That's my father."

Spider's eyebrows jumped, but he made no sound.

"Mom never told me, and I never met him face-to-face, but those letters ... Apparently she'd worked for him at some point, and obviously something happened between them. Well, you know how it goes." He paused. "I guess she never got desperate enough, or angry enough, to send them, but I did. I wrote him a letter of my own, packed hers in there with it, and sent it off, letting him know that she was gone but that I could still use his help. I was working construction at the time, basically just bulling scrap from the build site to the truck. I thought he might be my ticket out.

"Well, I got nothing. No 'I'm so happy to hear from you.' No 'I'm sorry about your mother.' Not even an 'I don't believe you.' What I got was ignored. I didn't cope with that too well, to be honest." He paused again. This was where the "So what did you do?" was supposed to come.

"If it helps," Spider said softly, "he never read the letters."

"What?" Cort replied, dumbstruck.

"Men like that?" Spider continued, "they don't read their own mail. Someone else decides what's worth his time and what he needs to be protected from." He nodded at Cort. "Like you."

Cort stared at him. "Okay. Either way, I had to ... " He trailed off. "You know," he said finally, "that's the first time anyone's ever said anything like that."

Spider shrugged apologetically. "Sorry."

"No, it's not that." Cort shook his head. "I just never ... never thought of that. And you're right. It makes sense. And to be honest, it makes what I did even worse."

Spider shrugged. "So what did you do?"

There was the cue, just a beat later than he'd expected it. Cort filed the new insight away under "to consider in the future" and set about wrapping up the story. "I decided that, if he wasn't going to respect me enough to answer my letter, I'd talk to him face-to-face."

"And?" Spider pressed.

"And so I went to his house with all of my mother's evidence. I knocked on the door as civilly as I could and I waited. After about ten minutes of that I lost my temper, so I swiped a sledgehammer from my worksite and went back, knocked in the front door and went through the house room by room, looking for him. By the time I came to my senses and realized that he wasn't hiding from me, he just wasn't home, the police were at the front door. Shit, of course he wasn't hiding from me. He had no idea that I existed." Cort sighed. "Anyway, I had enough time to drop my proof on his bedside table before they got hold of me and took me in for breaking and entering. When I got out of prison, I found out that he passed away just a few months after I knocked down his door. But in the meantime, he'd put me in his will. I've got a stipend to live off of until I'm thirty-five, then I get a million and a half. If I stay out of trouble."

Spider whistled. "Nice. So he did right by you at least."

"I guess. He gave twice that much to DePaul and the Art Institute. I'm grateful, don't get me wrong. But that's why this room we're sitting in is a problem. I'm pretty sure all of that is out the window now. Back to square one. Back to zero, basically."

"Yeah," Spider said, not unsympathetically. "That's too bad, man. I'm sorry."

"Thanks," Cort replied.

"But," Spider continued. "Not to be a prick, but that's not the same thing at all."

"What do you mean?" Cort said.

"Well, assuming both of us innocent men actually manage to stay out of prison, I'll have lost my only daughter for the rest of my life. Best I can hope for is she decides to find me once she's grown up. You basically have to get a job."

Cort laughed, then smothered it as inappropriate, contenting himself with a rueful smile. "That's true," he said. "Good point."

"Shit," Spider said. "What do you want with all that money anyway? Won't bring you nothing but trouble."

"I guess. I don't know. I guess I just wanted to live well for a while," Cort replied.

"Don't we all," Spider said, dropping to his side and then rolling over to lay on his back and stare at the ceiling. "And I'd say you deserve that after all the bullshit you been through. Too bad he had other plans for you."

Cort was silent, nodding absently as the comment sank in, then he straightened, frowning at Spider, his frown deepening under the other man's steady gaze.

"That's the third time ... " Cort began, pausing as a slow smile crept across his cellmate's face. "That's the third time," he repeated, "that you've said something like that. 'He won't let you' or 'He had other plans.'"

Spider nodded.

"What are you getting at?"

The big man shrugged. "Mostly I wanted to see if you'd pick up on it, and if it'd make any sense to you, like it does to me." Reading the puzzlement on Cort's face, he continued. "Basically, something happened today that changed things for me. Everything was going good, but someone put himself in the way and that threw my life out of whack. That's why I'm here. I'm sure of it. And I have a feeling it's the same for you. If it is, you'll know it. You'll feel it."

"Feel what?" Cort demanded. "What are you talking about?"

Spider held up his hands, and Cort fell silent, taking the time to draw in a breath and forcing calm upon himself.

"Recently," Spider said, his voice soft but pointed, "have you felt different? Made a decision you normally wouldn't make or done something you normally wouldn't do?"

Cort shrugged at him but said nothing.

"My guess is you have," Spider said. "But I'll let you be your own judge. All I can say is: I made some decisions in the past couple of days that aren't like me. And he made me pay for them. I don't know what he has against me. Maybe I did the man wrong at some point. It's possible. I'm not always the nicest guy. Whatever it is, he's buried me, for sure. Took my daughter and took my life."

"Who did?" Cort heard himself ask, somehow feeling that he already knew the answer.

"Fuck if I know," Spider replied easily. "Maybe he was just the wrong guy to insult on a train and now he wants to make me pay for making him feel small. Maybe he's the fucking devil. I'd believe either one without much trouble. But if you saw him, I think you'd know it."

Unbidden, the vision of the odd, gray man who'd been staring down at him from the top of the stairs after his ill-fated walk with Theresa sprang to Cort's mind. Smiling a thin-lipped smile and flashing him that odd, discomfiting peace sign ... ... "Skinny guy," Cort said. "Gaunt, even."

Spider's eyes came alive. "Like a fucking skeleton," he added. "Creepy round glasses and a long gray coat."

Cort was nodding now as Spider continued. "Looks like death. Shit, he might be Death for all I know. He smells like a fucking funeral parlor."

"Wait," Cort said. "What was that?"

"He stinks," Spider replied bluntly. "Like dead, dried flowers. Reeks of it."

And now something was pricking at Cort's brain. A name, somehow connected to the overwhelming smell of dead flowers. Something ... unusual.

"Robin Love," he said aloud.

"Yeah, he was," Spider replied. "From both of us."

"What?" Cort blinked, losing the thread of the conversation.

Before Spider could reply, a door slammed somewhere outside of Cort's line of sight, and the sound of hard-heeled shoes clicked toward them. Spider shot Cort a look that he couldn't translate, but before Cort could ask him what was going on or what he'd meant by his last comment, a uniformed cop appeared at the barred wall.

His gaze fell on Spider first. "Not you," he said. "You stay where you are." He turned to Cort. "Mr. Jamison, you can come with me."

"What?" Cort said, for what seemed like the hundredth time in the past half hour.

"You're free to go," the cop replied, "You're not being charged." His voice suggesting that he disapproved of the idea.

Still, he turned to unlock the door, his eyes pinning Spider to his bench. Spider, for his part, simply stared back, his own eyes full of disdain.

As the heavy door swung open, Cort was swept with a desire to leap out and sprint for freedom, knocking the cop down along the way and setting his cellmate free so that they could continue to uncover whatever it was they had brushed the surface of. He felt his body actually begin to sway in that direction and bit down on his tongue hard enough to draw blood. The urge passed and, simultaneously, realization dawned on him. He turned to see that the cop was regarding him strangely. "What?" Cort asked.

"Are you coming or not? Usually people are a little more anxious to get out of here."

Cort nodded and stepped out of the cell, then turned back to face Spider as the cop locked the door behind him. "Incidentally, that was a name, not a ... it's the person, not what he did. It's who we're looking for. Do whatever you will, or whatever you can, with that." Spider stared at him for a moment and then nodded quietly. Cort followed the cop down the hallway away from the cell. Behind him, he could hear the creak of the bench as Spider stood, and Cort imagined him crossing to the bars and gripping them in his large hands. "Thanks!" he heard Spider call. "Good luck, man. Go get him."

> **Author's Note:** Am I cheating, here? When I steer my characters in converging directions; make their paths cross to serve the story, am I taking unfair advantage? More to the point: If it passes by unnoticed, should it bother the rest of us, or should we simply be grateful that the story moves forward because I helped delay Cort a bit, or pushed Puck a few blocks out of his way?
>
> It's the little things, really, and oh how they add up:
>
> If Spider had attended Cate's party from the start and not worried so much about finding a gift that made him the equal of the other parents, or if Ben had called the police after Spider had finished his cigarette, he might still be with his daughter.
>
> But without Spider to gum up the works, Cort would have been processed and released too quickly. And that would have ruined the story.
>
> That Spider was there to cause problems for the police just as Cort arrived at the station slowed the process just enough to make the story work. And if I had to cheat just a little to make that true, well, you won't find guilt in me. I haven't changed anyone's nature, only their circumstances.

No one forces a homeless man to give up his most precious possession to save something that is, ultimately, worthless.

No one forces an old man to turn his back on his son or to bury the truth of what his life has been.

No one forces an ex-convict to fit in, just as no one forces him to believe that his child cannot love him if he doesn't become one of the people he has always hated.

And no one forces an intelligent, charismatic man to lie, scheme, and dodge responsibility, all the while denying to himself that he's doing any of it.

The most we can do is nudge—provide the stimulus. All I can do is beg the question. Ultimately, we all make our own choices, for better or worse, and so they have. Their bad decisions are *their* bad decisions. Their mistakes are their mistakes. And the consequences must be their consequences. In the end, it's the people who must own their own mistakes—who must admit their failings and identify their weaknesses and learn from them. And who must ultimately overcome them.

#

Cort was led down a series of halls before coming to a heavy door which, when opened, revealed a waiting room. A large window let in golden shafts of late afternoon sunlight that caught Cort by surprise and illuminated a familiar face that turned his surprise up a notch: Ryan.

"Hey man," Ryan said, standing from the straight-backed chair where he'd been sitting. "Glad to see you're okay." He drew closer and his eyes widened. "Jesus," he breathed. "Alright, mostly okay. You look like shit."

"Seems appropriate," Cort replied. "That's what I feel like." He crossed to the small counter set into the wall where a second policeman presented him with forms to sign and a small bag of personal items.

"Thanks for coming, anyway," Cort continued, glancing over his shoulder at Ryan before returning to the forms. "I don't know how things got so out of control."

"Yeah," Ryan replied. "By the time I heard the commotion and came out of the ballroom you were already in the back of a squad car and that girl you were with was being put in an ambulance."

Cort winced. "Jesus. I hope she's okay. I guess they thought I was ... " he stopped himself, not willing to say it out loud for fear the cops around him would hear and change their minds about letting him go.

"She's fine," Ryan replied. "Don't worry. That was the first place I went. I didn't get out in time to follow the cop car that took you away, so I followed the ambulance to St. Joseph's and hung around there, trying to figure out what was going on. Eventually my lawyer got them to tell us where you were being held. If it makes you feel any better, you definitely got the worst of it. She's got a couple of black eyes, but otherwise she's fine. I heard the cops talking outside her room before I headed over here. Sounds like she's not going to press charges. But I wouldn't call her for a couple days if I were you," he added with a smile.

"Thanks," Cort said sarcastically, extracting his meager possessions from the clear plastic bag they'd given him. "Hey," he said, turning to the officer behind the counter. "I had a black leather jacket and a pair of gloves with this."

The man just shrugged. "What you see is what we got. Were you wearing them when they brought you in?"

Cort shook his head. "I don't know. Probably not. Maybe I left them at the coat check."

The officer stared at him. "Yeah, we didn't get to that. Didn't pick up your dry cleaning for you either. Guess you should have taken care of that before you got yourself arrested."

"Yeah, yeah," Cort replied, smirking at the irony of the statement. "Fair enough." He pushed out the door, shivered in the cold, missing his jacket and gloves, and continued to sift through the bag, filing things away into the appropriate pockets as he waited for Ryan to catch up. After tucking his wallet into his back pocket and his keys into the front, he was left holding a wad of bills—presumably his change from the bar which someone must have collected and passed to the police. Clipped to it was an unfamiliar scrap of paper. For a moment, he took it to be his coat check ticket, with Allison's number on it, but it was not. He stared at it, feeling

Ryan's gaze over his shoulder. The front of the card read: "Lonnie's Bar: Now You're Home," along with an address and phone number. He flipped the card over and stared at the spiky handwriting that read, "Let her go. You may have seen her first, but you will always come in second. R.L."

In his mind, Cort saw the gaunt, gray, round-spectacled man smiling his tight smile and waggling two thin fingers at him, and he felt a chill sweep through him.

"Cort? What's the matter, man? What does it say?" He could hear Ryan's voice in the background, but it grew more distant by the second, and Cort realized that he was running down the street, sliding on the snow in his slick-soled dress shoes. He had no idea where he was going. He only hoped that he would get wherever it was in time.

Epoch

The words of sometime poets lend
soft caresses to the air.
They dance a solemn jig with me.
They whisper soft, "beware."

"This magic will consume you,"
echo their cries of sharp despair,
but their words benumb my agony.
They teach me not to care.

The spark and prick of verbiage
plays a song bent to impair,
and the electric sting of alcohol
makes firm my hollow stare,

so my streamline dances double time
resistant to the glares
of besotted men and liquor
forging pointed double dares.

Their challenge isn't challenging—
my muse no easy scare—
and at first the words flow strong
and mate with ease to rhyming pair.

But as they intertwine and weave—
form themes of light and air—
a single word chokes off my muse
and "Love" cuts short
the simple snatch of song
I've scrawled in translation of life.
Scarred, I search for meaning
as the clamor twists the knife.

To find my air, I make paths cross
in effort to repair—
but by the time I mend my moorings
I've turned boat to busted pair.

And the clock ticks isolation
as the truth finally comes clear—
my wallpaper rhymes have blasphemed
any hope of lovers' prayer.

And while its right to cross out lines
just penned, life's not as fair,
and none can ever hope to heal
my lonely solitaire.

So I'll sit here and watch you all—

backlit and unaware—

as I wish and ache and love you ...

and you don't know I'm there.

Author's Note: I wrote that some time ago, before this story took began. And while this hasn't been the romance I'd hoped for, I do love them— all of my characters—and I have hope that my new muse will help change things; help me find my love story. Even if that somehow fails to happen, Cort has shown me that there are always options, and that's for the better—provided you can be honest about it, and ready to move on.

Speaking of Cort, I can see him from where I'm sitting. Lonnie's was too crowded and had too many memories, so I've moved just down the street to a bar whose name I can't quite remember. It's a classier place—the juke is playing The Police instead of Guns and Roses. "Every Breath You Take" instead of "I Used to Love Her." More appropriate. If this keeps up, I may become a regular.

Cort has passed by several times, looking more frantic with each lap—each time through the chorus and each snowflake that finds a home on the windowpane. As I watch, he darts off once again in the direction of Lonnie's. Poor guy. He's smart enough, he's just a little behind. It's a terrible feeling to know the plot but not have the power to affect it—to see the finish line but be unable to reach it, or prevent someone else from getting there first.

I'll ask again: Am I cheating? To be honest, I don't see how. I am an observer and a recorder. Telling the story cannot make it happen. And when the characters need a nudge in the right direction, how can I be blamed for keeping the plot on track, even if it means making a phone call, or stealing a gun, or if necessary, pulling the trigger? It's all in service of the story.

Now there is only snow outside the window, whitewashing the city—covering everything in a pristine blanket that buries all of the filth and the sin. For a little while at least, it makes Chicago feel beautiful—innocent.

In an alley just a few blocks away, the snow gives an honorable burial to a homeless man who never realized that he was fighting a false battle—that there was no enemy and that, instead, his paranoia was an accomplice in the execution of the woman he most wanted to protect. I left him his little gold flower pin. White Heather may signify protection and good luck, but it couldn't provide that for Puck, or for his Jamie.

Outside a small house near a Brown Line station, the snow makes patterns in the air and on the windows, but it can't have anywhere near the same effect as the snow inside the owner's mind, whose empty bottle of bourbon has helped bury the memories that he found so unpleasant. We should be relieved that, from this moment forward, he will no longer have to struggle to forget the past. That will come naturally.

In a nearby jail cell, the snow has little effect. The cell's inhabitant has no idea that it's snowing at all, and even if it were ninety degrees and sunny it wouldn't brighten the pall that has fallen over him. He's locked in an eternal winter, the bitterness of loss and of his own folly giving him permanent frostbite. But he has earned every bit of his penance, and his girl will be better off without his stilted worldview to guide her. There's no redeeming a bloodied hand, and only fire will cleanse a bloodied soul.

Finally, on the street, searching the snow for the woman that he may finally be ready to admit that he loves, is the talker—the penniless playboy—now so breathless as to not be able to formulate the simplest of sentences. He searches so frantically, so passionately, that it's almost endearing. Particularly because, just as he sprints down the street yet again, the object of his frenzied search turns the corner and steps into the bar he has just passed—the very bar I'm sitting in, actually—brushing snow from her white-blonde hair as she scans the room.

These men have all lost something vital—not just their money or their family, their lives or their minds (although that's closer). Most crucially, they have lost the game. Lost my game. Their tragic, timely mistakes have cost them.

But, of course, I promised you five. Five men and five mistakes to go with our lunar eclipse. The four should be obvious. You likely picked them out as they passed by. And by now you may have guessed that the fifth man is Robin Love. However, I cannot lay the fifth mistake at his feet. I'm afraid that I must pin the final mistake on you, dear reader, for making assumptions about who is the hero and who the villain in our story. Though our four men have fallen mightily, our protagonist—our fifth man—has carried the day. And his success is my success. His victory will give me, finally, my long-desired love story. And if it doesn't ... well, suffice it to say that there are always options. But best not to worry about that just yet.

Back in the bar, Allison's eyes have finally lit on a familiar face, though not the one she may have expected. She frowns, searches the room once more, and then crosses to his table. And while it's possible that she may be holding Cort in some corner of her thoughts, I choose to believe that he will be as quickly eradicated as an ineffective muse. All it takes is an effort of will and the ability to do what is needed without hesitation. All it takes is desire.

Allison stands beside the table, smiling cautiously. "Hello, Robin Love," she says. "What are you doing here?"

I lay my glasses on the table—I don't care for the way they make me look anymore—and stand, smiling myself. "Hello, Allison," I say. "I've been waiting for you."

The End

FIVE MAN FUGUE is a work of fiction.

All names, characters, places, and incidents are products of the author's imagination or are used fictitiously. Any resemblance to current events or locales, or to living persons is entirely coincidental.

Very special thanks to the Chicago Literary Writers Network: Sue Fox, Kate Hawley, Stephen Markley, Willy Nast, Ian Penrose, Alexander Slagg, Denis Underwood, Anne Ungar and all the rest. Deep appreciation to Shire Brown and Heather VanHuizen for their immensely valuable contributions. To anyone who read early drafts and provided valuable feedback, including Melissa Dylan, Rob MacGregor, Jill Prinsen, Gary Reichardt, Patricia Vernier, and many more.

And, as always, to Emjoy for patience, support, and understanding.

C.D. Peterson is a writer, arts marketer, and recovering actor living in Chicago or Minneapolis, depending on when you ask. He enjoys walking in the woods with his dog, cooking with his wife, reading about things that could never happen, and imagining how to make those things possible. He is currently working on a piece of YA fiction about some very special kids, and dreaming about all of the stories that have yet to be written.

Made in the USA
Monee, IL
19 October 2022